"*Pink Whales* is a delicious, hilarious, voicey romp of a novel about Charlie, a wife and mother who doesn't feel she belongs in her new home in preppy New England. Sara Shukla has an absolutely killer sense of humor, and the voice is pitch perfect. I adored it."

—Annie Hartnett, author of *Unlikely Animals* and *Rabbit Cake*

"*Pink Whales* is a deep and delightful modern rom-com full of meaningful twists on love, redemption, family, and the meaning of home. A perfect read for the beach . . . or the yacht club."

—Byron Lane, author of *A Star Is Bored* and *Big Gay Wedding*

"*Pink Whales* is a can't-miss coastal romp where Charlie navigates the choppy waters of her new preppy town on a quest to save her marriage and bring her family together. I loved every page. Shukla has a gift for writing humor that hits deep while also exposing truth and the raw emotion that makes the story both relatable and unforgettable."

—Rachel Barenbaum, author of *Atomic Anna* and *A Bend in the Stars*

"Sara Shukla's *Pink Whales* is an equal parts hilarious and heartfelt portrait of class anxiety and late coming of age. With her irresistible dialogue and perfectly skewered characters, Shukla swept me into the seaside town of Rumford and all its preppy, pesky privilege. I loved reading this utterly delightful debut!"

—Liv Stratman, author of *Cheat Day*

"My house is a mess and my laundry piled to the ceiling, and it's all Sara Shukla's fault! I couldn't put it down. *Pink Whales* lets you go places you're not invited, drink more than you should, and escape to the beach on nearly every page. What's not to like?"

—Christine Simon, author of *Patron Saint of Second Chances*

pink
whales

pink
whales

A NOVEL

sara shukla

Little
a

Published by Little A, New York

www.apub.com

Amazon, the Amazon logo, and Little A are trademarks of Amazon.com, Inc., or its affiliates.

ISBN-13: 9781662514852 (hardcover)
ISBN-13: 9781662514869 (paperback)
ISBN-13: 9781662514845 (digital)

Cover design by Joanne O'Neill
Cover images: © Valeriya Zankovych / Shutterstock; © daseugen / Getty Images; © Cosmic_Design / Shutterstock; © anthonycz / Shutterstock; © FoxysGraphic / Getty

Printed in the United States of America

First edition

To Maya, Noah, and Leo—
Doc Brown was right

It is the inalienable right of every man, woman, and child to wear khaki. —*The Official Preppy Handbook*, (edited by) Lisa Birnbach, c. 1980

chapter 1

I didn't mean to misplace my kid. Not in public. I'd lost the coffee maker in the move, but that was understandable. My family's relocation to New England still didn't feel real, the chaos amplified by two young children and a husband whose brain lingered on shift at the clinic he'd joined, double-checking orders and charts in his head even while his body, as if in a fugue state, shuffled around our rented yellow cottage. Unable to face another day of opening boxes, unpacking boxes, breaking down boxes (or just breaking down), I herded the twins out the door of the dilapidated guesthouse we now called home. I felt like Ms. Pac-Man, jaw hinging haplessly, chasing two rogue ghosts down the tree-lined sidewalk grid into town.

On the walk, gulls cried over our heads. Kate threw her head back and yelped, "AAAIIIIIEEEE!" in reply, slicing through the still, dignified air. Toby screeched in response. I imagined white-haired men and women in their shingle-sided homes, ironed shirts tucked neatly into khakis, startling from their crossword puzzles, sloshing coffee from their cups and saucers onto antique rugs.

Taking the highway exit into Rumford was like beaming our beat-up Subaru Forester directly into a link from *Coastal Living*'s "Top Ten Seaside Towns." When Dev first sold me on Rumford, I'd pictured sunset-saturated photos of our children frolicking on the rocky coastline in white fisherman sweaters. I hadn't owned a white piece of clothing since the twins were born. Then, when we pulled up to the cottage on

Cedar Street, I'd marveled at the overgrown plantings. I'd said to Dev, "Things grow here because drunk undergrads don't pee on them."

Back in North Carolina, we'd intended to move from the block of student apartments next to the hospital. But Dev's call schedule had been relentless. I called it getting raptured, so sudden were his departures. Year after year, proximity won out over wanting a garden with little tomato plants. When both kids were sick, when the power went out during a thunderstorm, when Dev couldn't even respond to a text about picking up milk or toilet paper, I imagined him swooping down on a distressed patient with a defibrillator, arms outstretched like an eagle's wings. I'd seen enough episodes of *ER* to romanticize, when necessary, the human drama that could be monopolizing him, even as I understood that most of his work involved titrating meds and dictating electronic medical records, bursts of electricity confined to a computer's processing unit.

Still, when Dev said he wanted to leave, it hit me that our current way of life wasn't unlike being slowly suffocated by a favorite pillow. I was so familiar with the contours, it had taken time to realize I could barely breathe. In Rumford, I told myself, I wouldn't have to imagine Dev taking heroic measures on someone's nana while I ate dinner by myself or measured purple tablespoons of children's Motrin at two in the morning. I wouldn't be alone.

By the time the kids and I arrived at the Jib, a café on Market Street, my running shorts clung to my thighs like plastic wrap. This trip would be fast—in and out. I hadn't met anyone in town beyond our mail carrier, and I wasn't primed for first impressions. I adjusted the backpack I'd grabbed on my way out the door and winced as something sharp dug into my shoulder blade. It was a gardening shovel Kate had found in the new shed. She'd demanded I carry it with us at all times in the event she needed to dig an emergency snow cave. Never mind it was

July. Never mind Kate was six. When I told the kids we were moving to New England, to a town they'd never seen, an hour north of a city—Boston—they'd never heard of, Kate took an intense interest in survival training.

Toby stalled as I nudged the kids inside, and the door swung shut, trapping my backpack. I clawed at the bag with one arm, like it was caught in a bear trap.

"Use the shovel!" Kate suggested loudly.

After finally freeing myself, I scanned the café for a free table and noted four canvas tote bags, each monogrammed and nestled next to their owners like small, fashionable dogs. Could I monogram my JanSport backpack? If only it were so easy, to land someplace and solidify to match it, like Jell-O spreading into a mold.

I readied myself for some adult interaction. It had been seven days since the four of us traded the mountains of our university town for flat, tidy lawns and shingled sea captain homes. Five days since I'd had a conversation with another adult that didn't involve an invoice or a sandwich order. Two days since I'd laid eyes on Dev, though we technically shared the same bed. Two hours past when I should have had a cup of coffee—which was the one problem I could solve.

"Mama, look who's here!" Kate said. She stopped short, and Toby bounced off her.

I followed Kate's gaze. I'd texted Dev to let him know we were going into town, feeling like I should send evidence we were, in fact, settling in, even if each successive day made it look like more bombs had gone off inside our two-bedroom cottage. Dev hadn't replied, but that was nothing new. Maybe he'd managed to sneak away and meet us. But instead of finding my husband in a wrinkled button-down, dark curly hair brushing the top of wire-rimmed glasses, I saw Kate pointing to Santa.

To be fair, I was less surprised to see Santa.

On a table, a square sign printed on thick, cream-colored card stock lay propped against a coffee cup. The sign read: IT's CHRISTMAS IN JULY!

GET A JUMP ON THE HOLIDAYS AND HELP KIDS AT BRADLEY ELEMENTARY GET A JUMP ON SCHOOL SUPPLIES. Bradley was the town where Dev worked, a handful of miles and seemingly worlds away.

Two women flanked Santa, and a little girl with straight blonde hair and enviable posture sat on his lap. She looked bored. At Santa's feet, I spotted a fifth tote bag. Its looped canvas handles stood at attention like bunny ears.

One woman wore a linen dress, its navy-and-white stripes as crisp as her canvas bag, as precise as the ribbon in the little girl's hair. Her body was a study in lines: her blonde hair was expertly trimmed to an inch above her shoulders, her dress tailored to just above her knees. A pair of oversize tortoiseshell sunglasses held her hair back from her face, while her hands rested on her narrow hips. Clearly nothing that touched her body was the result of an impulse purchase from an Instagram ad at two in the morning.

The other woman held a camera so high tech it looked like it could transform into a robot and walk away. Her hair was darker and pulled into a tight, high ponytail. Her skin was smooth, her makeup minimal. She was shorter than the other woman, and looked like she could dominate a squash tournament at a moment's notice. A white quilted leather backpack lay beside the table, and I wasn't sure if it was for the camera or her gym clothes, both of which probably cost more than my student loan payment. Her tennis whites were fitted and flawless, and her teeth were bleached the same shade as her skort.

I felt sweaty, not dewy, and suddenly being barely a year past thirty felt borderline adolescent. Was it these women's actual ages— midthirties at least?—or did their dry-clean-only clothing simply make them seem more experienced?

I tried to straighten my spine, but the shovel dug in deeper. Glancing down, I saw a stain in the shape of small fingers near the hem of my rumpled T-shirt. *It's pizza,* I thought. We had pizza last night. We had pizza a *lot* of nights.

I gripped Kate's and Toby's hands and tried to lead them to a table in the back, but the currents of their tiny bodies pulled in opposite directions.

"Ivy, just a few more shots. Stop squirming," Navy Stripes said. To Tennis Whites: "Honestly, Poppy, if I hear him say *cap rate* one more time, I'm going to put Ambien in his single malt. Ivy, keep smiling."

The woman in tennis whites, Poppy, held the camera in the air, not actually taking any pictures, though she seemed to be the one in charge of the Santa operation. She looked like she could be in charge of any number of operations. Her taut arm balanced a clipboard as she smiled and set the camera on a tripod. Navy Stripes dropped two twenties into the donations jar, kissed Poppy on the cheek, and motioned for the little girl to follow. They made it look so easy, to move through the world like everything wasn't about to fall apart.

Santa's lap was available seating, and I hadn't let the kids out of my sight in almost a week. In the pilled red velvet, I saw my chance to do one thing by myself, with two free hands, while someone else poured coffee over ice for me. I plopped Kate and Toby onto Santa's knees, told them to smile, and assured Poppy I'd be right back.

She glanced at her gold chronograph watch. "We got this!" she said, and her smile let me relax just enough to step away.

In line behind Navy Stripes and her daughter, I leaned sideways and checked my reflection in the pastry display case, then looked away just as quickly. The bags under my eyes could hold groceries, and my dry shampoo that morning had sprayed out nothing but air.

Two teenage girls giggled about a late-night party. I listened, nostalgic for the days when a cup of coffee could cure a hangover, when my skin withstood all-nighters with such alarming elasticity.

I ordered an iced coffee. The ice maker at the cottage grumbled on and off without producing anything cold, and by midday I longed for the central AC of the south like a jilted lover. I turned to see if Poppy needed me, digging into my wallet for some bills to put into the donations jar. But Kate was the only one with her. Where there should have been two children, Santa's lap was half-full.

I blinked. Where the hell was Toby?

I scanned the shop for Toby's brown curls, a shade lighter than his father's though equally unruly. My chest felt hollow. I forced a slow, shaky breath and tried to think. Toby couldn't have gone far. It was a coffee shop. The bell on the door rang sharply. Toby was small for his age and could slip out a door quicker than a shadow. I held my breath and craned my neck to look out the window. Two thoughts flashed in my head: *If Dev was here, this wouldn't be happening.* Then, also, *I'm not telling Dev this happened again.*

"Charlie," the barista called.

The harbor was two blocks away, its water so smooth that just yesterday Toby asked if he could walk on it. The chipmunk scampering in my chest did a cartwheel.

But, as I lunged for the door, hand pressed to my rib cage, I caught sight of two toothpick legs sticking out from under a square table. I knew those toes; they'd been painted orange by his sister. Toby sat there, perfectly at home on the smudged tile floor at the feet of a well-dressed, oblivious man speaking heatedly into a Bluetooth earpiece. I let out my breath. *It's okay,* I thought. *He was here all along.*

Squatting, I motioned for Toby, but he shook his head. He started picking at something stuck to the underside of the table. I hissed his name and waved harder.

"Charlie," the barista repeated. She sounded bored. Was she going to throw out the coffee? Wait, was that gum Toby was pulling from the underside of the table?

The businessman sitting at the table stamped a tan Sperry boat shoe into the floor as he drove home a point about a 7.5 percent cap rate, and Toby startled. Before I could reach out for him, he darted on all fours like a squirrel across the aisle and under the next table, knocking a tote bag to its side and spilling its contents onto the floor.

It was Navy Stripes's bag. Of course it was. I frantically mouthed *sorry* in her general direction.

Suddenly the town, the coffee shop, the bags, it was all too much. I was sticky with dried sweat, I was severely undercaffeinated, and I wanted my son back. I crouched on my hands and knees and dove under the table. A chair groaned against the tile. My knee landed on something wet. I grabbed hold of Toby's ankle and pulled him to me before he reached the remains of an oatmeal raisin cookie. Emerging from under the table, I banged my head and let out a curse that would make a sailor blush.

Upright, I held Toby around the waist and tucked him into my elbow like a football. He kicked and screamed, 'Ccoookie!" I refused to make eye contact with the women whose table I'd dive-bombed, pivoting instead and squinting for my coffee at the end of the counter, my free hand outstretched like a running back.

Then I remembered I had another child. Kate was still frozen on Santa's lap. They stared at each other, Kate and Santa, neither willing to make the first move. I could already see Kate adding the big man to her flip-top notebook of worst-case scenarios.

"Kate!" I hissed. Toby writhed like an octopus, all arms and legs, clamped between my hip and elbow. I tried again. "Kate, hop down!"

Poppy, clipboard balanced on her forearm, glided toward Kate, hands outstretched to lift her from Santa's lap. But Kate recoiled and grabbed the poor man's beard instead. From the look on his face, it was real.

I heaved Toby over to his sister, palming my coffee as I passed the counter. When he realized he was close to Santa again, Toby kicked. His foot caught around a leg of the tripod where Poppy had set the camera. I spun to watch the entire setup clatter into the fake fireplace, upending a collection of soy candles. As I watched the candles topple, one after the other like environmentally conscious dominos, Toby's flailing limbs swept a half-full latte from the table to the floor. Lukewarm froth seeped into my canvas sneakers.

I shook my soggy sneaker and mumbled a defeated, "Sorry, so sorry," to anyone in earshot—Santa, Poppy, the postparty teenage girls making a note to refill their secret birth control prescriptions. I held out my own hard-won iced coffee as an offering for the spilled latte. But instead of taking it, Poppy scooped Kate from Santa's lap like a basketball.

"Don't be silly," she said, waving over one of the teens from behind the coffee counter. "They think it's a hoot to use the mop."

Poppy plopped Kate into an empty chair at the table with the other women.

This was not the plan. People in Rumford barely made eye contact. Dev called it "New England Charm." Could I simply make a run for it? I could go home, shower, change, sedate the children, then return us all to the coffee shop and sit back down.

But as Poppy looked at me expectantly, I fell into a seat, still holding Toby to my hip.

"Thanks," I said. I tried to smile. I wasn't sure what was actually happening on my face.

Poppy nodded at Kate with approval. "She's unfazed."

"Not much fazes Kate," I said. I gave a small wave with my free hand. "I'm Charlie. I'm fazed by many things."

When neither of the other women spoke, Poppy held out her hand. "I'm Poppy," she said. Her grip was firm, like her arm. "Are you summering? Have I seen you at the beach club?"

"We just moved here," I said. "We have a summer rental for now, on Cedar Street. But we're not, um, *summering*?"

Did I just use summer *as a verb?*

"Oh, the guesthouse!" Poppy said.

I turned the coffee cup around in my hands. "I call it the cottage since, you know, we're not visiting. And we don't know the couple who owns it. I heard they're in Europe? I was going to go to Europe once, when my brother graduated from college, but I got pregnant instead."

I sucked on the straw to stop talking. They didn't need my OB-GYN history. The truth was, we'd rented the "cottage" unseen. All we knew was that the owner's children were grown, and the empty nesters—whose main house was enormous—were traveling abroad, or had another house in France. They were renting out the guest cottage, and the real estate agent had made it all sound very *Great Gatsby* on the phone. She hadn't mentioned how the dishwasher was ancient enough to sound like a tsunami, or how the bedroom carpets were the color of tree moss.

"It's adorable. Isn't it, Heidi?" Poppy said. She looked to the woman sitting next to her, whose long honey-colored hair fell in waves over a gauzy black top. She pulled gold aviator sunglasses over her eyes in response. Poppy nodded as if she'd spoken out loud, and said, "I know just the one. I played house there as a kid. I wonder if they've updated it since then."

While they had not, in fact, updated anything since the early nineties as far as I could tell, I almost said I was playing house, too. I liked to imagine the four of us walking down Market Street together, mailing crayon rubbings of seashells to Dev's mother, popping into the little grocery store, which we'd soon learn to call the market. Rumford would be a place where I could stand beside a table made of reclaimed barnwood, ladle chowder from a stainless steel pot into four bowls made of bread.

In this scenario, too, the strange, simmering tension between Dev and me would simply dissipate as well, like so much steam from a perfectly seasoned chowder.

"So, Poppy, is this enough for your merit badge?" Navy Stripes asked, motioning toward the now-empty and clean Santa corner.

"For *community engagement*, yes, thank you for asking," Poppy replied. She said to me, "My boys, Pax and Dodge, they need to check some boxes for the upcoming school year."

I looked around, but I didn't see any boys, only Poppy.

Navy Stripes sipped her coffee, then made a face. "This is vanilla," she said, frowning. "You both know I gave up sugar."

Heidi swapped the cups without speaking.

"So what brought you here?" Poppy asked me. She was still the only one of the three who'd formally acknowledged my presence. "Usually the new faces in Rumford come from the dermatologist's office."

Heidi snorted. A church bell rang a few streets away. Navy Stripes flicked an annoyed glance at the man with the Bluetooth earpiece. I put my hand on Kate's head and smoothed her hair, until I realized Poppy was still looking at me, waiting.

"My husband took a job in Bradley, at a health care practice," I said. "We needed a change, and Rumford sounded nice, I guess. You know, small town, pretty sidewalks, lobster rolls . . ."

"That'll do it," Poppy said. She tapped the table for emphasis, like I had aced her pop quiz.

"He left out the part about his ex-girlfriend being his new boss and how she basically begged him to join her, but I'm sure it won't be weird at all," I said, immediately wishing I hadn't left my filter somewhere along the six-hundred-mile stretch of I-95 we'd traveled to get here.

But that was when Navy Stripes seemed to finally take note of me. As she turned, her hair swung like a golden curtain.

"Your husband," she said. "He's at the health care place in Bradley?"

Kate piped up. "My dad's a doctor," she said. "He fixes people."

Navy Stripes settled back in her chair, but she fixed me with a hungry look.

"Rumford is lovely, isn't it?" Poppy said. "Do you love it?"

I hesitated. It felt like I needed to give Poppy the right answer again or I'd disrupt some delicate balance in the very fabric of the community. Anyway, love was a complicated word. We'd only been here a week. I didn't not love it. I just didn't understand it, or how I fit into it, or, really, why exactly we were here.

"It helps if you know where to go," Poppy said when I didn't answer. "Like the yacht club! It's around the corner. I'm sure you've seen it."

10

"Totally," I said. "It's great."

I hadn't seen it. I didn't know about any clubs, other than a YMCA in Bradley, around the corner from the clinic. I did know I didn't want Kate and Toby to spend every summer watching Scooby-Doo and eating microwave popcorn like my brother, Simon, and I had. I hadn't admitted it to Dev, but part of moving to a small town appealed to me. Small towns had traditions, predictability. In a way, I was hoping the town would tell me what the heck to do.

"We'll have to drop by," I said. "The yacht club. I mean."

"Oh, you *do* have to be a member there," Poppy said, as if I couldn't have a puppy.

Navy Stripes put her elbows on the table and leaned forward. I leaned back reflexively.

"Charlie. It's Charlie, right?" She looked to Poppy, not me, for confirmation. "I'm Lacy. Come to the yacht club tomorrow night. I insist."

I looked from one woman to the other. "Are there, like, guest passes?"

"You can be Poppy's guest," Lacy said. She pushed back from the table and squared her bare shoulders. "You don't need a pass. But only if you promise to bring your husband."

Poppy clapped her hands. Heidi got up to throw away her coffee. These women were over the top and a little frightening, but I wasn't awash in invitations to do, well, anything. And maybe Dev would be excited to do something new. The only place he'd gone since we arrived in Rumford was work. Maybe this was just what we needed. We certainly needed something.

"Thanks," I said, focusing on keeping my voice steady, as if we were invited to exclusive parties after trashing a coffee shop every day. "That's so nice of you. I'm sorry about the mess we made here."

Poppy waved her hand. "Oh please, it's not like you burned the place down."

The door opened, and I took a deep breath, willing the salt air to fill me, to make Rumford feel more like home.

chapter 2

Back at the university hospital, I'd never dropped in on Dev during his shifts. There were always anxious residents waiting to ask him questions, machines beeping, people potentially emanating liquids. I felt woozy if the kids did more than scrape a knee on the sidewalk. All Dev had to ask was, "Is it gapey?" and I'd need to sit down

But Dev worked at a practice now. He wore khakis. And if he was still going to work twelve-hour days, just until he got the hang of things, I didn't need to wait at home. We could pop in and visit. I wanted to tell him about the coffee shop, the chaos we'd rained down, and the bizarre party invite.

Bradley, ten miles west, was overwhelmingly gray. The faded, grubby buildings, the craggy sidewalks; it was as if the musty sky melted onto the landscape, like a post–Industrial Surrealist painting. Some buildings looked outright abandoned, the windows boarded up. Yellow signs with red block letters hawked cash advances or pay-as-you-go cell phones. A row of connected brick buildings sat along the waterfront, draped with tattered signs advertising a for-profit college and a collection of storage units. When Dev had given us the grand tour, the highlight was the Dunkin' across the street. I promised the kids doughnut holes after our visit.

I texted a heads-up from the parking lot: We come bearing caffeine, surprise! I didn't wait to hear back. Dev usually took a while to reply when he was at work.

The glass double doors of Bradley Health Care opened into a waiting room. A cooking show played softly on a mounted TV. The pale-yellow walls were lined with gray plastic chairs—the kind that stuck to your thighs when you stood. A small collection of kids' toys sat untouched in a corner. A bulletin board held a pinned informational pamphlet that read EVERYONE DESERVES TO FEEL SAFE AT HOME, and a poster of a flowchart for treatment with something called buprenorphine. Beside a poster about the dangers of smoking that looked like it had been there since the eighties, a more modern rectangular sign announced, NO VAPING. The receptionist sat behind a smudged glass panel saying something over the phone in Spanish. I decided not to bother her.

The door to the waiting room swung open, and Dev's black Converse sneakers squeaked across the floor. He tucked the front of his dark-blue scrubs shirt into his pants—a familiar move. He looked tired, but when he saw me, there was a hint of that boyish grin that had drawn me to him years ago. Between his glasses, his constant need of a haircut, and his lingering British accent—he moved to the US when he was a teenager—my friends, early on, had nicknamed him Hot Harry Potter. To be fair, they worked in restaurants, and were usually high.

"You're a lifesaver," Dev purred into the amber-colored cup. I tried to remember the last time he talked to me the way he did to four shots of espresso.

"Nice to see you, too," I said. "Hey, didn't you leave the house in clothes? Did something . . . get on you?" I took a step back.

"Elvis spilled her coffee on my shirt," he said, as if it fully explained how he'd arrived in a button-down then ended up in doctor pajamas. "No one bled or puked on me. Not yet, anyway."

"Well, the day is young," I said.

It was Presley "Elvis" Keen who told Dev about the opening at the clinic. She took the job first, the year before, then implored Dev to join when her partners announced their sudden retirement. It was Presley who had possibly spent more nights next to Dev than I had, if you counted med school study groups and overnight residency rotations. There were also other kinds of overnights, but that was before we met. Whenever I brought this up, Dev said I was being ridiculous. *She's just Elvis,* he'd remind me, as if calling someone "Elvis" precluded you from sleeping with them. Again.

Dev swallowed half the coffee in the cup as Kate and Toby wrapped their limbs around his long legs. "I only have a few minutes," he said. He rubbed his eyes, then opened them extrawide as if that would help him stay awake. "We have a backlog of patients."

In the waiting room, an elderly couple watched the cooking show. A young woman in leggings and a tank top sat while her toddler stared at a phone. The automatic doors opened behind me and three more people came in and sat down. Dev smelled like coffee and hand sanitizer.

I'd just wanted to set eyes on him, but I suddenly felt self-conscious about demanding his attention, interrupting what was obviously another nonstop day to tell him about a party invitation.

Meanwhile, Kate had started in on one of her spiels about proper leech removal. "Dad, did you ever see one in medical school? They suck your blood. Maybe all of it, if you wait long enough. And you can't pour salt on them and make them shrivel up like slugs because, get this, Daddy, they'll barf on you and spread bacteria all over. Like Toby at Disney World."

"Hey!" Toby swatted her on the arm, but Kate was on a roll.

"So, you have to use your fingernail to *press* against your skin and break the seal. Then you can flick it off like a booger." Kate giggled triumphantly. She had not inherited my squeamishness.

But Dev was looking over my shoulder at someone slouching in a chair. It was a young man, in his twenties, baseball cap pulled over his eyes. He held one of his shoes in his lap. That couldn't be good.

I realized I wanted to impress Dev a little bit, too. "So, guess what happened today—"

I didn't get far before the swinging door leading to the exam rooms banged open.

"Dev, did the social worker call you?" Presley Keen, all six feet of her, looked at Dev intently with a razor-sharp focus. She'd always managed to look like an off-duty supermodel someone had simply thrown a white coat on, but today, with her auburn, naturally highlighted, no-nonsense hair pinned in place, mascara smudged around her eyes—Southern Belle Presley was intimidating, if I was being honest. But her eyes softened when she saw us, and the rigidity in her body dissipated a fraction before she threw her arms around me.

"Charlie! I'm so happy to see you," Presley said, squeezing me like I was a teddy bear she thought she'd never see again. "Oh, it's just, I have this patient back there—I'm so sorry, I have to run. It's been a day, and we're behind. Let's get together soon!" She put her hand on Dev's arm, and I pretended not to notice. "Dev, tell me as soon as the social worker calls you, okay?"

Presley straightened her spine like she was pulling up a zipper. Then she banged through the door back into the treatment area.

"So, what's up?" Dev asked. His eyes darted over to the man beside me, the one who was missing a shoe.

"What? Nothing. I mean, we wanted to see you. And there's this thing—"

The swinging door banged open again. Presley popped her head out.

"Dev, did you order the script for room eight?"

"I was just about to."

Presley smiled at me and the kids. "Right. Okay, no prob. I got it."

The door flipped shut, and Dev downed the rest of the coffee. The host on the cooking show measured out ingredients. Someone coughed. Why was it so hard for me to just talk to Dev? We weren't strangers. Maybe I should surprise him later about the party. Spontaneity was good for a marriage. Like deciding practically overnight to move to New England, for example.

I blurted, "The kids wanted to know, um, do you think you'll be home for dinner?"

Dev looked at his watch, nudged his glasses into place with his wrist, then glanced back around the room. "I don't know. It depends. I'll try, though. Kate, take care of everyone. No leeches."

Kate gave him a salute. "I won't let Toby run away again, Daddy," she said.

"What?"

"Gotta go!" I pulled the kids backward, retreating through the automatic doors.

—⁊⁊—

Growing up, I moved around a lot. Then, for a stretch I'd hoped was permanent, my family settled in coastal North Carolina. My mother, Lillian West, tutored child actors who were doing stints on teen soap operas, all parties confident they were on the verge of something greater, artistically speaking. My father, Edgar, doggedly pitched abstract concepts for big-box home improvement store commercials which were, according to my parents, vastly underappreciated. Fortunately, he was paid for his accounting skills.

The summer before I started high school, a storm felled an oak tree that landed in the middle of my family's kitchen. My parents rented an RV—"Bessie"—that we could live in while the house got repaired. We traveled to national parks all summer, and while my parents raved about rivers and rock formations and natural beauty, I imagined the sleepovers I'd host that fall, how I'd serve ice cream sundaes from our big new kitchen island, share the ghost stories I'd heard around campground bonfires, and embellish my two torrid (and very PG) summer romances.

Instead, my parents flipped the script. They bought the RV and sold our three-bedroom ranch. My mother said she felt freed from convention. (We lived on a cul-de-sac.) My father declared we'd save the money for college funds. I said I'd take out loans, go to community college, be an escort—anything to not share a mobile bunk with my younger brother while cramming AP calc.

17

No one achieves greatness by blending in was my mother's mantra. She'd crowed it when I needed a uniform for team sports and when I got a job scooping ice cream so I could buy Abercrombie jeans. *Comfort is the enemy of success,* she maintained, as I scheduled study sessions with friends during the airing of *Dawson's Creek*, savoring their upholstered couches and the dank smell of their decidedly immobile basements.

In other words, I rebelled at my parents' free-spirited pivot by being aggressively basic.

My parents held out hope for my brother, Simon, to prove less traditional. They left PFLAG pamphlets around the house, despite my insistence that Simon was going steady with all three Jennifers in the eighth grade. When Simon did come out, he waited until college, not wanting our parents to take credit. While I'd married a doctor, had two kids, and pined after a life that didn't feel like scrambled eggs, Simon grew a nonironic beard and moved by himself after college to Montana. Most of his possessions fit in a backpack, and none were bespoke.

At that point, nest empty, my folks decided the logical next step was to become retiree social media influencers. They painted large, blobby spots on Bessie and started a YouTube channel called *Senior Moments*. Between weeks of travel—from the Grand Canyon to New Orleans jazz bars, which they chronicled in bite-size vlog uploads—they set up camp for free in expansive Walmart parking lots. They favored Atlanta, an international airport hub with mild enough weather to leave Bessie unattended for weeks at a time.

The kids called my mother by her nickname, Lilly, and my father GP, which became how I often thought of them in my own head, like they were characters, even to me. I loved my parents dearly, and genuinely got a kick out of their adventures now that I no longer had to share a living space with them. And compared to their escapades, Rumford felt even more muted and buttoned up.

In my first year of college, I read Shirley Jackson's story "The Lottery" for an English class. The scenes of the small community coming together for terrifying rituals haunted me for months. Back then,

I was already an outsider, returning home for Thanksgiving to an RV, not a gated suburb like my suite mates. I'd felt expendable—ripe for a stoning if ever a sacrifice was needed. Rumford was so quaint, so tidy, not a hydrangea out of place, that it brought me back to that feeling. I wondered what it was hiding.

—⁓—

Back at the cottage I watched Kate and Toby scour the grass for worms. My phone buzzed, and the screen lit up with a caller ID photo of my mother.

"Hi, Mom. Where are you?"

"We're still at chez Walmart, Charlie. We jet to Thailand tomorrow, so there's no point in relocating Bessie. You would not believe the humidity, sugar, my hair is practically floating."

I pictured my petite mother in the black denim overalls and slip-on Vans she favored, like a silver-haired middle school stage manager.

"How was Italy?" I asked, twirling a dandelion stem between my fingers. "Where does it rank among your best places to jet-set post-menopause? Hold on. Toby, you have to stay in the yard. We talked about this."

I put my toes in the grass, and James Dean padded over and lapped at a bowl of water. James Dean is what people whose parents pressure them to take artistic risks end up naming their fourteen-pound rescue dachshund.

"Oh, it was so much more than a ranking, Charlie," my mother said. "Your father and I are showing people the real deal. Instead of traipsing up and down with travelers' checks tucked into our undies—"

"Wait, what?"

"I'm just saying we're not intrepid tourists, sugar. In Italy, we settled into one town for a week. We drank espresso in tiny cups, struck up *intimate* conversations. We asked a shopkeeper named Enzo to teach us how to make pasta. We milled flour. Wait until our next installment, Charlie. You've never seen such adorable ravioli."

"Sounds great," I said. "We had pasta the other night, too." I decided not to mention it was mac 'n' cheese from a box, the kind that turns to neon concrete if you don't wash the bowls right away.

"Enzo eats pasta every day, and he's fit as a fiddle," my mother said. "Wait until you see him on the vlog. I told him, if he's ever in Montana . . ."

"Mom, you can't use your YouTube channel to matchmake for Simon."

"Well, how is he going to meet a nice young man out in those mountains, Charlie?"

I tried to imagine my brother, who ate freeze-dried meals meant for astronauts while leading backpacking hikes at Yellowstone, with a svelte Italian pasta maker. I could hear my mother rustling through a plastic bag on the other end of the phone.

"What's new with you, sugar?" Lilly asked. "How are my Yankee grandchildren?"

"Your grandchildren terrorized a coffee shop Santa, but it scored us an invite to a yacht club party." I flicked the flattened dandelion stem into the grass. The kids lay on their bellies, staring down at something Kate held in her hands.

"Oh, I'm sure Santa deserved it," she said. "And a party sounds delightful."

More rustling on the other end of the phone.

"You must be open to unexpected possibilities. It's what I always say. Dare to be fully yourself, and the rest will follow."

"You and Dad make a living being comfortable wherever you land," I said. "I'm afraid I'm going to make a fool of myself for free. Even the children in Rumford look like tiny adults. Between the twins looking more like Dev than me, and me looking like the teenage babysitter compared to the other mothers there, I was afraid someone would ask if I was free next Saturday. And the thing is, I probably will be. Dev has been so distracted. It's like he doesn't even see me."

Lilly opened and closed cabinets as she spoke. "Transitions are stressful, sugar, but change can bring couples closer, too. I wish your father and I had taken risks together sooner. Some healthy risk can invite passion—"

"Okay, okay," I said quickly. "Say no more, please. I'll be open. I promise. Bring it on, Rumford Yacht Club."

"That's the spirit!" Lilly crooned. "And your father's back. Ed, start sprinkling the flour. Charlie, we better get started. This could take a while. Ciao, sugar. See you after Thailand!"

"Wait, what do you mean *see* us?" But it was too late; she'd hung up. We hadn't talked concretely of a visiting date yet; I just wanted to feel settled first. I wondered if my parents might leave Bessie at a chez Walmart nearby when they visited. I had been able to overlook my mother gracing our graduate student apartment complex with her leopard-print bathrobe as she had shuffled between the RV and our one full-size bathroom. Cedar Street was another matter.

I squinted as the sun flashed in my eyes. Shielding my face with my free hand, I saw what Kate was holding: a small mirror, the kind Lilly gave her from free-gift weekends at the Clinique counter.

"Kate, where's Toby?"

"He took James Dean for a walk into town," Kate said. "I've been trying to signal you with this mirror. Three is the universal code for distress."

Scrambling up, I wondered if *yacht club party* was in any of Kate's survival guidebooks.

chapter 3

"When will Sidney be here?"

"Soon," I promised Kate. I pulled open the freezer door to double-check our stock of frozen pizza. Sidney was the daughter of our real estate agent, and our new babysitter. I was starting to worry I'd spend the evening playing The Floor Is Lava! with Sidney and the kids instead of going out with Dev. He was an hour late, and I still hadn't technically told him about the party.

"Sidney has long hair and pierced ears," Kate said, staring into Toby's eyes with practiced intensity. "She's in high school, Toby."

I considered my limited wardrobe options for the yacht club. Should I have bought boat shoes, or was that like wearing the band's T-shirt to the concert? What if there was an actual dress code? I imagined showing up in a T-shirt and being handed a boxy blazer from a lending closet.

The doorbell rang, and Kate shrieked with glee.

— ∽ —

When we met, Dev was in medical school, training to be a doctor. I was training to be a bartender. Dev was part of a group of students who took a table in my section at the brewpub every Tuesday. I liked the way he scrunched his nose to keep his glasses in place. I liked his mop of thick, dark curls. I liked the way his soft brown eyes followed me as

I poured beer from the bar and loaded empty pint glasses onto black circular trays.

One night, I used one of the five ballpoint pens in the back pocket of my jeans to sketch a beer glass wearing a stethoscope on a paper napkin. I served his IPA on top of it and walked away. When he smiled and showed the girl next to him, I wanted to hide under the bar. The best tips were on two-dollar Tuesdays, but if she was his girlfriend, I would change my schedule, perhaps find a new job entirely. It was Presley, of course, and she and Dev were just friends—by then.

One by one that night, Dev's friends left the table, and he stayed. We sat at the far corner of the bar and talked while I wrapped flatware for the next day. When he kissed me against the bricks outside the restaurant, he cupped both hands at the top of my neck, his fingers already at home in my messy hair. I pulled him the two blocks to my apartment.

Until then, I'd had an on-off thing with one of the waiters. It was never serious—he wore a hemp necklace. Flushed with thoughts of the previous night, not to mention that morning, I went to work and poured two secret shots behind the bar. I handed one to the waiter and told him I was no longer available—I'd met an older man. Dev was thirty at the time. I was twenty-five.

"He's going to be a doctor," I said. "He's known what he wants to be since he was seven."

The waiter had asked what I wanted to be when I was seven.

"A Muppet," I answered, before taking a shot and lugging a rack of pint glasses to the dishwashing station.

Until Dev, I'd been adrift in a postcollege, preadult haze, sharing an apartment with a PhD student who was never there. Dev was like an island I could huddle on, someplace safe I could ignore the lapping waves of things left undone in my own life.

I'd followed friends to Chapel Hill on a whim of a business plan. But when that didn't exactly work out, and I still had to eat, I found myself behind a bar. To my surprise, I liked it. I liked not having to do anything of consequence with my hands, other than pouring pints. I'd always been drawn to making things that were small in scale—things I could hold in my hands, that I could take with me. But the tiny acrylic animals I'd started painting on pieces of canvas the size of coasters collected dust in a box under my bed.

Dev's trajectory felt reassuringly textbook compared to mine. His father, originally from southern India, met his mother in London, where he trained in cardiac surgery. After his dad died in an accident when Dev was thirteen, his mother moved him and his brother, Jay, across the pond to Georgetown, where she'd accepted a job in the classics department. Not one to dwell in details such as emotions, she preferred to plaster a new life over the grief of the past one.

At med school in North Carolina, Dev had acquired an endearingly childlike joy around Southern staples like bourbon and barbecue, while his wardrobe still consisted solely of two pairs of 501 jeans and a pile of polo shirts. Jay was already a doctor by then, lauded for his international relief work. Dev's mother taught Chaucer and ran a squash club. When I met her for the first time, I pretended to understand both.

I liked how Dev didn't quite fit into a box I already knew, not in the standard rumpled khakis and floppy-haircut-that-wasn't-a-haircut way of Southern college men. Dev knew how to straddle different worlds, and I wanted to absorb his apparent ease by osmosis. I studied him like a road map—his determination, his confidence, the unflagging focus he directed at the people around him, including me. He made me feel grounded just by proximity.

Dev drew energy from his work, even when the hours would have turned my brain into baby food. He'd describe assisting on an hours-long surgical procedure during a med school rotation, likening it to a flow state. The only thing I could imagine close to it was how I could lose myself to hundreds of tiny brushstrokes, watching a rabbit materialize hair by hair onto a four-by-four-inch square of canvas. I had my tiny tools, and he had his, I supposed; his just came with more intensive cleanup. And higher stakes. I could put the art I used to make in a drawer and forget about it, but his patients needed to walk out of the hospital. At night, he'd run his hand along my spine and describe, in detail, closing up an incision or doing something that sounded obscene with a needle, until I'd demand he do something different with his mouth.

We'd been seeing each other for four weeks when he told me about his father, and how he'd gone into medicine in part to feel close to him. We were talking after my shift, and he spoke to the dingy ceiling of the brewpub even as his fingers traced lines up and down my forearm.

"It's like I was always supposed to do it. Does that sound stupid?" he asked.

"Well, I don't know anything about destiny," I said, "because I work at a bar."

He'd laughed into my hair, whispered, "I can be your destiny," and kissed my ear, and I realized I was in love with him. Nothing had ever felt so effortless.

—∞—

Six months later, I was halfway through a secret application to art school, and Dev was two weeks away from starting residency, when I found out I was pregnant. It wasn't that my application was going to stay a secret. But what was the point of telling Dev about my dream program—which wasn't in North Carolina—if I wasn't even sure I'd get in? I'd planned on crossing that bridge when I came to it. When the test turned positive, I felt like I'd detonated dynamite under it instead.

It was the day before med school graduation. We were supposed to go to a party. Dev burst into the apartment like a tornado, whipping off scrubs, showering, pulling on one of his two pairs of jeans. He'd called out that Elvis wanted to meet for a drink first with her professor boyfriend, and was I ready to go? I sat on the couch, legs curled under me, staring into space.

I told him he didn't have to worry about it—the baby, not the party. We hadn't known each other that long. I'd get my own RV, a small one, and caravan with my parents, I said. I'd bring the baby up on the road; he'd never have to see me again. I joked to keep from crying. I couldn't look at him.

"I know we were careful, and it's probably embarrassing because you aced Biology 101 and everything," I said. "But there was that time, when we went camping . . . Anyway, really, it's fine. Babies like moving vehicles. That's what I hear. People say that."

I kept my eyes trained on my hands, turning the ring on my pointer finger around and around in a nervous circle. Dev was the best person I knew, and the thought of making someone who was half of him, however unplanned, made me feel giddy, and not just from nerves. Surely this wasn't part of Dev's plan, however, and I wanted to make it easier for him to just say it, to not draw things out.

When I met his eyes, though, Dev was smiling. He looked like someone had handed him a puppy, one he hadn't asked for, and one that had immediately peed on the rug, but still.

"Are you done?" he asked.

"I don't know." It was all I could think to say. "I don't know what I am."

He'd pulled me up from the couch and wrapped his arms around me. He felt so solid. He said, "I guess you'll need to meet my mother at graduation this weekend."

At that point, I didn't know "the baby" was actually "babies." When Kate and Toby made their arrival, a perfect little twofer of best-laid-plans TNT, I was relieved in a way. I rode the wave of what others needed of me as a new mom, a new wife, and called it an identity. I didn't have the time or emotional capacity to think about who I was, or what I really wanted. I stuck my MFA application in a proverbial drawer along with my paintbrushes. I cut way back on my job at the bar but didn't give it up entirely, subbing in for summer lunch shifts when there were plenty of adrift college students to babysit. The extra money helped, and I liked how I didn't have to choose who to be when I was there. I could explain the difference between a hefeweizen and a saison to a visiting professor, then ask about her research. I could live vicariously, if only for the night, in someone else's life experiences. And when someone complained about the fries being soggy or the new sour beer being sour, I only had to wait for them to leave, not read them a bedtime story. If pressed, I preferred characterizing myself as "flexible" rather than "lost."

When Dev finished residency, he took a job at the university hospital, and we stayed put. Our life was busy and loud and messy, and it didn't include the Caribbean vacations Dev's work friends could escape to, or the jaunts to Europe my parents had started posting about on YouTube. I'd wait at home for Dev to get out of work and we'd laugh about something goofy Toby did that day, or marvel at the mosquito net prototype Kate made from the pot holder loom kit Lilly sent her. The labor of my days was tangible, and ever-present, and we were together, even when life didn't look anything like what either of us might have planned.

Then, something shifted.

Dev started to stay at the hospital until after the kids' bedtimes, and would come home with brows furrowed. When I'd ask him about work, he'd turn evasive. Well after I'd gone to bed, he'd stay up, lost to a Netflix show about chefs traveling to remote destinations to forage mushrooms. He started drinking bourbon from a mug.

The energy, the good kind, that had run between us since the night we met—it was like it flatlined and just lay there, vibrating with a low hum of tension neither of us knew how to name. When Dev announced he wanted to take this new job, to make a clean break and move up north, the first thing I felt—again—was relief. If he wanted to leave everything else, I reasoned, it meant the problem couldn't be me.

Kate squealed from under a blanket when we heard Dev's key turn in the door, and I almost squealed with her. All day I'd imagined us on the walk home from the party, full of gin and tonics and lobster rolls, lazily holding hands and talking about how this move was a great decision, how it let us reprioritize our family, reenergize our relationship. We were marriage ninjas, really.

Dev dropped his bag onto the floor, his shoulders slumped. James Dean scampered over to bury his nose in the bag and emerged with a Clif Bar wrapper. Then Dev headed straight to our bedroom, stepping over the three pairs of legs sticking out from the couch-cushion shelter.

I made a move toward him, but he put his hands up in the air in a "no touching" signal.

"Sorry," he said. He turned on the shower. "Let me just rinse the pesky MRSA off first."

"Always the gentleman," I said, wiping my hands on my shirt even though we hadn't touched. I eyed the clothes I'd thrown over the bed. "Hey! Fun thing about showering—we actually have a thing. At the yacht club. I mean, it's a party. I was going to tell you, but you stayed at work so late . . . Maybe you noticed the extra pair of legs sticking out of the couch shelter? I got a babysitter and everything."

I spread out my hands like I'd made a full Thanksgiving meal. Then I held up the dress I'd found on sale at Anthropologie before we moved. It was speckled with small yellow elephants. I squinted.

"Could these pass as anchors from a distance?"

"Absolutely," Dev said, not turning around. He threw his shirt into the trash bag–lined laundry bin.

It felt a little like when I took Toby to a checkup and didn't tell him about the shots. If I acted like it was no big deal that I was just springing this on him, maybe Dev would follow my lead.

"It'll be fun. I promise," I said. "We can drink gin and tonics! That's what people drink at yacht clubs, right? Didn't you go to one, when you spent summers in Annapolis?"

As Dev stepped into the shower, I grabbed one of his shirts from the closet and laid it on the bed next to my dress. It was a light flannel, and appeared marginally more festive than the collection of black T-shirts stuffed into his dresser drawer.

"Work seemed busy when we stopped by today. Want to tell me anything about what you did? A day in the life?" If we were to leave the cottage and be around people again, we would need to at least present as a couple who knew more about each other than a Netflix algorithm.

"You sure?"

"Why, is it gross?" I peeked into the bathroom.

Dev allowed a small smile. "Only some of it."

"I can take it. This is the new me," I said as I pulled on my dress.

"Well, my first patient swore she had a kidney stone," Dev said, from behind the shower curtain. "She reported all the right symptoms. But then she asked for 'that one that starts with a D.'"

"Dayquil?"

"Dilaudid," he said. "It's an opiate."

"Right. Of course. So, straightforward?"

"I mean, kidney stones hurt like hell. But, to quote Dr. Presley 'Elvis' Keen, 'It's not Burger King. You can't just order an opiate your way.'"

While I wondered what else Dr. Presley "Elvis" Keen was telling him, he said, almost to himself, "I've been here for a week, and I've had patients ask for more drugs by name than I knew in college."

"I only knew Midol and weed," I said. I brushed my hair one last time and checked my mascara in the bathroom mirror, breathing in the smell of Dev's shampoo.

"I diagnosed someone with hep C. I referred a patient to another clinic for Suboxone, because she's pregnant and withdrawing could make her miscarry. I talked to people not that much older than me about high blood pressure, cholesterol, asthma, and chronic pain—not that I could help them actually solve anything." His voice sounded tired and flat. "My last patient of the day seemed like a college kid—I mean, he was twenty-one. Athletic."

Okay, I thought, *this can't be so bad. A follow-up for a dislocated shoulder, or an old-fashioned ACL tear.*

"He had an abscess on his foot," Dev said. "I swear it's from inject-ing drugs."

Or not.

"We can skip tonight," I offered. "It's not like I sent a formal RSVP."

But Dev said quickly, in a tone I tried to tell myself was simply muffled by the shower, "No, it'll be fun."

I walked back into the bedroom and slipped a charm bracelet I'd made in college around my wrist, telling myself the tiny diary keys could be nautical, like for treasure chests. Then I glanced back into the bathroom. In the gap between the shower curtain and the wall, Dev leaned under the steaming showerhead. He let the water run down his head and over his shoulders, and I listened to it splash onto the bottom of the porcelain tub. For what felt like five minutes, he didn't move to wash his hair or pick up the soap.

The party would probably be a small group, quiet and restrained like the houses on the streets leading up to it. And, I reassured myself, Dev's work would settle down in the same way. It had to. Wasn't that the point of all this?

chapter 4

Rumford Yacht Club was nestled between waterfront manors, homes that somehow managed to look tasteful and quaint at first glance while being sneakily enormous in square footage. As Dev and I walked, we passed at least a dozen black BMWs and Audis with out-of-state license plates tucked into driveways. It baffled me that the largest dwellings—the ones sitting on the most prime waterfront real estate—were people's second homes, that they simply sat empty for most of the year.

On Harbor Street, a row of maple trees shielded the day-to-day goings-on of the clubhouse from direct view. While the lawn out front was absolutely teeming with people, a gravel drive led back to where I assumed the real party was taking place. Until moving to Rumford, I'd only inhabited spaces of this kind of wealth in my imagination, like in high school, when Simon and I would bike at night to the neighborhood with the big houses, sneak into their backyards, and pretend to sip drinks brought to us by pool boys.

The stillness in the air on the walk over made speech feel compulsive, like it was vibrating in my throat, and Dev's silence had only amplified my uncertainty about what awaited us.

"When the kids start school, I can go to Pilates or something. I think it's what I've been missing," I blurted.

Finally, Dev looked at me and laughed. Our arms brushed, and I remembered when his touch would send heat up my arm, how it would travel through my limbs and make me want to cover every inch of my body with his. I hoped, again, that this night would be the reboot we needed.

Dozens of cars packed the street, and I stared as a man tossed a bag and some wet sandals into the back of his SUV before stripping the long-sleeve UV shirt off his back. He pulled a blue button-down from a hanger. I craned my neck to see what else he had stored in the car, and what he was going to do about his shorts, but Dev nudged me before I could find out.

"Are you on a guest list or something?"

I had no idea. But I wasn't going to tell him that. "It's not a frat party," I said instead, ushering him down the driveway like I knew exactly what I was doing.

The clubhouse itself was two stories—its myriad shingles weathered to varying shades of tan by wind and salt spray. A row of three dormer windows lined the second story, upside-down Vs pointing to the heavens, and on the first floor, a wraparound porch extended from both sides and around the rear of the building, promising a gorgeous sunset view from every angle. The porch's railing and posts were painted white, a crisp contrast to the shingled exterior. A second-story balcony, also white, faced the water and lent shade to the deck below.

Past a white flagpole shaped like a *T*, closer to the water, I could make out the silhouettes of small boats—ones that looked like they could fit just one or two people, some maybe three or four. I wondered how it all worked, this foreign language of putting bathtubs into the water and making them fly across the bay.

Turning back to the club, I gazed at a pair of french doors framed with bright white siding that led inside—to what? Charmingly worn leather couches? A Gatsby tower of martinis? Was I even allowed inside?

Next to us on the lawn, a foursome with sweaters draped across their shoulders chatted animatedly, their cheeks ruddy and hair artfully wind-tossed, like they'd wrapped a cologne commercial that very minute. Someone mentioned docking in the "BVI," and it took me a second to register that this was not something that required antibiotics.

Another group held life jackets, as if they'd simply hopped off their sailboat to enjoy a freshly muddled cocktail.

Women wore tiny diamonds spaced evenly on thin chains or pink tassels that dangled from necklaces and earrings onto crisp linen. Flowing dresses, many with ruffled shoulder straps or cap sleeves, nearly all in dizzying patterns of fluorescents, floated above gold and leather sandals. I wanted to run my hand down one of the bright patterned dresses and ask the woman next to me if she actually owned a steam wand, or if she'd bought the dress that same day. Everything about the ladies on the lawn was smooth: their dresses, their hair, their foreheads.

The men wore polos or pressed button-up shirts, basically anything with a collar. Folded sunglasses hung from their shirts' open necklines or lay perched on heads. The amount of khaki didn't surprise me, but the cranberry-colored pants were a delightful development. And the belts—I'd never seen so many belts. Leather belts, fabric belts, belts with flags on them.

I had so many questions. What did all those flags mean? How had we moved from the south with so little pastel? I brushed my hands over the yellow elephants shuffling around my hips. I'd never seen casual look so goddamn elegant. Even the baseball hats—red with a little yellow island on the front, many sun-lightened to varying shades of pink—conveyed some kind of status. I just wasn't sure what.

"What's up with the hats?" I mumbled. It wasn't entirely rhetorical; I thought Dev would know. While summer camp for me was concrete and asphalt, riding bikes with Simon to the community pool, Dev spent summers at sailing camp in Maryland.

"Let's get some drinks," I said, not waiting for him to answer. "We can explore. Maybe make out behind a boat or something."

"Aye aye, skipper," Dev said, grinning just enough to make me feel like I could still right our ship like an old-timey sea captain.

I parked us in a line at an outside bar, a cloth-draped wooden countertop set up on the lawn. I was still trying to determine where to stand, how to stand, or where to look, when I realized Lacy—a.k.a.

Navy Stripes, keeper of crisp blue ribbons and bestower of yacht club invites—was less than six feet away. I didn't know if I should approach her, thank her, or run from her.

Lacy's hair lay in the same perfect symmetry as in the coffee shop, an inch above her shoulders, smooth in defiance of the moisture in the air. She reached skyward to emphasize the size of something, yet her drink refused to spill over the sides of her shimmering cup. Her skin glowed beneath a seersucker maxi dress. Her red lipstick was crisp and bold. She looked positively regal, like she was holding court.

She said, apparently finishing a story, "Then Warren moored *Penelope* and we both agreed to pretend it never happened." The others—Poppy, Heidi, and another woman I hadn't yet had the pleasure of humiliating myself in front of—chuckled as long as was appropriate, confirming it was exactly the right mix of hilarious (very) and embarrassing (only a touch) to be endearing.

"So what'll it be?" Dev asked.

"What?"

"I said mixed drinks are inside. Beer and wine only outside. Can you make do without a gin and tonic?"

I was about to suggest we leave and grab a bottle of wine from the store on Market Street instead. We could take it to the rocky public beach, just the two of us. That was something I knew how to navigate—at least I used to. But Poppy called my name.

"Charlie! You made it. Lacy, I told you she'd come."

Poppy bounded over and pulled me into a hug. Her bare skin was warm, her cheeks flushed. She smelled like sunshine and coffee. Wait. I sniffed again. It was Kahlua.

"Your dress is *adorable*," Poppy cooed. "You remember Lacy. And did you meet Heidi?"

Heidi hadn't uttered a word during my apology tour after tearing the café asunder, but I supposed we'd technically met. Where Poppy was on the shorter side, and fit, Heidi was tall and slender—and she was holding two drinks. She raised them in what I hoped was a greeting.

"Welcome," Lacy said. She fixed her eyes on Dev, who was still waiting in line at the bar. "Both of you."

"And this is Bitsy van der Koff," Poppy said.

Bitsy, who had coiffed hair and pearl earrings the size of Gobstoppers, said, "Are you here for the season?"

"Oh, I'm just normal," I answered, suddenly groping for a way to appear normal in any way. I got the impression none of these women had ever summered as an ice cream scooper.

"I mean, I live here now, but not only for the summer. I'll be here in winter. And spring." I waved. "Still here."

Heidi's eyes shifted toward the bar. Bitsy van der Whatever walked away without making eye contact again. Like a nervous puppy, I fumbled for something else to say.

"I grew up in the south—I mean, kind of all over, but mostly in the south—so I'm looking forward to snow. That's a thing here, right? I've never even owned snow boots. Or boat shoes." I turned to make sure Dev wasn't miming me digging a hole. "You need so many shoes up here."

After a beat, Poppy said, again, "That's a cute dress."

"Oh, I don't know. I don't think elephants can swim," I said. My face burned against the cool sea breeze, and I felt the underarms of my dress dampen, threatening to drown the elephants.

Lacy set down her drink. "What a beautiful night. Can you even stand it?" The women nodded knowingly, like someone had finally said something that made sense.

I wondered if someone from the club would appear with a bottle of champagne to refill Lacy's plastic cup. Dev joined us then holding two beers, one of which, I noted, was already only half-full.

"This is my husband, Dev," I said. "The one I mentioned at the coffee shop. I mean, he's my only husband."

Lacy looked at Dev like he was a treat. "So, you're the new doctor in Bradley."

"I suppose I am," Dev said, handing me one of the beers. I waited for him to say more, but instead he reached into his pocket and pulled out his phone. It was buzzing with a call, and I could see the name "Elvis" on its lit-up lock screen. He threw me a look of apology and excused himself.

"Work," I explained, holding my free hand out like it was fine—totally understandable—that he was taking a call at that very moment. "Never stops."

We were next to a table with spreads of crackers, soft cheeses, grapes, and I was dying to start piling bits and pieces onto a plate. I hadn't eaten dinner beyond a piece of the kids' frozen pizza; surely there was a lobster roll here somewhere, too. But when I realized none of the women were eating, my mouth decided it would keep talking instead.

"So, yes, Dev's a doctor at the clinic. It's the one near the hospital. But he doesn't work *at* the hospital. He sends some patients *to* the hospital, I think." How many times had I just said *hospital?*

Lacy brought her cup to her red lips. It was full again. How had I missed it?

"Where's he from?" Lacy said, in the same tone I imagined she'd use to ask where I'd found such cute shoes.

"Georgetown," I answered, even though I suspected it wasn't what she really wanted to know. "By way of London." I gave a pointed smile. The one time someone asked this in reference to Kate and Toby at a mommy-and-me music class, I answered with "my uterus."

"Love the accent. And how great for your family, having a doctor," Poppy said quickly, clutching her drink with both hands. Her tight ponytail bobbed with enthusiasm. "Paxton sprained his wrist last week on our backyard zip line. If Davis was a physician instead of an investment banker, maybe we could have avoided a night in the ER to make sure it wasn't broken. Pax had a lacrosse tournament that weekend, so stakes were high."

"Doesn't he have a lacrosse tournament every weekend?" Heidi asked.

"Stakes are always high," Poppy confirmed.

"He'll be back over any second," I said, trying and failing to hide my annoyance when beckoning Dev back over with my eyes didn't work. He shook his head and grinned slightly as he listened to whatever Presley was saying, at seven at night, on a Friday.

Poppy grabbed the elbow of a tall man in a fitted pink polo shirt. "This is *my* husband, Davis," she said. "He sailed in the race today, so please forgive his swarthiness."

Clean-cut and as evenly tan as Poppy, Davis looked the opposite of salty. His boat shoes had seen better days, but looking like they were run over by a car somehow added value; even I understood that much. He held two plastic cups sloshing with mudslides.

"Babe, I've been waiting for these!" Poppy held one out in Lacy's direction, but when Lacy tilted her head and hissed, "No sugar," Poppy thrust it at me instead.

Dev returned, and I waited for him to smirk or raise an eyebrow as I accepted the chocolate syrup monstrosity. Drinks masquerading as dessert had never been my thing; it was a joke between us. But he didn't seem to notice this time, so I sipped my alcoholic milkshake while Davis rhapsodized about sailing—*freedom, trying to master something that's impossible to tame.* I was pretty sure I'd read similar sentiments in a Jon Krakauer book, but Dev nodded like it made perfect sense.

"I'm sure you must be swamped at the clinic," Lacy said. "What with the partners retiring."

Dev looked surprised. "You know about them?"

Lacy smiled. "It's a small town."

"Oh, maybe you know Presley, too," I said. "That's who Dev was talking to. I guess you could say she's the one you can thank that we're here. Not that you need to thank anyone. But maybe you've seen her around? She's, um, really tall, like Dev."

Dev gave me a questioning look, and I realized how nonsensical I sounded. We both knew Presley hadn't set foot in any yacht clubs. She hardly did anything but work.

"No doctors in this bunch," Lacy said, shrugging at Poppy and Heidi like their choice of employment was a significant inconvenience.

"Can we go out on the pier to look at the boats? Dev, I wonder if they're the kind you used to sail." What I meant was, *Dev, please come back to Earth and help make sense of this new life for me.*

"Oh sure, the dock," Davis said. "Dev, follow me."

Where I grew up, the piers were wide and long—they had ice cream bars and pinball games. The yacht club dock was narrow, stretching from the lawn into the mouth of the harbor. It was for business, for going to and from boats, enough room on the walkway for the carrying of necessities—bags? life jackets? martini shakers?—but not lingering in the middle, and certainly not for making out under. At the end there was nothing to hold on to or balance against, presumably so you could step directly off it and onto a boat. But it also seemed like you could simply make the wrong move, lean the wrong way, and disappear right into the shimmering blue-gray harbor.

I moved to follow Dev, but Lacy laid a cool hand on my arm. "Don't be a stranger, Dr. Dev," Lacy said as he turned and walked away. "Charlie, you must be dying for a tour."

chapter 5

Lacy started walking without waiting for an answer, so I followed her and the other women to the edge of the lawn. The grass gave way to large rocks, and the water near the shore was so murky, I couldn't see the bottom.

"*Penelope* is third on the left," Lacy said, pointing to a cluster of sailboats. They all looked the same to me, but I picked out the biggest and decided it must be Lacy's.

"It's gorgeous," I said.

"She," Lacy said.

"Who?"

"*Penelope*, of course. We'll have you and Dev out on her sometime."

I wasn't sure how I felt about being trapped on a boat, at sea, with Lacy. "How do you get out there? To . . . her, the boat?"

"You take the launch," Lacy said.

I giggled, imagining being shot from a cannon. I threw back more of the mudslide.

Poppy sighed. "Summer after junior year, I dated the boy who drove the launch boat. His name was Ames. One time, we stayed on a little island out there, drinking his dad's vodka until sunrise. The next day he yakked into his dry bag between passengers." Poppy raised her drink, and melted whipped cream sloshed over the side, barely missing her rattan espadrilles. "To summer love!"

Growing up in Rumford sounded a little like one of the teen dramedies my mother used to work for, and not in a bad way. My bare shoulders warm from the setting sun, I watched Dev's lanky silhouette on the dock as he climbed onto a dinghy with Davis. Rumford did seem like the perfect place for a summer fling. Is it called a summer fling if you just start having sex with your husband again?

Lacy, Heidi, and Poppy suddenly moved so close, I knew I should have used more than herbal deodorant. "It's fortunate you met us so quickly, Charlie," Lacy said. "We're all adults, obviously, but it can be hard to be new here. Our children have been friends since they were born."

"When I moved here from California, in high school, I felt so lost. Thank God I found tennis," Poppy said with a kind of reverence. "Don't worry, though. Bitsy van der Koff didn't even speak to me until I married Davis, and now we're committee cochairs."

Blame it on bouncing from place to place as a kid, on my parents' wanderlust, on the RV, I suppose, but I'd never quite landed with an actual "friend group." I'd always enjoyed having a smattering of friends in different places—ones I met on the road, artsy friends from college who moved on to New York or LA, restaurant pals who were passing through. That way, I'd never really felt excluded, which was a neat trick for never really getting close to people.

"I think everyone should have the opportunity to have a life like this," Lacy said conspiratorially, like there was going to be some kind of entrance exam at the end of the summer.

Lacy had lowered her voice, making me edge even closer. My toe caught on a small rock, I imagined tipping over, plunging into the water. I took another sip of the mudslide.

A boy ambled over to Heidi's side, his hair the same shade of straw. He was older than the twins by a few years, and he pulled at a blue blazer as Heidi straightened his collar. I clocked a giant diamond on her ring finger, so I asked, "Is your husband here, too, Heidi?"

Lacy's eyes flicked to Heidi's son. The boy dug his foot in the grass. I worried I'd said the wrong thing—maybe they were divorced, and that ring was from a second, or, who knows, third marriage. Maybe he was in prison for a white-collar crime. I didn't know anything about these women's lives.

"My dad's on a trip," the boy said.

"Business or pleasure?" I asked nervously, because now I was an airline attendant. I raised the cup to my lips, but it was empty.

The corners of Heidi's mouth lifted into a smile, like someone was pulling tiny strings. "Teague is sailing around the world," she said. "He took some time off from work, and he's clear off the grid for now. Living his best life and all that."

Poppy rubbed Heidi's arm. "Teague is such a great sailor, Heidi. Really goal oriented. He'll be home before you know it. He just has to stay the course."

Was this the kind of life Lacy thought everyone should have? The thought of just taking off because you wanted to was a little dizzying.

"It really is lovely," Lacy said, her voice like velvet. "We should all be so determined. Hayes, why don't you go find Ivy and the boys?"

"Charlie, are your kids here?" Poppy asked as Hayes trudged away.

"I didn't want to worry about Toby running off or Kate reporting any safety violations," I said. I wondered which boat Davis had ferried my husband to, when they'd come back, and what I needed to do to keep him from formulating a nautical escape plan. "Maybe next time?"

"Rumford is a special place to grow up," Lacy said. "You just have to know where to go." Poppy nodded solemnly, like this was essential information. Heidi stared past them.

"Like the beach club," Poppy said. "There's a camp for kids, and so many activities."

"Kate loves camping," I said. What I meant was, she had a guidebook.

Poppy listed more clubs, counting them off on her fingers. "So there's the beach club, the tennis club—or squash, if you prefer. There's the racquet club, but don't be fooled, it's not for tennis. For country clubs, you have the Dunes, the Walrus, the Tri—that's the Trident. It's my favorite of the three, but you should see what suits you."

I nodded vigorously, trying to keep up.

"And in the offseason, for school, Heidi's Ellery and my Ivy go to Bridge Academy," Lacy said. "Your kids could fit right in."

The grass under my feet tilted a little. I passed Bridge Academy's tidy campus when I left town to grocery shop for items made with nonartisanal ingredients. Bridge was like a small college for children.

"It sounds lovely," I managed to say. I'd planned on enrolling the kids in public school. No way in hell could we afford an academy of any sort, but it did sound lovely.

"This club is lovely, too," I said, this time with a hint of genuine longing in my voice. It wasn't the yachts or the fancy clothes, or it wasn't *just* those things. It was having a place to go, not being alone with the seagulls, or in the cottage, waiting for Dev to come home.

Across the lawn, a group of teenage boys appeared on the far side of the club. All six of them emerged with button-down shirts, khaki or faded red shorts, and worn-in leather boat shoes. Their hair was wet, impatiently run under a showerhead to rinse away the dried-in salt from a day out on the water. *There must be a changing room at the club,* I thought, *maybe a Brooks Brothers.*

I imagined Toby as an adolescent, stepping smoothly from a boat onto the dock like it was second nature. He'd wear rumpled cranberry shorts held to his narrow hips by one of those navy fabric belts studded with miniature sail flags. Kate would come home from college for the summer and teach in the sailing school. They'd be sun-kissed, their skin glowing. We'd meet for lunch on a Sunday, sip unsweetened iced teas on the club's covered back porch, so accustomed to the ridiculous beauty of the harbor, I wouldn't even comment on it anymore.

I'd spent enough of my life hovering around the perimeter of things. I didn't want my kids to feel like I had, especially not here—watching everyone else live their neat little lives as if through a snow globe. They could be anyone in this new life. Who knows, maybe I could, too. Maybe *that* was what we all needed.

"Applications for the club already closed in the spring. Bitsy van der Koff is membership chair and," Poppy lowered her voice, "she's kind of a bitch about it."

"Oh," I found myself saying. "Maybe if I just introduce myself again . . ."

Lacy smiled with teeth so white they made my eyes hurt. "Didn't I say everyone should have the opportunity to have a life like this? You and Dr. Dev can be our guests at the events that really matter. And you better get cracking, Charlie. The best party of the year is just six weeks away."

"That's incredible," I said, a bit stunned. "I hope I can repay the favor." And for a bizarre second, I thought Lacy might pet me.

"That's what friends are for, right?"

Friends? I felt like I'd been dropped into the yacht club next to Lacy—tall, imposing, beautiful, connected Lacy—from another planet. I felt like E.T., extending my pointer finger, croaking, "Friennnnd."

Six weeks felt like a lifetime away. Anything could happen.

The women moved on to talking about a cooler that Heidi swore could fit two bottles of prosecco upright, next to a liter of Gatorade, for soccer games. I took the opportunity to slink away, to pass like a jellyfish, pale and wobbly, through a cluster of neon starfish dresses. I needed some air that didn't feel filtered through a hedge fund and a drink I could see through. I headed to the outside bar to ask for a water, something to clear my head before I went in search of Dev and told him about this latest development.

A man ahead of me leaned on the white tablecloth. I waited for him to step aside, but he lingered, chatting with the bartender. His blond hair was damp, raked back from his face. A wet spot from the bar spread on the elbow of his untucked shirt. He was barefoot.

When he turned and caught me staring, I managed to raise my empty cup toward the bar.

"Ray," the man said, "I think our friend here needs something."

I forgot about asking for water. I briefly forgot about finding Dev.

"Nothing with chocolate sauce, please," I managed to say. "And extra limes if you have them."

I patted the sides of the elephant dress, wondering if I needed to pay. Barefoot Guy said something I couldn't hear, and the bartender nodded. A breeze from the harbor blew loose strands of hair into my face. From beneath the white cover of the bar, the bartender pulled out a small glass bottle with a tiny gold dragon on the label. He poured it into two plastic cups.

"I don't know if I should be taking shots," I said. "It doesn't seem like that kind of party."

"I'd sip it," the man said, handing me the cup. "Unless you want someone to drag you out of the harbor tomorrow morning."

The barefoot man stepped aside. I stood still, holding my cup, as he nodded his head sideways.

"Well, come on," he said. "We're in this together now."

chapter 6

I glanced around, but I didn't see Dev anywhere in the crowd. Did he set sail with Davis? There was something interesting about this man who seemed to have just dropped into the yacht club and, what, forgotten his shoes? He clearly wasn't worried about being handed a blazer from a lending library.

Five minutes, I thought, as I followed Barefoot Guy to the edge of the lawn. I *was* there to make friends. And to have a little fun. And maybe I was a little bit drunk.

I stood under the cover of a maple tree, the new drink cool in my hand. The harbor glowed with an absurd blend of pink and purple, like someone had swiped their palm across neon sidewalk chalk.

"I like your elephants," Barefoot Guy said, nodding at my dress.

"Thanks," I said. "I like your shoes."

He wiggled his toes in the grass. "I left them on the boat."

I took another sip from the plastic cup, savoring the crisp burn of the tequila. *Look at where we live,* I thought. A glowing seascape in which ocean creatures smiled and adorned accessories. Men went on sabbatical from the rat race to sail around the world while their wives stowed bubbly wine in travel coolers at soccer tournaments. What was it Lacy had said? *Everyone should have the opportunity to have a life like this.* That statement had felt a little ridiculous, but maybe there was something to it. At the very least this felt like *my* chance to live this way. Maybe I could find an L.L.Bean outlet, let loose, get a tote bag.

For now, I kicked my own sandals off. I sipped my drink and rocked my heels into the cushy grass.

"Thanks for the drink," I said, trying to hold eye contact without blushing. Who did he think he was, having eyes like the sea glass Kate collected from the beach? Still, it looked like he hadn't shaved in a few days, not that it wasn't working in his favor. Something about the way he didn't seem as self-consciously scrubbed as the other men at the club made me drop my guard just a little.

"I'm Charlie. I just moved here." I held out my hand.

"Oliver," he said. His hand was cool from the drink.

"Are you local, or are you summering?" I couldn't help myself. "Did I say it right? I didn't know it was a verb until recently."

"You can say it any way you want," he said with a half smile. "And no, I'm weekending."

"Where do you, um, week?" I asked. I shook my head. "Where do you live in real life?"

"New York. In real life. Here, hold this."

He handed me his cup and rolled his shirtsleeves past the soggy elbow. His forearms were tan and firm, like he did things with them, like they held more than a golf club. The wake of an incoming motor reached the dock, and the sailboats bobbed like rubber ducks. I felt myself sway with them.

"Much better," Oliver said. He leaned in to retrieve his drink. He smelled like salt and fresh limes. "I grew up in Rumford," he told me. "I haven't lived here for years. When I visit I do odd jobs, restore antique furniture. Back in the city, I make some of my own."

"Where in New York do you live?" I asked. "My brother went to college there." I wanted to ask about what he made, to tell him I made things, too—at least, I used to. But talking about the things I made always felt a little like opening my underwear drawer.

"I was in Brooklyn," he said. "I'm between places now. I was with someone, a chef, but there was someone else. In the walk-in freezer."

"Ouch," I said. *Well, that was personal.* I put my hand in my pocket, then took it back out again. Was he flirting with me?

"I'm staying in a friend's studio while he's filming in Iceland. He likes to Airbnb it on the weekends, so I come here. Mostly I sleep on my boat and keep to myself. I forgot about the race this weekend."

He swept his hand from the dock to the lawn. He was the third person I'd seen make a similar gesture, but it was less "can you believe how lucky we are" and more "eh, what're you gonna do." It took an edge off the intimidation factor, like maybe finding *my* way there wasn't a total impossibility.

Oliver wore khaki shorts, like most of the men at the club, but his white shirt was rumpled like he'd hastily grabbed it out of a duffel to pull over his broad shoulders. I'd smoothed my own wrinkled dress by holding it in the bathroom while Dev showered. In this hoard of pastel seahorses and fabric belts with whales that knew no seasons, Oliver seemed at ease standing apart. How did he do it? I was exhausted from trying so hard, and Oliver's confident aloofness—aided by the tequila— continued to loosen something inside of me.

"I need to ask you something," I said. "The hats. Are they party favors?"

What I meant was, *Can I have one?*

"Kind of," he said. "They're from the race. Or other races."

"Was there a 5K?"

Oliver smiled with half of his mouth again. "A sailing race."

I couldn't help it. Laughter rolled out of me in manic-sounding waves. I put a hand to my face, but I couldn't stop, not until some of the tension I'd been carrying released itself into the humid air. I wiped my eyes and looked to see whether Oliver was backing away, scanning for someone else who he could pretend needed him, but he just stood there, looking bemused, like he had no better place to be. I supposed I should try to explain.

"It's my first time at this yacht club. At any yacht club. I know, don't be shocked," I said, holding up my hand. It wasn't like with Lacy, how I kept stumbling, reaching for the right words then cringing as they came out wrong. I took another sip of the drink, then pulled out a lime and waved it around between my fingers.

"I have no idea what to say or do. I'm wearing a dress with yellow elephants, my six-year-old did my pedicure, and no one in my family has a cool sailing hat. I don't even have a red visor. I hate drinks that taste like dessert. The sugar makes my teeth feel like carpet." I took a breath, sucked the alcohol out of the lime, and dropped it on the lawn next to my toes. It was all the things I would have said to Dev, if only I could find him. "It's nice, too, I mean, I'm relieved . . . it's nice to talk with someone who doesn't seem so . . . perfect. But honestly, I'd also love to be so perfect. That would be okay, too."

The side of Oliver's mouth curved again. "Who says I'm not perfect?"

I groaned. "Sorry, I didn't mean it like that. It's just . . . looking around, it feels like no one here, you know, gets cheated on, crashes on couches, forgoes shoes, buys generic toilet paper."

He raised his eyebrows.

"I buy generic toilet paper," I admitted. "If you don't, it's fine." I needed to stop drinking.

"No, I get it," he said. "This crowd is polished within an inch of its life." He motioned for me to lean close. I held my breath, afraid I'd try to sniff him like a Yankee Candle. "Between you and me, it's a front for an elaborately choreographed network of swingers. It's why people never leave."

"Shut up." I was 96 percent sure he was joking.

"I'm kidding," he admitted, taking another sip. "I mean, those four *are* sleeping together." He pointed to two couples comparing pretend backhand tennis swings. "But it's probably for the best. I like your bracelet, by the way."

I snorted a little. Then I realized he was being serious this time. I turned my wrist back and forth, making the tiny keys jingle.

"Do you have that many secrets?" He leaned back against the maple, as if he really expected me to answer. I felt flushed, from the drink, from the sun.

"I used to make jewelry," I said. "With friends. We made custom charms, sold them in a couple of local boutiques, near where I went to college. They wanted to start doing pendants—for necklaces, mostly—like for kids' names or birthdays. You know, like those car decals with stick figures for every member of the family, but with overpriced jewelry."

I wasn't sure why I was opening up to this barefoot stranger about the thing that had crushed me. I assumed he could just take my embarrassment and hurt back to Brooklyn or wherever and I'd never see him again.

"One of them had a family connection near Chapel Hill, a boutique that wanted to partner with us, so I followed them there. I thought we'd get back to making some of the weirder stuff we did in college. I liked finding things and making something new out of them." I held up my wrist, letting the tiny keys clink softly like a wind chime. "Anyway, I started making these small paintings on the side, and we talked about doing a show together. But in the end, I wasn't—I mean, what I wanted to make—it wasn't a good fit. We were business partners by then I suppose, not friends. And they wanted to go in a different direction."

What I managed to not say out loud was that I'd learned a valuable lesson from the fallout. Everyone says "be true to yourself," like it's this magical key to happiness, but the truth is, not everyone actually wants that. Not everyone is going to like it.

"That's cold," Oliver said. "I'm sorry."

"Not as cold as a walk-in freezer," I said, attempting to joke my way through my awkwardly vulnerable admission. "Anyway, it was a long time ago. And it brought me to my true love. Bartending!"

Oliver snorted into his drink, and I felt another tiny thrill. I wasn't doing anything wrong, I assured myself. This was just fun. I was allowed to have fun. And I had to admit, it was nice to talk about myself. It was nice to have someone seem interested.

"What did you love about it?" he asked.

"About bartending?"

He just looked at me again, waiting. So, I told him the truth. "I could be whoever I wanted, for a few minutes at a time."

"And who are you now?"

"I think I'm taking suggestions."

"Oh great, is there a comment card I can fill out, or . . ." He looked around, waving an imaginary card as if looking for a box in which to place it, and he brushed the keys on my bracelet with his index finger.

This guy with his questions, and his hands, sheesh. I felt a confused kind of fuzziness that I wasn't sure I could entirely blame on the tequila, and I decided I'd probably absconded from the party for long enough.

"I should go," I said, turning back to the club. "But thanks for the drink."

By the time I finally found Dev, the harbor had almost swallowed the sun. The bulbs lining the edge of the club's awning glowed softly against the violet light of the evening. I desperately needed to find a bathroom after all those drinks, but first, I stood on my toes and leaned into Dev's ear—literally leaned, holding on to his shoulder for support.

"What did I miss?" I said. "Did *you* make any new friends?"

I gulped the rest of the drink I was holding. If he hadn't wanted to tell me what Presley's call was about, I didn't need to mention meeting anyone named Oliver, whom I'd probably never see again, anyway. Also, Dev smelled like Scotch.

"We went out to Davis's boat. I kind of wanted to stay out there forever."

"I'm glad you didn't," I said, trying not to take it personally. "Did you take the *launch* boat? I know what that is, by the way. I know lots of things."

"Solid work there, skipper. You'll be hoisting that mainsail in no time," Dev said. He put his arm around my shoulders, and I leaned into him again, on purpose this time. "Where are your shoes, by the way?"

I glanced toward the line of maple trees where I'd apparently left my sandals sitting in the grass, but before I found a way to answer, Davis appeared again and slapped Dev on the shoulder

"Plug your ears," he said. "Almost time for colors."

I looked around. Everything was white—the tent, the table covers. And you couldn't *hear* colors. How much had they had to drink out there? "Are they in the water? The colors?"

Before Dev could answer, a boom ripped through the silent air. I yelped and put my hand to my mouth, throwing Dev's arm from around my shoulders and looking around in panic. The clamor of voices ceased, all at once, and a polo-shirted staff member slowly lowered the American flag. I wanted to tell Dev about Lacy's offer, how we could come to the club all summer, or whenever there was a party, which was basically all summer. We could be boat people. Boat-adjacent, at the very least. In that moment, I could see it all clicking into place. I just didn't know when I was allowed to speak again.

The staff member holding the now-folded flag called out, "Carry on," and, like someone flipped a switch, the buzz of activity resumed at full volume.

"What just happened?" I hissed. My heart was still pounding.

"They did that in Annapolis," Dev said, stifling a yawn. "They lower the flag and shoot a cannon. You get used to it."

"Do you, though?" I felt bewildered, again, and right back to remembering how little I knew about this secret club. "Is there an admiral, like in *Mary Poppins*?" Maybe this was our cue to call it a night. I didn't think I could metabolize any more surprises. I told Dev we could go, if he wanted to. But first, I still had to find a bathroom.

I walked around the side of the porch, near where that group of boys had emerged. Tiny stones dug into my bare feet as the grass gave way to gravel and a pair of shingle-sided outdoor changing rooms, each with a small row of showers and bathroom stalls inside. I slipped into one gratefully.

I was washing my hands when I heard the crunch of footsteps on the gravel, the muffled sound of someone crying. I turned off the water and froze.

"Heidi, you have to get it together."

It was Lacy, her voice like ice. She was clearly in charge of every room she entered, even the alfresco bathroom. I hoped I never got on her bad side. Heidi stifled a sob. I didn't want to walk past them like nothing was happening, and I didn't want to interrupt, so I just stood there behind the wall.

"Freaking out doesn't change anything, Heidi. Teague isn't coming back anytime soon. And life won't be any easier for you if they know the truth."

Not coming back? The truth? But Poppy had gushed about Heidi's husband's sailing adventure. It didn't seem like a secret. Did he have a secret family? *Was* he in prison for a white-collar crime? Anything felt possible at that point in the night.

Heidi sniffed. "I wish you wouldn't bring him up so much. I worry, and I just want to pretend it's not happening. What if someone has, you know, a sharpened toothbrush or something?"

"Heidi, it's rehab, not *Shawshank*."

I could practically hear Lacy's eyes roll. So, Teague wasn't really on a hedge fund sabbatical—not for pleasure, anyway. And he wasn't galivanting with a mistress. I wondered what he was in rehab for.

"Seriously, Heidi. Pull yourself together. Pretend he's a client. You have to fight for what's best for him without being emotional. And you have to keep his business confidential. Isn't that how lawyers work?"

"But he's not a client," Heidi whimpered. "And I was a real estate lawyer."

"Look." Lacy's voice softened. Heidi hiccuped. "I'm sure it's hard for you or whatever right now. But he's going to be fine. Everything will go back to normal. Until then, it's better for them to believe Teague is rounding Cape Horn than sitting on a plastic chair in 'group' with people wearing gray sweatpants. Now, let's get back out there. We'll say you're crying because you drank too much wine. That much is true, anyway."

Heidi hiccuped again and agreed.

I listened to their steps recede. My mouth was dry, the air thick and salty as I walked over to the maple trees to retrieve my shoes. While "fake it till you make it" was sort of a guiding principle of my life thus far—I was seven months pregnant with the twins before I told Dev my knowledge of prom came not from personal experience but teen rom-coms—this was next-level secret keeping.

The sun was beneath the horizon, and I could just make out the lean lines of Dev's body as he waited for me on the gravel driveway that led back to the now-empty street.

I reached down for my sandals, and lying in the grass next to them was a faded red hat. I smiled—a party favor. I pressed the hat and sandal straps into my palm and walked out barefoot.

chapter 7

In the time it took me to pay Sidney and latch the front door, Dev was already in shorts and an old Georgetown T-shirt, uncapping a bottle of beer from the fridge. I joined him in the kitchen and leaned against the countertop, the edge of the granite cold and hard on my back. I longed to change out of my dress, but I was afraid if I took the extra minutes I would lose Dev to sleep or to his new favorite documentary series, about the lone chef foraging for mushrooms on an island in Norway.

"I got pulled into a group of people on the way out of the club," I said. "I think they thought I was someone else. I didn't know what to say about second-home kitchen renovations, so I just nodded like that toy bird Toby has, the one that dips its head over and over into a glass of water. My neck hurts. And just before I slipped away I told someone I wore velvet house loafers as a joke, and they replied with, 'Oh, what color?'"

Dev laughed. "That does sound painful," he said, taking a long sip but not moving any closer to me. I swear I could see his eyes searching for the remote.

"So, what did *you* think?" I asked, eyeing his beer and wondering how much he'd already had to drink that night.

I felt a whisper of cool air on my ankle and thought for a second he'd gotten the AC unit to work, but it was just the refrigerator. I poured a glass of water, and the plumbing made a high-pitched protest.

"The sailboats remind me of being a kid at summer camp," he said. He reached to the upper cabinets to stretch. His fingers grazed the dusty tops, and his T-shirt rose and fell over the waistband of his shorts. Not so long ago I would have taken it as an invitation to launch myself across the narrow kitchen. But the night hadn't closed the distance between us like I'd hoped. I just felt confused in new ways.

"Can we, like, sign one out? A sailboat? Is that how yacht clubs work?" I asked.

"Sadly, no. You have to own one already. Then you can moor it there. Maybe—if there's an opening. I asked Davis about it. If we want to get a boat in the next five to ten years, we should get on the wait-list now."

"Some club," I mumbled. I poured another water. "Those mud-slides were like melted McDonald's sundaes. I'm kind of wound up. Tell me more?"

Dev brushed his hair back with the palm of his hand and it fell right back over his forehead. "There was this guy, Warren. Did you meet him? He's something."

"Lacy's husband? You talked to him? When?"

"When I couldn't find you. He saw me with Davis and introduced himself. Then he just rode me about the clinic, didn't even buy me a drink first." Dev smiled, but he looked tired. "I gave him the *Rocky* version."

"The what?"

"The one where my patients are working hard to overcome difficult circumstances, no matter the odds. Like it's not all stacked against them in the first place. It's the *Rocky* version of health care. It's the one people like him want to hear."

I imagined someone in a hospital johnny, the young man from the waiting room with the baseball cap, arms raised above his head in triumph at the top of a long flight of stairs. Even I had to admit, Rumford served up the illusion that anything was possible. It wasn't just shiny; it was glittering.

"Some things do seem easier here," I said. "If you know the right people, I guess. All these clubs with membership lists, cute little drinks and theme nights. It's like college Greek life for grown-ups. It *is* a kind of escape. Just go sailing around the globe like Heidi's husband instead of . . ."

I stopped myself, considering the more complicated truth of what I'd overheard.

"Must be nice," Dev said, almost to himself, "to just . . . take off." He put the empty bottle in the sink, then he walked down the hallway and into our darkened bedroom.

His words were like a gut punch. If that was really how he felt, what were we even doing? I needed Dev to think it could be kind of magical here, too. This move was my turn to take a leap of faith for him—for us. In my mind, our unspoken deal was that if we did this, if I did this, he'd come back to me. Standing there in the kitchen, I wasn't supposed to feel even more alone.

chapter 8

A few days later, I was starting to think I should've hopped a jet to Thailand with my parents. At night, as the Norwegian chef in Dev's docuseries started explaining how *allemannsretten* was a right-to-roam law, meaning he could forage for mushrooms all day every day if he wanted to, I'd started browsing online clearance sales on my phone—foraging, as it were, for discounted neon-printed dresses. And I would do anything for my children, but if I spent another day with only them, as the cottage slowly came apart at the seams, I was going to start climbing the peeling wallpaper.

I went for a long walk that morning to get out of the house, before Dev had to go to work.

The harbor was a pane of smoky blue glass, and I matched my breathing to the steady beat of my sneakers. I thought about how I hadn't always been so devoid of *allemannsretten* in my own life. I used to fantasize about a cozy space, a café maybe, walls dotted with my tiny canvases. No one could say, "I don't know where I'd put it," or "I don't know how to get it home," because each would be smaller than a library book. I didn't have much to fall back on, though, and when it came to paying rent, *allemannsretten* was never going to cut it.

When I returned, Dev was already halfway out the door.

"I think the shower's on the fritz again," he said as we passed each other.

"Cool, love you too," I said, wiping sweat from my brow into my hair.

In the kitchen, Kate bounced between the table and the counter to retrieve a frozen waffle from the toaster. She jingled softly like a cat's toy.

"Kate? Why do you sound like a Christmas elf?"

"So the bear will hear me coming." Kate tore off a piece of waffle before setting it on her plate.

I looked out the kitchen window and saw a squirrel. "Honey, I don't think Rumford has bears. They can't swim." I hesitated. "Can they?"

Kate sighed, as if to say we'd been over this before. "Only when they need to."

As I hydrated with coffee, Toby nibbled a chunk of waffle into a neat square and fed it to his plastic dinosaur. Kate jingled her way from the kitchen to the living room. I'd waited all week for someone to reach out about the beach club—any club, really. I'd have jumped for a club soda by Thursday.

And then—finally. A ding from my phone.

Poppy: Girl! Where have you been all week? Get your ass over to the beach club. Everyone is here. 🍸 😎

I stared at the text as I sat in the kitchen of our summer rental cottage with the shitty plumbing and creaky cabinets. Poppy had a point. Why hadn't I just gone there earlier that week? What was I waiting for? The ice maker let out an empty growl. I rinsed out last night's empty beer bottles for the recycling bin, and then texted back: On my way! Just tell me where to go and what to do.

Poppy sent the address, and I didn't even shower from my walk before gathering the kids and heading out the door. I texted Dev to join us there after work, still holding out hope for the power of spontaneity.

—◦◦◦—

The kids and I rode our bikes from Cedar Street, gliding by short gravel driveways and shingled cottages with painted white shutters. A quarter mile past the yacht club, Fifth Street Beach Club lay behind a nondescript wooden privacy fence in an otherwise quiet—it was all quiet—part of town. The last house on the street before the club was a saltbox, painted a pale shade of yellow. To the right of the front door, a small sign identified it as a historic site, once the home of a nineteenth-century sea captain. *I bet his wife wished he'd worked a little bit less, too,* I thought.

We pulled our bikes up to a small parking lot strewn with crushed sun-bleached shells. Kate took my hand and squeezed, and I realized we were both a little nervous. There wasn't a "Making New Friends" chapter in her books about bears.

The first thing I noted was that Fifth Street Beach Club was more club than beach. There was a bar: a snack bar with hanging bags of chips and pictures of strawberry and chocolate ice cream on Popsicle sticks, but also a *bar* bar. A line of juice boxes sat beside four pitchers of sangria, red-orange and packed with ice and chunks of fruit. High-top tables perched ready and waiting to balance sweating glasses of rosé. A row of outdoor grills, concrete topped with black grates, cradled bricks of charcoal and piles of ash. On the far side of the club, close to the sand, light-blue cabanas sat in a row like uniformly sized Monopoly houses. Matching umbrellas, tied closed, pointed skyward like soldiers' bayonets in formation over lounge chairs with navy-and-white-striped cushions. It was all so orderly. It was unlike any beach I'd ever been to.

Both kids remained glued to my legs. Toby pointed wordlessly at a wooden pirate ship the size of a Ford Explorer, a slide sticking out of its hull. A group of boys threw a football and chased each other until they fell into a clean-cut pileup of sandy arms and legs. A stack of boat shoes and leather sandals sat next to the volleyball court, where six teenagers tried to keep a ball in the air. I put a hand to my belly, sure I'd never lunged that confidently in a bikini at any age.

Kate eyed a cluster of younger children digging a giant hole in the sand with sturdy, wood-handled shovels. She'd been begging me for a real shovel, not the plastic kind we got at the grocery store. The sand was white and soft. The shoreline was as still as bathwater.

"Mama, can we go in?" Kate asked.

I thought she meant the water, then I realized we were still frozen at the entrance. I stepped forward and shut the gate. A teenage girl with a tight ponytail and a perky smile approached. She held a clipboard and a pen with a little blue pom-pom at the end.

"I can sign you in," she said. "What's your last name?"

"Oh," I said. "I'm not a member. I was just . . . told to come. Like *Field of Dreams*?"

The girl smiled politely and checked something at the bottom of her clipboard.

"Charlie? Poppy listed you as her guest."

"That's me," I said, a little too enthusiastically.

I looked around for Poppy, or anyone I could simply pretend to know. Women in linen pants and gauzy tank tops converged on lounge chairs in small groups. Others hovered on the patio near the bar. Most of the other moms—I assumed they were moms with the number of kids running around—wore trim sundresses and tasteful cover-ups with bright, busy patterns. The men were ubiquitous in khaki shorts or seersucker trunks, differentiated mainly by the pastel of their polo shirts.

"So other than that section, feel free to make yourself at home," the girl was saying. "You can use cash for the bar today if you don't have a member account. And welcome!"

"You too!" I said. "I mean . . . thank you."

I wiped my brow with my hand and straightened my shorts, dislodging my bikini bottom. If this really was what Poppy did every day, I could see why. Lounge chairs at the ready, refreshments for the taking—it was like passing through the Matrix of beach life.

"Charlie! You made it!" Poppy waved a clipboard near the bar. I shuffled the kids toward the blinding white of Poppy's tennis dress while Toby clutched the frayed hem of my shorts.

Poppy reached for two juice boxes. "Kids, would you guys like some apple juice? It's organic. So are the snacks." She winked at me. "So's the sangria!"

The kids took their drinks and Poppy pointed to a picnic table where some other boys and girls piled orange crackers shaped like bunnies onto crisp blue napkins. Kate and Toby sidled up to the bench, and I offered up a silent prayer for the universal love language of crunchy communal snacks.

"Thanks," I said to Poppy. "It's nice to finally see them with other kids."

"Oh, you should have just come here," Poppy said, like I'd spent every day since moving to Rumford purposely avoiding the beach club where, apparently, every single other person in town was simply lounging.

Poppy dipped to keep one of many clipboards from slipping. "I'd lose my mind without it. Kate and Toby will love the kids' camp. The lifeguards play games with them and organize an annual volleyball tournament. The winners get to work the snack bar for a day. Pax and Dodge just adore it. I even let them skip lacrosse practice."

Poppy beamed. I guessed if you didn't grow up knowing food service would be an integral part of paying for college, handing ice cream bars to hyped-up kids like Toby could be a novelty.

I chided myself for not reaching out sooner, for waiting for Poppy—for anyone—to text me first. Poppy seemed open and kind, not to mention an intriguing combination of charmingly aloof and deadly competitive. While I still felt like I had to pass some kind of initiation with Lacy—and Heidi, well, I wasn't sure she even remembered my name—Poppy seemed like someone who'd actually enjoy being peppered with questions about Rumford. She certainly seemed to have all the answers. Maybe she could be my Rumford whisperer.

"What about the little houses over there?" I asked, nodding at the cabanas. The girl at the door said they were off limits, which only made me want to zigzag through and touch each and every one.

"There is quite a wait-list for the cabanas," Poppy said. "Families hand them down, so they don't open up very often. Someone has to die or go through a really nasty divorce." She lowered her voice. "Between you and me, I have dibs on the Whitneys' cabana if Jenna runs off to Jackson Hole with her ski instructor again this year."

I laughed, but Poppy looked determined. "My brother is a ski instructor. In Montana," I said. "But he'd have to find someone's husband to run off with, so . . ."

"Wouldn't that be so funny," Poppy said. She held her smile but kept her eyes trained on the cabana.

I asked about the clipboards. There were so many of them.

"You should sign up for a committee," she said. "It's why all the free snacks and drinks are out today. First, make sure we have your information for the directory." She handed me a series of clipboards. "Then there's the family day committee, the kids' club, beach volleyball, STEAM Wednesdays . . . When I tell you I stay busy, Charlie, I mean it."

Poppy piled three more clipboards into my arms, then scooted over to chat with Davis.

I dumped them onto the bar counter, and when I looked up from signing, Heidi was next to me pouring a cup of sangria. Even in the shade of a giant straw hat her lipstick was bright and precise, her hair in beachy waves. My own lips felt dry, my skin slick with sunscreen. I'd grabbed the cranberry sailing hat before running out the door. I hoped I was pulling it off.

"Hi, Heidi, nice to see you again!" I said, trying to match Poppy's enthusiasm but feeling more like a yellow bird in a Disney cartoon. Heidi raised her cup in greeting, then fished out an orange slice and sucked the wine-infused pulp.

"Babe, is that your breakfast?" Poppy asked.

"Please," Heidi said. "I don't eat breakfast."

Hayes, Heidi's son, whom I recognized from the yacht club, scuffed his flip-flops on the sandy patio next to us, then brightened when he saw Poppy.

"Poppy, my dad sent a postcard from South Africa yesterday."

If it was possible, Poppy's smile grew in wattage. "Hayes, I can't wait to see it!"

She put her arm around Hayes. "Charlie, it's so sweet. Heidi's kids put a world map in their foyer. They tape up postcards that Teague sends along his journey."

"You can't miss it," Heidi said flatly. "It's there every time you walk in the door." Poppy shot her a sympathetic look over the boy's head.

"That's . . . nice?" I said. I didn't mean to say it like a question.

"The nanny did it for them," Heidi said. "Super nice of her. It certainly is a constant reminder of where Teague is." She downed the rest of her sangria.

Poppy squeezed Heidi's pale arm. "Hayes, why don't you bring a juice box to your sister over there?"

Hayes took an armful of juice boxes and dumped them unceremoniously onto the picnic table. The little girl next to Kate made a face at Hayes, and Kate laughed. She had to be Heidi's daughter. She wore a bright-yellow bathing suit, and a matching ribbon hung loosely in her blonde ponytail. I watched her and Kate share a frosted cupcake, each digging their finger into the icing, licking it, then giggling. Maybe if Kate could make a new friend, she wouldn't worry so much about wildlife.

Heidi pulled another orange from her sangria, and I wished I had something to say about juice cleanses. Instead what came out of my mouth was, "Kate and I talk a lot about how to find water in the desert."

Heidi called to the kids' table, "Ellery, show your friends the pirate ship."

Kate shoved a handful of crackers into her cargo pocket. They joined another little girl, hair held back from her round face by a headband with a giant navy bow. I recognized her from the Jib.

"Aren't they cute together? That's Ivy," Poppy said, reappearing with a fresh clipboard. "She's Lacy's daughter. Lacy must still be at her family's cabana. She should be back any minute."

My phone buzzed in my back pocket. *Maybe it's Dev,* I thought. But the screen showed my mother, on FaceTime. Lilly didn't usually call from abroad; she claimed it interfered with their flow. Worried, I picked up.

"Mom, is everything okay?" I said as quietly as possible.

"Oh, sugar, you would not believe," Lilly said, not quietly at all. She sounded breathless. I searched the screen for a clue, the industrial pea-green wall of a Thai hospital, the inside of a van. But the blur behind my mother, who appeared to be power walking, looked floral. Was that a hydrangea?

Lilly said, "Well, we're back Stateside a little early, dear. Your father contracted a nasty case of traveler's you-know-what in Bangkok. I told him to stick to the *kai jeow,* because that stall was packed, but he *had* to try some sun-dried squid from the man all by himself at the end of the row. He's always been a sucker for the underdog." Lilly shook her head. "He made it through the flight home, but can you ask Dev if one can take too many Imodium? Because let me tell you, I've been behind the wheel, and the RV has not been a place of reprieve."

I grimaced. I needed to get away from Heidi and Poppy for this call.

"Could you keep an eye on Kate and Toby for a second?" I said. I pointed to my phone while trying to muffle the sound.

Poppy tapped the clipboard against her hand. "On it, girl. Why don't you see if you can find Lacy? She was getting life jackets for Paxton and Dodge from her cabana, and they're itching to get out on the paddleboards before we have to leave for lacrosse."

I mouthed *thank you* and gave her a thumbs-up, then I walked away quickly before anyone else overheard my mother proselytizing on why one should always bring wet wipes in a carry-on bag. I slipped between two cabanas, leaning against one that seemed empty, so the check-in girl with the rule book wouldn't see me lingering in the off-limits zone.

"Then I bought a Fitbit on sale," Lilly said, between breaths. "Now I can track my steps while both Bessie and your father recover." She waved the phone to share an aggressive blur of pink and violet petals.

Something beeped, and Lilly waved her FitBit arm in victory. I half listened to her carouse about a jet-setting couple who she feared was impinging on their travel vlogging territory.

"I know your father hates to discuss the capitalistic aspects of our mobile lifestyle, but the fact is, we have to stay relevant if we want to fund our next experience," Lilly said. "Authenticity still takes means, Charlie Parker. It's like a human centipede."

"Oh God, Mom, that's not what you think it is."

The device on Lilly's wrist screeched again. Claiming spotty service, I ended the call before she could say more. I turned and pressed my forehead into the cabana I'd been leaning against. Would it kill my folks to go on a cruise and eat defrosted cocktail shrimp?

My phone buzzed again. What on earth could she have left out of that conversation? But it actually *was* Dev this time. He was at the club! And he wanted to know where I was.

I still needed to find Lacy, but the cabanas were identical; it wasn't like they had name tags. Just like everything in Rumford, you were simply supposed to *know*. I startled as something banged inside the cabana I'd been leaning on—the one I'd assumed was empty.

Holding my breath, I poked my head around the side of the cabana. I peeked into the open door, but instead of Lacy I found a man with damp blond hair and no shoes. I tried and failed to look away as he pulled a white T-shirt over his shoulders, its frayed hem catching on the top of his black board shorts.

I pivoted sideways and flattened my body on the outside wall of the cabana like I was the Pink Panther, just as Oliver called out, "Hey, Yellow Elephants."

chapter 9

I peeled my sweaty T-shirt from the wood siding and cursed under my breath. Lacy was still at large, and Dev was waiting for me, but I couldn't just scamper away after Oliver had seen me. Could I?

Inside the tiny house it smelled like coconut sunscreen and something musky. A wet suit hung in the corner.

"Nice hat," Oliver said.

"Thank you," I said, touching the faded brim. "I happen to race boats. Lots of them. I was just looking for someone. I wasn't, you know, lurking."

Oliver raised one eyebrow and wiped his hands on a towel. We stood there for a few seconds. He'd missed a spot of sunscreen on his neck, below his ear. I could just reach out, swipe it with my thumb. I crossed my arms over my chest instead. What was I even doing? Did these clubs turn everyone into a teenager?

Oliver smiled with half of his mouth, and I tried to breathe like a normal person. He asked, "Is your name really Charlie Parker?"

"Parker is my middle name, yes. My parents wanted us to be artists, my brother and me," I said. "And not defined by gender. Please don't ask me how I know Simon was conceived during their Nina Simone era." I ran my fingers along the sandy frame of an aluminum beach chair. "In college, I ran out of Sociology 101 to tell Simon our names were culturally appropriated."

"Are you?"

"Culturally appropriated?"

He laughed. "An artist." Oliver tossed the sunscreen onto a heap of towels.

"I don't know." I answered on an exhale. I didn't want him to ask me more about it, so I snuck in a question of my own. "What's a Figawi?"

It was written on my hat. His hat. Whatever.

"Where the fuck are we?"

I looked around. "Rumford?"

"No, the hat." He laughed. "It's a race from Hyannis to Nantucket."

Oliver wiped a hand over his chin and down his neck, rubbing in the sunscreen. I felt a sense of loss that it was gone.

"The story goes, three friends tried to sail the route first, but they got lost in the fog. *Where the Figawi?* You have to work on your accent, Yellow Elephants. Watch out or you'll be a local before you know it," he said, before cracking a smile and squeezing past me through the narrow doorway.

I didn't move as Oliver picked up a paddleboard the size of a dining room table and weaved it through the lounge chairs before plopping it into the water. The onshore wind blew the edges of his T-shirt away from his shorts, and I watched him glide away on top of the glassy bay until he was the size of one of Toby's LEGO men. Remembering that was I supposed to be meeting Dev back at the patio, I turned, feeling flustered. No wonder the cabanas were off limits.

"Enjoying the view?" Lacy asked, suddenly behind me. I whirled around, and Lacy's eyes flicked over my shoulder toward the bay. "Poppy said you were over here. Weren't you supposed to be looking for *me*?"

"I was! Poppy sent me to retrieve you," I stammered. Who was I, Lassie? I tried to sound casual. "I . . . didn't know where your cabana was. Was Dev with Poppy, by any chance? Did you see him?"

Without answering, Lacy turned and started walking back toward the patio. I hurried to follow her.

"This club is great," I said, my nervous chatter picking right back up where it left off. "I'd love to get involved. I signed up for some committees, or something. I'm not sure what I signed. I signed a lot of things. Um, I really do have to find—"

"If Poppy has you on her radar, you'll be here every day," Lacy said. "Did you at least sign up for camp? You can drop the kids off in the morning. It's the only way I work out all summer."

"Oh cool, like spin class?"

Lacy laughed, so I did, too. Then she lowered her voice. "Wait until you meet Sean. He'll make you wish you were dead."

Lacy said it like it was a turn-on. I tried to look enthusiastic instead of scared. "Charlie, look who I found while you were off hiding in the cabanas," she said loudly as she led me over to a high-top table—and my husband.

"Hiding? What?" I said. "No, I was just—hi! I wasn't *hiding* in the cabanas," I repeated. Dev wore a black polo shirt and jeans. Not exactly beach club attire, but at least he was there. "Did you bring your bathing suit?"

He shook his head and said, "Maybe next time," while Heidi leaned into the table next to him, elbows resting on the sticky surface.

"I'm so glad you made it. The kids are going to want to come every day," I told Dev, giving him a long hug—maybe longer than necessary. "There's a camp, with theme days, I think—I signed a clipboard about it. Also, volleyball, a snack bar, a *bar* bar."

Dev pointed to the sangria. "Can I have one of those?"

I poured him a cup, then tried not to stare as Dev downed half the drink. He turned the cup around in his hand absentmindedly.

"Rough day at the office?" I said. "I thought you just had to go over a few things with Presley."

Dev cleared his throat but didn't answer, looking down at the cup of sangria instead of me. It was like he quietly pulled away, without moving an inch.

"What you must see at the clinic," Lacy said. She sighed and put her hand to her cheek as if resting her elbow on an imaginary table. "That part of town really is due for some TLC."

She said it like what they direly needed was a Chipotle, not access to decent health insurance and sustainable jobs. I thought about what Dev said the other night, about how he changed the way he talked about his work, depending on the situation or the person. In that moment, I couldn't say I blamed him. Maybe it was best to not get into it here.

I pointed to Kate, who was on the beach next to the shallow sand-pit, a semicircle of kids giving her their undivided attention. "Did you see Kate? She's leading a quicksand seminar."

"Maybe Poppy could start a committee," Heidi said into her elbow, and I laughed too loudly. Lacy put her arm around Heidi's shoulders and pulled her upright. She motioned Poppy over, and they propped Heidi up on either side like bookends.

I helped myself to Dev's sangria, then I topped it off, all the while musing on how to bring him into some kind of conversation that would get him more excited about the club. Then I really started to question my grip on reality.

Was anyone else seeing my mother, here in Rumford, marching triumphantly toward us in her signature overalls—pink this time—her cropped hair dyed to match? I prayed that I was simply having some kind of medical event, until Lacy's head turned as well, and her eyes went wide.

My mother arrived at our table phone-first, already speaking, and I realized with a distinct sinking feeling that she was recording. For her vlog. For YouTube. At Fifth Street Beach Club.

This had to be some kind of serious membership code violation.

"Ladies and gentlemen, I have arrived, but I will keep you posted on our on-again off-again 'summah' in New England," my mother said, winking to the phone, before signing off. Then she threw her arms in the air and cried, "Surprise!" before squeezing me, and then Dev, into a hug. "What an absolutely lovely little town. The houses, the streets, that little market. I gave myself a quick walking tour—took all of thirty minutes—and I'm just in love."

"Mom, where did you come from?" I looked at Dev as if he could explain this apparition, and he looked back at me, equally clueless. "I thought you parked Bessie at chez Walmart!"

"I beg your pardon?" I heard Poppy say.

"We *were* at chez Walmart, dear, then we decided to go right to chez Cedar Street. Coming home from Thailand early, we didn't know what to do with ourselves, so we said, why not visit Charlie and Dev and those glorious grandchildren? I told you, I drove while your father rested. Are the kids here, too? Tell me, is Kate running the place yet?"

"But how did you know where to find me?" I sputtered.

"Find My Phone, of course, Charlie, keep up!" Lilly said cheerily.

"Of course," I said, thinking, *This is the way my social life ends.* She kicked her slip-on Vans sneakers into the sand and I wondered, not without some measure of dread, if she was going to whip a bathing suit out of her neon green fanny pack.

Lacy stood with one hand on her hip, like she was watching a mildly amusing movie. Heidi had put her head back down on the table. Poppy—thank goodness for Poppy—reached her hand forward.

"You must be Charlie's mother. I'm Poppy. Welcome to Rumford."

"Firm grip," my mother remarked, shaking Poppy's hand. "Good for you, dear! How do *you* feel about being on camera? I want to know the story of this club, this town, oh, just tell me everything."

She pulled her phone out again, and Heidi and Lacy exchanged a look. Poppy straightened her skirt and looked ready to launch into a monologue, but I jumped in. "Maybe another time, Poppy? Mom, I really don't think you can film here." The sudden apparition of my mother, in director mode no less, was my cue to exit the beach club, stage as-soon-as-possible, and I grabbed Dev by the arm. I'd save the grand tour another day.

"I'll just grab the kids," I said, realizing too late that the quicksand seminar had disbanded. "Dev, do you see them—"

"I saw Bart van der Koff chasing Ivy around the cabanas," Lacy grumbled. "Where are the lifeguards? Why aren't they playing with the children?"

Heidi slurred, "That Bart van der Koff is trouble. He'd better be careful or he'll end up sailing around the world."

In a valiant but misguided attempt to take the attention off my mother as I scanned the beach and volleyball court, Dev said, "Heidi, isn't your husband a sailor? Charlie told me he's on a voyage or something. That sounds like an interesting story."

I tried to keep a straight face as I kicked him beneath the table. Heidi's straw hat fell forward, covering her face. Horrified, I watched her shoulders shake. I assumed she was sobbing. I looked to make sure my mother wasn't filming again.

"I'm sorry, Heidi," I said. "It's none of our business, you know, whatever he's doing. Not that he's doing anything. I'm sure the Indian Ocean is lovely this time of year."

Dev gave me a bewildered look. Then I realized Lacy was smirking. And Heidi, far from sobbing, was laughing. She reached under her Ray-Bans to wipe tears from her eyes. I wondered how deep Kate had made the sandpit, if it could fit an adult-size woman of my height.

"Charlie," Lacy said slowly, "do you really think Teague is sailing around the world?"

I didn't know what to say. If I said I knew it was a lie, I'd have to admit to eavesdropping at the yacht club. But if I said yes, I'd make them think I did in fact believe he was drinking a piña colada and evading pirates off the coast of Cape Town. Again, I wished desperately for a rule book, a memo even, for being a Person of Rumford.

"I mean, isn't it what you said? The other night at the yacht club?"

Heidi laid her hand on my arm, as if to say, *You're cute.* She said, "Dev, to answer your question, Teague has been out at sea for six weeks." She used exaggerated air quotes for "out at sea."

"It's just a story Heidi's telling the children," Lacy said dismissively. "We all know Teague is in rehab, obviously."

Dev threw me a questioning look, and I tried to subliminally convey some sense of *I don't understand either, please just go with it*, hoping the sentiment would reach my mother as well.

"But, what about the postcards?" I asked, as if the answer could make me feel anything but more confused and humiliated.

"I send the postcards," Heidi said, glaring at Lacy. "My in-laws feel strongly the kids don't need to know where Teague really is. I went along with it and sent a couple of postcards after he left. I wasn't in the best place, you might say. Then the nanny made the map, and it turned into a whole fucking thing. Anders Anderson can pay for their therapy one day, like he pays for everything else. As Lacy would be more than happy to explain, it is a truly elaborate hoax."

Heidi leaned back onto the table, but she missed it by a couple of inches. She reached out and grabbed Dev's elbow before she could topple over.

"Thank you, Dr. Dev," she said, almost formally. "That'll be all."

Lacy leaned forward, as if to say more, but Heidi started to tip, so she straightened up again.

We watched the kids reappear as Kate dragged Ellery out of the makeshift sandpit using the paddle. My mother pulled her phone out to start filming again.

"Looks like Ellery could use a friend like Kate," Heidi said.

Couldn't we all, I thought. I put my arm around my mother before she could hit record and steered her away from the table. "I think it's time for us to go. *Now.*"

chapter 10

Turning onto Cedar Street we immediately encountered Bessie dwarfing the narrow expanse of the road and preventing two-way traffic. My father sat meditating, eyes closed, on a beach chair in our driveway.

Lilly smacked my father on the arm. "Up and at 'em, Ed! I've returned with our illustrious grandchildren!"

"The best time to cross a piranha-infested river is at night," Kate announced. "In case you were wondering."

"Kate, I am always wondering," Lilly assured her.

Inside, Dev made everyone tea, then walked away as it steeped. I pulled out two chairs, but instead of sitting next to me he paced the kitchen, unable to relax. My parents sat at the table, sharing the same cup.

I had no idea how long they planned on staying—it could just as easily be an hour or a month. I prayed it was closer to an hour. It wasn't that I worried so much about their effect on my newfound social inroads—well, it wasn't only that. My parents shared everything; they always had. They blazed through open doors holding hands. I knew Lilly would pick up on how Dev and I weren't connecting, and I didn't want to account for it out loud. I wasn't sure I knew how to.

"Edgar, you have to get it right before we shoot in Cape Cod," my mother said, seemingly picking back up on a conversation they'd had earlier that day. "A quahog is a clam, but a clam isn't necessarily a quahog."

"It doesn't make any sense, Lilly. Is a quahog the big one or the little one?"

"Think *hog*, Ed! It's the big one."

"And are those the ones with bellies and feces still attached? Because after recent events I'm not sure I'm comfortable . . ."

Toby turned to Kate. "Faces?" He looked a little horrified.

Kate whispered back, "Feces. It means poop!"

They dissolved into giggles, and both of my parents beamed at them like they were two presents on Christmas morning.

When Dev reappeared in gym shorts and told me he was going on a run, the world turned fully upside down. Dev wasn't a runner. Dev was a reader of medical journals, a watcher of mushroom foragers from the comfort of our living room. He bought a road bike once, after the twins were born. It sat in our apartment for two years before I sold it, and even then he didn't notice it was gone. I watched incredulously as he headed out the door.

Lilly explained that they'd scored a gratis week at a recently renovated resort in the Maldives, and their flight would leave out of Boston in a few days. The resort was looking to increase its exposure to more mature demographics, having been recently trashed by a twenty-three-year-old influencer after her boyfriend's Instagram story accidentally showed him in a compromising position with her best friend.

"*Senior Moments* to the rescue!" Lilly sang. Kate and Toby clapped. "We come with a drama-free guarantee, but the offer is only on the table this week. You know what I always say, when opportunity knocks, you get up and open the door before it can change its mind."

I laughed. Was that what I was doing? Showing up to the beach club for the rest of the summer certainly seemed easier than learning how to navigate my increasingly unfamiliar life at home.

The next day, while my parents loudly debated the title of their next vlog series at the kitchen table—my money was on "Caped Cod Crusaders"—Dev came home from work, kicked his bag under the table, and took a beer into the shower with him. Lilly and I exchanged a look. That I was being replaced by a shower beer was concerning on any number of levels.

She sidled up to me on the couch. "Sugar, are you two doing all right?"

I hesitated. What could I say? Their visit made it even more plain to me how Dev and I were not exactly functioning as a team.

"Your guess is as good as mine," I admitted, pulling my knees up to my chest. "Let's just say, we could use a week in the Maldives."

"Well, couldn't we all, sweetheart," Lilly said. "I remember what it's like to have small children, Charlie. When you were seven, your father and I once didn't talk for an entire week after a particularly fraught neighborhood barbecue."

I laughed. "Is that why we only stayed in Charleston for a year?"

Lilly smiled but didn't take the bait. "Do you want to talk about it?"

I could hear the shower running, knew Dev would be in there for a while.

"Dev's always been like my center of gravity," I said, trying to keep my voice steady. "Now, I walk into a room, and we're just orbiting each other. It's like he doesn't even see me."

I demonstrated with my index fingers, moving them around in opposing circles, until Lilly took my hand and squeezed.

"We moved around so much when Simon and I were kids," I said. "And it wasn't always easy, but it *was* like a little reset. I could settle into some new version of myself and leave the old one behind, like a systems upgrade. I guess I hoped this would work the same way."

Across the room, Kate and Toby pretended to recap the morning's bike ride in the glow of my mother's ring light.

"Just remember, change doesn't have to change you, sugar. It lets you open a little and expand. But you'll always be you," Lilly said.

"What if that's what I'm afraid of?" I said. *What if I'm not what Dev wants anymore* was what I didn't say. I trailed off, thinking about those few minutes talking to Oliver. If I was being honest, it just felt nice to be a version of myself that someone noticed. Then I immediately felt guilty.

"These things can take time, sugar," Lilly said. "But—" She stood up, my hand still in hers, and pulled me up off the couch. Kate giggled from across the room as she watched Lilly shake her hips. "I find that sitting around doesn't help one bit. Get out there, Charlie. Find something you can say yes to. You and Dev will find your way back to each other when the time is right."

After Lilly called out, "Hey, Siri, play that song about scrubs," she, Kate, and I had an impromptu living room dance party, while Toby wandered to the other side of the room and picked up my iPad. I stopped dancing and imagined the kids spending the summer watching videos of other children playing, transfixed by weird unboxing videos on YouTube, and shivered. Was I basically doing the same thing, staring at my phone and waiting for Dev to come home late from work?

Heidi said her daughter could use a friend like Kate. I would say yes to that, like Lilly suggested. I'd make something happen. "Speaking of open doors, we have plans this week. With a new friend. You and Dad have prep to do anyway, right?"

Lilly raised her cup of oolong tea as she shimmied around the coffee table. "That's the spirit."

I texted Poppy for Heidi's phone number. I needed a playdate, too.

chapter 11

The arches of Heidi's gambrel-style house gave it fairy-tale-mansion vibes. As soon as I parked in the U-shaped driveway after picking up Kate, Toby, and Ellery from beach club camp, the children hopped out and barreled through a side door like they'd been there a million times before. In the car, Kate had blabbered on and on about the structure of the beach club camp; she was a sucker for a daily itinerary. And Toby was basking in the attention of the high school–aged lifeguards. It was one weight lifted from my shoulders; they'd found their happy place. I was determined to find mine.

Entering Heidi's house through the side door, I stepped into a mud-room the size of our kitchen. A small woman with dark hair pulled into a tight bun was picking up the shoes and towels the kids had dropped on the threshold. From the kitchen, Ellery was already calling out a list of snack options as Kate and Toby replied "yay" or "nay" like Pilgrim settlers at a town council meeting.

"Hi," I said to the woman. "Sorry my kids just blew through here. I'm Charlie. I'm looking for Heidi?"

The woman smiled, then disappeared to another room without speaking. I listened for Heidi, who was surely here somewhere, over the roar of a vacuum kicking into gear. Heidi's kitchen was like being inside a Grecian urn. Everything was white: the massive island, the floor, the cabinets, the doors that looked like cabinets camouflaging the largest fridge I'd ever seen. I ran my hand over the cool marble countertop, then looked for a napkin to wipe away the smudge of my fingerprints.

Ellery, Kate, and Toby perched on tall chairs around the island, hands already submerged in an overflowing bowl of popcorn. Another voice called out from a pantry the size of a walk-in closet.

"Ellery, I don't see the mini brownies. Your mom said to stick with one snack today, anyway. Between you and me, I think she finally caught wind of the beach club snack bar tab." A petite woman in her fifties with close-cropped brown hair poked her head out of the pantry door. "Oh hello," she said to me. "I'm Jeannine, Heidi's nanny."

I introduced myself, feeling panicked that maybe Heidi wasn't even there. Looking at Jeannine's outfit of leggings and cotton tunic, her sensible footwear, I suspected I had more in common with her than with Heidi anyway, even if Jeannine was my senior by about fifteen years.

Jeannine turned to Ellery and said, "Sweetie, dinner is early tonight. Hayes has his Russian math tutor, so Hunter left lasagna."

"Can I, um, do anything to help?" I stood next to Kate at the kitchen counter feeling useless, wondering how many people worked for Heidi. "I don't know how to make lasagna, though."

"Just make yourself comfortable," Jeannine said. She winked at Ellery. "My own son is all grown up, a ripe old age of twenty-one. Washing lunch boxes from beach camp is nothing."

"Can we go play?" Ellery asked Jeannine.

"Of course, but remember, no food upstairs," she said gently, holding up an empty package of pretzels. "Mom's orders."

As Jeannine wiped the popcorn from the counter into her hand and dumped it along with the pretzel bag into a garbage can sneakily masquerading as another cabinet, I heard a clacking sound descend the stairs in the adjacent room.

"Jeannine," Heidi called out, "did you find anything else in Ellery's room today? The last thing I need is a bunch of ants up there."

Jeannine glanced at me sideways and answered, "All clear." I smiled at Jeannine not calling Ellery out on the contraband pretzels—I liked her.

"Well, at least that's something," Heidi said. Then spotting me, she said, "Oh, hi, Charlie. That's right, you're here for a playdate. Are the kids upstairs already?"

Who did she think was picking up her daughter? Maybe Heidi had so much help she forgot sometimes.

"Thanks for having us, Heidi," I said. "I mean them. The kids."

"Jeannine can drop them off when she takes Hayes to his math tutor," Heidi said. Then she looked out the window. "They mowed the grass *again* today?"

I felt like a mismatched accessory in the marble kitchen. I looked to Jeannine, as if she had the answer as to what I should do next, and Heidi noticed my hesitation.

"Oh, do you want to stay?"

I fumbled. "No, I mean, I thought, maybe but it's fine. Jeannine, do you have enough car seats? Or I can take Toby with me now. We need, um, caulk—"

Heidi waved her hand. "Stay. I just assumed." She went to the fridge and pulled out two bottles of sparkling water, breaking the line of neatly arranged bottled beverages.

Jeannine said, "I almost forgot. Heidi, I found these in your closet, when I put away the silk scarves Ellery used for dress-up. I guess she's getting more creative in her hiding places."

Jeannine handed Heidi a plastic bag containing a handful of primary-colored gummy bears, then she returned to rinsing Ellery's camp lunch box in the farmhouse sink.

"Have you heard from him?" Heidi asked in a low voice.

Jeannine shook her head quickly. She said, "Not yet," then she left the room.

I assumed they were talking about Teague. I couldn't see Heidi's expression. When she turned around, she raised one eyebrow and held up the bag of gummies.

"These are definitely *not* for Ellery."

I laughed as I realized what she meant, pleasantly surprised at the sight of Heidi, in her marble kitchen, stuffing a bag of pot gummies into the pocket of her skinny jeans. Good for her.

In the living room, Heidi straightened an eight-by-ten framed photo over the mantel. The four of them—Teague, Heidi, Ellery, and Hayes—stood in matching navy and white, arms draped around each other on the lawn of the yacht club. The sun lit their faces. Sailboats blurred in the background. Teague's left arm wrapped around Heidi's waist while his right hoisted Ellery in the air. Hayes laughed up at his father, smitten. They looked like a staged family used to sell frames, too happy and blond to be real.

"What a great picture," I said. "You all look so . . . coordinated."

Heidi stood facing the photo. "That was last summer," she said. Teague was handsome, I noted; they looked like a family who had everything figured out. I wondered when Heidi knew he was keeping something from her, what she saw now when she looked at the photo.

Heidi cleared her throat and turned around. "I asked Elena to keep the wall art dusted, but she forgets to straighten the frames afterward."

I took the cue to stick to the practical. "Is Elena your housekeeper? I ran into her when we came in. Your home is beautiful, Heidi. It's so well decorated. Our house looks like an IKEA and Dev's mother's basement threw up in it. This must be a lot to keep up with on your own," I said, not thinking. I winced. "I mean—sorry, I don't mean to keep bringing it up."

Honestly, how could I *not* talk about Teague's absence? He was nowhere and everywhere all at once.

"It's fine," Heidi said. "Teague's parents hired a battalion when he went away. We already had Jeannine for the kids and Elena for the house, because I was working, but they doubled their hours. And his parents insisted on Hunter. They told him they'd pay for culinary school if he cooked for us. Win-win!" Her smile was like cracked glass.

"Wow," I said. I thought about the frozen chicken nuggets I'd planned for dinner. And how I'd still need to clean the bathroom after the kids went to bed.

"They wanted to make sure I'd stick around," Heidi said. She laughed dryly. "It's not like Teague did any of those chores when he was here. I took a leave of absence from my law firm when things got . . . complicated. But it's nice to not worry about all that now, I guess." After a beat, she added, "It's not like I don't know how to take care of my family."

"Of course not," I said. "I didn't think . . ." But it didn't seem like Heidi was actually talking to me.

"Mr. and Mrs. Anders Anderson to the rescue," she said, raising her Pellegrino.

It wasn't the same, but I understood how something could feel off in a family, like a piece was suddenly missing from the puzzle, even though no one could admit to seeing the blank space. I knew how alone that could make a person feel. Dev had woken up early to go running every morning that week. I supposed it was better than foraging, but, to me, his new hobby felt like just another way of avoiding being in the house.

I started to ask what Heidi did most mornings while the kids were at camp, or with Jeannine, but a giant thump made the ceiling quake. It was followed by another. I looked at Heidi. "Should I check on the kids?"

Heidi shook her head. "They're jumping from the climbing wall. I had it installed in the hallway for Hayes. He's had some extra energy to release since Teague went away."

I nodded. Of course my children were jumping from an indoor climbing wall on the second story of this house. Suddenly, I craved a minute alone to let all of this sink in and, hopefully, stop asking such awkward questions. I held up the empty green bottle of sparkling water. "I'm just going to pop into the bathroom."

"We're having the downstairs powder room redone," Heidi said. "Well, *I* am. You can use the one in the master. Here, stash these back in the closet on your way." She thrust the bag of gummies into my hand.

It's not snooping if she told you to do it, I thought as I slunk through Heidi's bedroom and into the walk-in closet. Teague's clothes hung neatly on one side, a row of pressed white and light-blue button-downs, crisp suit pants. A column of drawers held folded ties and rolled socks. Heidi's clothes were on the other side. If Dev was "away," I'd need to swap our clothes around so his undisturbed 501s wouldn't be the first thing I saw every time I opened the closet to get dressed by myself. I quickly stuffed the bag of pot gummies into a top drawer.

Heidi's bathroom was also marble; I could roll out a pie dough on the slab of countertop. I washed my hands and scanned the array of glass-encased beauty products, serums, and lotions with names I didn't recognize, then stared at my reflection. In the superior lighting, my skin looked dry. I pumped something from a tiny bottle and smoothed it onto my cheeks. It smelled like freshly cut cucumber.

I pulled out my phone to text Dev, wondering when he'd be home. His answer? Late. Meeting after work.

I typed: Again? Then deleted it. I tried About what? but deleted again. After I typed then deleted Would you rather stay at work with Presley than be home with me? I put my phone away and shifted my gaze to the glass-encased shower, hoping to distract myself with Heidi's high-end hair care products. A flash of red caught my eye. I pulled open the shower door to get a better look. Surely it wasn't what I thought. There were two iridescent bottles of shampoo and conditioner I had never encountered at CVS. The one wedged in between, though, was startlingly familiar. Why did Heidi have a bottle of ketchup in her shower?

The pristine white of literally everything in this bathroom only made the ketchup feel even more out of place, if that was possible. I reached in and picked up the bottle. I sniffed it, just to make sure. But as I put it back, it slipped between my fingers. A line of red squirted across the floor, and as the bottle knocked over the wastebasket, something white and plastic fell out. This time, I had no doubt what it was. I'd bought five of them on Dev's graduation weekend, the plus sign on the tests startlingly clear each time.

My mouth fell open. Teague had been "away" for two months. The timing was possible, I supposed, though I had trouble assuming they were in the best place for that kind of goodbye before he left. This test was negative anyway, which I could only assume had been good news. I tucked the test back into the basket, used toilet paper to wipe up the mess, then I placed the ketchup back in the shower.

I returned to the living room, but where there had been an empty stretch of hardwood floor—I'd stood right there, looking at the family portrait just minutes ago—was now a trapdoor the size of a refrigerator box, raised diagonally on hinges like an open dragon's mouth of finished hickory.

I inched closer, slowly, as if the jaws might snap closed, and found Heidi languidly climbing back up a set of wood stairs, a bottle of wine in her right hand.

"I thought we could use a drink." She tapped a button on the wall and the trapdoor closed.

"Heidi, where did you come from? What just happened?"

"I didn't want to break up the floor space with stairs to the basement. So I had this made instead. Now I can keep my house pretty *and* my wine at an optimal temperature."

She smiled slyly. This woman, her skin as spotless as her marble countertops, ketchup in her shower, had some tricks up her sleeve. She opened the bottle and poured two glasses.

"I'll show you some other time. It's pretty fucking great. This guy, Oliver something, he made it for me just after Teague went away. I should see when he'll be in town again."

I tried to not spit take my wine, picturing Oliver in Heidi's house, tool belt sagging on a pair of Carhartts. Maybe it was time to share something more personal—not that, obviously. But something that showed I could relate in some way. "We moved around a lot when I was growing up, and for a stretch it felt like the only consistent thing in my life was Ben Folds and that sad piano song. But looking back, my parents were there for us, too, for my brother and me. I'm sure your kids feel that from you, Heidi. Despite what they can't control."

"I don't know anyone named Ben," Heidi deadpanned, but her eyes softened, so I kept going.

"In college, I dated this guy from Georgia for five months without ever telling him how the 'cozy' home I referred to in North Carolina was a recreational vehicle," I said, staring at the space where the trapdoor had been. "Or that it was actually, at the time, in Sonoma."

Heidi seemed to consider this, taking a sip of her wine. Then she said, "Now I honestly have no idea what you're talking about."

I laughed and tried again. "I guess I was thinking about how things can be so complicated and, well, kept under a trapdoor at the same time. Great when it's wine. But . . . we had brunch with Dev's mother just before we decided to move. That's how we communicate with her, mostly, over brunch." Heidi sat on the edge of the white couch as I continued.

"I tried to ask if she thought Dev seemed, I don't know . . . off. Like something was wrong. He was working all the time, not sleeping. He'd always been so relaxed, and focused, and suddenly he never sat still. I thought maybe she'd have some insight, from when his dad died."

I caught myself. This was the most I'd said to Heidi, to anyone in Rumford, about what was going on with us. It was a lot to unload on the first playdate.

Heidi drained her glass and looked at me expectantly. "And?"

"And she asked if I wanted another scone."

Heidi snorted. She looked me up and down, taking in my cutoff shorts and messy ponytail. "How's it work for you?" She tilted her head. "Brunch."

I winced. "Dev's mother doesn't know what to make of me. I don't know if it's a British thing or just a Dev's mom thing. My parents have zero boundaries—not conversationally, not emotionally—so it's like I'm fly-fishing when I'm around her, just blurting out feelings then reeling them back in."

"Sounds fucking exhausting," Heidi said.

"I still feel like an unannounced visitor when we show up at the brownstone," I admitted. "Even when I wear a cardigan."

Heidi squinted. "I can't see you in a cardigan."

I laughed. "Rumford makes me feel like I need a hell of a lot more than a cardigan. I do have ketchup, but I think I'm not using it the right way." *Did I really just say that?* Great, now she'd think—or know—I was snooping.

"I'll have you know, it's a detoxifier, and I wash my fucking hair with it," Heidi said, with a hint of a smile. "Sometimes we all need to feel alive, Charlie. Anyway, I only use it on the mornings when Elena cleans the bathrooms. Marble is porous."

She seemed to wait to see if I'd ask a follow-up question, if I'd noticed anything else in that bathroom, but I told my face to remain neutral.

"I get it," I said quietly. She nodded, almost imperceptibly.

"Teague and I were having problems for a while before he went away," she said. "You should know that. Rumford can smooth over a lot." She trailed her fingers along the edge of the couch. "But not everything."

It was my turn to drain my wineglass.

"And with Teague, you know, *away*, sometimes people don't know what to say. They act like it's my fault that it's awkward to just come over to the house. Everyone except for . . ." Heidi waved her hand like it didn't matter, and I certainly wasn't going to press her on who exactly had been so happy to visit. "Anyway, you won't tell anyone? Lacy doesn't know that part."

"Of course not," I said. Then, after a beat, I added, "I'm also exceptionally good at awkward, so I'll come over anytime."

She was quiet for a moment. I'd all but strong-armed this playdate, but I wondered if it was possible Heidi wanted company as much as I did. Simultaneously, I worried I'd pushed too hard, made her reveal something she hadn't wanted to. Heidi stood up, and I readied myself to collect the kids and make my best attempt at a smooth exit.

"You should come to the Garage next week, Charlie. Drop the kids at the beach club for camp. Bring water and don't eat a big breakfast."

"I'll be there," I said. "It sounds . . . fun?"

I had passed some sort of test, evidently. It felt good, like this time I was being invited into something. And yet. I couldn't help wondering, how many secrets would I be expected to carry as I became friends with these women? I twirled the empty wineglass in my fingers. The stem was like a clear toothpick—if I held on too tightly, it would snap.

chapter 12

I arrived at the Garage ten minutes early after parking outside an industrial-looking building, a box of gray concrete. It was located just outside of town, closer to Dev's practice than to any of the clubs where I'd pictured the ladies of the Rumford hive dropping dollars to break a sweat. But either I'd found the place, or the Range Rovers I'd parked next to were waiting to be taken inside and broken down for parts.

I desperately hoped the Garage wasn't some kind of dance studio. When Dev and I started dating, Presley had invited me to Zumba. I'd felt so self-conscious, I'd accidentally thrown an elbow into the instructor's face as she encouraged me to let go and swing my arms. And since having the twins, I'd let working out go the way of the vast number of the things I meant to get back to but never did.

Dev was running every day before work now, rain or shine. In the evenings, we'd fallen into a routine distinctly lacking in endorphins. Dev would set his bag on the floor and kick it under the hall table. He would walk to the bedroom without saying a word, peel off his clothes, dump them into the trash bag–lined basket, then stand at the sink as the shower warmed up, a towel wrapped around his waist and his skin prickly and cold. In the shower he'd lather soap into his hair and let it run over the length of his body, flooding his skin and whatever had touched it that day with steaming water. After about five minutes of standing still, doing nothing for the first time in however many hours he'd been at work, he would turn off the faucet.

Kate started charting his arrivals and departures on a whiteboard in the kitchen, tasking me with entering data when she was already in bed. On the nights Dev stayed late, when I'd ask what for, he'd mumble something about billing, or paperwork. There was always paperwork. Too many nights I'd be asleep by the time he was finished cleaning up, and he'd update me the next morning on the Norwegian chef's progress, or lack thereof. I worried we were more and more like ships passing in the Netflix watch list.

Standing outside the Garage, in the morning sun, I thought about how I'd spent most of my life on the perimeter of things. No way I was going to pass up the invitation to do something that, apparently, only a select few knew about, even if it likely involved synchronized dancing to boy bands. Rumford was like an obstacle course of clubs and invites and rules that everyone just seemed to know, and I was determined to hurdle jump them all.

My running shorts swished as I followed a woman in black leggings and a sports bra to an unmarked door. Inside, Poppy bent at the waist and touched her toes like an evenly tanned, human U-lock, glowing in white bike shorts and a tight white tank top. Lacy and Heidi, both wearing different variations of black Lycra that likely cost more than my car payment, stood beside a set of banged-up lockers. I used the toe of my sneaker to trace an outline of a body, framed in sweat, on the mat-covered floor. A sweat angel.

I tugged at the hem of my T-shirt, wishing I'd grabbed literally anything out of my laundry pile besides the size-large GYM AND TONIC T-shirt I got as part of a bar promo event, or at least that didn't feature a giant lizard holding a glass tumbler. My worn-out shorts were missing the drawstring that usually held them on my hips—a casualty to Kate's latest project, I assumed—and they sagged where they should have hugged. I pushed the hair out of my eyes, surveyed the women in $100 mesh-paneled leggings and perfectly sculpted sports bras once more, and considered slipping right back out the door.

"Bring it in!" a man shouted, so loud it made me freeze.

Lacy saw me and opened her mouth to say something, then she closed it in what looked like actual trepidation. The women moved toward a dirty whiteboard, the kind I hung on the door of my college dorm room. I half expected to see a black-and-white poster of Einstein or Jim Belushi stuck to the cinder blocks, too. The gulf between the sparse decor and the women who populated the Garage was baffling. What kind of gym was this?

I craned my head over the group of women as they huddled together, my stomach now a mass of nerves. The whiteboard showed a list of exercises scrawled in black dry-erase marker and the guy with the impressive vocal projection, the only male in the space, stood beside it wearing a disconcertingly grim expression.

I squinted to read the board. A hundred push-ups. Fifty pull-ups. Two hundred sit-ups. A mile run. Fifty burpees, whatever those were. And at the bottom: X2. Maybe these were workouts for the next two weeks.

"Here's your next hour of hell, folks," the trainer said. His voice echoed off the bare walls. "I see some new faces," he said, looking directly at me. "Don't blow it up too quickly."

I nodded. I didn't want to blow anything up.

"Okay, let's do this," barked the trainer. The women fanned out across the mat-covered floor, positioning themselves at arm's length. I moved to the back row and took the corner spot next to Heidi.

"Heidi, what's happening?" I felt like we were about to break into a flash mob dance and I didn't know the moves.

"Sean's going to start the timer," Heidi said. She glanced at Sean, the trainer, like he was going to call her out for talking during class. "Then you do the workout as fast as you can without dying."

"Wait," I said. "The workout? Like, what's on the board? *All* of the things on the board?"

"Correct."

"*Without* dying?"

"Ideally. Did you sign a waiver?"

95

I gaped at her. Sean raised his arm, a small remote control in his hand. He yelled, "Begin!" Blocky red numbers flashed on a timer that hung from the wall. I watched Heidi drop to the floor and start doing push-ups, her body a perfect diagonal.

I lay on the musty-smelling mat and wondered whose and which sweaty body part had touched down before I put my face there. I dug my toes into the mat, locked my core, and pushed up with shaky arms. When the room exploded with a bass beat that reverberated through my veins, my arms unlocked, and my face smashed into the mat. Sean surveyed the troops on the floor and nodded his head in time with the pulsing beat. I wasn't sure whether it thrilled or terrified me. I sat up and draped my arms over my knees to catch my breath just as the booming growl from the speaker demanded, "WAKE UP AND SMELL THE PUSSY!"

Zumba this was not.

Hard-core rap pulsated through every atom of the room, and these women who knew when to offer sherry over cognac and set Google Alerts on their iPhones for Lilly Pulitzer trunk shows hustled like plebes at West Point to a soundtrack that would make even my renegade mother blush.

"WAKE UP AND SMELL THE PUSS-AAAYYYY!"

A few songs in, Poppy, whom I had never seen curse, maybe not even frown, gave a war cry as she boosted herself up from the mat and headed toward the door for the mile run. I ditched the rest of my sit-ups to join her, my eyes blurry with sweat, my legs wobbly like a human-size Gumby doll. I pulled my T-shirt up to wipe my face and check that my ears weren't bleeding, barreling in what I thought was the direction of the open door, and slammed with spectacularly hard force straight into a foldout table full of stainless steel water bottles. They toppled and rolled en masse onto the mat-covered floor.

I stood frozen as bottles fanned out in every direction—under benches, behind lockers, and head-on into a regiment of women doing push-ups and sit-ups. It was excellent timing, really, for the lot of them to look up while my T-shirt was still bunched around my face—and I realized my shorts had dropped well beyond a sag, the worn-out elastic holding on for dear life halfway down my not-so-toned glutes. I reached one hand down to grab my shorts and lunged with the other, attempting to block the final water bottles before they fell like lemmings from the table. But I tripped, my shorts still dangerously low, and fell face-first onto the sweaty mat.

I waited in shock for one of the women to scream, "*This* is why we wear Lycra!" A handful of them glared at me, but others simply batted the bottles away in a panic, trying not to lose too much time on the ticking clock. I sat up, my body humming with humiliation, and pulled up my shorts. I shot the trainer, Sean, a look that I hoped conveyed some combination of helplessness and apology, moving to pick up the water bottles, but he barked, "Nope!" and pointed at the door. My stomach dropped as I thought he was telling me I had to leave. That was it. No second chances at the Garage.

"No excuses," he boomed over the speakers. "Get that run in, newbie. Let's go."

One hand on my waistband, I made a break for the door without looking back. My breath felt like it was being sucked out of my lungs by a Dyson, but I sprinted ahead, hoping the lack of oxygen would induce temporary amnesia.

"Poppy," I croaked. "Where's the mile run?"

Poppy looked back in surprise. "Oh, Charlie! You're so fast!"

"I wanted to run," I panted. I didn't say *with you* or *away from this place*. What was the point of all this?

Then the smell hit me, so thick it felt like actual matter. I was sucking wind through my open mouth when all of a sudden it felt full of rotting fish. I gagged.

"There's a storage facility next door, for fish trucks," Poppy said. "It gets a bit rank. Perks of coastal living!"

"Poppy," I panted, one hand raised to cover my mouth, the other hovering near my shorts. "You pay to do this every day?"

Poppy nodded resolutely in rhythm with her pumping legs. "It keeps me challenged, Charlie. Sean gets results like no one else. Sometimes I do it just to remember I can. You know, to prove to myself that Paxton and Dodge—even Davis—they aren't the only ones who can compete."

I tried to nod but was afraid if I moved more than my legs I'd black out.

"I played lacrosse in college," Poppy said. Her breathing was steady, like we were best friends Oprah and Gayle going for a power walk.

"I was a captain. I was fierce, Charlie. Now I drive Paxton and Dodge to lacrosse practice. I cheer at games and tournaments. I support their passion, I really do. But some days? This is the only place I feel like my true self."

I thought of Poppy as a powerhouse—the clipboards alone. But seeing her here, away from all that, I considered the ways in which she'd ceded her competitive drive over to the twins' exploits, relegating her victories to this foul-smelling concrete box.

"But you play tennis, right?" I managed to choke out.

"I do, but most of the time I play doubles with Davis. Don't get me wrong, we're an awesome team. You make choices, right? You stick together and make it work. In tennis, and in life." She turned and winked at me. "But this space, the Garage, is all mine."

With that, Poppy took off at a sprint to finish the run, leaving me to wonder how long it had been since I had a space of my own, one that conjured some molecule of my whole self. I honestly didn't know. In that moment I was only certain about two things: one, if I gave up now, I'd collapse in a heap and probably end up in a fish truck, and two, good for Poppy that this hellhole was her happy place, but it sure wasn't mine.

I made it back to the gym and moved my body up and down from the floor like a snake with no bones, willing myself to drop to the sweaty mat then rise again. As the clock on the wall counted down, I even started to reconsider. Maybe Poppy did have a point. Maybe this was a way to get out of my head and simply exist in my body. Maybe this was what freedom felt like.

Maybe I was going to puke.

When Sean called time, I collapsed next to Heidi, who looked invigorated, her eyes bright like a rabbit.

I managed to get out a single word: "How?"

"Eyes on the prize," Heidi said. "The white party gala is just around the corner, and that dress isn't going to wear itself. With Teague away, I have to show these bitches nothing has changed."

I tried to laugh, but what came out sounded like dust releasing from my lungs.

Lacy walked over from the watercooler after filling a clear bottle. A single lemon slice floated inside. "Who the hell knocked over all the water bottles? I had to dig mine out from under the bench press," she said, making a face. I pretended to look at my watch, pushing its tiny buttons at random as if to chart my nonexistent workout stats.

"I think Sean bumped it. He was probably distracted by my ass in these new leggings," Heidi said, sounding bored, but flashing a quick smile as she met my eyes. She was covering for me.

"That's hilarious," Poppy said. "Good for you, girl. I didn't even notice. I don't take anything in when I'm in the zone."

I looked away, taking stock while my heart rate found a more reasonable rhythm. I hadn't died. And not everyone—not Lacy, anyway—had seen me half-naked. It was enough to count the morning as a win. Sean was picking up the last of the fallen water bottles and setting them back on the table for women to grab on their way out the door.

"We don't tell just anyone about the Garage, Charlie," Lacy said, pulling a black Nike to her sculpted backside, stretching her quad. "Glad to see you survived."

Did I, though? I thought, still on the floor. I saw Sean approaching us then. Was he going to call me out? Ask if I needed a discount code for workout shorts with a functioning waistband? I planned on thanking him, but not with an audience. I looked around for an easy exit, but wasn't confident my legs could carry me.

"I'm going to run before Sean talks to me in his normal voice. It kills the vibe," Lacy said. "But Charlie, you and Dev should join us on *Penelope* this weekend. Bring the kids. Warren and Dev can talk business, and we can talk everything else."

I blinked once for yes, because sailing was still the one thing about which Dev had expressed enthusiasm. Then I lay on the floor with my eyes closed. I'd been through something with these women. Was this it? Was I in? Would we all go get smoothies or something?

By the time I opened my eyes, though, it was just me and Sean. Up close, under his beard, he looked straight out of college. Most of those women could probably buy the Garage right out from under him, but they sure did whatever he said, no questions asked. It was like fifty shades of sweat.

"You okay?" he said, smiling at me. As it turned out, I much preferred his normal voice.

"I, um . . . I think so?" I stood up, and stayed up—another victory. "I'm sorry about the table, all the water bottles. I would have helped you pick them up if my legs were functional before now."

Sean laughed. "Don't worry about it. You don't want to know what I've had to clean up at this place."

"I absolutely do not," I said, leaning against the table, then straightening back up too quickly when a solitary water bottle trembled. I felt lightheaded again, and Sean reached out to steady me.

"It's not for everyone. But damn, these ladies punish themselves harder than my UMass football team," he said.

"I felt better after childbirth," I admitted. "With twins."

Sean laughed. "It's why the first class is free. It's a mental buy-in first. But Heidi covered you for the month, if you're up for coming back."

"Really?" I croaked.

Sean shrugged, like he'd stopped trying to figure these women out a long time ago.

chapter 13

Simon and I had first joked about *The Official Preppy Handbook* when his college roommate went through a sustained madras phase, never completely sure if it was real or legend. But, not only was it real, I found a used copy online while anticipating my sailing debut on the SS *Penelope*. I did not tell Simon.

I paged through the slim paperback the night before we were scheduled to set sail with Lacy and Warren. I just needed an authority to tell me something, anything, as I zigzagged between the beach club and the gym club and the yacht club and whatever club was next. I lost hours at night to online sales featuring "splashy" flower prints in green, pink, orange, or white, or small repeating motifs of sailboats, tennis racquets, or animals that became adorable when shrunk and/or embroidered—like hedgehogs.

The book itself was satire, I knew this, but desperate times called for desperate life rafts. When I found myself genuinely questioning whether embroidered ducks *always* had to accompany muted beige (and how could one mute *beige?*), I tossed the book onto the couch cushion and pulled up YouTube on my phone, to see how my parents fared in the Maldives. I was bored and feeling lost in the hours between when Dev said he'd be home and when he actually walked in the door.

I checked for a *Senior Moments* vlog update. *They* always arrived right on schedule. On the screen, my father sat half-submerged in a blue square. His bright-yellow UV shirt floated uncooperatively around his belly, and he beat it back down into the water.

"Lilly, move three steps to the right."

"Fine, Ed." My mother shuffled and stretched her arms skyward. "How's this?"

"No, my right."

"Ed, I'll fall off the side of the infinity deck. These things need finite lines, you know. Not everyone has the core stability of a twenty-two-year-old."

My mother turned to the camera and smiled. She knew what she was doing. That back-and-forth was part of their virtual charm, though I knew it was also, to use one of Lilly's favorite words, "authentic." They didn't much believe in editing, on film or life in general.

I slammed the laptop shut. Watching my parents' banter and hearing about their wellness regime filled me with a bizarre envy. I picked up my phone to ask Dev—again—if he was coming home soon, then I decided to text Simon instead.

Me: I tried that thing you suggested for the ice maker, to see if there was a frozen clog. I tried to melt it with my hair dryer, but that only blew a fuse. Am I doing home repair right?

Simon: I hear you can buy bagged ice at the supermarket now. Maybe it's even that circular kind where you are. Great for cocktails.

Me: Haha. Speaking of fancy, did you see Mom and Dad's infinity pool in the Maldives? They're so influence-y.

Simon: What are they influencing?

Me: Your love life if Lilly has her way. Something about a yoga instructor?

Simon: That's why I live out here.

I thought about everything I'd done that day: made meals, cleaned up meals, said no to snacks, given in to snacks, cleaned up snacks, applied sunscreen, scrubbed off sunscreen, brushed teeth, read stories, cleaned up dog shit inside and cleaned up dog shit outside. I wanted all of it—the house with the yard not maintained by a building manager, the boo-boos that were invisible but desperately needed a Band-Aid. But I also wanted someone to want me for more than napkins, leashed walks, or page views.

—⁓—

On Dev's first day of residency, I woke up at 4:30 a.m. to make him coffee. We'd recently learned I was pregnant with not just one unexpected baby, but twins, and the anxiety of two (two!) new lives growing in my belly while a new life was forming around us had me in some serious throes of insomnia. I was also in negotiations with Dev's mother to plan a simple yet tasteful—and don't forget quick—wedding, while dodging reminders from my own mother about how I shouldn't feel hemmed in by tradition (when some hint of tradition was what I desperately wanted in order to make it all feel legitimate).

When Dev appeared in the kitchen, collared shirt tucked into his pants, white coat slung over one arm, he was like an apparition of a fully functional adult man. I couldn't believe my luck that, somehow, he was mine. I presented the mug of coffee to him like a gift and cooed, "Have a good day at the office, dear."

He'd leaned in and kissed me. Then he took one sip of the coffee and spat it back out. He laughed and wiped coffee from his formerly clean shirt, mumbling, "Charlie, did you forget to use a filter?"

I was wearing one of his old Georgetown T-shirts over my rapidly expanding belly, and I pulled it up around my face to hide the tears that sprang to my eyes. This was supposed to be about Dev, not about my face leaking again before the sun had even risen. And while I tried to lay some blame on my rollercoaster hormones, the truth was, I had no idea how I was going to do any of this. How was I going to care for a baby (make that two babies!), be someone's partner, still be some percentage of myself, if I couldn't even make coffee?

Dev set the cup on the counter and pulled me to him, like it was the easiest thing in the world to just be in that tiny kitchen together. He held me like it was *my* first day, not his.

"It's . . . so much. Residency. Babies. Plural! Me," I murmured into his chest. "I think you should pick the best three out of four. And I'm not sure I make the cut."

"Don't be ridiculous," he'd said, smoothing my hair back and kissing me on the forehead. "I want all of it. Four out of four. But especially you. None of it matters without you, Charlie."

—⁂—

Maybe, I thought now, he hadn't been so sure after all. In Rumford, I was doing all the things a fully functional person should. My quads shook from five billion squats at the Garage, and I'd signed a clipboard for STEAM day at the beach club. The ice maker had worked for an entire day. I'd scored us an invite on a sailboat, for crying out loud. Now I just needed Dev to see it all, to be part of it with me—to actually talk to me.

When his car crunched onto the gravel drive, I stuffed the handbook between the couch cushions. I could see the next twenty minutes play out like a grainy rerun of bag drop, shower drink, TV. Tonight, though. Tonight could be different.

Before Dev opened the door, I ran to the bathroom. I splashed cold water on my face and swapped my old T-shirt for one I hadn't slept in the past two nights. When I emerged, he was already in the kitchen pouring a drink. He rubbed his eyes, ran his hand through his hair, and leaned onto the counter. It took him a few seconds to notice me.

"Hey," he said. "You're up."

"It's all these workouts," I said. "When I'm there, I think I'm going to die, but then, later, I have more energy. It's the almost-dying that really stirs something up."

I busied myself pouring a water. Dev took a piece of cold pizza from the fridge with one hand and picked up a mug of bourbon with the other. I hadn't noticed when exactly he'd switched from beer to bourbon postshift.

"How much is it, by the way? The gym. And that beach club place? Elvis and I were talking budget today. Until we can turn some things around, we might have to start cutting our checks last, that is, unless we secure this grant."

This was not how I wanted the night to go. I didn't want to talk about paychecks, or Presley. I waved my hand. "Heidi said not to worry about the Garage for now. She probably has some kind of frequent customer credit built up. She's over thirty and has a thigh gap."

Dev paused, then he nodded as if that was a reasonable kind of transaction. He took a sip from the mug, and I could smell the bourbon from where I stood. I bit my lip.

"I saw you put a recurring meeting on the calendar," I said. "For Wednesdays? Is there something I forgot about?"

Dev looked caught off guard. "I put that on *our* calendar?"

"You did," I said slowly. "Why? Is it a secret?" I tried to say it like I was only kidding, simultaneously trying *not* to think of Presley leaning over his shoulder at the shared desk, after hours, most of the lights already turned off, the whole place empty but for them.

"Of course not. It's just more work stuff," he said, his voice a little gruff, his eyes not meeting mine. He shifted his weight, fingers tapping on the mug as he held it to his chest. It was like he closed an imaginary door, and I wasn't going to get more out of him. I took the mug from his hands and took a sip. I was breathing a little too quickly, and I didn't want him to notice.

"Wednesdays are grill nights at the beach club anyway, and Poppy's been asking us to join. She always has way too many steak tips and veggie kabobs, and she said it doesn't feel like she's winning grill night unless she's feeding two families."

Dev looked relieved. "That sounds fun."

"It is," I said. "I'd be having even more fun if you were there with me some evening." I gave him back the mug.

"And miss three hours of returning calls, checking labs, and finishing charts? Are you mad?" Dev's eyes creased with a hint of a tired smile, and I told my racing brain to relax, ordered the nervous flush creeping up my neck to recede. I reached out to touch him on the arm, then pulled my hand back. "Wait, what kind of day was it?"

He frowned. "Let me take my shirt off."

"By all means," I said as he smirked and unbuttoned his dress shirt, throwing it inside out into the carpeted hallway. He wore a plain white T-shirt underneath, and between the simplicity of it, and the way he nudged his glasses back into place with the back of his wrist, I could almost trick myself into thinking we'd just started dating and were huddled in my cramped apartment kitchen, like I was about to ask him if he'd played high school sports or still listened to Dave Matthews Band.

I reached for the bottle of bourbon and, instead of putting it away, poured a bit more into the mug. "Let's play a game," I said.

"A game," he repeated. "Here, in the kitchen?"

I nodded. "Tell me one thing about your day. A good thing. And I'll take a drink. But it has to be something good, and not something gross. Is that too many parameters?"

Dev pretended to contemplate, scrunching his nose in the way that always made me soften toward him, muttering, "Not something gross . . . not something gross . . . this could take a while." Then he said, "Okay. We got a patient into outpatient rehab."

"That's great!"

"It's something," he said, passing me the cup. I took a swig of bourbon, then placed it back in his hands. The sugar and firewood left a pleasant burn on my tongue. Dev took off his glasses and set them aside. Leaning against the counter, he rubbed the back of his neck then arched his back, raising his hands to the upper cabinets and twisting, like he was trying to dislodge a pinball from behind one of his shoulder blades. I stepped across the kitchen and hopped onto the countertop to sit behind him, digging my thumbs into the ropes of his neck. I let my knees rest on either side of his hips.

He leaned back without quite touching me.

"I still have to shower," he mumbled, but he didn't move.

I paused. "Emergently?"

He shook his head, so I moved my hands down to his shoulders. It was the closest we'd been in some time, at least when we weren't sitting next to each other on the couch, inviting the Norwegian chef into our marriage.

"Okay, tell me more, sir," I said. "What kind of heroics did you perform?"

"Nothing heroic," he said softly. "I spent the morning making phone calls, between seeing other patients. Honestly it was mostly a lot of extra paperwork." He spoke slowly, pausing as I let my palms rest on his shoulders and swept my thumbs to the pressure points at the base of his neck. He exhaled slowly as I pressed.

"A heroic amount of paperwork?" I asked, my voice low.

"So much paperwork, it would blow your mind," Dev said, fully leaning into me now as I worked my way down his back. "Your turn."

"Okay," I said. "Don't be intimidated. But I tried out for Poppy's beach volleyball team today. Now drink."

Dev took a sip obediently, then he let his hand drop to my knee. "Wait, what do you mean you tried out?"

"Poppy doesn't take just anyone off the street, Dev."

"Right, of course not," he said. "Well, did you make the cut?"

I snorted. "God no. I was terrible. I was in the first round of cuts. But I had fun goofing off and borrowing one of her skorts. I made the team in my heart. Your turn again."

Dev laughed softly, and I let myself pretend we really were back in our old apartment, that it was still just the two of us, before life fanned out in so many directions. Then the ice maker in the cottage grumbled, and the dryer banged so loudly James Dean hid under the couch.

"Wait, I'm going again," I said. "I have a surprise. Tomorrow, we're going to sail with Lacy and Warren on *Penelope*. I only had to do push-ups at the Garage until my arm bones disintegrated to make it happen." I held up my hands in a ta-da gesture, then I let an arm hang at a right angle, my forearm limp.

Dev turned around and actually smiled. "That *is* good news. Except for your arms. I liked your arms."

"Drink then," I said. "Them's the rules." Dev raised his cup, his eyes finding mine over the rim of the mug.

"We're meeting them at the yacht club dock in the morning, so Presley will have to survive without you during Saturday's riveting session of catching up on paperwork. And maybe don't stay up too late with your chef friend either," I said. I thought, then—potentially aided by the rapid intake of bourbon—of Oliver in that stupid cabana, how his stupid white T-shirt caught on his board shorts, how they hung on his stupid hips. I pushed it away. There were far too many people in this conversation, and in my head, when it should only be Dev and me.

I took the hem of Dev's T-shirt and gave it a tug. "You should shower," I said. "We should shower."

Dev swallowed the rest of the bourbon in his mug and grinned at me before running down the hallway.

I watched from the doorway as he dropped his work clothes in the appropriate hazmat baskets and stepped into the shower. I stared at the contours of his silhouette through the curtain, the long line of his back, his broad shoulders. He shook his head as the water hit it, spraying droplets onto the bathroom mirror. He looked out at me from the gap in the curtain.

"Are you coming?"

I threw my clothes in the direction of our bedroom and hopped in. My face came up to his shoulders, which meant I couldn't look up at him without getting water in my eyes. So, I put my hands around his back, eyes closed. I felt his arms rest on my shoulders, his chin skimming the top of my head. Why wasn't *this* the nighttime routine? Screw foraging.

I was leaning in, closing the small space between us, when he reached for the shampoo and squeezed some onto his head.

"What the fuck??" He pulled away abruptly.

I opened my eyes. Dev was looking at me, baffled, watery red ketchup dripping from his hair, down his cheeks, onto his chest. The smell was overpowering. The drain looked like we were reenacting *Psycho*.

"Charlie, were you meal prepping for grill night in the shower?" Dev asked, bursting into confused laughter. I felt like he'd caught me reading *The Official Preppy Handbook*. I was not going to try to explain this one. And unless he was turned on by cheeseburgers, I may have ruined the moment.

"It's a detoxifier, and it's organic," I said. I grabbed the bottle and squirted it at his chest. "You can just rinse it away."

chapter 14

While the night hadn't turned into the steamy reconnection I'd hoped for, unless you counted the amount of shower steam involved in washing off ketchup, Dev still had to be a little bit impressed with me, I thought the next morning. Only a few weeks in Rumford and I'd procured our passage on the Queen *Penelope*.

"Dev! We have to go! Lacy and Warren are at the yacht club waiting for us." I looked at my phone. I'd already texted that we were on our way ten minutes ago.

"Ready, mateys?" I asked, dumping bowls of Cheerios into the sink.

"Arrrrrrrr!" Kate and Toby growled, shaking their fists.

Dev strode out of the bedroom with a red bandanna wrapped around his forehead, his curls pushed back and up so they stuck out in every direction. It was more Springsteen than Sparrow, but I had zero complaints.

Kate squealed, "Daddy, you're a pirate!"

Kate was in her element—we all knew how to punch a shark on the nose, should it come to that. Toby was under strict orders to stay below deck except when I had my hands on him. As if all this wasn't enough, I was wearing white jeans.

As I gathered and filled water bottles, Dev picked up his phone and chuckled at something on the screen.

"What's so funny?" I said.

"Elvis." He shook his head.

I set a water bottle on the counter more loudly than was necessary. "What about her?"

"It's nothing," he said, putting his phone in his pocket. "Let's just go."

I bristled. "Try me," I said.

He cleared his throat. "She's at Costco, restocking the bathrooms for the office, likely out of her own pocket—which I told her not to do. But she's timing herself, like it's *Supermarket Sweep*. It's an old inside joke. She's sending me stats from the paper products aisle."

When I didn't meet this apparent hilarity with a chuckle of my own, Dev added, "Anyway, it's dumb. Sorry. You all set?"

I tried to hide my annoyance and hold on to the glimmer of the better, more connected vibe we'd gotten last night, but I felt something heavy lodge itself in my chest. "You know what," I said, handing him the bag I'd filled with water bottles and extra clothes for the kids. "I am ready. And please. Can we just not talk about Presley—or work—for once? Just for today?" I walked to the door before he could answer. We had someplace to be.

—⁓—

In short order, I was convinced I'd missed my calling as a model in a Ralph Lauren ad. The wind picked up sea spray as *Penelope* skimmed across the bay, and I closed my eyes as it tickled my face. The sailboat was twice as spacious as I'd imagined, both above and below deck, and it was sparklingly clean. One of Lacy's white cashmere sweaters draped over my shoulders, faded sailing race hat on my head, I could definitely sign on to *this* kind of mobile lifestyle. Warren nodded in approval from across the boat.

"I thought you were new to this," he said.

"It's from a friend," I said quickly.

"I thought you said you found it," Dev said.

"I did find it. At the yacht club. From a friend." *Could we lay off the hat?* "Warren, what's the big sail called again?" I asked, half listening as he answered.

Dev put his hand on the long metal beam that held the bottom of the mainsail—the big center one—in place. "Charlie, the boom moves back and forth when we let out the lines and use the wind to turn the boat. It's called tacking. Listen for Warren or me to call out; you really don't want the boom to whack you."

"When we're cruising, it'll be so smooth," Lacy called from below deck. "Don't worry. You'll love it, Charlie."

I was already sold. Maybe we'd get a boat of our own. We could do boat stuff, be boat people. It could be *our* thing. I hopped down the ladder to see if I could help Lacy below deck as we motored out of the harbor.

In the kitchen—because there was a *kitchen* on the boat—Lacy unloaded cans of seltzer from a monogrammed zip-top Yeti cooler and wedged them into a compact stainless steel fridge. Next, she stowed boxes of crackers and cookies into an upper cabinet. Wood shelves and cushioned benches flanked the cabin walls, adorned with blue-and-white-striped throw pillows. Kate and Toby sat on either side of a table as Ivy laid out a deck of UNO cards.

"This is nicer than my college apartment," I murmured.

Lacy laughed like I was joking. "It's not the Ritz, but we like to teach Ivy to be flexible," she said. "It's a two bed, one bath, and the Wi-Fi is spotty."

"Can I do anything to help?"

"Only this." Lacy handed me a teardrop-shaped travel mug. "Ready to leave the world behind?"

"That I can do," I said, thinking it was coffee she'd handed me until the sharp sweetness of rosé hit my tongue.

Back on deck, I held on to a skinny steel railing and made my way along the side of the boat to find Dev near the front as he tied a complicated knot with a thick rope. Be the nice normal couple, I told myself. Don't be weird or tense—not out at sea, not in front of Lacy and Warren.

"You should take that rope to dinner first," I said as Dev worked it with his fingers and gave it a good pull.

"Take this *line* to dinner, you mean?" Dev said. He smiled, clearly trying to close some of the distance between us. "Just, they're called lines, not ropes. You don't want Warren to reprimand you. I might have to push him overboard."

"Obviously. Lines," I said. "What else should I know about the lifestyle?"

"Well," he said, "we're on the bow. Did you know that?"

"Nope. I thought we were on the front."

"And Warren is at the helm."

"If you say so," I said. *See?* I thought. This was easy. We'd be fine today.

Warren called Dev to help with something, and I turned my attention back to Lacy, who had draped herself on a bench, at the *helm*, legs outstretched, shoes off. That I could do with zero instruction.

A short while later, the sails were full. We were, in fact, cruising. Lacy kept refilling my cup with rosé. My mouth felt both loose and fuzzy. I planned on switching to water soon, just like I planned on checking on the kids, who, last I noticed, were playing hide-and-seek in the rooms down below. But for the time being, Lacy was being as generous with the gossip as she was with the wine, and I was hypnotized.

"You've already missed the Fourth of July, Charlie. The winter is so long here; it's like that show about climate change with all the bad weather and dragons," Lacy said.

I giggled. "*Game of Thrones*?"

"Whatever," she said, waving her hand.

I didn't see a need to correct her. I did stash the comment away to tell Dev later. We'd watched a lot of that show while up in the middle of the night with babies, facing them away from the screen during the inappropriate parts—so, pretty much all of it. For now, I kept my attention on Lacy.

"Anyway, the Fourth is the best weekend. We 'rough it.' We pile into our Whalers and motor over to the island—you know, the one you can see from the yacht club." Lacy lowered her voice. "You can get there in a dinghy, but no thank you."

She laughed loudly, so I followed suit, as if we, too, had a Whaler or a dinghy or even a paddleboat.

"Anyway, Teague always organizes it. Though, obviously, not this year. Heidi took the kids to Wellfleet instead. By herself." Lacy furrowed her brow as if she couldn't quite understand why. "Don't get me started on Heidi," Lacy said. Then she sighed and continued. "It was fine when it was the four of us. Teague chilled Heidi out, you know? Until he let his little habit get away from him. When he went to rehab, God, Heidi lost it. Teague's parents hired an army. Heidi quit her job, and she doesn't have any responsibilities now, other than to *exist*, until Teague comes home."

"That's terrible," I said softly, remembering Heidi's empty, museum-like house. I'd seen Heidi either at the Garage or the beach club every day that week. It hadn't occurred to me that maybe she was trying to avoid being at home.

"It really is," Lacy said. "It's a drag on everyone. And, between you and me," she leaned even closer, until I could smell the wine on her breath, "we all lost out when Teague dropped the ball."

I swallowed more wine to drown out the part of myself that felt guilty nodding along. Did Teague's addiction really put such a cramp in Lacy's social scene? Were they so awash with money and access and toys that rehab amounted to an inconvenience? A bummer?

Lacy looked at Warren, making sure his attention was elsewhere. "Warren invested a chunk of our trust with Teague, before he left for rehab. Teague was trying to show he was still at the top of his game, but let's just say he wasn't in a place to make responsible decisions with other people's money."

"Oh," I said. "That does not sound good."

Lacy waved her hand. "There's always another investment opportunity around the corner. And I've taken over our finances, obviously. Still, after what happened to Teague, Warren wants to do something meaningful. He has a project that could revitalize Bradley." She paused and raised her sunglasses. "Mixed-use condos. They'd be higher end than anything there now, and the project could raise the property value of the entire downtown. Those couple of blocks by the waterfront are just begging for it, don't you think?"

I had questions, such as how, exactly, are high-end condos meaningful? Wouldn't raising the property values make it impossible for the current residents to stay—in which case, who was it really helping? I thought about the patients Dev told me about, the ones I'd seen on my rushed visits to the clinic. A first-floor Starbucks wasn't going to fix what ailed them.

"I'd appreciate you keeping this between us, for now," Lacy said. "Unless you think Dev would be interested. I always think, why don't men simply ask for help? Teague and Warren, I mean, in this case, but really any of them. We don't always know what they're really thinking, these husbands."

I swallowed uncomfortably. "What about Poppy and Davis?" I said, wanting to take the focus off Dev, and secrets. "They seem like a great couple. Super enthusiastic about everything."

"Well, Davis is gay, obviously, but they make it work. Socially they're a blast."

I almost spat out my wine. "I'm sorry . . . what?"

A satisfied smile spread across Lacy's face. "You didn't know? Charlie, keep up."

"But, what? Why?" Why would Poppy, who seemed so confident, so capable, stay in a marriage like that? Why would Davis, who seemed equally a catch? It was like my brain was off balance. *No*, I realized, the actual boat had begun rocking more noticeably underneath me. It was both.

"Why are they still married?" Lacy said, placing a finger on her chin like I'd asked her why I should join the PTA. "First of all, Davis has a massive trust fund. Do you know how many lacrosse tournaments it can fund? They *both* get off on lacrosse tournaments."

I honestly didn't know if she was joking. I didn't know what a joke was anymore. The boat was really undulating, and I steadied myself by holding on to a handrail.

"Anyway, he's not *totally* gay," Lacy said. "Maybe bi? I don't really get it, but whatever. At the end of the day, Davis is an excellent tennis partner. And have you seen their house? Stunning. They've decided to take separate vacations twice a year and have flings." Lacy shrugged as if to say, *To each his own.*

"Does everyone know?"

"I hope not," Lacy said. "They try to keep it among friends. Their relationship status, I mean, not the sex. Although . . ." Lacy trailed off suggestively. "Just kidding. It's been less than a year since this all came to light. Was it a bump in the road? Yes. Do they let it get in the way? No. Unlike some people."

I tipped my mug all the way back.

"Now," Lacy said, "let's bring the boys a beer and let them pretend they're in charge."

"Mama?" Kate called from below deck.

"Be right down," I said. My head was spinning, trying to process all that Lacy had told me.

I stared out at the water, lost in my own thoughts. The wind was picking up, and I could hear Warren shouting directions to Dev.

"Mama?" Kate called again, more insistently this time.

I reluctantly pulled myself to my feet and climbed down the short, shallow ladder to the cabin.

Once there, I immediately wanted to retreat.

Toby sat perched on the edge of the bench, his face an unfortunate shade of off-white that looked much better on leather cushions than small children. His eyes were sallow. Ivy sat next to him, trying to distract him with her iPad while Toby stared, unfocused.

"Toby, sweetie? Honey, are you okay?"

He whimpered in reply.

Water, I thought. *I should get him some water.* I turned on the faucet in the sink but nothing came out. I squatted to pull open the mini fridge, praying I'd find something more than wine and Pamplemousses seltzer. Then I heard Toby gag. My own stomach dropped instinctually, and I shot straight up, banging my head on an upper cabinet.

"Shit!" The boat rocked to the right. I fell against the counter, my hip bone colliding with the edge. I grumbled another panicked curse in front of the kids.

Toby whimpered again. He hadn't actually thrown up. It was fine. I'd bring him the water, and I'd tell the guys to turn *Penelope* around and head back home. Toby and Kate hadn't been on a boat before. They just had to get their sea legs. Kate hovered by the bottom of the stairs, not sure whether to comfort her brother or give him a wide berth. I lunged over to the bench, grabbing the table as *Penelope* lurched beneath me. You really could feel the waves in the cabin more than above deck. *No wonder Toby is a little queasy,* I thought, starting to feel iffy myself.

Lacy called into the cabin from above, "Everything okay down there?"

"Totally," I said. "All good!"

"Mommy?" Kate did not look convinced.

"Toby's just a little woozy, Kate. A little seasick."

"He looks a lot green," she insisted.

"He's fine," I repeated. "He'll be fine." I didn't want to make a scene. Through the opening at the top of the stairs I could see Dev and Warren talking above deck, their faces serious. Dev wasn't going to see me trying to get his attention from down here.

"I'll be back in a sec," I told Kate, intending to climb back up the ladder and discreetly request Dev's presence. "I'll find Toby some water, and we'll be right—"

And that was when Toby threw up all over my white jeans.

"Oh, sweetie," I said, rubbing his back, not sure whether to breathe through my nose or my mouth, both terrible options in the enclosed space. Ivy delicately stowed the iPad on a shelf behind the bench and scooted to the side.

"Sorry, Mommy," Toby mumbled. He looked as confused about what to do as the rest of us.

"It's okay, don't worry, buddy," I said. "It's just what pirates do sometimes. Let me get you a towel."

Not seeing any beach towels, I grabbed a throw blanket from the other bench. I tried to mop up some of the vomit, but the navy yarn of the blanket just spread it around instead of absorbing anything. Then, I realized I couldn't throw it in the washing machine or hose it down when I was done. I was on a fucking boat. Could I toss it in the ocean without anyone noticing?

"Paper towels," I said aloud. "There must be paper towels."

Kate stood by the stairs, gripping the railing, legs spread for balance.

"Mommy, I don't feel so good either," she said.

I tried to quell the rising panic in my chest. I hoped it was only panic that was rising.

"Okay, honey, go sit by Toby, okay?" Then I added, "But not too close?"

The soiled jeans would have to stay on for now, but I had to get Lacy's sweater away from my face. I pulled from the back and yanked it over my head. Maybe I could sneak it home somehow and wash it. For now, I left it on the floor in the galley kitchen while I scanned the counter for paper towels, maybe a trash bag, anything that wasn't dry clean only.

I steadied myself with one hand on the counter and pulled at cabinets with the other, but none opened more than an inch. They were latched from the inside, like when I babyproofed our kitchen so the kids wouldn't eat dishwasher pods. I pulled at a lower cabinet, tried to wedge my fingers in to find the clasp, then the boat lurched suddenly, and I slammed my hand into the door as I fell against it.

"Goddammit," I groaned.

"Mommy, I feel funny," Kate said again.

I banged on the cabinet, trying to get it open, but between the rocking of the boat and my panicked hands, it was useless. I saw the soft-top Yeti cooler, the one with the giant monogram, on the counter by the fridge. I lunged over to Toby and Kate, both of whom shared the same expression of confused misery.

I squatted on the floor to balance and looked at both of them. "You're going to have to share."

Before they could argue, they both vomited into the Yeti. I patted their heads, repeating, "It's okay, it's okay," direly regretting the rosé.

I told Kate to hug the cooler between them while I went to get Dev. He couldn't cure seasickness, I knew that much about the limits of modern medicine, but he could at least help me figure out how to clean up the mess. We were guests on this boat, and our kids, poor things, had made it look like a frat party.

chapter 15

I poked my head out of the cabin and sucked in the fresh air, hoping to displace the sour stench from my lungs. Then I remembered, the smell was *on* me. Lacy stood at the helm, hands on the giant metal wheel, while Dev and Warren worked together to yank the lines attached to the mast and the sails. They looked like puppeteers trying to assert control over a giant marionette. Warren clamped one of the lines and took the wheel back from Lacy. Dev stood in the cockpit, thick tri-colored lines in his hands. He braced himself with one leg and leaned back.

Warren said, "Dev, be honest, man. It can't be easy. From what I hear, there's a line out the door of the clinic, like Walmart on Black Friday."

I doubted Warren had *ever* stood in line at a Walmart, even on a Tuesday. I waved, trying to catch Dev's attention. His brow was furrowed, and it felt like he was avoiding looking in my direction.

"It's fine." Dev's voice was clipped. "Really. We can handle it."

What if Warren wants to throw some money at the clinic, like a tax write-off, I thought. I had always been too busy throwing my money at rent or groceries to know what, exactly, qualified as a tax write-off. Could that be part of the condo deal? Improving current infrastructure? Whatever the reason, Warren didn't let up on Dev, even as I competed for his attention.

"Um, guys, Dev," I said. "I need some—"

"That Keen girl who took over the place. Does she even know what she's doing? She looks like a grown-up Tinkerbell in a white coat, and Bradley is no fairy tale."

While Warren looked amused with his own wordplay, Dev didn't hesitate to shoot back.

"That's bullshit, actually. Nothing fazes Elvis. She's on top of everything, and we don't need any help. Like I said, we're the partners now. And we've got it under control."

I stared at Dev like I wasn't sure I knew him. He was defending Presley with this burst of passionate intensity, while I was right there, within arm's reach, trying to get his attention to help me rescue our children from the perils of the sea. *I* was his partner. And I, singular, had *nothing* under control.

"Tacking!" Warren yelled.

"Shit, Charlie!" Dev reached out and pulled me down by my T-shirt hem. I ducked as the boom swooshed over my head. Warren turned the wheel, and I grabbed onto a handhold as the boat shifted direction more sharply than I thought possible. What happened to cruising? A whitecap sprayed over the side of the boat, and Warren looked like he was enjoying himself. I prayed he was pointing us toward dry land.

"Hey, listen, I need—" I tried again, but the wind was loud, and Warren was louder.

"It seems to me, Dev, a lot of the clinic's clientele would be better served at the hospital anyway. It's on the bus route. And how many of your patients even have private health insurance? Must be hard on the ole bottom line. Tacking!" Warren yelled again.

I felt Dev's hand on my head, pushing me under as the boom swung around again.

"What the fuck?" I snapped at him.

"I didn't want you to get hit," Dev said. He sounded impatient, and he pulled another line through another swivel thingy that probably had a fancy-sounding name I'd never remember. "If you're going to be up here, you have to pay attention, Charlie."

"Pay attention to what, exactly?" I said, my voice heated. Even the vomitorium was better than this.

"What's that smell?" Dev said, looking around.

"Do you want me to pay attention to how you'll leap to Presley's defense and guard whatever you two have going on over there like it's the Temple of Doom? Because obviously, I wouldn't understand?" I was yelling now, sure Lacy and Warren were staring, and we were making it super *awkward*, and I knew how Lacy felt about awkward, but I couldn't stop. "Meanwhile, our kids are puking their guts out down below. And it's all over me. That's what you smell, Dev." *I will not cry on this sailboat,* I thought. I will *not* cry on this sailboat.

Another whitecap crashed against the boat and sprayed us with more water. Dev swiped the bandanna from his head and wiped his face. His glasses were covered in water droplets.

"Are the kids okay?" His face looked pained.

"Yes, they just . . . they don't quite have their sea legs yet," I said glumly.

"I got caught up in what Warren was saying, and we hit some weather. We're heading back in," he said, gripping the lines more tightly than seemed necessary. "Look, I just don't think Elvis would want me talking about the clinic like it's town gossip."

"Well, good thing no one would think that, because you never *talk* about it!" I said, still heated, giving in to anger instead of tears. "You just schedule your secret meetings, and between apparently deciding to train for a marathon and zoning the fuck out to mushroom foraging porn, you can't even stand to be in the same room with me—"

Dev said, "Charlie, you don't understand . . ." at the same time Warren yelled, "Tacking!" again.

"I got it!" I yelled at the both of them, ducking my head.

Dev didn't need Warren's help, and I didn't need *his* help either. I took care of the kids on my own all the time. I retreated down the stairs before I said something I couldn't take back in front of the whole crew, or really did start crying, either of which would be more humiliating than I could stomach, given current circumstances.

I swung my shaking body down the ladder, and my foot landed on the vomit-covered sweater I had dumped on the galley floor. I slipped, slamming onto my ass as *Penelope* bucked indignantly against another oncoming wave.

"Goddamn shit motherfucker," I said in defeat. I looked apologetically at the kids, but Kate nodded like she understood. Someone did, at least.

"Charlie? Sounds like you could use a refill." Lacy climbed down after me. "Let's just leave Warren and Dev to talk business."

"Lacy, I'm sorry, but we have some business down here," I said into my elbow as the smell hit me once again. "I was trying to take care of it."

"I see." Lacy took in Kate, Toby, and the Yeti.

"I'm so sorry about the cooler," I said, pulling myself up. "I couldn't open the cabinets to get a bag or something. I don't, I didn't know—"

I felt Lacy's hand on my arm. I took a deep breath, then desperately wished I hadn't.

"Charlie, don't be silly, it's fine. We have four of those coolers at home. We'll throw the mess into it, zip it up, and trash it at the club. Voilà!"

I blinked. Was Lacy really turning a $200 cooler into a reinforced Glad bag? I watched in equal parts horror and appreciation as Lacy took the blue blanket by its unsoiled edges and mopped up the floor below Toby's feet. She then picked up the white sweater I had borrowed with a Ziploc bag around her hand, like she was picking up a Shih Tzu's sidewalk deposit rather than a fistful of cashmere, and plopped it into the cooler on top of the blanket.

"We're almost back in the harbor," Lacy said to Kate and Toby. "You'll feel as good as new. I promise. It'll be like this never happened."

Ivy sat conscientiously next to Kate, rubbing her back. She'd probably been there the whole time I was above deck trying to spar for Dev's attention. Ivy whispered something in Kate's ear, making her smile.

"Thank you, Ivy," I said, "for being a good friend." I smiled at Lacy, too. My club invites may not be long for this world, but I wasn't cleaning up this mess on my own after all.

"Now," Lacy said, fixing her eyes on me. "Looks like you need a change of pants."

I looked down at my ruined white jeans. I'd found them on clearance and by some miracle they fit perfectly, but now I never wanted to see them again.

"Good thing I always have extra on board," Lacy said. She went into the front room and opened a cubby to reveal a full miniature closet system. "When California Closets did the house, I thought why not do the boat, too?"

I ran my hand over folded white jeans, polos, cream-colored sweaters, and pullovers with thin pink stripes. Was that a Chanel handbag? *The Official Preppy Handbook* would have a field day. Lacy selected a crisp, folded pair of white jeans, and I took them gratefully.

I slid my own ill-fated jeans down my thighs right there in front of the kids and Lacy, then I dropped them into the Yeti. I sucked in my stomach and pulled the button closed on the fresh pair. "They're perfect," I managed to say, though they were so tight around my waist I worried I might rupture my spleen.

"I . . . I'm sorry about all this," I said again. I felt so stupid, thinking Dev and I could leave our problems behind on shore. "This disaster, and also the one between Dev and me. I'm assuming you heard us up there. I guess *Penelope* isn't the only one hitting a bit of a squall."

"Please, who isn't?" Lacy said, shaking her head. "And those look good on you. You should keep them."

I rose from below deck, grateful for fresh air and Lacy's spare pair of pants, to the scene above: Dev and Warren drinking the beers we'd left on deck before things got hairy. Dev stared out at the choppy waves as Warren motored us back into the calmer waters of the harbor. He had no idea the fresh hell I'd just cleaned up. He'd been up here playing sea captain while I dealt with the messy, smelly, and unseen business of our life together. It was suddenly so clear. He was always someplace else, even when he was right next to me.

"Hey," I said loudly. If this was the only way to get his attention, so be it. "I was thinking, Warren might have some decent advice for the business side of the clinic. Dev, weren't you just telling me how Presley shops at Costco out of pocket to stock the bathrooms? I mean, you both went to med school, not business school."

I had to make a life for us here, too, and one way to do that was to build bridges with Lacy. I felt like I owed her something now, and besides, a conversation wouldn't hurt anyone. While the sun shone behind him, making the still water of the harbor sparkle, Dev's face clouded with confusion.

Kate poked her head up from the cabin. "Can we get ice cream sandwiches at the club?"

I marveled at her iron stomach. She was more resilient than any of us. Warren, looking as smug as the baby-blue sweater draped over his shoulders, told Dev he'd drop by the clinic that week, "just to circle back." Lacy ascended the stairs with the Yeti. She threw me a knowing look, like it was our little secret that my children's lunch, half of her nautical throw pillow covers, and an entire outfit were zipped inside.

"I think we all deserve a treat," Lacy said.

chapter 16

After a few days of awkwardly going through the motions with Dev at the cottage—which was easy to do, since he was never there—I decided to stop by the clinic unannounced. The white party gala was being held at one of the country clubs that night. It was always a white party, Heidi had explained to me before handing me a dress to wear. And even though we'd hardly talked to each other since being on the Sailboat of Unfortunate Events, I wanted to make extra sure Dev remembered that it was that night, and he knew what time we needed to be there.

Part of it, too, was that I still thought of the clinic as Presley's place. I wouldn't mind if she overheard me telling Dev about the gala, and if she imagined us there—together, as *partners*—well, that was okay, too.

There were only a few people in the waiting room. I stared at the swinging door—could I just walk in and look for Dev, like I belonged there, too? It didn't feel that way. I was wearing the white jeans Lacy had given me on the boat, hoping to stretch them a little, and a turquoise-striped tank. More preppy than my usual getup, I suddenly felt self-conscious.

I texted Dev: Hey. Coffee? I thought maybe I could catch you while the kids are at Heidi's house. I'm nearby picking up our gala dresses from the dry cleaner.

No response. At home, it was like he couldn't even be in the same room with me. We passed each other like ghosts in the night. I didn't know how to ask him what was really going on, what he talked to

Presley about during off-hours, why he left the room when she called. I was afraid of what the answer would be. At night, the chef foraged farther and farther into the forest, still not finding what he was searching for.

I waited the length of a commercial break on the talk show playing on the waiting room television, then, when Dev didn't reply, I walked back outside and paced next to the car. Just as I was thinking I should give up and leave, Presley exited from a side door. She wore gym shorts and a T-shirt, and, not seeing me, she jogged across the street to the Dunkin'. Less than a minute later she emerged with two giant iced coffees. But she didn't go back into the clinic. Instead, she walked toward a big fenced-in area a block away. A park, maybe? I pictured Dev's phone sitting in his messenger bag, ignored on a park bench, as Presley handed him the sweating plastic cup. *Et tu, iced coffee.*

I darted out of the parking lot, crossed the street, and walked in the direction of the park. On the side of a big cement basketball court, on the other side of the chain-link fence, Presley—just Presley—called out to a gaggle of teenagers as they jostled for the ball on the opposite side of the court. As I approached, she waved at me and jogged over.

"Hey, Charlie! What a fun surprise," she said, holding one of the now-sweating cups of iced coffee.

"Isn't Gatorade the preferred beverage of basketball?" I said.

"Girl, I'm trying to be a New Englander!" Presley said in a fake whisper, her Southern accent even stronger than I remembered. Then, in a normal voice, "How'm I doing?"

"Better than me," I said. "Hey, listen, is Dev here? I was hoping to grab a few minutes with him. I thought you guys would be seeing patients. I texted him, but he isn't responding. Then when I saw you here . . ."

Presley took a gulp of the iced coffee. "Shoot, he took off a few hours early today, Charlie. For, um, he has that thing, with . . . He didn't tell you?"

"Tell me what?" I said, like it was nothing, like it was completely normal that I had no idea what she was talking about.

The teenage boys were yelling for Presley to join them, and she gave them the one-minute sign with her index finger. "Don't make me hold up a different finger!" she shouted. Then, to me, "Sorry, girl, what were you saying?"

I tried again, but even to my own ears, I sounded shaky. "What was Dev going to tell me? I just, I must have forgotten."

The boys continued to haggle Presley, and she turned and called out, "I'm just waiting on Jake, so you can play a freaking game of horse while you're waiting, Anton!" The boys laughed and continued to wrestle over the ball.

"Look, I'm sorry, Charlie, but you should just ask him. It's not my business." She checked her watch. "But hey, do you want to stay and play? I'm just waiting on the other coach. He's a doc, too, at the hospital. Girl, it's worth sticking around to see his abs when he takes his shirt off after the first quarter."

I suddenly felt silly. The other vat of iced coffee that Presley had picked up from the doughnut shop was sitting on the bench, waiting, I assumed now for Jake, and his abs—not Dev. But I still had no idea where Dev was, or why he wasn't answering my text. Or why it was that Presley knew where he was—and I didn't.

—◊—

"I'm sorry we're late," Dev said, later that night.

We sat in the parking lot of Rumford's most exclusive country club, the Trident. The gala had started an hour ago.

"I got stuck," Dev said. "There's this . . . it's hard to explain right now. Do you want me to?"

"Nope," I said. I didn't. Not then.

"Roger that." Dev looked relieved.

I'd thought about canceling on the gala after talking to Presley. What were we supposed to do, smile and dance and pretend like everything was fine? But just as quickly, I'd decided against it. Whatever the real problem was—that we'd only gotten married because I was pregnant; that we'd stayed together because we had these two babies, and we were sleep deprived, and they were all-consuming, and one thing had simply led to another; that this wasn't the life he wanted; that he thought moving would solve it, but—oops—he'd moved *with* me (an unfortunate if crushing, to me, oversight). It would have to wait one more night to lay bare, for my fears to be confirmed.

The thing was, I wanted one fairy-tale evening, even if it meant pretending, or simply not acknowledging all of it, for one more night. I wanted to wear the dress, I wanted to dance, and I wanted to pretend that Dev wanted to be there, with me. If my life was going to fall apart this last week of summer, I would make it wait one more day.

This way, Dev also didn't have to *not* mention that Warren had stopped by twice that week and Dev had avoided him (I heard about it from Lacy), and I didn't need to share that I'd dropped by the clinic, when he was strangely MIA, and had a chat with Presley that made everything even murkier.

Dev wore a white button-down shirt tucked into light-gray pants, which were the best we could do on short notice. Poppy had offered to loan him a pair from Davis, but Dev was so tall and lanky, it would never work. Given recent events, I wasn't entirely confident about white clothing myself, but rules were rules.

Dev looked down, as if double-checking whether he'd actually changed out of work clothes. I'd practically thrown the shirt and pants at him when he raced in the door. "I couldn't find my belt," he said.

"I think Kate has a thing going with drawstrings and belts," I said. "Maybe she's making a zip line. Could be fun." I wiped some drops of water from his shoulders. His hair was still wet.

The entrance to the Tri Club was white marble streaked with meandering veins of gray. Tall, thick columns rose from the floor. A three-tier cast iron chandelier hung suspended from the vaulted ceiling, and lights dripped from it like frosted ice cubes. Tiny seahorses adorned the light sconces, and in the dining room, which seemed endless, I could see huge floor-to-ceiling windows, entire walls of dark which, in daylight, framed the endless blue of the Atlantic Ocean. The room was cleared of tables and chairs and instead dotted with high-top tables for people to rest plates and empty glasses on as they chatted. My stomach rumbled, but I wasn't sure if it was hunger or nerves.

"What was it like to go to places like this when you were a teenager?" I said. "Because for me this would have been the stuff of novels, or movies about regular girls who found out they were secret royalty."

"It had its moments. But it wasn't always a fairy tale," Dev said. Before I could ask what exactly he meant, he grinned and put his arm out for me to take, like we were about to promenade. I took it, feeling a mix of happy and sad and hopeful and devastated that I knew I had no chance of making sense of. I looked for someone I knew, someone I wanted to talk to and clink champagne glasses with, but unfortunately landed on Warren, who was talking to an older man whose tuft of white hair matched his white bow tie. Warren waved us over with such fervor that we couldn't pretend we hadn't seen him.

As we joined them, the man in the bow tie said, apparently finishing his thought, "But that's why they call it *hard* work. These people, they don't know the meaning of the word, am I right?"

Warren looked like he was about to reply, for better or worse, but then the man turned to Dev and said, without introducing himself, "You, son, your people know about hard work. At least, well, who *are* your people?" The man was looking at Dev as if his ambiguous ethnicity was a joke Dev was playing on him.

Dev's jawline tensed, and he said simply, "The British?"

The man looked confused, then he burst into surprised laughter. Warren cleared his throat and said awkwardly, "They lost the war, but they worked hard, didn't they? Dev, have you met Al Westinghouse?"

I felt the blood rush to my face. Who was this guy, tossing around his casual racism like it was small talk? And why did he make Warren so nervous that he'd simply try to paper over it? Giving Warren my best death stare, and avoiding Al Westinghouse completely—which, to be fair, was relatively easy seeing as he hadn't acknowledged my existence—I told Dev I needed him and pulled him aside.

"I'm going to go get us some drinks," he said abruptly, his jaw still tight, face unreadable, before turning and walking away.

"Wait," I said, and I moved to follow him, but he gave a slight shake of his head. I ducked down a carpeted hallway into the bathroom instead, thinking I'd give Dev a minute, if that was what he wanted, then I'd find him. Al Whatever had just lobbed a bomb that felt like it made everything screech to a halt, and yet outside the bathroom door, the party was still going at full tilt. I didn't know how to reconcile both realities at once. I suspected this was what Dev meant when he said spaces like this weren't always a fairy tale. I also didn't want to let that smug dinosaur ruin our night.

The room was empty, thank goodness. Standing under an air-conditioning vent, I waited for my face to return to a normal temperature. I wondered if despite, well, everything, the evening could still be okay. If I could make that happen for us. I shook out my shoulders and pretended to wave off a comment about our late arrival. *"Oh, Dev had a last-minute emergency at work. You know how it goes when human lives are on the line."*

Dev would get us something from the bar, something undiluted by fruit juice or garnish. We could make the rounds, because I knew people—other people. I was wearing the right dress. Kate and Toby were home with Sidney, meaning neither of our children would spontaneously disappear, or construct a life raft from the rattan auction baskets "just in case." Even James Dean would be happy tonight. We'd been out of the house so much lately, I thought about asking if there was a club—just one more—that I could join for dogs on his behalf. A tiny voice in my head whispered. *Maybe, just maybe, if you show Dev all of this, he'll want you again, too.*

You've got this. Keep it simple, I told my mirror self, just as the door blew open.

"Christ, Heidi, leave some champagne for the rest of us."

Lacy pulled Heidi by the elbow. Heidi cackled and stumbled across the carpet of the lounge before sinking into one of the couches. Lacy met my eyes in the mirror and rolled hers. She made sure Heidi was temporarily parked, then stood next to me and reapplied dark-red lipstick. Lacy glowed in a floor-length gown with clear sequins, like a golden mermaid who'd grown a pair of toned, thoroughly waxed legs. Beside her, I suddenly worried I looked like I was getting married at a courthouse.

"Teague's counselor called today," Lacy said, by way of explanation. She lowered her voice. "Teague failed a drug test."

"Anders Anderson to the rescue once again," Heidi said from the settee. She'd taken her heels off and propped up her feet.

I whispered back, "Don't you get thrown out for that kind of thing?"

Lacy sighed in annoyance. "Anders went to business school with the CEO, so . . ." She rubbed her thumb and forefingers together. I wondered how much it took to bribe a rehab facility.

"Relapse is part of the process," Heidi said in a singsong voice.

Lacy pursed her lips in the mirror. "Heidi's not taking it well."

"I can't believe she's here," I said, more to myself than to Lacy.

Lacy shrugged. She blotted her lipstick on a tissue. "The gala's been planned for almost a year. Heidi's the one who chaired the committee. The show must go on. Right, Heidi?"

Heidi put a hand to her forehead in a wobbly salute. She was drunk, but her blowout was impeccable.

I said, "I'll see if they have some water bottles at the bar, Heidi."

"What for?" I heard Heidi ask as the door swung shut behind me.

I passed back through the foyer into the huge banquet room, high round tables each draped with a white cloth and anchored by a small explosion of white flowers. Paper lanterns glowed like orbs from the thick wood rafters. Caterers dressed in black circulated with trays of champagne. I stared at the far wall, a double row of windows, panels of dark sky and clouded ocean that ran seemingly the length of our cottage. I didn't see any water, but when a passing server offered me a glass of champagne, I gladly accepted it.

I'd find Dev, then I'd find Poppy, I decided. She always knew what to do. I scanned the room. Averting my eyes from Warren and his all-white three-piece suit, I spotted Dev's still-wet hair on the far side of the dining room and watched him walk through a set of frosted glass french doors. I moved to follow him, grabbing a second glass of champagne as I got closer. The room was packed with women. They buzzed and hovered around long tables. Some hunched protectively over clipboards. The tables, dotted with oversize baskets, stretched from one end of the room to the other.

I picked up a clipboard, and a woman with an aggressively tight ponytail and huge diamond earrings threw me a reproachful look. The heading was "Girls Spa Weekend," and the reigning silent auction bid was more than our rent. I quickly put it back down, and the woman with the ponytail snatched it up.

The air around the silent auction was thick with perfume and passive aggression, so I slipped out the glass doors that led to the deck. Closing my eyes, I inhaled the cool, salty air. I heard waves crashing, and as my eyes adjusted, I could make out the blurred edges of white-caps on the rocky shore.

Then I heard Dev. Laughing? He leaned against a banister separating the club from a short lawn that ended in a rocky cliff. Heidi and Lacy perched beside him, soft pashmina scarves enveloping their bare shoulders like glowing white boa constrictors. Poppy and Davis were out there, too. Poppy wore a tight white dress with cap sleeves that accentuated her biceps, and Davis popped the collar of his white sports coat up around his neck as the wind blew from the sea.

It was happening! My worlds were colliding, and I hadn't even had to orchestrate it.

"Charlie, there you are! We found Dr. Dev," Heidi said. "Lacy is being very bad in front of Dr. Dev. He's going to write her up. He's going to give her a doctor ticket. But don't worry, she can pay it."

Lacy held a lit cigarette in her left hand. She hung it over the deck and the tip glowed in the dark. She rolled her eyes as she brought the cigarette to her lips.

"I think he's seen worse," I said.

Dev laughed a little too hard. Lacy tapped some ash over the side of the beam into the dark grass. "Just don't tell Warren," she said.

I looked toward the door.

"He's getting us drinks," Lacy said. "But last I saw, he was talking to my father. I could smoke a whole pack before he comes back."

As I tried to picture what Lacy's father might look like, Heidi fumbled with the clasp of a small white bag. She cursed, then her elbow knocked her champagne glass from the railing onto the lawn where, from the sound of it, it broke into pieces. It was too dark to see the grass clearly. Heidi cursed again and took Lacy's glass out of her hand.

Dev looked at me, as if to ask whether anyone was going to do anything, but I just said to the group, "So what did I miss?"

Poppy said, "Charlie, we were asking Dev for stories."

"Oh, I like this game," I said. "Did he already tell you about the time he learned to intubate on Superman?"

Poppy and Davis both looked at Dev expectantly. "I did an ER rotation on Halloween, during med school," Dev said. Lacy took a drag on her cigarette, and Heidi gazed over Dev's shoulder, her attention half there, half elsewhere.

I remembered how we were still operating on a moratorium on talking about work, how it had, in fact, been my idea. But everyone was looking at him, waiting for more.

"There's the list of unexpected items people get stuck in . . . places they shouldn't," I offered.

"If you've seen one, you've seen them all," Dev said, while Heidi murmured, "I doubt that."

"The poisoned grapes," I said. He used to tell these stories all the time. During residency, he and his colleagues would one-up each other over drinks and french fries at happy hour, recounting bizarre injuries and diagnoses like they were office gossip.

"Don't leave us hanging," Davis said.

Dev shrugged. "A woman had what was likely a GI bug, but she blamed it on the last thing she ate. A grape. She thought it was poisoned. She brought the bunch from home so we could test it. I gave her fluids, ordered a psych consult. She really just needed some help."

"Huh," Davis said, looking mildly disappointed.

"Did you test it?" Heidi asked.

Dev shook his head and offered up a small smile, like it was a consolation prize. "Her husband got so tired of her ranting about the grapes, he ate them, one by one."

"The things we do for love," Heidi said, staring past Dev into the black ocean.

"Dev, do you ever get grossed out?" Poppy asked.

Dev turned his drink around in his hands, like he wasn't sure how to answer. "It's not really like that," he said.

I prodded him again. "C'mon. What about the eyeball one?"

Lacy, Heidi, Poppy, and Davis all looked to Dev like children being told a gruesome bedtime story.

Dev grimaced. "Are you sure?"

Poppy nodded. I put my hands together in a prayer and gave Dev my best puppy-dog eyes.

"It was in med school. I examined a patient, and everything seemed okay, at first. He wasn't in any emergent danger, not that I could see, anyway."

I tried not to make a face.

"Vitals were normal, no visible wounds. But as I finished up the physical exam, I realized he was missing something."

"Oh my God," Poppy said.

"What was it, Dr. Dev?" Heidi grasped the railing, either out of suspense or simply for balance.

I soaked it in. They were hanging on Dev's every word.

"He only had one eye," Dev said. "Where the other one should have been, um, it looked like a fresh extraction. But neat. If you can imagine."

"I absolutely can't," Davis said.

"Where was it, Dr. Dev?" Heidi asked. "Where was the eye?"

When Dev looked at me, I jumped in for the big reveal and announced, "He said he ate it."

Poppy squealed. Davis put his hand up for a high five. Heidi's mouth hung open. Lacy exhaled a stream of fresh smoke. Once everyone had recovered, Lacy said, "No stories from Bradley, Dev? Surely you must see some things there."

Dev hesitated. "I see a lot of patients struggling with comorbid conditions—problems that exacerbate each other. It doesn't exactly lend itself to stories."

Lacy put her hand to her chin like she was leaning onto a table, looking at Dev like an overdressed therapist.

"But, you know, it's a systemic issue. Lack of access, delayed care, mental health. It's more like a puzzle of not enough resources and too many needs. People just need help, most of the time. More help than we can give them." Dev's voice had changed, intensified.

"It certainly sounds complicated," Lacy said. I didn't love her tone of voice: cloy and slightly patronizing.

"It's not, though," he said. "There aren't any actual resources going into those neighborhoods. I mean, the cost of catering at this party alone could—"

"Don't you ever want to just walk away?" Lacy interrupted, raising her eyebrows at him. "Give everyone a magic pill?"

Dev cleared his throat. "I think that's what the previous docs tried to do."

Lacy leaned forward even more. I glanced at Heidi and changed the subject. "Are the grounds open during the day?" I said.

"Yes, it's gorgeous," Poppy said longingly. "The boys play croquet, just over there." She pointed straight ahead, then she swept her hand to the right. "The lawn curves around this way, and it leads to the private beach. After Memorial Day, they put tables and umbrellas in the sand. You and Dev should totally apply next year." My stomach fluttered at the idea of "next year."

"Shit!" It was Heidi. She leaned over the banister next to Dev. "I dropped my bag."

Heidi turned and lifted her leg to the railing. She tried to get her foot onto the top of it, and her dress rode up her thigh.

"Shit," Heidi said again, this time with less conviction.

"Have no fear, ladies," Poppy said. "I've jumped this railing before. Last summer Dodge pretended my Hermès scarf was a kite."

She handed her wineglass and handbag to Davis, slipped off her heels, and hiked her dress up a few inches. Looking straight ahead, she exhaled, bounded the few steps to the railing, anchored her hands on top, and neatly vaulted over. It was so perfectly executed, I clapped. And it happened so fast, I forgot about Heidi's wineglass.

"Ow! Shit!" Poppy yelled, her voice two octaves higher than usual. "I didn't stick the landing."

"Do you see my bag?" Heidi asked.

"Heidi, shut up," Lacy hissed. "Poppy, are you okay?"

"Babe, come back up here and get your wine before I drink it all," Davis teased. Lacy hit him on the arm, and sauvignon blanc splashed onto his white shirtsleeve.

"I think I landed on a piece of glass," Poppy said. "I can't see."

"But do you see my bag? It's white. Like my dress," Heidi asked again.

This time Lacy hit Heidi on the arm. "Poppy, don't move. Are you bleeding?"

"I told you I can't see! I think so? Ew, I'm afraid to touch it. Let me try to stand," Poppy said. Then she squealed. "Ow ow ow!"

"Good thing there's a doctor in the house," Davis said.

Dev was already rolling up his shirtsleeves and pulling out his phone to use as a flashlight. I mouthed *thank you*.

"You're too sweet, Dev," Poppy said from the ground. "Oh, Heidi, here's your bag!"

Heidi let out a whoop. Lacy lit another cigarette. I held my breath as she exhaled.

chapter 17

Dev kneeled next to Poppy, taking her right ankle in his hand and using the flashlight on his phone to illuminate her foot. It was smeared with red, from her heel to the ball of her foot.

"Is it gapey?" I asked, my voice wobbly. I gripped the railing and told myself to breathe slowly. I would not pass out at the sight of all that blood.

"I need something to clean it with," Dev said. I marveled at how his voice remained the tenor of someone making a grocery list. "I can't see how deep the cut is. Does anyone have a water?" He looked up and surveyed the group, quickly muttering, "Right, never mind."

Lacy grabbed one end of Heidi's pashmina and pulled. It slid easily from her shoulders. She tossed the scarf to Dev, and he used it to wipe Poppy's foot.

"So what's the plan for that tennis tournament," Dev said, holding Poppy's foot on his knee and speaking to her as if they were making small talk at the beach club. He leaned in close to her heel, shining the light directly on it. I watched through my fingers. "Are you and Davis playing doubles?"

As Poppy listed their five-point strategy, Dev pulled a sliver of glass from the bottom of her foot. It happened between points three and four, and Poppy barely paused. Then he wrapped the pashmina tightly around Poppy's foot, securing it at her ankle. He hoisted her onto the wooden railing so her bare feet wouldn't touch the grass again. Her legs dangled over the deck.

"Davis, help her down," Dev said.

Davis downed Poppy's wine in two gulps to free up his hands. Then he ducked under her arm so she could dismount the railing and lean on his shoulder. She held her left knee up in the air, foot suspended, like she was a Rockette mid-dance. Then she beamed at Dev as he swung his long legs back over the railing and onto the deck.

"Oof." Poppy tried to stand.

"You could maybe use a stitch or two, but it's not an emergency," Dev said. "Just get it properly cleaned up. You should wash it with soap under running water in the bathroom for now."

Poppy looked at Davis with grim determination. "I can't turn the Trident ladies lounge into a first aid station. The tournament. Bitsy van der Koff is right inside and she can't see me like this."

Davis nodded in agreement. "Let's just go to the ER right now, babe. We can leave through the side door."

Lacy held up her hand. "Davis is wasted, Poppy. He can't drive you anywhere."

"I can't risk it," Poppy said. "I *can't* not play in the tournament. And it's not like I'm going to go win the dance contest now anyway."

Everyone was silent for a moment. Waves crashed lightly against the cliffside rocks. I understood Poppy's anxiety around being able to perform, and compete, but waited for her to acquiesce. Or call an Uber. I also desperately hoped there wasn't really a dance contest.

Then Dev spoke up. "I can take you. To the ER."

Poppy, Davis, Lacy, and I swiveled our heads in Dev's direction, while Heidi stared lovingly at her rescued handbag.

"Elvis is moonlighting. She's on shift there tonight. I'll just call her." He looked at me, in some combination of apology and asking permission. I nodded, too shocked to manage my own face.

"A medical concierge," Poppy said. "Sign me up."

"Dev, you're a lifesaver." Davis clapped him on the shoulder, jostling Poppy, who hopped on her right foot to stay balanced.

"Do you have to go immediately, Poppy? Warren hoped to get a word with Dev tonight," Lacy said, glancing at the doors leading inside with annoyance. "He's got to be here somewhere."

"I've been training for months," Poppy said. "You understand, right, Charlie? I'll make it up to you, I swear."

"Of course," I said to Poppy. To Dev. To everyone. I cared about Poppy, and her tennis record. But as I watched Dev shuffle off with her around his shoulder, I couldn't help feeling like he simply *wanted* to leave. That he couldn't go a whole night pretending to be happy. That it was preferable to return to his natural habitat. He sounded so blasé—relieved, really—to go spend the night with his work wife in the emergency room instead of at this party—with me. I followed as Lacy yanked Heidi back inside. We found Warren in the dining room holding a warm glass of wine meant, some time ago, for Lacy. I pushed a strand of hair from my face and smoothed my dress with my shaky hands. I certainly didn't want to trail Lacy all night.

I wandered around and signed my name to two silent auction baskets which weren't yet in the triple digits, hoping someone would come along after me and bid for a cooking lesson or personal stylist consult I couldn't afford.

Heidi appeared with a shot of something, and I took it. A group of moms I recognized from the beach club, led by Bitsy van der Koff, lined up for group photos. I threw my arm around Heidi, at the end of the photo train, and tried to swivel my hip and point my knee like the others. It was more or less like I'd always imagined prom: posing for photos, hoping no one could tell how much I'd had to drink in a short period of time.

I texted Poppy to see how she was doing, and she wrote back: Dev is the best! Then she sent a selfie in which she held a can of seltzer Dev must have retrieved from the doctors' lounge. I hoped she'd thank us in her acceptance speech when she won the tennis trophy.

I laughed along with whatever story Bitsy van der Koff was telling about her son Bart shimmying up the mast of a sailboat—and nearly falling off it (how was this funny, exactly?)—no longer caring about how Bitsy was constitutionally unable to make eye contact with me.

Also, my hand was empty again.

I walked through the dining room back to the bar. I flashed a smile at anyone who made eye contact. I'd be all over social media later, I was taking so many group photos. I hoped everyone knew my name so they could tag me. Friend requests would pour in. I'd need a social assistant.

At the bar, I wedged myself between two columns—one made of white marble and one in the form of a tall man wearing white clothing. Neither the column nor the man budged when I nudged my way through, so I slammed my hand on the bar, then laughed at myself.

How much had I had to drink? I tried to count, to remember, and decided it didn't matter.

"You mean business," said my elderly neighbor to the right, his white hair an excellent complement to his suit jacket.

"I *mean* a vodka tonic," I said. "With all of the limes." I craned my neck for the bartender. It was loud, and I didn't feel like pretending to listen to someone else's husband teach me about the stock market.

The bartender popped through a swinging door and stood in front of me, but the man behind me ordered before I could raise a finger.

"Whiskey, rocks, and a vodka tonic."

Fine, I thought. I was about to say a perfunctory *Thanks* so I could rejoin the hive of women when the man reached over me, across the bar, and plunked six lime wedges into my glass.

"That enough?" he asked.

Looking up, finally, I took in the blond hair raked back from his face. His eyes looked more gray than blue in the light of the bar. I held eye contact for a beat longer than felt necessary for a drink order, then quickly looked down. Oliver was wearing Adidas sambas, and they were in fact white.

"Yes," I stammered. "Hi. I didn't see you there."

Oliver smiled that ridiculous half smile. He looked me up and down.

"You're fancy," he said. Then he asked, "Where's your man?"

"He left," I said simply. Then, less simply, I nervously tried to explain. "There was an incident on the back deck involving broken glass and an ill-fated vault over the fence." I took a long gulp. "It's Poppy's foot, and there's a tennis tournament, and Dev has a work wife. I don't know. He's like her FastPass—are those still a thing?—and Presley is Space Mountain. Does that make sense?"

"Absolutely not," Oliver said.

"The point is," I said slowly, with resignation, "he is not here."

Oliver nodded toward a window in the foyer, away from the crowded bar. I followed him, happy for a five-minute break from speed dating the gaggle of club moms.

Heidi emerged from the restroom with another full glass of champagne. She weaved over to where we stood and balanced on her heels, very close to Oliver. While I felt a flutter of anxiety, I was fairly certain Heidi wouldn't tell Dev how, after he left, I was found chatting it up with a hot James Bond villain.

"Olivvvveerrr." Heidi drew out his name. Ah, she was plastered. She unwrapped a pashmina—another one?—from her shoulders and tried to lasso him, but the scarf fell limply between them instead. Heidi waved her hand and left it there, as if it had disappeared over the railing just like her handbag and she wasn't going to put in the effort this time.

I waited for Oliver to pick it up. Heidi was a damsel in distress, a rich, thin one in a designer dress.

But it was my eyes Oliver met over his glass of whiskey as he smiled into his drink, trying not to laugh. I felt my cheeks go warm.

"Ollie," Heidi said. "Can I call you Ollie?"

"Not really," Oliver said, but Heidi was too busy petting his bicep to register his answer.

"Ollie, when are you going to come back and finish my wine cellar?" Heidi said. "Bring your tool belt." She reached out and put her hands on Oliver's waist. "You'll need different pants." She giggled.

Oliver raised one eyebrow in my direction, and I snorted into my vodka tonic. I put my arm around Heidi's waist, hoping to steady her. Oliver did pick up Heidi's scarf then, and he wrapped it lightly around her shoulders.

"Now if you'll excuse me." Heidi pointed into the dining room, her finger swiveling in a circle. "Al Westinghouse wants an update on Teague, and I needed a pick-me-up first." She swung out from my arm more gracefully than I would have imagined possible given all she'd had to drink, and her heels clacked against the marble floor.

Oliver's face looked like I felt four (six?) drinks in: relaxed, warm, open. I took stock of where I was standing and realized I hardly recognized myself. Who was this Charlie-by-the-sea? I thought about all that Dev was missing. He was missing so much! I didn't want to miss anything else. I wanted to let go of all the stress and anxiety and worry about who I was to Dev, to Rumford, to myself, and just enjoy what was happening without feeling like I was going to lose it at any moment. To facilitate this, I downed half the vodka tonic.

I grabbed Oliver's forearm, just to see if it was as solid as it looked. (It was.) The noise in the room receded as I met his eyes and took a deep breath. It was time I simply asked for what I really wanted.

"Were you here for the small plates?" I asked. "Were they very small? We were late. I'm starving."

Oliver laughed. I let myself feel that familiar ease with him. It took me a second to realize I was actually leaning into him a few inches more than was natural, so I overcorrected back onto the windowsill. I tried to make it look like I'd meant to half sit on the ledge. I just needed a second to steady myself.

"Sadly, I missed the small plates," he said. He sipped his drink and set it down next to me on the thick windowsill. His hand brushed my hip.

"Hold on a sec," he said.

Oliver walked around the corner and came back with a plate of four oysters. I braced myself as he squeezed a lemon over the plate in a zigzag, hitting each one. I'd never been an oyster person, but I'd had enough of holding back.

"They were still on ice," he said, and I let my trepidation pass as an age-appropriate concern for food safety.

I reached out. We each took one. Oliver met my eyes and said, "Cheers, Yellow Elephants," then raised it to his lips. I did the same. I tilted my head and threw it back, not unlike the shot Heidi gave me earlier that night.

"I could do that more often," I said, almost to myself.

Oliver laughed and handed me the plate. Then he reached toward my face. I struggled to catch my breath; he was so close. Why was he so close? His forefinger brushed something from the side of my chin. God, I hoped it wasn't oyster goo.

"Your hands are full now, so," he said.

I wished, and simultaneously dreaded, that he would break eye contact. The ocean was too loud. Was the oyster *that* immersive? No, the windows were closed and the roaring was coming from the insides of my ears. I put the plate back down so my hands would be free. For what, I wasn't sure. I couldn't just keep staring at him. Could I? I wasn't entirely sure what was happening, but I did know that it felt like the first time someone had really seen me all night. I didn't want it to stop.

"This is the second big party I've been to in Rumford," I said, to fill the silence, "but I have never seen anyone eat."

"What about the yacht club?" Oliver asked. "Weren't you there for the lobster rolls?"

I shrugged. "I ate mudslides instead."

"And limes," Oliver said.

"I never forget a good lime," I said. "You know, I've still never been inside the yacht club. Is there a kitchen? I do know there's a bar, because there's always a bar."

Oliver put down his glass again.

"Let's change that, Yellow Elephants." He tilted his head to the door, and I realized the only thing that sounded more fun than staying at the party was, in fact, leaving it.

The last person I saw at the gala was Lacy, watching me over the brim of her champagne flute, as I followed Oliver out of the Tri Club and into the night.

chapter 18

Oliver and I half walked, half jogged the handful of blocks to the yacht club, laughing and shushing each other like teenagers sneaking out past curfew. I'd taken off my shoes when we hit the road, and I paused on the back porch of the club to catch my breath. The harbor was so dark I could barely make out the line where the sea met the sky. Everything felt murky and undefined, like a dream. I felt my thoughts lap slowly like the waves, drawing near, then receding.

"You wanted in. Right, Charlie?"

He stood in the shadow of the open door, and I realized it was the first time he'd used my real name. I didn't mind it. His white shirt glowed against the light from his phone. I was giddy, and felt like a carefree version of myself, like the me who used to sneak into those landscape architect-sanctioned pools with Simon, giggling all the way. The only time I felt comfortable in properties of the rich and famous, apparently, was illicitly, and in the moonlight.

The room was empty other than a pair of dark-leather couches. I imagined it full of tables and chairs, men in navy sports coats clinking glasses, women in Vineyard Vines shifts. A wood cabinet with glass panels displayed shelves upon shelves of trophies.

"Why do you have a key?" I asked. "Do all members get one? Is it *literally* the keys to the kingdom?"

I threw myself onto one of the leather couches, lying flat and putting my feet up on the armrest.

"I did some work here a few summers ago," he said. "I built that trophy case you're staring at. They never asked for the key back." The room was shrouded in shadows but light enough to highlight his white shirtsleeve rolled to his forearm. He walked to the bar and ran his fingers along the bottles.

"What are the trophies for?" I asked. "And why does everything around here have a trophy or title associated with it?" I sat up and put my feet on the cool wood floor.

"It's for racing, mostly," Oliver said. "Why, do you want one of those, too?"

"Shut up," I said. "I'll have you know I had a *day* on a boat and I earned that hat."

Oliver grabbed a "something clear" from the bar and two glasses. Before he poured, I watched him take a swig straight from the bottle. He wiped his mouth with the inside of his forearm, then smiled at me, whispering, "Don't tell."

The lower half of my body went warm, and I thought about lying flat on the cool floor.

"Are you going to refill it with water so no one notices?" I said.

Oliver laughed, and this time I had more trouble looking away. "You're always sneaking around, Yellow Elephants. You don't need to."

His disarming irreverence for this bizarre place—I found it alluring, and intimidating, and fascinating, all at once. Asking permission felt like all I did. For Oliver, Rumford was there for the taking, but he didn't *need* it. Did I really need it? Should I care so much? What *did* I need? A jug of coffee? A beta blocker?

"Okay, fine," I said. "Then make me a drink while I show myself around. That's an order, not a request."

Barefoot, I ran from the couch to poke my head into the hallway.

"Darling, did you lower the jib and pack up the boom before we took the dinghy to the Vineyard from the sailing yacht?" I called out, my voice high and somehow British. "I think I left my Hermès life jacket aboard the schooner! It can't get wet out there; it's purely for photos. Can we send someone to fetch it?"

I waltzed my way into another room and paused at a door labeled HEAD.

"Winston! I've found where I left my head last week. Silly me, it was simply in the head closet all along!" I opened the door and was slightly disappointed to only find a bathroom.

"If you're done there, I have a drink for you, skipper," Oliver said.

I made to run across the room, to the bar, but midsprint I tripped on a bag that was sitting in the middle of the floor. I pitched forward in the dark, landing on my hands and knees.

"Owwww!" I groaned. I rubbed the knee that connected with the dark, wide-paneled oak floor, hoping I hadn't torn Heidi's dress. "The membership gods heard me. I've angered them."

Oliver left the glasses on the bar and walked over to hold out his hand. I gripped his palm, more concerned now about the red in my cheeks, the warmth threading its way up my arm into my chest, than the purple blooming on my knee. Oliver kicked the bag against the wall, and I recognized the embroidered monogram: *LH*, as in Lacy. No wonder she always had a chic, tiny handbag. She could leave supplies at every club in town.

I hobbled to lean against the bar, then hoisted myself up onto the counter. Oliver handed me a glass.

"Wait," he said, as I raised the glass to my lips. He took the glass back from me. From a mini fridge below the bar he pulled out three lime wedges, dropped them into my glass, then held it up to his own face.

"You can still see through it," he said. The side of his mouth curved slightly as he handed it back to me.

"Come to think of it, *I'm* supposed to be the bartender here," I said.

"Maybe you don't have to do everything yourself."

I kept the glass held high, in front of my mouth, and I tried to look anywhere but straight at Oliver. The wall was covered with triangular flags painted on pieces of wood, more symbols of a world I'd never truly understand.

"They're family burgees," Oliver said, following my gaze. He shifted toward me. "So is this what you want?"

I choked on my drink, then realized Oliver was talking about the club. He nodded at the dark room.

Was this what I wanted? I was so tired of thinking about it. I was so tired of wanting things I wasn't sure I could have.

The cold of his glass touched my bare knee, and I felt it everywhere. He was standing in front of me now. I was still sitting on the bar. I thought about how he brushed my hip in the window seat at the club. Maybe it hadn't been an accident.

I could hear a fan on the ceiling. I could hear him breathing. I felt my knees inch away from each other, like they weren't connected to the rest of me. Oliver took another step forward. I registered the fabric of his white pants on my bare legs. His fingertips grazed my left knee as he set his drink on the bar beside me. I still held my own drink in front of my face, like a shield. My ears roared like I was a rock in the harbor, the waves crashing over me so swiftly I couldn't focus.

Oliver took my glass. He sipped from it before setting it down.

"It's good," I croaked. "The drink, I mean."

"Good." Oliver's voice was low.

I closed my eyes. He was so close. I was afraid to open them to see how close. I smelled salt, and limes, and soap, and the humid wood of the club. I tilted my head to the ceiling, opened my eyes to the rotating fan overhead. I watched it turn: one, two, three, four.

It felt good to want, to be wanted, to feel something so much that it put blinders on my own self-consciousness, on the million ways I talked myself into or out of making decisions, the myriad ways I doubted myself. It was how I felt when I met Dev. It was oblivion.

Oliver's hand, cold from the drink, moved from the side of the bar to the side of my leg, and that was when I caught my breath.

What was I doing? Why was I doing this? It was real. That line, the line I didn't want to cross. There it was. There it went.

I felt like I was in quicksand. How was I supposed to pull myself out? I put my head down, put my hand on Oliver's chest, and pushed him back a few inches. I knew I could lean into him again, a fraction, and I'd be lost. But this wasn't a role I was playing—it was just me, just Charlie. I shifted my gaze sideways. I stared at the stupid trophies, lined up in the floor-to-ceiling cabinet.

I breathed into the space between our bodies.

"It's just . . ."

I didn't know what to say. What do you say to quicksand?

chapter 19

I woke the next morning to James Dean licking the side of my face, and Kate standing over me with a glass of water.

"Mama, you look like you need to hydrate. You should drink *before* you feel thirsty, you know."

When the bed made me dizzy, I'd fallen asleep halfway upright on the couch, trying to convince James Dean to spoon me, all fourteen pounds of him. I nodded like my dry mouth was the result of a missed Dixie cup of water at bedtime, not a wide-open bar.

"Also, your phone is blowing up," Kate said, hand on her hip.

I squinted, trying to make sense of the missed texts accumulating on the screen.

"I only read the first one," Kate called from the kitchen, refilling the glass. "It says Lilly and GP are going to the Big Apple!"

My phone buzzed with a call, and I swiped to answer without looking, expecting to hear my mother reporting on how many times my father had already made them stop to take in a highway vista "with intention."

"Charlie! Where are you? We're already here setting up without you." It was Lacy, and she sounded annoyed. Already? Where was "here"? What was she setting up? I looked around the living room, as if the answer was lying among the piles of LEGOs and broken crayons.

"Oh, um, right . . . I'll be right there," I said into the phone. My head felt like someone had positioned the chute of a cement mixer full of sludge next to my ear and hit pour. I wasn't sure I could move from the couch, unless it was to leave my body. "Wait. Where should I be?"

Lacy laughed. "Charlie, you're so funny. The block party. Don't you remember? We discussed it last night. I mean, you didn't even know. She didn't even know," Lacy said to someone, her voice moving away from the phone.

I rubbed my eyes. The sludge in my head throbbed. Too much about the previous night was blurry. I drank the second glass of water Kate left. The drinks, the yacht club. Oliver. *Oliver.* I swallowed to keep the water down.

Even Lacy's tone nauseated me. I wondered how many other women were buzzing around her. She lowered her voice in a way that made me squirm. "Charlie, I know you left a little early last night, but we talked about this *before* you disappeared." Then, at full volume, "Don't you remember? The block party—it's *always* the day after the white party. Hello? The countdown to the bacchanal is on, Charlie. Ticktock."

"Totally," I rasped. "Ticktock."

"I'm making Bloody Marys, Charlie." Heidi must have grabbed Lacy's phone. "Get your ass over here and we'll fill you in." Then she hung up.

I had my marching orders. At least it was a reason to get out of the house. But first, I stood up. Slowly.

"Coffee's almost ready."

I spun around, then regretted it, steadying myself on the edge of the couch. Had Dev been in the kitchen the whole time? My heart was pounding. *It's not a tiger,* I thought. I hadn't let anything with Oliver turn into a tiger. It was, at best, a squirrel. At worst, a feisty raccoon.

I shuffled into the kitchen. Dev's back was turned as he waited for the coffee to brew. He looked like he'd already been out for a run, his hair damp, his T-shirt clinging to his back. I wanted him to pull me into a hug and rest his chin on the top of my head. I wanted to slip my hand underneath his threadbare Georgetown T-shirt, the one I used to steal when I was pregnant, to feel his warm skin and the solidness of his lower back under my palm, to breathe him in and let sense memory take over until I felt whole again.

But no, I would take the sludge. I deserved the sludge now. Plus just the thought of him tensing as I moved nearer was enough to keep me on my side of the kitchen, like a boxer before a match.

I hadn't completely let go with Oliver, but it had gotten so, so close. I could pretend all I wanted, for a night, that I lived in a pastel-painted world without consequence, but there was always going to be the next morning. And now—looking at Dev as he poured coffee into my favorite mug, cartoons humming in the background—I felt the weight of all I could really lose.

"When did you get home?" I asked.

Dev yawned in reply, raising an arm to cover his mouth. "It was late. You were on the couch. I tried to wake you, but you said you weren't allowed in the bed."

I grimaced, lowering my face into the coffee cup and breathing in the bitter steam. "I must have been dreaming," I said. "You still got up to run?"

"I couldn't sleep," he said, with a hint of irritation that I wasn't sure was directed toward me, or sleep. Then, more softly, he said, "I'm sorry I bailed."

"It's fine, the kids could have woken me up. Kate knows that," I mumbled.

"No, Charlie, I mean last night," Dev said.

I glanced up from the deep eye contact I was making with my coffee.

"Elvis gave me shit for leaving you at the gala," he said, tapping restlessly on his mug with his wedding band finger. He leaned against the counter.

Grasping at indignation instead of the guilt that was churning in my gut, imagining Dev sitting in the ER lounge, recounting details of our night to Presley while I bounced from person to person at the gala explaining why he wasn't there with me, I said, "Sounds like I missed a heart-to-heart, but Dev, I don't need Presley to stick up for me. If you didn't want to stay, you could have just told me."

"It's not that. I thought you'd want me to help Poppy. I'd already made us late. I wasn't even wearing white pants."

"Your pants were fine," I said. "I don't know if I could be married to someone who owned an entirely white three-piece suit like Warren."

"If my pants were any darker that old man would have handed me his empty glass and asked for another highball," Dev said.

I groaned. "I'm sorry. I was looking for you, after. Who was that guy?"

"According to Poppy he's a piece of work, but an incredibly loaded one. And Elvis just overheard me talking to Poppy about cutting out early, by the way. You didn't miss any heart-to-heart."

"You *were* Poppy's knight in shining armor," I said, now feeling chastened in addition to confused, regretful, and massively hungover. "She sent me a selfie." I busied myself getting milk from the fridge, pouring enough to make the coffee turn caramel colored. "She appreciated the star treatment. The private room. The seltzer. Still, Presley must have been on her A game."

Dev looked at me, confused. "I got Poppy the seltzer. And the room."

"Oh. Okay."

"Elvis was hardly with us, Charlie. She was working."

"Okay," I said again. I tried to ease the pounding in my head by leaning it against the cool door of the fridge. I took a gulp of the coffee. It was all I needed to drink for the rest of my life. People didn't make stupid potentially life-altering mistakes on coffee. They just got a lot of shit done.

Dev glanced at the kids to make sure they were absorbed in cartoons. He lowered his voice. "Charlie, I stayed with Poppy because Elvis was busy treating the guy in the next room who'd been shot in the head."

I pulled back from the fridge and stared at him.

"You're kidding."

"It was an accident. This is Bradley we're talking about." He held his finger to his lips. "We don't talk about that kind of thing in Rumford."

I shook my head. "No, we don't," I said softly. "What happened?"

"Well, he got in a scuffle outside a party. I don't believe it had a guest list. He went home, drank a beer. He smoked some weed. His buddy said, 'Hey, man, maybe you should get your head looked at.' So he came into the ER. He waited in line."

"Okay."

"To be fair, I don't think he realized his brain was showing, just a little bit," Dev said. "Elvis told me about it later." He recounted it like it was an everyday honest mistake. How "normal" was this to him?

"Sorry. What? Doesn't that make you, I don't know, upset, I guess?" I asked.

Dev drank his coffee, not making eye contact. He shrugged. "It's just work."

I wanted to shake him. I wanted to push into his chest with the palms of my hands until he pushed back—something, anything, to suggest that he cared more than he was showing. Maybe it would dislodge whatever he was keeping from me, like a coin stuck in a piggy bank. There was something he wasn't telling me, and I was tired of letting it seem like it didn't matter, that it didn't affect every aspect of our relationship. But if I'd had it in me to do any of that, I'd dropped it somewhere on the walk from the Trident to the yacht club. If our marriage was a piggy bank, I felt like now I was the one holding the hammer.

—⁓—

The walk to Market Street was supposed to help me get myself together while Dev took the kids and James Dean for their own walk in the opposite direction. I felt dizzy and sat on a stone wall, hoping I wouldn't be sick on the pristine sidewalk. My phone had buzzed seven times in two blocks. Defeated, I pulled it out of my bag and sifted through group texts.

They were hanging streamers. Could someone bring a stepladder? There had to be a goldfish toss. There was always a goldfish toss. Who could pick up thirty goldfish? By chance, a shot in the dark, did I have a cotton candy machine?

I said I was on my way. Dev and the kids would meet me in an hour. Maybe I'd know what to say to him by then.

I took a minute to distract myself and scroll Facebook. The last thing I needed, among so many things, was evidence of my talking to Oliver in the background of anyone's champagne selfies. A group photo topped my news feed, a line of women poured into white dresses, their pale necks stretched like geese in a row, toned arms draped over tanned shoulders. I tapped to enlarge the photo. *Where was I? Was I smiling? Were my eyes open?* I'd tried to look relaxed when Bitsy van der Koff waved everyone in. In fact, I was pretty sure by that point in the night I was *too* relaxed.

A text came in from my mother as I scrolled.

Lilly: Already on the Palisades Parkway, sugar, en route to the inaugural "recreational nomads" conference. We'll FaceTime the kids later with Lady Liberty in the background. An espresso in Washington Square Park is all I need, but your father will want to sightsee.

I couldn't believe my parents were driving Bessie anywhere near Manhattan. And an off-label version of Comic-Con for up-and-coming RV lifestyle gurus? It all made my head hurt more.

I scrolled back to the party pictures and scrutinized the row of women. There was Heidi holding two glasses of champagne. Lacy stood at the center looking like she owned them all. I was there; I knew I was. I had been at the end, next to Heidi. I read the comments.

Best night ever!

Best ladies ever!

#Blessed to have these friends!

In the photo everyone shared, I realized Bitsy had cropped me out. My phone buzzed again.

Lilly: Dropping a pin at the Liberty Harbor RV Park. Oops just missed the exit. Looks like we're taking Bessie for an impromptu tour downtown instead!

I put my phone away.

Market Street was closed to traffic, and women in chino shorts scurried back and forth setting up for the street circus. A barrel of water with apples crowding the surface sat outside the market. Across the street, outside the Jib, two teenagers set up a ring toss booth. Red and white streamers wrapped every post and wooden railing: the boutique with the overpriced loafers, the souvenir shop, Death by a Thousand Watercolor Sailboats. Dev's name for the studio made me want to laugh and cry at the same time. That first week in Rumford, I'd decided I'd buy Dev one of the tiny watercolors for Christmas, a shared joke we could hang on the wall of our first real house together. My chest ached thinking about it all.

"Charlie! There you are!" Lacy climbed down from a stepladder outside of the real estate office. "Where's Dev? He's coming, isn't he? Surely you caught up with him last night." Lacy looked at me expectantly, and I felt a chill run through my body despite the blazing sun.

"Oh my God, Charlie, I have to thank Dev again for helping me," Poppy called, her bandaged foot nestled in a loosely tied running sneaker as she led a small pony by a rope. Heidi sat on a folding chair next to a cotton candy machine. Aviator sunglasses covered half her face as she put stickers on rubber ducks then tossed them back into a white tote bag.

"He was so sweet, Charlie," Poppy said. She mimed a tennis swing, shifting her weight between legs. "I'll be good as new for the tournament."

"I heard," I said. "That's great, Poppy. And yes, Dev is coming later with the kids. We did catch up because, you know, he's my husband."

"No offense, Poppy, but your pony smells like shit," Heidi said.

"Shhhh," Poppy hissed. "Don't let her hear you. And she's a *miniature horse*, not a pony."

"A morse." Heidi snorted.

Poppy huffed. "She's a horse. Just miniature. Like a mini cupcake. All the sweetness, just petite."

I stared at them, bantering over a miniature horse as Market Street morphed into an upscale carnival of yore. Maybe this was all a dream. I sniffed, but the miniature horse smelled real enough to make me glad I'd skipped breakfast. Everything was real. Everything had happened—last night included.

"Is the market open?" I asked. "I think I'm going to need more coffee."

"Heidi's got some," Lacy said, unrolling another streamer. "She made us wait for you, Charlie."

Poppy tied the horse's lead to a railing, then she took my arm and led me over to Heidi's black SUV, like I was the one in need of watering. Inside the flattened hatchback, a travel picnic table with short screw-on legs held a box of coffee with a pour spout, as well as four mono-grammed pastel travel mugs. I wanted to sweep the Easter egg–colored cylinders aside and wrap my lips around the box's spout. I was sweating from the morning's humidity, and I wondered if the others could smell the alcohol leaving my body.

"Ladies, it's time to rally," Lacy said. She checked her watch. "The kids will start arriving soon. We all know from past experience there is only one way to get through the block party. Every summer, it happens on the heels of the gala. Every summer, the children are underslept from lax babysitters, and the adults are underslept from lax morals."

Poppy and Heidi giggled. I felt my face go hot. I reached for a mug.

"Not so fast," Lacy said. She held up one hand like a crossing guard.

"Oh, sorry," I said, not sure what I was apologizing for.

"Charlie, we're not amateurs," Heidi said. She reached into a brown paper bag behind the box of coffee. She pulled out a bottle of Kahlua. Poppy clapped her hands. Lacy smiled. I groaned.

"Oh God, Heidi, I don't think I can drink any more. Maybe ever again."

Poppy handed me a mug, and I realized it was monogrammed with a *C*. I looked at Heidi, who shrugged like it was nothing, but allowed a dash of a smile under her dark sunglasses. She'd made me a mug. She'd thought of me. I raised the cylinder to my lips.

"To Kahluffee!" Poppy cheered, raising her travel mug.

Lacy leaned close and said, in a low voice, "Maybe you prefer whiskey?" She winked, then turned and walked back to the streamers. Oliver was drinking whiskey at the gala, I remembered in a panic. It was official, then—Lacy must have been watching more closely than I thought.

I shivered, the sweat on my chest a cold sheen of sugar and alcohol and regret. I'd have to run interference between Lacy and Dev when he arrived. And later, I'd tell her we went looking for a corkscrew, a pizza, Oliver's shoes—did he have a cat? I tipped the mug back again. I had never been a fan of the circus, and I wasn't going to start now.

chapter 20

Dev arrived an hour or so later, a kid swinging from each of his arms, as I scooped live goldfish into fishbowls the size of duckpin bowling balls. I set down the flimsy green net, wiped my hands on my shorts, and took another sip from the freshly monogrammed—and freshly refilled—travel mug.

I watched as Dev lifted Kate and Toby into the air, one on each arm, as they walked. The kids' sneakers grazed the sidewalk, and their bodies wiggled in the air like noodles. Kate appeared to be lecturing about something, and Toby was trying to walk in a different direction while tethered to Dev's hand. Dev lifted Toby in the air and used the hand holding his to push his glasses back in place, nodding along to whatever Kate was going on about. I watched them, my little family. I wanted to wrap my arms and legs around Dev's torso as his arms lifted, to hide in the space between his waist and his arms like a koala on a eucalyptus tree.

Then I saw Oliver, in a crisp white shirt, cross Market Street. We briefly made eye contact and his mouth lifted in a half smile. I looked away quickly, moving to take Kate's hand. Oliver went into the market, and I desperately hoped he'd take his coffee to go, ideally straight back to Brooklyn.

"Mama!" Kate called out, breaking my trance. "This is the best party I've ever been to. Ellery already told me how to win the ring toss. She said she practiced at home." Kate lowered her voice. "Her mom has lots of bottles in the secret basement, but don't worry, Ellery puts them back in kind of the same spaces." Then, loud again, "And can I have a goldfish?"

Before I could gather my wits to respond, Kate let go of Dev's hand and ran to the goldfish toss.

"Hey, horsey!" Toby yelled.

"It's a morse," I said without thinking.

"A what?" Dev kept a tight grip as Toby tried to wriggle the rest of his body toward the miniature horse. He took in the streamers, the games, and the popcorn machine. "This is aggressively festive."

I held up my hands. "It's what we do here."

"Hey, morsey!" Toby called. Dev reached into his back pocket with his free hand.

"We brought you something." He pulled out a can of lime seltzer. "I forgot, I pilfered it for you last night from the lounge, so you wouldn't feel left out."

Dev leaned in to hand me the can, and before I could think better of it, I pulled back the tab on the seltzer, wanting to wash the Kahluffee from my mouth before he got any closer. The can erupted in a spray of fizz, soaking the front of my T-shirt.

"Toby might have bounced it a little," Dev said apologetically. As I rung out my T-shirt, I said a prayer to the universe that the seltzer would be the only thing that blew up in my face that day.

—⁂—

For a while, it was exactly the kind of morning I'd envisioned on our first day in Rumford. Kate ran from station to station with Ellery. I showed Dev the goldfish, the giant Jenga game, the porches strewn with balloons and red streamers. I pointed out people I'd hoped for him to meet at the gala, and told him about their kids, what they did for a living, whether or not they had a coveted cabana location at the beach club. The goal was to keep him busy, and keep him away from Lacy, and keep me a football field away from Oliver.

There was one caramel apple left on the table nearby when Toby dismounted the morse. I reached out to get it at the same moment as another woman. Hair in a low ponytail, shirt tucked into knee-length chino shorts, she looked like a fellow mom I might run into at Target, someone with whom I'd share a nod of mutually acknowledged quiet desperation as we filled our respective carts with Goldfish and apple-sauce snack packs. "It's all yours," I said, stepping back. "My kids have already had enough sugar to last a week."

The woman smiled and handed the caramel apple to a little girl by her side. She started to thank me, then she stopped when she saw Dev. She hesitated, like she wasn't sure if she should say anything. Dev waited, too. What was going on? My phone buzzed again in my pocket, and I ignored it.

"Hey, Doc," she said finally. She gestured to the little girl who was already biting into the sugary orb. "This is Maisy."

Dev crouched down to the little girl. "Maisy, I've heard such nice things about you," he said. The girl's mouth was full of caramel, but she gave him a sticky smile.

"She's back with me now," the woman said, her voice low.

"That's great," Dev said. "For both of you." The mom nodded. She took her daughter's hand and led her away.

I motioned Dev over to the ring toss while Toby climbed the stack of hay bales.

"Does she work with you? You could have introduced me."

Dev cleared his throat. He fidgeted with a rubber ring, then aimed and tossed it into the far corner of the booth. It bounced off the side and slipped between two bottles. "I can't really talk about it," he mumbled.

"You know, I don't know anyone you work with except Presley. Isn't that kind of weird? And you *can* talk to me about . . . whatever." I tossed a ring that landed and teetered on top of a bottle, then slid to the side. I dropped the rest of my rings back into the bucket. I guess we weren't pretending to be at the circus anymore. "How long do we do this, Dev? Last I checked, I didn't marry a CIA agent."

Dev let out a breath, then he nudged me to the side of the ring toss, next to an empty hay bale. He looked to make sure the woman and her daughter were on the other side of Market Street. "She's a patient, Charlie. She's a nurse, actually, but not with us. She almost lost custody of her daughter."

"Nasty divorce?"

"Drugs, actually," he said, picking straw out of the bale with restless fingers. "Maisy was living with her grandparents when I saw her."

"Oh," I said slowly. "That kind of custody."

Dev let the straw fall to the ground and wiped his hands on his jeans. "She's a nurse at the hospital. A really good one, apparently. She injured her back lifting a patient. Got addicted to oxycodone. This was all before we moved here."

As the woman and her daughter waited in line for the morse, I pictured her in a kitchen full of gleaming copper pots. She looked like the type of mom who set out decorative gourds every year on the first day of October. As if reading my mind, he said, "We see all kinds of people trying to dig themselves out of holes, and trust me, none of them look like Post Malone."

"Honestly, she looks like she could run the PTA," I said.

"People surprise you with what they can keep secret," Dev said.

My chest felt tight again, and I leaned into the hay bale and let the straws dig into my back through my T-shirt. I still didn't know all of what Dev was keeping from me, but my own secret, still raw, felt stupid and selfish. My phone buzzed again, and I looked down to check it, relieved for someplace to put my eyes.

Lilly: On the West Side Highway now in dear old Bessie. Don't fret, though, your father is taking this detour in stride. Just pretending all the honks are the other drivers saying hello.

"I think my parents missed an exit and drove Bessie through Downtown Manhattan," I mumbled. "My mother does always say, *A mistake is just another word for opportunity.* Somehow it works for them."

Dev stared at his hands. "Charlie, I know this hasn't been easy. The truth is, the docs who Elvis took over for, they prescribed pills like candy." He pulled another handful of straw from the pile and sifted it onto the ground piece by piece. "Some days it's like half the patients I see in a day are addicted to something. Often they're there for something else, but it's all part of the picture. It's everyone. It's guys who were laid off and can't find work. It's parents who were recovering from surgery and got overprescribed. It's kids who dropped out of college."

Dev nudged his glasses back, ran his hand through his hair. He seemed visibly uncomfortable talking about all of it. But he took a breath and kept going.

"We're the cleanup crew, Elvis and me. People like Maisy's mom got addicted without realizing it. She was in pain, so they gave her a script and sent her out the door. She lost her job, almost lost her daughter. And she's not unique. It's like we direct traffic all day to Suboxone clinics, detox, rehabs." He brushed his hands off on his jeans again. "Everyone's trying their best to just live their fucking lives. Then one thing leads to another."

I wondered if this was how it happened with Teague, reasonable intentions spiraling out of control. It was the way of so many things, really.

I watched Dev glance at his phone, then silence a call. I wasn't sure what intentions Dev had anymore, or if he'd ever had any—I'd just crashed my way into his life. And he'd found his way back to Presley, anyway. I knew it had to be her calling him.

"So did Presley forget to mention all this when she begged you to come up here?" I asked, my voice sounding a little bratty even to myself. "Or did one thing just lead to another in that regard, too? If you'd just talk to me, if you didn't shut down every time you start to talk about work—which is all you ever do, and all you ever talk about, by the way, even though you never actually talk about it, which means we *never* talk."

Dev just shook his head. He looked exasperated. "Charlie, do you really think this is all fun and games here, like an actual carnival? That everyone is going to galas and sailing on yachts? I can't spike my coffee and turn everything into a party."

Was this what Dev really thought of me? "Of course I don't think that. And the Kahluffee was not my idea. It just happened. So many things here . . . they just happen."

Dev looked at me. "Charlie, you sound like a teenager." It would have stung more had he not sounded so tired. Or, if he was wrong. Guilt rippled through my chest again.

The carnival around us faded: the noise, the stares I imagined lasering in our direction as we quarreled amid the hay bales, the gingham tablecloths and outrageously expensive lightweight cashmere sweaters which—I still didn't understand how—could be worn in August.

Wounded, I hissed, "I wouldn't know about that either, because some of us didn't get to be teenagers who went to parties and got to act like the world was our fucking oyster, just for a day, or a night. Maybe if I had, I wouldn't have almost—"

I stopped. This was *not* going anywhere good. I'd spent hours upon hours wishing Dev would be around, and now, I just needed him to go. I didn't trust myself.

Dev's phone buzzed again. He still didn't pick it up.

"You should go help Presley," I said. "Go do whatever you two do together. Maybe add another meeting to the calendar that you can't explain. I'll see you at home later. Or not. I'll tell the kids. We have plenty to keep us busy. But you should just go."

He looked at me, like he wasn't sure what to say, what to do, what I wanted from him, all of which was probably true. What really broke me into little pieces, though, was that he looked relieved. I was so intent on keeping Dev from Lacy and Oliver, the joke was on me. I'd simply driven him away myself.

I set my hand on the hay bale and took a shaky breath. Crying at the circus was for children who were afraid of clowns, and I steadfastly refused to do it. Who could be depressed or resentful or lonely or lost on a day like this? Not I.

I'd tell Toby we could go back to the morse. We could ride it all day if he wanted to. We could be morse people. Goldfish for everyone! We'd party like it was 1991, when circuses weren't pretty widely acknowledged to be problematic in a number of ways.

I turned around to tell Toby the plan, but then I realized, an invisible bungee cord tightening around my chest, I had another problem. Toby wasn't climbing the hay bales. He was gone.

chapter 21

"He was right here, climbing on the hay!" I said to no one, and also everyone.

He was! He had been. If it were Kate who'd wandered off in this bustle, she'd simply find a responsible adult and talk their ear off about how she didn't *need* to find her parents, because she knew how to take care of herself, but she knew her parents would be worried, so for *their* sake, could the adult help? Toby, though. Toby could be anywhere.

I breathlessly asked two teens by the ring toss if they'd seen a little boy in an orange T-shirt. They shook their heads.

I saw Poppy talking to Bitsy van der Koff outside of Death By a Thousand Watercolor Sailboats. I grabbed her by the arm. "Have you seen Toby? He's gone."

"What do you mean gone?"

"I mean *gone* gone." My voice was so shrill that the kids nearby stared at me in alarm. "He does this. He's like the guy who Irish good-byes the party, except it's a store or a street fair and it's often in proximity to heavy machinery and bodies of water and he's a *child*. And I'm his mom, and I lose him, Poppy. I . . . I lose people."

Poppy took my hand from her arm and squeezed it, her grip firm and reassuring. "Charlie, calm down. Breathe. First of all, you're not alone. We're on it."

Bitsy walked briskly away, but Poppy smiled reassuringly. "*I'm* on it," she said, nodding across the street, where Bart van der Koff tried to balance on top of the giant Jenga tower. Bitsy gave him a stern look and a lecture as it toppled, probably listing their health insurance deductibles in descending order.

Poppy snapped her fingers, and I swear a group of women parted like the red (okay, white) sea, and Heidi appeared by her side.

"I'll check the market. Heidi, you're on the morse corral. We'll cover the obvious spots Toby might turn up or return to. Charlie, you walk the perimeter. I'll text Lacy and station her at the Market Street entrance."

I peered onto porches, under bushes, and inside plastic wagons. I scanned every table adorned with sugar-laden food, every cotton candy machine or bucket full of lollipops. I poked my head inside the post office and the gift store. He wasn't anywhere.

I forced air into my lungs. I'd exhausted Market Street, and if Toby returned there, or simply turned up, someone would spot him. *I'm not alone,* I repeated. My mother always told me to find a mantra. *I'm not alone.*

I squeezed between the post office and real estate office building to see if Toby had wandered away from the fray. There were oak trees there, on a grassy patch leading to the wharf. Toby liked to gather the acorns; he carried them in his pockets to feed squirrels on our walks. I scanned the trees and the green space, hoping to see Toby crouched over a pile of sticks and crumpled leaves, making what he called *squirrel trail mix,* without a care in the world.

But the only person I saw there was the one I desperately did not want to find. Oliver leaned onto one of the trees, his back to the festivities as he brought something to his lips. I flattened myself against the building while I scanned the grass leading to the harbor.

Then I spotted him—Toby!—cross-legged in the middle of the wharf, staring up at the clouds. I barreled past Oliver, nearly knocking him sideways as I dashed to the wharf and scooped Toby up into my arms. I checked each of his limbs, and I kissed his head. He was fine. He was perfectly fine. And I felt like a perfect failure.

It wasn't until after the world returned to its axis, until I could breathe normally again, that I realized what Oliver was doing. While the folks of Rumford transformed the town square into a Norman Rockwell painting, Oliver was leaning against an oak tree and smoking a joint like one of the Outsiders.

With Toby perched on my hip, yelling inches from my face for me to "Look up, look up at the sky," because there was a dinosaur, just like his dinosaur, in the clouds, I turned my head and saw Oliver exhale a plume of smoke, then I watched it disappear.

—⁓—

I schlepped back to Market Street with Toby, contemplating whether anyone made BabyBjörns for children over forty pounds.

"I knew you'd find him," Lacy said, like I'd simply misplaced my sunglasses. She set to arranging the small paper bags full of popcorn into a more symmetrical order on a gingham-draped foldout table.

"I found your Kahluffee mug by the market." Heidi said, squeezing my arm. "Who's the real hero?"

Poppy held her hand up to Toby for a high five.

When I looked down to confirm that he was still at my side, a candy apple had materialized in his other hand. I had no idea where it came from.

"Thanks for mobilizing," I said. "Toby, how on earth did you get all the way over to the wharf?" I ran my hand through his matted curls. Whatever breeze the harbor had granted in the morning was gone.

"My fweet!" Toby said, his mouth full of caramel apple.

"Where's Dev?" Poppy asked. "I looked for him when I made the rounds for Toby."

"Don't ask," I grumbled. I thought about repurposing the plotline of some old *ER* episode, some fake emergency he had to attend to, but I was just too tired. "We should find Kate and head home anyway. I think we've stayed too long at the circus."

But Toby whimpered in reply, then cried out in a panic. "Rory!"

Crouching on one knee, I said, "Look, buddy, we can ride the morsey one more time if you want to, but then we need to go home."

But Toby's eyes went wide, his mouth still full of caramel apple. I couldn't understand what he was saying. Tears ran down his cheeks and into the dried caramel around his mouth. He wiped his face on my shirt, leaving a brown smear. Kate ran over with another caramel apple. Where were all these damn apples coming from?

"Where's Daddy? Today is supposed to be an off day. It says so on the chart. Toby, what's wrong?"

"I lost Rory," he snuffled. "And he can't swim."

"Kate, can you please translate?" I was about to throw my own tantrum.

"Mama, he left his toy dinosaur by the water. Rory—that's the dinosaur—can't swim. His arms are too small. Because he's a T. rex," Kate said, decoding his distress like a cipher. Then she stage whispered, *"And he's plastic."*

I blinked. "You got all that?" Kate shrugged and took a bite of her caramel apple.

Lacy lifted her sunglasses. "Charlie, we throw this block party every year so we don't have to entertain our children the day after the gala. It's a safe space. Stay and let yourself enjoy it." Her voice was like honey. "No need to stress over *all* the men in your life."

"I don't have *men*," I stammered. "And I'm not stressed. Why would I be stressed? I didn't . . . I just . . . I need to go rescue a dinosaur. Poppy, would you keep an eye on Kate and Toby while I go get it?" I pointed in the direction of the wharf. "Especially Toby?"

Poppy gave me a pert salute. Heidi held up her Kahluffee cup. Lacy lowered her sunglasses.

—⁓—

I retraced my steps to the wharf, and I located the green plastic dinosaur perched on one of the planks near the water's edge. Easy peasy. I wedged it under my arm, then, knowing Poppy had her eagle eyes on Toby for the moment, I sat down. I let my legs dangle off the edge of the wharf, willed time to slow for just a moment. Even though I'd found my kid, and his dinosaur, *I* still felt so irretrievably lost.

"Forget something?"

I startled, and Oliver grabbed my upper arm before I lost my balance.

"No!" I said. "I mean, yes. But I found it." Realizing that could come across as potentially flirty, I added, "I don't mean . . . you."

Oliver took his hand from my arm, but instead of straightening up and walking away, he sat down right next to me.

When I stiffened, he scooted over an arm's length to the right. "Better?"

I rolled my eyes. "I saw you earlier, smoking by the oak trees. Not a fan of the circus?"

Oliver stretched his arms behind him and leaned back. He closed his eyes, tilted his face to the sun. "Are you going to tell my mom?"

"Shut up," I said. He was so obnoxiously charming. "Look, I'm sorry about last night. I was confused, I guess. I was drunk, for sure. I was a lot of things."

Oliver's eyes were a little glassy, a little red. He smiled like a kid at, well, a carnival. Then he leaned so close, so suddenly, that I jerked my body away without thinking. Before I knew what was happening, gravity took over, and I was no longer on the wharf. Shocks of cold water enveloped me, head to toe.

My toes in the mud and seaweed slipping past my ankles, I broke the surface and wiped hair out of my eyes to see Oliver's outstretched hand. His face, a mix of surprise and delight. Instead of taking his hand, I splashed him as hard as I could, which, given the state of things, only made him giggle more. Then, out of options, I let him hoist me back onto the wharf, where I lay flat and closed my eyes, catching my breath. The sun warmed the water on my arms and legs, and my T-shirt hung soggy on my chest. If I remained perfectly still, I thought, maybe we could simply pretend nothing had happened, like when someone farts during yoga.

Oliver said, still laughing, "I was just trying to give you the weed, Yellow Elephants."

Then I heard another voice.

"Charlie," Lacy said, looking positively smug, hand on her hip. "If you're done here, we're going to start setting up for the bonfire, and we desperately need you."

"Desperately," Oliver repeated under his breath, eyeing me with a slight half smile.

I scrambled to stand up. Did I look like a soggy adulterer, or simply a dummy who'd fallen into the water in proximity to an absurdly hot carpenter?

"I was on my way back," I said. "I got the dinosaur, but I slipped."

"Clearly," Lacy said.

I wrung out my T-shirt for the second time that day but only succeeded in lifting it up to expose my midriff and part of my bra.

"Whatever, we'll say you were bobbing for apples. It gets competitive. Ask Poppy." Lacy lifted her hand in a wave at the same time she turned and said, "Nice seeing you, Oliver." Then she walked away like there was no question I would follow her.

I tried hard to not look back as I followed Lacy to Market Street, but I stole one quick glance while she complained about how Heidi had dropped her David Yurman ring into the cotton candy machine. Oliver lay back on the wharf next to the spot where I'd left a swamp angel, hands tucked under his head like a New England Tom Sawyer, feet bare, perfectly relaxed and staring up at the clouds. When he turned his head in my direction, I snapped mine back to nod at whatever Lacy was saying.

"So, Heidi and Poppy are gathering the kids for a cotton candy–eating contest so she can find her ring. And we agreed you should definitely come to book club this week, for some girl time." She eyed me over her giant sunglasses. "Looks like you could use it."

"Okay sure, thanks for the invite," I said, even though it sounded more like a mandate.

Then, like she was talking about the weather, Lacy added, "Warren and Davis are setting up the bonfire, by the way; we don't really need you for it. Just looking out for you, girl." And then in a whisper: "I knew you wouldn't want to do something you'd regret."

As I opened and closed my mouth like one of the goldfish, dread swelling in my chest, Kate ran over holding my travel mug of Kahluffee.

"Hey, Mama," Kate said, licking her lips. "I was thirsty after the caramel apple. Your coffee is yummy. Can I have my own?"

I grabbed the travel mug and tossed it into a trash barrel, monogram and all.

chapter 22

As sunset neared, everyone started to gather near the stretch of sand beside the wharf.

Dev was nowhere in sight—he was still with Presley, I assumed. He didn't text. I'd gone home to change into dry clothes, holding out hope he'd be there. At six, I told the kids we would have to go to the bonfire without him. When Kate shrugged and Toby nodded, like I'd told them I'd ordered pepperoni pizza instead of cheese, I realized they were so used to Dev being gone, it hardly registered. So much for Kate's flowchart. I threw a leash on James Dean and brought him along with me instead.

Back at the wharf, Warren and Davis stacked wooden pallets into a shifty-looking pile on the sand, like a pyrotechnic Jenga tower. Bart van der Koff eyed it greedily, like he wanted to shout, "Parkour" and leap over it. We waited on the grassy patch where I'd seen Oliver smoking. If someone handed me weed in a toilet paper roll now, I'd smoke it down to a stub, so great was my wish to escape and just go back home.

Lacy waved me over to where she stood with Heidi and Poppy, near the edge of the grass. Kate and Toby plopped down on a blanket next to Ellery and Ivy. We all were waiting now—for what, I wasn't sure.

—⁓—

The last bonfire I'd attended was actually just before we moved to Rumford. The medical department held a reception every year for the residency graduation. It was at a vineyard, and alumni or current hospital staff always attended, so we went, even though Dev had been quiet, or snappy, or not sleeping, or generally miles from a festive headspace for a few weeks at that point. Presley had traveled from Massachusetts for the party and shared the news with their residency friend group: her partners at the clinic had left her high and dry, retiring early. According to Dev, she needed help, and she was recruiting like her life depended on it.

While the residents, attendings, and academics mingled aggressively, I'd claimed a quiet Adirondack chair beside a firepit. The clouds stretched like cotton balls over the mountains and the sky turned a deep, blissful pink. Dev seemed more interested in brooding at the bar than joining the festivities, and the sunset was peaceful enough to blur the confusion and hurt I felt into something mutable—that is, up until Presley plopped down into the chair next to me. The straps of her dress hung askew, sagging off her shoulders, and she dropped a pair of sandals into the grass. She looked at me like she'd lost her puppy.

"Oh, Charlie, I miss Dev so much." Then she added, "And you!"

Presley reached out to pat my arm, but she missed and kneaded the chair's armrest instead. Doctor parties were always open bar, and no one in Dev's line of work did anything halfway—it didn't matter if it was Monopoly or Malbec. As Presley tried to focus on my face through a haze of wine and bonfire smoke, she said, "Dev's been so stressed, right? About the asthma thing?" Presley mouthed the word *asthma* like it didn't fit comfortably in her mouth. "But JFC girl, we *all* make mistakes. Even Dev. He's always been so hard on himself. Perfection is the enemy of . . . I don't know . . . living your damn life, right, Charlie? *We* know that. Don't let him tell you otherwise."

"Sure . . . I mean no." I had no idea what she was talking about. I tried to breathe in but coughed on bonfire smoke instead. Why did Presley, who lived thousands of miles away, know things about my husband which I, who lived *with* him, did not? But Presley was already switching gears.

"God, it feels good to let off some steam," she said. "It's a little tense up north, Charlie. Let me tell you." Presley held her thumb and forefinger an inch apart to emphasize the little bit of tension, which I guessed was more like an armful. Then she dropped a charred marshmallow into her sandals. She cursed and tried to rub the goo off in the grass before shrugging, standing up unsteadily, and zigzagging back toward the other doctors. She scooped up a half-full glass of wine from a tray which, I was pretty sure, was meant for the dishwasher.

When Dev told me the next day that he wanted to take a job at Presley's clinic, that he wanted us all to move to Massachusetts, that Presley had implored him to come, I felt the air leave my lungs just like the night before. I had a million questions. *What? Why? How?* And again, *Why?* Dev said he needed a change. And Presley needed a new partner; she'd asked him, specifically, to join her. He'd never meant to stay at the university hospital, anyway. What I heard was that he never meant to stay there with me. And despite the uncertainty gnawing at my gut, I said okay. Picking up and moving my life someplace else was the only coping strategy I knew. While moving around as a kid made me feel out of control, volunteering for it in this case made me feel like I had agency. Starting over, I told myself, I could be the person he'd want, the one he fell in love with, not just the one he'd fallen into a life with.

And how was all that going? I wondered now, as I stood wearing a dress with cartoon sea creatures on it, in a town so utterly unlike a bonfire: so self-contained and controlled—usually. Warren grinned unnervingly at the stack of pallets he was about to light. His teeth shone white, his hair combed back from his face. It didn't feel implausible he would start speaking in tongues. Waiting for Warren to initiate an exorcism or call on the Puritan spirits of Rumford Past, I thought, maybe I could have him conjure me a John Goodman in Mayflower garb to stand beside at the bonfire, a phantom husband.

"It's time," Lacy said.

"For what?"

"Charlie, where's Dr. Dev?" Lacy said.

I opened my mouth but nothing came out. I took out my phone to silence it. I'd apparently gone down some kind of road here, and if Dev were to join us now, I didn't know how I'd begin to explain it. He wasn't the only one I didn't understand anymore.

"It's *time*," Lacy said again, glaring at Warren.

Warren stepped back from the pallet pile. He and Davis checked their watches.

"Mama," Kate called. "It's time!"

"Time for what?" I said, but everyone was silent. I plugged my ears in case there was a cannon involved.

Warren gave the thumbs-up to Lacy. She handed him a piece of rolled newspaper. Davis took out a lighter. Warren lit the newspaper and waved it over his head in a circle. He let out a whoop. I shivered. There was something deeply disconcerting about a man in a pink polo shirt, a man who used a smidge too much hair product and wore a Bluetooth earpiece at the beach, letting out an unbridled war cry while waving the open flame of a rolled-up weekend edition of the *Wall Street Journal* into the night.

Warren pointed the makeshift torch around the circle, and one by one, the adults pulled out a pair of sunglasses and put them on. The flames reflected back at me from where each pair of eyes should be, and it was like they could see nothing and through me all at once.

Warren tossed the flaming collection of stock indexes into the center of the pallets, and the entire stack erupted into flames. Laughter poured out of him in jarringly high-pitched waves, like something deep inside had been uncorked.

I stumbled backward as Warren let out another whoop. I felt dizzy, and the flaming pallets blurred before me. Then Poppy looked straight into the pit and practically growled. She threw her head back and pumped her arms into the air. Davis stared at her with admiration, then opened up and hooted like he was at Wimbledon. Heidi let out a shrill, rallying cry. I stared, uncomprehending, as she whipped the sweater from around her shoulders and tossed it into the growing flames. Then she reached into a bag and did the same with what looked like a man's dress shirt. Poppy and Davis shared a look, then Davis tossed a bouquet of white roses into the flames as casually as if he were bowling.

What in the world was going on? I had never seen them let go like this before. It was some bizarre ritual, and I didn't know how far they were going to take it. I picked up James Dean, hugging him protectively to my chest.

Lacy nodded at Warren, and he tossed a small tote bag into the center of the pallets. It had a zip-top, ensuring they were the only ones who'd ever know what was inside.

Do I have to make an offering, I wondered. What did this place want from me that it didn't already have?

Lacy reminded me of a wolf, smiling through her teeth and vibrating with a predatory energy that was just waiting for a reason to pounce. She didn't offer up an unbridled scream into the red-orange heat. Even when it came to combustion, she remained terrifyingly in control.

The bonfire rose into the sky, like the heavens hinged open and someone high above Rumford was sucking the whirling smoke through a straw. Heidi closed her eyes, like she was saying a prayer. Poppy and Davis performed an elaborate high five. The kids danced, their thin bodies like enchanted saplings, twiglike arms in the air.

Was this a cleansing, too, of Rumford's communal summer sins? A hall pass for what had yet to boil over? There was still a week left of summer. Who—what—did they need to appease? What were they going to do?

"Charlie, take a paper, but don't unfold it," Lacy breathed into my ear. "It's time to find out who's the chosen one."

She held out a sea captain's hat, pinching the stiff brim. Folded scraps of paper filled the soft pouch of the cap.

Holy shit.

It's happening, I thought, as I recalled the "The Lottery" again with a resigned kind of dread. I should have seen it coming.

I took a scrap of paper. I crushed it into my sweaty palm. The other women did the same as the children held hands and jumped in a circle. The fire reflected off their white shorts, gave their tan skin a sheen, as the flames licked higher into the woozy, smoky gray sky. I felt myself sway a little. If Dev were here, I would know this insanity wasn't real, whatever it was. We'd share a look across the specks of ash floating through the air, merely visitors to this mania, and we'd laugh about it later. But he wasn't there. These were my people now.

This place, this new home, these people—they were all I had. And they were very possibly about to stone me to death.

"Ladies," Lacy said. She stood with her back to the fire. It looked like it was emanating from within her, flames reaching out from her smooth, sculpted calves. "Unfold your paper."

I held my scrap at arm's length. I opened it like I was peeking under a bandage, bracing myself, eyes half-closed. All I heard for a moment was the roar of the fire, the sharp bursts as the flames sought out moisture pockets in the wood and spit sparks into the night.

"Charlie! You won!"

Poppy's palm filled my field of vision when I opened my eyes. Her triple-stacked platinum wedding rings hovered in the air for a high five. I sat down on the ground instead.

"Who is it?" Heidi swung her head back and forth. Her hair seemed precipitously close to the flames. I buried my face in my hands. Whatever I won, I didn't want it. I didn't want any of it.

Lacy grabbed me by the arm and pulled me back up to standing.

"Charlie, stop looking so grim. You won!"

I mouthed *What?* unable to project the word through my vocal cords.

"A cabana!" Lacy said. "Didn't we tell you?"

I shook my head. *A cabana? Are they going to burn me in it?*

"My family has an extra," Lacy said. "We keep it for guests. For the last week of summer, someone wins it. That's you! You're *meant* to be here with us, Charlie."

I was relieved, and still a little terrified—I was afraid she might be right.

chapter 23

When we finally arrived back home, I let the kids sleep in their clothes, smelling of bonfire smoke and the exhilaration of doing something grown-up while the actual adults acted like children, playing with fire and yelling to imaginary gods.

Dev was on the couch, eyes closed, an empty bottle of IPA in his lap. He'd fallen asleep with his head propped on his hand, elbow on the couch's armrest. On the TV, the Norwegian chef, returned from his time in the woods, chopped mushrooms into neat little piles on a giant slab of wood.

Pouring a glass of water in the kitchen, I refused to poke my head out the back door and check the recycling bin. I didn't want to know how many bottles had preceded the one in Dev's lap. I took Dev's beer and put it on the side table, then I crawled onto the couch, and replaced it with my head. I pressed my check into the smooth cotton of his T-shirt, and he shifted under me, waking up. He took off his glasses, set them on the side table next to the bottle, and laid his hand on my shoulder.

"Hi," he said.

"Hi."

The ice maker gave a death rattle, and as I waited for Dev to say something, the only sound was the wind outside. He ran his fingers through my hair, and it felt almost foreign, his touch on my scalp. I was so exhausted. I just wanted to pull him over me like a blanket.

His voice rough with sleep, he said, almost like he was talking to himself, "So, there's this young guy. One of the ones who we got into outpatient rehab. And he's been going to meetings."

Dev kept moving his fingers through my hair as he spoke. Maybe the bonfire had borne some magic into the evening after all, some spirit of disengaged married couples. I lay still and listened.

"He called when Elvis was doing paperwork," Dev said. "That's why she called me. That was the call I didn't answer, at the block party. The clinic was closed. But Elvis gave him her cell a while back. She wanted him to call for help if he needed it. So when he texted her, that's what she thought it was, that something was wrong . . ."

Dev's voice trailed off as he traced his fingers behind my ears, down my neck. I steeled myself for whatever bad news had kept him away the rest of the evening.

"He asked for penicillin," Dev said, his chest rising and falling. "His girlfriend's toddler had an ear infection. He thought, since he had Elvis's cell, and it was the weekend, he could help. He wanted to help."

"Huh. That's sweet," I mumbled. I tried to let the day, the week, the month rise from me like smoke. Maybe it would get sucked out the window and taken out to sea. The beat of rain on the windowsill was like a white-noise machine.

I barely heard it when Dev said, "I left, because I didn't want to have missed something . . ."

Then he cleared his throat and shifted beneath me. He picked up the beer bottle from the table and brought it to his lips, then seemed to remember it was empty.

"Anyway, I stayed to help Elvis work on the grant. If we get it, it would help her, us, get through the next year. It would give us some time back in our days."

"You don't smell like the clinic," I said. I took his hand and wrapped his arm around my shoulder. His T-shirt smelled like he'd been outside: grass, dirt, and a hint of smoke that must have already seeped from my clothes onto his.

"I sat in the backyard for a bit," Dev said. "When I got home."

"With Presley?"

"Nope."

"By yourself?"

Dev was quiet for a moment, and my body felt heavy. He'd sat outside in the dark, by himself, rather than coming to meet me. Then he said in a noticeably forced upbeat tone, "So, what did you guys get up to tonight? You smell good, like a roasted marshmallow."

I yawned and sat up. My head, my heart, felt too tired to find the words I needed.

"Oh, the usual," I said. "I thought they might kill me, but I won a cabana instead."

chapter 24

It rained on and off the next day, as if the bonfire had knocked something loose in the heavens, and the clouds that night leaked with the same unpredictability as the cottage's kitchen faucet.

The kids and I spent the rainy morning watching a marathon of *Man vs. Wild* shows. I hoped Kate would one day, far in the future, find a partner on whom she'd bestow as much wonder as she did Bear Grylls when he ate a cricket.

But for now, she snuggled against me. She had been asking about Dev lately, what exactly he was doing when he wasn't home with us, and mostly I didn't know what to tell her. At least that morning I could answer, "He's on a five-mile run. In the rain."

Meanwhile, the texts about book club at Heidi's house started at noon.

"Do they ever take a break?" Dev asked as he toweled off postrun.

"Do you?" I'd replied, which didn't help the overall vibe.

I crammed the book in a day. It was a convenient place to put my eyes while Dev buried his in his laptop. I orbited around him, focusing on discrete tasks like laundry or home repair—things with a beginning and end. I'd hoped Simon could talk me through installing a new kitchen faucet, but he hadn't returned my calls.

If Dev wasn't looking at his laptop, he was pacing the living room, on the phone with Presley. The couple of times I tried to ask him what was so pressing, all he offered was a tight smile and a clipped reassurance.

"It's nothing."

"It's boring."

"It's fine."

"Work stuff."

The night was cool, after the rain, and I grabbed one of Dev's hoodies off the rack as I walked out the door, thankful for at least one social event that didn't warrant a value pack of shapewear. All I wanted to do that night was curl up on Heidi's white couch with a glass of wine, wrap the hoodie around my legs, and get out of my own head for a few hours.

I hadn't been able to shake the image of Lacy, flames from the bonfire rising around her, like a witch standing impervious to the fire meant to consume her. Nothing could touch Lacy. I wondered what it must feel like, to walk through the world like you were there to direct the elements, not be done in by them.

—⁂—

Inside Heidi's kitchen, I could hardly see the white marble of the island under the array of wine bottles, the trays of canapés. Sliced pieces of tropical fruit shimmered on silver ovals.

"Hi, Jeannine," I said, trying my best to sound perky.

"Oh, Charlie, nice to see you," Jeannine said as she spooned something mushy and peach hued into a dozen champagne flutes, then topped each off with prosecco.

"Those look festive." I pointed to the flutes of Crayola-colored fizz.

"Heidi said the book was a beach read," Jeannine said as she spooned. "It's a little overcast out there tonight, so I said, let me make my Bellinis, and your friends will feel like they're on what's-his-name's private island." I couldn't tell if Jeannine meant Richard Branson or an actual person who lived nearby.

Happy to delay joining the others for a few more minutes, I said, "Let me help." I transferred fruit from a cutting board to the platter. Jeannine hummed as she poured more prosecco.

"Can I get a side of your good mood with my Bellini, please?" I said.

"My son is back home," Jeannine said, flashing a smile between plops of pureed peach. "He hit a rough patch, but he's home now. It puts a spring in my step. You know how it is, Charlie. They're always your babies."

I smiled, happy for her. I couldn't even imagine my babies starting school soon: Kate transferring her survival skills to a classroom, all those little animals in captivity after a summer on sailboats and sand dunes. I thought back to what Lacy said at that first yacht club party, about Kate and Toby going to Bridge Academy. It felt like building a fortress around them and sending them to the wolves all at once.

I picked up a Bellini, but just looking at it made my teeth hurt. I felt the same about the book selection—it was just too much. There were too many characters, too many twists in who wanted whom, who screwed over whom. I had enough trouble navigating my real life these days.

Jeannine eyed my hoodie as she placed the glasses on a serving tray. To be fair, it fit Dev's height perfectly but hung on my frame like a child's hooded bath towel.

"Do you want to go change, dear? The downstairs powder room is still a work in progress plumbing-wise, but you can scoot in there and put on your resort wear."

"Oh. I can take this off," I said. I moved my arms to pull the hoodie over my head. But as it rose over my shirt, covering my face, I heard Jeannine say, "Oh!" and I paused.

"What?" I said, my voice muffled by the plush cotton.

"Hon, you're going to want to stick with the sweatshirt."

I scrunched the hoodie back under my neck and looked down. The white of my belly glowed between gashes in my black tank top. Before I left, Kate had been practicing first aid on Toby with strips of fabric, tying off imaginary snake bites. Apparently she'd fashioned tourniquets from my laundry pile.

"You'll be fine, hon," Jeannine said, pulling the shirt back down for me. "Just have another Bellini."

I picked up the skinny glass, and I pulled at the neck of the hoodie. The rain may have cooled the air outside, but it was downright muggy inside Heidi's house. The oven must have been keeping an untold number of tiny appetizers warm. I turned before leaving the kitchen.

"Jeannine, what did you mean by resort wear?"

"Oh, never mind, hon, you look great. Go ahead and join the other girls in the living room." Jeannine smiled. I knew that smile. I'd plastered it on my face the other morning as I sent Kate to beach club camp looking like the Crocodile Hunter's apprentice in a full khaki jumpsuit.

I swallowed the lump in my throat and followed the laughter, crisp like the clink of the champagne glasses on the tray Jeannine balanced behind me. The living room felt like it was a hundred degrees. I pushed the hoodie's loose sleeves up my arms. I scanned the room for a window I could discreetly crack.

That was when I realized I was the only one in the room wearing a shirt, let alone oversize terry cloth sleeves.

Heidi perched by the mantel next to a roaring fire—wearing a neon-orange bikini and nothing else. A trim straw hat shielded her eyes from the recessed lighting. Lacy and Poppy sat on the couch, bare arms outstretched for Bellinis as Jeannine passed with the tray. Had Poppy gotten a spray tan? Lacy wore a black one-piece and espadrilles. I reflexively scrunched my toes, like I could hide my chipped pedicure under the rubber strap of my dirty flip-flops.

"Charlie, are you wearing a bikini under that thing?" Heidi tipped her hat up so she could see.

I tried to laugh. "Um, no. I thought, it's been raining, and, you know, it's a book club? So I wore . . . clothes."

"Did we not tell you? Heidi, I thought you told her," Lacy said, but Heidi just shrugged. "Poppy?" Lacy raised her eyebrows behind giant tortoiseshell sunglasses. "Do I have to do everything around here?"

Poppy scooted forward on the couch. "Charlie, the book is a beach read, so it's a vacay theme. There's always a theme. Gosh, sorry. I spaced. I've been so distracted this week, with Davis going out of town, and the end of summer around the corner. It always makes me anxious."

I found a chair farthest from the fireplace. The ragged safety-scissors tears in my T-shirt would not pass as vacay chic. I pulled my hair back into a ponytail, plucked a flower from Heidi's hibiscus, and put it behind my ear. At least I'd read the book. Maybe that would make up for my shoddy excuse for resort wear.

"So, what did you think of the twist at the end of the story?" I said. "Pretty unbelievable, right?" Actually, the twist had been logistically impossible, but my word choice gave wiggle room in case someone actually liked it. When no one replied, I said, "Sorry, did you guys already talk about the book?"

Jeannine set a tray of tropical fruit onto the glass coffee table. Poppy plucked a yellow star-shaped piece and tucked it onto the side of her drink. "These are so cute, Heidi," she chirped.

Lacy nibbled on a kiwi. She set her Bellini in front of Poppy and asked Jeannine for a glass of champagne, reminded everyone she was off added sugar and had never felt better.

I tried again. "I mean, when Mackenzie left Jackson at the island chapel, I thought it was the end, but when she went on the honeymoon anyway, with Clementine? *And* they found that dead body in the hot springs?" I sat back in the chair, adding, "It was wild, right?"

I waited while the other women exchanged glances. "Sounds like it," Lacy said. A smirk formed at the edges of her coral lipstick. Poppy looked at me like she'd whiffed a tennis serve. Heidi cackled. Lacy crossed her legs and straightened her back. "None of us actually read the book, Charlie."

Jeannine took an empty tray from a side table. From behind the other women, she threw me a sympathetic look before returning to the kitchen. The flower fell from my hair onto my leg. I squeezed the leathery red hibiscus petal, felt it begin to disintegrate between my sweaty fingers.

"We pick books that make for a good theme night," Heidi said. "I had these fruits delivered overnight from Mexico. Do you really think I could scoop out a dozen pineapples for piña coladas if I had to read a whole damn book?"

Heidi nodded to another side table. It was lined with pineapple husks, hollowed out and filled with a frothy liquid. A paper umbrella stuck through a maraschino cherry floated on top.

"Lacy's orders," Heidi said in a singsong voice, "even if she won't drink one."

"Oh," I managed. "Yum." Yum was for kids' drinks. This felt like a children's party.

"I read the Goodreads reviews when you suggested the book, Heidi," Lacy said. "No thank you. But what a fun party."

Poppy picked up her vibrating phone from the coffee table. "Pax, I'm at book club. No, spraying Febreze on the crotch of your lacrosse uniform is not enough." She put her hand over the phone. "The boys are helpless." She got up and paced between windows, walking Pax through buttons on the washing machine and the proper amount of liquid detergent.

"Have you tried the one with cucumber and mint?" Heidi asked, pointing to the tray of tiny pieces of bread.

"I will, okay?" Lacy said. She stared at Heidi, who shoved a canapé between her expertly lined lips. Lacy turned her steely gaze back to me. Her hair was so shiny. I wondered if she'd gotten a blowout for book club. "Is Dr. Dev off saving the world yet again tonight?"

I put my hands inside the kangaroo pocket of the hoodie. "He's at home," I said. The irony of it didn't escape me—I'd pined for him to be home all summer, and now that he was, I couldn't get out of the house fast enough. "He's just doing some extra admin work. Balancing the books and whatnot."

Lacy repositioned the tortoiseshell sunglasses on her head. "Do you really think the clinic is worth all the time he puts into it? It just seems like he's not always there for you. I worry about you, Charlie."

I looked at my hands. My fingers were stained pink from fidgeting with the petals of the hibiscus. What was I supposed to say? That I worried, too? That the bottle of bourbon Dev bought last week was already half-empty? That before breakfast he'd snapped at Toby for leaving two plastic giraffes in the coffee maker? (It was part of a zoo.) Old Dev would have made a game of taking the giraffes out of the coffee maker, finding them a new home in the smoothie maker we never used, sprinkling some flax seeds and pretending it was zebra poop. Before I had to answer out loud, though, Lacy kept talking.

"I have good news, however. We found an investor, for the condo project. He's offered Warren partnership. It could mean great things for Bradley."

"Great things for yours and Warren's bank account," Heidi mumbled.

"Teague is still Warren's business partner," Lacy said. "Don't forget. A rising tide lifts all boats. Even pretend ones."

Heidi's mouth formed a straight line. She finished her Bellini and set the empty glass on the mantel.

Lacy crossed her legs and looked at me again. "Speaking of rising tides, this could be good for you and Dev, too. Think about it, Charlie. Warren went to business school with plenty of consultants and pharma execs."

I stuck what remained of the flower into the hoodie's pocket. "It does sound like the partners that retired last year didn't leave the clinic in the best shape. Maybe they'd have some advice?"

The way Lacy looked at me then, I felt like a puppy whose toy had rolled under the couch, like I was cute, if a little slow. Lacy stirred the pineapple drink Heidi handed her, swirling the tiny umbrella back and forth. She didn't bring it near her mouth. "Here's the thing," she said. "The clinic, to be frank, is an eyesore. From a real estate perspective, it simply doesn't add value. If these condos are going to move forward, the clinic, unfortunately, it has to go."

I moved my head to look like I understood what Lacy was saying until my brain could catch up. What she was saying was absurd. The clinic couldn't just "go." It wasn't a Monopoly piece they could pick up and move to another square.

"It's obviously a waste of prime waterfront-adjacent property. There must be other places where people can get prescription refills." Lacy's eyes flicked to Heidi, but Heidi stared into the fireplace. "These condos can only happen in one location. *They* can't move to a strip mall on the other side of the highway. Plus, I've already started planning the interiors for the model units."

Heidi chimed in. "Reading up on vases and mid-censh table lamps?"

Lacy shot her a look. "You know my style is modern."

"You can't be serious," I stammered, finally finding my voice. "The practice is walkable from downtown. It's on the bus route. It's a block away from the hospital. Patients can't just pick up and move the already limited health care they have across town, and making room for a Froyo place will solve literally none of their problems."

"Look, I get that it's not *ideal*," Lacy said impatiently. "But we don't have all the time in the world. This investor has a tight deadline. Warren needs to guarantee the clinic's closure or relocation by the last weekend in August."

"But that's *next* weekend," I said. My head was spinning, and not from the alcohol this time, at least not entirely.

"Oh, are you girls talking about the bacch?" Poppy put down her phone and sat back down on the couch.

I blinked. "The what?"

"Next weekend," Poppy said. "The bacch."

"It's the same weekend, yes." Lacy sighed.

"What are you talking about?" I said, panic creeping into my voice.

"The yacht bacch," Poppy said, as if making it rhyme made it clearer. "Last year's theme was nauti by nature." Heidi handed Poppy a pineapple, and she continued, "It's the last hurrah of summer. After this weekend, it's like the real world comes crashing down again—school lunches, the end of daylight savings, cardigans." She made a face. "So first, we have a bacchanal at the yacht club. The bacch."

"It's a masquerade," Poppy said. She picked another star fruit from the tray and held it over one eye. "Just cute little masks. It's not like you don't know who everyone is. It's still Rumford. But it's one last weekend to pretend whatever happened over the summer doesn't really count."

"Not that you have anything to hide, Charlie," Lacy said. She pulled her sunglasses down from her head, but I could feel her eyes on me like laser beams. The room was so fucking hot. I had to get out of there. And I had an idea of what I needed to help me get through the rest of the evening.

"I'm going to get more piña coladas," I said, trying to sound breezy instead of panicky and asthmatic. "Back in a sec."

chapter 25

Jeannine had said the downstairs bathroom was still indisposed, so no one questioned my beeline to Heidi's master suite. I looked over my shoulder to make sure no one had followed me down the hallway, then I poked my head into the closet where I knew Heidi stashed the gummies. If Oliver could smoke a joint at the block party, I could scam a couple of Heidi's pot gummies to make it through the rest of this book club.

I dug my hand between slippery silk scarves until I heard the crinkle of plastic. Bingo. I folded three bears into a tissue and stuffed it into my pocket.

The last time I'd gotten high was before I met Dev, and it wasn't on edibles. One day I was smoking weed with the dishwasher guys after my lunch shift, the next I was staring at a pregnancy test. But the feeling of weightlessness I remembered, a fuzzy mix of possibility and calm, was the exact opposite of everything pressing down on me in that moment.

I popped a tiny green bear into my mouth and chewed.

—◊—

Back in the living room, I waited for the gummy to kick in. I looked across the room. Were the paper lanterns Heidi strung across the ceiling glowing more than before? Was I seeing auras? I squinted. Nope. And there were at least two more hours of book club before I could leave without calling attention to myself, probably three before Dev would be asleep, and I could return home without having to talk, or to acknowledge how we weren't really talking, beyond the night after the bonfire when we were both half-asleep. I'd tell him what Lacy said, about the condos, of course, but surely it could wait until the morning.

As Lacy and Poppy debated the pros and cons of various Caribbean islands, I started to feel many things that were unfortunately not high: annoyed, overheated, bereft of an opinion on which sainted island had the best sushi.

"Charlie, which is your fave?" Poppy said.

"I don't know," I admitted. "Which one has the giant slide? That always looked fun."

"Lacy, don't you think Saint John is the most underrated?" Poppy asked.

Lacy put her hand to her chin, as if it was a question that actually had a wrong answer. I shoved an entire piece of star fruit in my mouth, wishing it was a bag of M&M's. I grabbed a paper fan from a side table. It was so hot. Honestly, who builds a fire in the middle of summer? All for a book that wasn't even hot. The romance was lame! I laughed at my own double entendre. I should say more things. I should say them out loud.

Wait. *Was* I speaking out loud?

No one was looking at me. But what else was new? I tried to fan myself more quickly, to make the air ripple against my face, but my hand felt disconnected from my wrist. *Perfect,* I thought, *like I need another thing to go wrong. C'mon, hand.*

I was feeling a teensy bit more relaxed now, sure, but it was probably just because the room felt like a sauna.

"Charlie, don't you think the future is in concierge medicine, anyway?" Lacy said, like we were already in midconversation.

"I'm more a rideshare kind of girl myself," I said.

Lacy nodded like we'd agreed on something. "Clients are the new patients. Dev needs autonomy. He shouldn't have to work with whoever walks in the door." She made a face, like an expired container of yogurt could walk in the clinic and ask for antibiotics. "Besides, there are other perks. Ever since Bart tried to poach those lobster traps, the van der Koffs bring their doctor to Nantucket with them. Just in case."

"Their lawyer, too," Heidi said.

"I mean, if you don't have a house on the Vineyard already, it could come in handy, that's all I'm saying." Lacy took a canapé between her thumb and forefinger, but instead of eating it, she handed it to Poppy. "They're delicious," she said.

Heidi smiled, her lips as tight as her orange bikini. "These piña coladas aren't going to drink themselves, ladies."

I squirmed in my chair. Sweat rolled down my back. I felt suffocated by the heat coming from the roaring fireplace, from this conversation. And what was going on between Lacy and Heidi? Was passive aggression contagious in such a small town, like those midwestern teenagers who all developed tics at the same time? I should wash my hands. I didn't want to catch it.

"Have you thought any more about Bridge Academy, Charlie?" Lacy said.

"Their robotics program is top notch." Poppy nodded solemnly.

"So is the tuition," I said before I could stop myself. I put the paper fan in front of my mouth, like it could contain whatever I said next.

"Well, I don't want to overstep," Lacy said. I waited for her to overstep.

"I'm not sure how much Dev makes at the clinic, but I imagine Medicaid doesn't give the most lucrative kickbacks." She unfolded an expensive-looking black linen coverup from the couch and draped it across her shoulders. "If he let the clinic go and started his own concierge practice, or if he transitioned to consulting, he'd probably triple his salary. It's something to think about."

"If he's a concierge, does he have to do restaurant recommendations, too?" I said. It came out more pointed than it was in my head. In my head, it was hilarious.

Lacy smiled stiffly. I tugged on the sleeves of the hoodie. My head felt too light. My body felt too stuffy. I wanted to take both shirts off and throw them into the fire. I started to do just that, then remembered what was underneath. I crossed my legs, but the skin behind my knee was slick with sweat.

"Do they learn magic at Bridge Academy?" I asked.

"Teague was the valedictorian," Heidi said, her voice flat.

In college, I had watched my suite mates stumble home from frat houses at four in the morning, sleep through lectures, bomb exams. They could fail sideways; they knew they'd be okay. I always wondered what that must be like. Teague was not living his best life at the moment, but I would also bet my public school tax dollars that he was doing reiki and drinking celery juice. Certainly no one was plotting to move his rehab to a strip mall across town.

I palmed the second gummy and stuck it in my mouth.

Heidi went to check on the next round of canapés in the kitchen, and Poppy took another call from Pax, or maybe Dodge, about laundering a jockstrap. My phone buzzed in my hand, and on the off chance it was Bridge Academy checking in, I silenced the call. Lacy leaned forward, balanced at the edge of the couch. I tried to scoot backward, but there was nowhere to go. I was trapped like a dumb animal, my chair a delicately upholstered cell.

"Don't tell Heidi I'm telling you this," Lacy said.

I nodded. Lacy set her sunglasses on the coffee table. The way she looked directly at me was like staring into the sun.

Lacy lowered her voice. "These condos. The ones in Bradley. Warren and Teague were going to develop them together. The project was put on hold when Teague went away, and his share of the capital is tied up now. We can't access it. It's essential that we close the deal with this investor. He's offering to cover Teague's portion."

I wasn't sure why Lacy was telling *me* any of this. I didn't know anything about finance. "Lacy, I think I need to tell you something." I stifled a giggle. "I do not own a Bluetooth headpiece. I used to work in a bar, and before that I made very tiny paintings."

The lanterns were glowing now, and Lacy's confused face glowed red. What a fun trick. I reached out to touch one, to see if I could pinch the glow between my fingers, like Lacy choosing a canapé. Maybe I could eat the light. I was pretty sure light was sugar-free. My hand hovered in the air in front of my face. I couldn't get my fingers on anything solid.

"Charlie. Are you with me? Anyway, we just need to have Teague sign off on it, since he's still technically a partner."

I wiped my cheek. It came away dry, but I could swear my pores were dripping. Did Lacy notice? Would it be weird if I touched Lacy's face to see if she was dripping, too?

"The other doctor at the clinic. With Dev. What's her name? Ringo?"

"Oh. Elvis?" The name felt strange in my mouth. I tried it again. "El-vis."

"Whatever. Warren approached her already. She's on a goddamn mission. Don't ask me why. Warren offered her connections to any hospital in Boston. He knows people in Connecticut, if she wants something more rural. Charlie, he'd do the same for Dev. Just say the word." Lacy snapped her fingers.

I squinted at Lacy's fingers. "What word did Elvis say? She knows a lot of words."

"Charlie, if this whole deal fails because of whatever loyalty Dev has for this Elvis person? It just doesn't seem right, or fair, to you. I'm looking out for you. Just like on *Penelope*. We have to look out for each other."

Lacy put her hand on my knee. I focused every muscle in my leg to remain still. I tried to assimilate Lacy's words with the buzz filling my head like so many bees. I felt trapped, and I could feel the hum of panic filling me like I was a helium balloon. If I gave Lacy a piece of what she wanted, would she release me? My whole body felt clammy. Was my heart supposed to beat this fast?

When I didn't reply, Lacy leaned even closer. "She's like a dog in a fight, isn't she? Does she feel the same way about your husband?"

Now I felt like Lacy had reached her hand into my chest. I looked down to check, but Lacy sat across from me, hands folded over her waxed knees. I moved my mouth, but nothing came out.

"She's still single," Lacy said. "And she's so pretty. She could meet someone no problem. But it's like she's *waiting* for him, right? She's so pretty, don't you think? So tall, just like Dev. Are they the same height? And that hint of a Southern accent, so cute next to Dev's British one."

I pushed hair out of my eyes, but it wasn't there. I brushed at my face again, like my bangs were a phantom limb. I could feel the flames from the fire licking my cheeks. I batted them away.

"If they don't secure the grant Elvis applied for, they can't stay open the rest of the year anyway," I said. The admission came out of me like a gust of wind. I tried to breathe it back in, but the air felt too sluggish. My mouth was lined with cotton balls, my nose a desert tumbleweed. I put my hand on my chest and tried to keep my heart inside of it. *Stay in there, you,* I thought to my pounding heart. *Don't embarrass me.*

The spell broken, I dashed into the hallway and found myself smack in front of a giant world map. Teague's map! I could hug it. Red push-pins clustered like mosquito bites along the East Coast, stretching from Massachusetts to the mid-Atlantic. There were more in the Caribbean, a smaller smattering in South America. Strings connected the pins to corresponding postcards on the perimeter of the map. It was like a crime map tracking a particularly unhinged travel agent.

"If I follow the lines, I can make sense of all of it," I said out loud. "I can fix all of this." It was suddenly so obvious. It was all connected. I just needed to *find* Teague. Heidi would be happy. Dev would love me again, because he was in the fixing-people business. Lacy wouldn't need Mystery Scrooge McDuck's moneybags. She'd leave me alone.

I swept my eyes along the red lines again. The key to Teague's whereabouts was in this map. I'd seen *Homeland*. There was always a pattern. *This* was how I would make it in Rumford. *It's all connected,* I repeated to myself. I could feel it. The lines of red yarn blurred. I stared harder.

I traced the strings crisscrossing the fake map with my finger. They were so taut. They were like Poppy's forearms. Did the *strings* work out at the Garage? I squeezed my midsection beneath the hoodie. I was squishy, like a gummy bear. My head felt squishy, too. I felt like I was out at sea, like Fake Teague.

"Heidi, can we break out the Veuve already?" Lacy called out—I was sure of it—from one of the postcards, on her own little Caribbean island. I bet it was nice there.

Break out, I thought. *Break. Out.* I touched one of the strings. *That's it. I need to break. Teague. Out.*

All of a sudden, I knew right where he was, and where I needed to go to rescue him.

From the hall, I watched Heidi push the button to open the secret wine hatch. Her sandals clacked down the wood stairs. They were so loud, like expensive, buttery leather gunshots. Lacy and Poppy remained on the couch, their backs to both me *and* the secret wine cellar. I knew I could make it, but only if I moved fast. I pulled the hood up over my head and bolted toward the open trapdoor.

chapter 26

I was down the wine cellar stairs before anyone saw me, carrying my flip-flops and tiptoeing on bare feet like a cartoon character. I slid to the floor and pressed my back to the far end of the long, white freezer chest that lay against the wall. I peered past the corner of the freezer and watched Heidi ascend the stairs, a bottle cradled in her arm. Now was my chance.

"Teague!" I whispered into the semidarkness. "Teague, you don't know me. I am a friend! Can you tell me where you are?"

Because Teague had been here all along. He was in the wine dungeon. It was a *dungeon* dungeon! I just had to find where, exactly. I opened the door to the wine locker, but I did not find a hedge fund manager in a navy-blue half-zip sweater awaiting rescue.

"Teague, it's o-kay." I tried to enunciate, but my mouth felt like maybe it wasn't my mouth. "I'm here to help." I let out my breath in a huff. I pulled on a couple of bottles in case there was a secret door. Satisfied that Teague did not need to remain chilled at fifty-five degrees, I let the door of the wine room close behind me and stood facing the freezer chest, my back to the stairs leading up to the living room. The freezer reminded me of a coffin, a long white rectangle low to the ground, sealed shut. I shivered even though I was still warm from the fireplace. "Teague?"

I knocked on the top of the freezer. My phone buzzed with a text. Maybe it was him. "Teague!" I hissed. I looked at the screen. My phone said it was Simon. My phone said he was coming to visit. My phone said he'd be at our place in the morning. Now I *knew* I was high.

Without warning, the dungeon went black, the trapdoor closing. My heart leaped into my throat. I swallowed, willing my whole heart to return to my chest. *"Stay there,"* I demanded, speaking both to my heart, and to Teague, who I was now 1oo percent sure was in the freezer. I felt along the wall for the light switch. The room flooded with yellow, but I was still alone with the freezer chest. The air conditioner kicked on, humming from the wine room. I was afraid to turn my back on the freezer. I wasn't going to *open* it. Gross. But I should keep watch. Maybe Teague would send me a sign from inside.

I heard footsteps overhead. Or, wait. *Wait.* Maybe that sound was knocking from inside the freezer chest.

"Teague . . . is that you?"

Clack, clack.

"Teague, is it all my fault? Knock twice for yes." My voice shook. My hands shook. I placed them on top of the freezer chest. "I just wanted someone to care that I was here. I don't know what Dev is thinking. My parents are globe-trotting. Simon doesn't need anyone. When Lacy made me feel like I was on the inside here, I think it did something to my insides. Maybe my outsides, too. All my sides, *okay,* *Teague?"* I was finally being honest with someone, but that someone was inside a freezer chest. We all had to start somewhere.

Clack.

I started pacing.

"The thing is, Poppy was really nice to me. And Heidi, too, once I got to know her. You did a number on her, Teague, let's be honest. Lacy is a little bit terrible. Maybe a lot? The thing is, I think I might be terrible, too. I told Lacy we have money problems. We're not supposed to talk about money here, Teague. We're supposed to have it."

I waited. Silence.

"Look, Teague, I just did not want them to roast me on the fire like a goddamn rotisserie chicken. You saw her smile. You know she would. I panicked."

I lowered to my knees and smushed my face onto the closed lid of the freezer chest.

"And don't even get me started on that thing with Oliver."

Clack, clack.

"Fuck you, Teague," I muttered. "Nobody's perfect."

Oliver. Hold the phone. Oliver made the magic trapdoor for Heidi. But he hadn't finished the job. Heidi told me so, at the kids' first play-date. Did Oliver want to trap me in a wine dungeon? Had he been planning this all along? Worse, did I want Oliver to trap me in a wine dungeon?

I turned around, my back to the freezer, and took out my phone. I would call him. I would simply get to the bottom of this like a reasonable person. "Oliver," I hissed into the darkness when he picked up, "I'm in your wine dungeon. Your plan worked. I know why you didn't build a way out. But now you need to come over here and get me out."

"Charlie?"

"Oliver?"

"Who's Oliver?"

I held the phone away from my ear, then brought it back.

"Dev?"

What was Dev doing with Oliver? "Teague, are you fucking with me?" I hissed. I felt my heart again, racing, pumping, trying to escape. I was not a doctor, but I was pretty sure I shouldn't be able to feel it pulsating like a kick drum.

"Charlie, what the hell is going on?"

"Dev," I moaned. "Dev, I have to tell you something."

"Charlie?" He sounded worried. "Are you okay?"

"No. Yes. I don't know." I heard the clacking again, but I wasn't going to let Teague stop me. "It's my heart, Dev. I think it fell out. It started beating too fast, and now I think it's in the pocket of this hoodie.

213

Also, it's your hoodie, and I need to give it back to you, because everyone here is in bikinis."

"Is this a joke? Charlie, aren't you at book club?" He said something else I couldn't understand, like he'd moved his mouth away from the phone.

"The thing is, I want to keep my heart, Dev. I need you to put it back in for me. It fell out, but I didn't mean for it to happen, and I want it back in." I was crying. I didn't know how to explain everything that felt wrong. I only knew it all hurt and I wanted it to stop. I wanted to be put back together.

"But Dev," I said miserably. "You have to be careful. My heart can't stay in this hoodie. But you can't make a mess either. Not in Heidi's white kitchen. Marble is porous."

"Do you need to go over there?"

Hold on. That wasn't Dev. And it wasn't Teague. That was Presley's voice. Why was Presley on the phone?

Was she? Was Dev? Were they—?

Clack.

I hung up. Teague was messing with me. Surely none of this was happening. I sat down on the stairs. I pulled the hoodie over my face and breathed in drugstore shampoo and coffee. I wanted to stretch it over my entire body. I curled up like a turtle. Then I wobbled and rolled down three steps. I landed against the freezer and decided to stay there, certain no one would be coming to rescue me.

—⁓—

"Charlie?"

Teague's voice was too high. Was he defrosting? I patted the floor around me. Surely Heidi kept a stash of hand towels in the wine dungeon. I didn't want him to drip. The floor would get slippery.

"Charlie. Are you okay?"

I pulled the hood back from my eyes and pushed myself up to sitting. Heidi put her hand on my shoulder.

"I was wondering where you went," she said. "You should come back upstairs. There are still so many fucking pineapples." Instead of pulling me up to standing, though, Heidi slid down the side of the freezer chest and sat on the cold floor next to me. She wore a gauzy coverup over her bikini. She had to be freezing. I craped my arm around Heidi's shoulders and pulled her close. The thin fabric of her coverup was like air between my fingers. Air that I could touch. I rolled the edge of Heidi's sleeve back and forth between my thumb and forefinger and thought about how it would feel to hold a cloud

Heidi let out a sigh. Then she said, "I fucked Oliver down here."

I let the sleeve fall from my fingers. I felt the concrete floor under me again, the freezer at my back. "Oh," I said. "Okay."

"I know you saw the pregnancy test," Heidi said. "The first time you came over. I appreciated you not saying anything then. It was negative, anyway. I was just late, and paranoid. Teague hadn't been away very long, when . . . and I was a mess."

"Okay," I said again. I took her hand. It was freezing, so I put it in the pocket of my hoodie. She rested her head on my shoulder.

"You should know, Teague and I were talking about separating before he went away," she said. "The drugs were a problem, but they weren't *the* problem. We were broken before."

"Did you want to be with Oliver?"

"Not really," Heidi said. "I just wanted to feel something."

"Did you?"

"What do you think?"

I laughed. I ran my fingers down Heidi's hair. It was like expensively highlighted silk, softer than the scarves in the closet. *The closet.*

"Oh, Heidi. I have to tell you something. I may have helped myself to your bag of gummies."

Heidi snorted. "Good."

She stood and held her hand out and pulled me upright. I took one last look at the freezer chest. I felt like I'd failed someone, but it wasn't Teague. I wondered how long I'd been curled up there in the wine dungeon before Heidi found me. Surely I hadn't really called Dev, thinking it was Oliver, prompted by a phantom, frozen version of Heidi's estranged husband. It was some kind of weird fever dream. I'd leave all that nonsense beneath the trapdoor.

"Stick a fork in me and hand me a piña colada with a tiny umbrella," I said as I followed Heidi up the stairs.

Everything was going to be fine, I reassured myself, and I believed it for a good ten seconds—until I found Dev, sitting in the chair I'd left vacant, facing Lacy on the couch.

chapter 27

"Charlie, where did you run off to?" Lacy said. "We didn't finish our conversation."

My heart jumped. I put one hand on my chest and one on Dev's shoulder—to make extra double sure he was really there. I was still, unfortunately, a little high.

"Dev, you're all wet," I said.

"It's raining again." He looked at me like he was trying to make sense of why, exactly, he was sitting in Heidi's living room being handed a piece of star fruit.

"But we're on a tropical island. Isn't it obvious? Did you bring your swimsuit?" I giggled.

Dev's damp bangs rested on the frames of his glasses. When he shook them out of his eyes, water droplets flew to either side. I thought of how James Dean wiggled himself dry after a bath. I knew I should be serious—he looked so serious. But I was so very tired of trying so very hard to do everything right.

"Did you come to join the party?" I said. "If you read the book, you're going to be disappointed."

Dev looked up at me, confused. Maybe concerned? It was sweet of him to be concerned. "You called me," he said.

I reached out to brush the hair out of his eyes, but I ended up swatting at the air between us instead.

"You said there was something wrong with your heart. And porous countertops. You sounded off, Charlie. You said I had to come get you."

"Ohhh," I said. "Did you come to see Heidi's kitchen? It's gorgeous." The kitchen made me think of the pineapple drinks. My mouth was still so dry. "Dev, do you want a piña colada?"

"What? No. Is that what's going on? How many did you have?"

"Not even one! Not yet. You know I hate dessert drinks, but these have little umbrellas in them! What do you mean what I had? Ohhh," I said again, "you mean—"

"Charlie wanted to see the wine cellar," Heidi interjected. "Then we got to talking about the book. Riveting. You know, book club and all."

Lacy rolled her eyes, but Heidi handed me a piña colada. I'd thank her for covering for me later. I'd leave out the part about trying to rescue and defrost Teague like a chicken nugget.

"Your timing is impeccable, Dev," Lacy said, like this all happened just for her. "I was just talking to Charlie tonight about the enormous growth potential Warren and I see in Bradley. It's like this pineapple, really." She shoved a pineapple into Dev's hand before he could protest, then she ran a manicured finger down the pointy husk.

"It's rough around the edges, but it could be something entirely different. Before we can fill it with something sweet, we need to scoop out the tough core. We can't make the drink *around* it. Surely you understand."

I elbowed Dev, and I loud whispered, *"She means the clinic."*

"I got that, thanks," he said, without a hint of appreciation.

I remembered something, and my chest started burning again. There'd been a voice on the phone—and it hadn't been Dev. I said to Lacy, "He'll have to talk to his partner about it. Not me, his other partner. The one he talks to."

Dev got up from the chair. "Charlie, we should go." He took my hand, but I pulled it away.

Lacy settled into the couch, ready for a show.

"Were you seriously with Presley? While I was here?" I shook my head, trying to clear it like an Etch A Sketch. "Wait. If you're here now, who's with the kids?"

"Elvis is at the house," Dev said. It felt like a bomb going off inside my chest, in the cavity where my heart used to be. "Don't worry, the kids are asleep. She didn't come over until they were asleep."

"Is that supposed to make it *better*?"

"Charlie, don't overreact," Dev said, too quietly, too calmly.

"But you invited her over. At night. When I wasn't home."

My face felt like it was on fire again, and the buzzing had returned to my ears. My legs felt like marshmallows, and I gripped the back of the armchair. I'd spent all this time feeling guilty about being alone with Oliver for, like, five whole minutes, and Presley, what, had a spare key?

Dev looked at the glowing logs in the fireplace instead of at me. "Why is there a fire going? It's August." He rubbed his eyes under his glasses. "Charlie, she insisted, okay? She brought decaf. We talked. I can explain, but look, I don't want to get into it here."

"You had coffee. And she's, like, hanging out while our kids sleep. Does this happen a lot? Let me guess, you wanted to show her your mushroom-foraging porn."

"Your what now?" Heidi said, then mouthed *sorry*.

"Were you even going to tell me?"

Dev lowered his voice again. "Look, it's not a big deal. It's the first time she's dropped by. Of course I was going to tell you."

I nodded like a parrot. "Not a big deal," I repeated. "First time. Cool cool cool." My eyes burned. Everyone was looking at me. I was sweating again, damp and shaky under the hoodie. I wanted to shed the weight of something, words and feelings if not clothing.

"They're really close," I said to the room, to the other women, to myself. "They have a whole history. Lacy's right; she's really pretty. And really tall. She could be a supermodel, but oops, she's a doctor instead. She's really capable. She gets shit done. I get woozy when I see blood. It's gross! I hate it! I don't really get it, what they do, because Dev doesn't talk to me about it. Like, whatever she came over to my house to talk about? He won't talk about it with me. But you know, I don't understand much of anything anyway. For example, I don't understand this book club, and I literally don't know how to sit on a couch in a bikini."

The room was blurring even more as my eyes filled with tears.

"But Presley isn't perfect either. The clinic is operating at a loss," I heard myself say. "I hear you talk about it, Dev, because, again, you talk to her. I know she hasn't taken her full salary in three months. I know you're counting on this grant to keep the practice open. I know that your lease is up for renewal. And I know that's what you don't want to tell Warren."

Dev stared at me. I couldn't stop now that I'd started. I just wanted to make him feel something. I wanted to see him react, not shut down or retreat.

"Presley begged us, well, *you*, to come up here, for us to move. That's what you told me. No one thought to mention the not insignificant fact that the practice is underwater. It's sinking. It's the *Titanic*, if the iceberg was a big fucking pile of oxy."

Dev took his glasses off and put them back on; it was what he did when he didn't know what to say. He stared at me. "Jesus, Charlie."

Lacy leaned back, like a lion settling in to gnaw on its limp prey. Poppy returned from another laundry coaching session in the hallway and plopped back onto the couch. "So, what did I miss? Dev, when did you get here?" she said. Heidi answered her with a pointed look.

I tried to suck the words back into my mouth, like my outburst was nothing but a melting piña colada, while Lacy smiled with her teeth.

chapter 28

When we walked in the door, Presley was in leggings and a T-shirt, not exactly booty-call clothes. And she wasn't watching my Netflix queue. I dodged her in a beeline for the kitchen. If Presley hadn't been there, I might have stuck my head in the sink and swallowed water directly from the faucet. Instead I refilled the glass three times and kept drinking while Presley said goodbye to Dev.

I heard her say, "You have to tell her, Dev."

I heard Dev say, "Yeah. I know."

I heard the door shut. And the glass break as I dropped it in the sink.

I woke up the next morning alone in the bed, still wearing Dev's hoodie.

—⁂—

I reread Simon's text from the night before, confirming I hadn't hallucinated it. The fact that he'd be at the house any minute was like a marital deus ex machina—it was the perfect distraction.

I busied myself throwing towels and snacks into a tote bag. I needed to show Simon I had my shit together, and what better way than to take him directly to the beach club, to stay at the cottage as little as humanly possible, even if inside I still felt like one of those midwestern towns leveled by a tornado the week before prom.

Dev had to work for a few hours during the day, so I could conceivably avoid being near him until when we'd all inevitably go to dinner that night. And while I was determined to do everything possible to avoid being in the same room with him for the time being, I knew I couldn't entirely sidestep the fact that the night before had actually happened. I just didn't know what to do about it, what to say, or if I even really, truly wanted to know why Presley had come over, what she'd meant by *You have to tell her*. Was I ready to hear it?

"Did Simon Uber from the airport?" Dev called out from the living room, having just come back from an extralong run.

"He said he was renting a car," I answered from the kitchen. "You know he's a control freak. He doesn't like other people driving him around." I pawed at something hard and cylindrical under a towel in my bag, thinking it was an errant seltzer. I found a flashlight instead, and Kate's compass, and set them on the table.

"Mama, I need those," Kate said, passing through the kitchen and plopping them back into the bag. Before I could inquire as to why, Dev called out again.

"Then who's in the car with him?"

Simon was never *with* anyone. Forgetting my same-room rule, I careened around the corner and pressed my face to the window. I stared as my brother stepped out of the passenger side—the passenger side?—his beard and angular chin bringing to mind an REI catalog model. He'd grown his hair out to almost shoulder length and tied it back with an elastic. He put his hand on top of the open door, then leaned back into the car to say something to the driver. That was an awfully nice smile to give to an Uber driver. I looked at Dev. He shrugged.

"Did he say he was bringing someone?" Dev asked.

"He never says anything," I said. "About anyone. He only told me he was coming to visit last night." I could feel the air thicken between us again at the mention of last night.

"Charlie," Dev said, brows knit. "About that."

But I just shook my head. "Not yet," I said. Dev hesitated, but he nodded.

A tall, slim man with skin a shade darker than Dev's and a trim haircut stepped from the car. He looked at the cottage, then back at Simon.

"Did Simon just wink at him?" I said. "Simon doesn't wink. What is happening?"

"Maybe he met someone," Dev said with a shrug. "It happens."

My stomach dropped, and my heart continued its game of Ping-Pong in my chest, but when I saw the man outside give Simon a quick kiss before they walked up to the house, I hissed, "Am I still high?"

"You're right here, Mama," Toby called from the couch.

"Everyone, get your bathing suits," I said, feeling like the walls of the cottage were already closing in on me. "We're getting out of here."

—⚭—

The man's name was Victor. He was Simon's boyfriend. The words felt strange next to each other, like peanut butter pizza; I repeated them to myself on the way to the beach club. Simon had a boyfriend. He'd been single since college. He didn't even have a dog. He liked space, and order, and not being accountable to anyone but himself. I told myself it wasn't personal; his intimacy issues couldn't be 100 percent traced back to sharing RV bunk beds with me for the bulk of his adolescence. Nature/nurture and all that.

Now I tried not to fixate on how close together they sat on the lounge chair, how easily Victor's hand rested on Simon's leg, like they'd known each other for years, not days. It reminded me of how Dev and I had been, when everything was new. The day after we met—by which I mean the morning after Dev left my apartment—he texted during class saying he could barely stay awake. I offered to bring him coffee before my shift at the bar. When he met me outside the hospital, he wrapped his fingers around mine and brought my hand to his mouth, just standing there, like it was second nature to be so comfortable wanting someone. I had breathed it in like it was oxygen. Now I just heard Presley's voice: *You have to tell her.* I blinked away tears.

As I passed around cups of sangria, Simon explained how he and Victor met through none other than our tirelessly matchmaking mother.

"Did you tell her?" I asked.

"God no," Simon said, smiling. "Not yet."

Victor was our parents' Uber driver in New York—after they drove Bessie through downtown rush hour, my father insisted they only travel in four-door sedans the rest of the weekend. Lilly chatted Victor up, and he told them how he worked in finance until six months prior, when his mother had passed away unexpectedly. Life felt short, he'd said; he didn't want to waste it wearing a Patagonia vest inside some office building when he could wear it climbing a mountain instead. Inside the Holland Tunnel, he'd explained how he quit his job and started taking lessons on all sorts of things—from rock climbing to film. He drove an Uber on weekends to supplement living off his savings for a little while. He'd felt a little lost, and wanted to get out of the city, but didn't have a good enough reason. While Simon rubbed sunscreen on his arms, Victor said Lilly had actually sold him on one of Simon's backpacking tours, and then given him my brother's personal cell.

"Let me guess," I said. "She refused to get out of the car until you promised to take Simon's number."

Victor's laugh was warm and inviting. "She said she'd withhold my five-star rating if I didn't call."

Kate ran over and pulled Victor to the pirate ship. She was brandishing a wooden sword, and Victor looked at Simon like he really had no choice. He giggled like a kid, then chased Kate back to the ship. Simon watched them, smiling like no one else was there.

"We'll never hear the end of it from Lilly," Simon said, shaking his head.

"This really all happened in the past week?"

"What can I say, I'm an excellent hiking guide," Simon said, ignoring my snort-laugh. "I flew back with him, to Manhattan, last night. I didn't tell you ahead of time, because I didn't know if I was being unhinged, which clearly I am. But I have to say, other than sounding like a pair of extra butlers from *Downton Abbey* . . ."

"Simon and Victor," I said. "Totally."

He shrugged. "I like him." On the pirate ship, Victor pretended to walk the plank, and Simon tried to hide another smile.

"It's okay to be happy, you know," I said. "You've been alone out in those woods for a while."

Simon put his cup down on the patio and leaned back in the chair. "Charlie, you do know I'm not the Unabomber, right? I live in Bozeman. Next to an organic coffee shop. You'd see if you visited."

Victor jumped off the end of the plank and pretended to flail in the sand. He motioned for Kate to throw him a rope. She was in heaven. Watching them play so unselfconsciously, I missed Dev so much, so suddenly, it caught me off guard.

"Do you have more sunscreen?" Simon asked, rummaging around in my tote bag until he pulled out *The Official Preppy Handbook* in one hand and Kate's compass in the other.

"Always be prepared, huh?" he said, tossing the compass back into my bag but holding on to the worn paperback book. "Char, is this your beach read?"

I tried to snatch the book, but Simon leaned away from me and held it out of reach. The last time I'd seen that gingham book cover, I'd stuck it in a place no one would look. I had to have a talk with Kate. What was she doing in my underwear drawer?

"It's a joke," I said, reaching for the book again and nearly knocking Simon's sangria over on the patio.

I glanced around, hoping no one else was listening as Simon opened to a random page and read aloud. *"Monogramming: when your own initials will do."* He pointed the book at my tote bag. "Charlie, you've been paying attention."

"Simon, shut up and give it back," I hissed. I wasn't sure which was worse: having bought the book in the first place or feeling like a thirty-one-year-old loser whose brother was about to ruin my pool party with the popular kids.

"There are so many things you can monogram," Simon muttered, running his finger down the coffee-stained page. "But *not* dog collars or cashmere scarves. So much for James Dean's Christmas present."

I held out my hand, and Simon reluctantly placed the book on my flat palm.

"There are two whole pages about sweaters," he said. "One is dog-eared. Are you sure it's a joke?"

I stuffed the book back into my tote, under a newly monogrammed towel I was absolutely not going to unroll. When I didn't answer with a snide remark or even defend myself further, Simon looked at me. "Charlie Parker, how much Kool-Aid have you had? Are you doing all right here?"

I felt caught. Here was Simon, life goals falling into place, and then . . . me, just trying to keep my head above water. "Look, you know how Kate has her survival guides?" I said. Simon nodded. "I felt like I landed here, and I needed one, too. I know it's stupid. But look around, Simon. How else am I supposed to know velour is not, nor ever will be, preppy?"

Before Simon could answer, as if there was an answer, Poppy plopped down onto the side of my lounge chair. "Charlie, check out the new hot lifeguard," she said. She pulled her sunglasses down her nose and stared at Victor. He'd taken off his white T-shirt and was waving it like a flag, surrendering to Kate and her friends. He was the only adult interacting with the children.

"Poppy, this is my brother, Simon," I said, whacking him on the arm as delayed payback for the book waving, then I pointed to the ship. "That's Victor, Simon's boyfriend."

"Oh, he's adorable," Poppy said. "Good for you, Simon." She held up her hand for a high five. "I've got to run to tennis, Charlie, but I wanted to give you this, to say thank you to Dev for the other night. The tournament is next week, and it's thanks to him that I'm playing. It really means a lot."

She handed me a piece of folded white card stock with a plastic gift card to a restaurant nestled inside.

"It's this amazing Italian place. You'll love it." She leaned closer. "It's kind of near the Garage, but it smells great once you get inside, I promise."

Simon raised his eyebrows, and before he could comment I said, "We can go tonight! Great timing, Poppy," and I hopped up to get us more sangria.

Simon lay back on his lounge chair. "Wish I brought a book," he said.

I smacked him on the head as I walked to the bar, where I found Lacy scowling at her cell phone. Her thumbs moved over the screen like she was trying to squish a spider.

"Lacy, about last night," I said. "I think I said some things."

"Whatever, no one's marriage is perfect." Lacy didn't look up from her phone.

"What? No. I meant about the clinic. I was, um, not quite myself, and—"

"It's bullshit. He doesn't believe I can make it happen," Lacy said from behind her tortoiseshell sunglasses. Did she mean Warren? "He always does this. The bacch is in two days. He's such a narcissist, with his deadlines and stipulations. I'm not a child."

It took a moment for me to realize she was talking about the investor, not about anything I was saying, or anything I'd already said. Maybe what I'd blurted at book club wouldn't even matter. Maybe the deal would fall apart anyway. It was another thing I'd leave for just one more day. I leaned on the table trying to appear relaxed, but I jostled the pile of masks she'd laid out, and one slid to the stone patio. I picked it up and ran my fingers along the rhinestones.

"I had these shipped overnight from some rando on Etsy," Lacy said. She held a black bedazzled mask to her eyes. "They're for the bacch."

Of course, there were party favors.

"I don't *need* a mask, right?" I said. "My brother's in town and we're going to dinner. I'm not sure I'm in the best state overall to wrangle a hot glue gun tonight."

Lacy stared at me. "It's the *bacch*," she emphasized, as if I'd asked for permission to attend naked.

On the beach, Kate stood at the mast of the wooden pirate ship, waving a white flag. I squinted then groaned as I realized the flag had come straight from my underwear drawer.

chapter 29

A low light fell onto the restaurant bar where Dev sat waiting for us that night. He wore a button- down shirt, wrinkled but fitted to his slim chest. An empty barstool sat angled next to him, like he'd pulled it out just for me. I slid onto it, summoning the positive attitude of someone whose biggest problem was choosing between noodles and gnocchi.

"Simon and Victor are at the table," I said, forcing an awkward smile. In a half-hearted attempt to ease the tension (or at least to give a good show of it) before we had to sit at a small table together, I leaned in to give him a hug, but pulled back when I felt a hand—not Dev's—on my back.

"Hey, Charlie!"

My brain struggled to catch up with my face, which was reacting in a way I didn't hide quickly enough. Presley and Dev were, what— having a drink? Before we met for dinner? I understood suddenly, like falling into a sinkhole, whom the barstool had been meant for.

Meanwhile, Presley grabbed me in a hug, and I let it happen, too shocked to do anything but play along like the whole meet-cute was entirely expected.

"Charlie, you are such a saint to let me tag along," Presley said, letting me go. "Dev said your brother was visiting, so it wasn't like a date night, and the thought of just being out with people?" Presley pursed her lips and blew a strand of hair from her face. "Girl, I just really needed it."

I nodded like Dev had already told me, like we'd discussed this already. Like we discussed literally anything anymore. I was pretty sure my smile looked deranged. "Of course! So great. We're just over there," I said. I pointed to Simon and Victor, and Presley hopped over to introduce herself.

Dev looked at me like he worried if he moved too suddenly, I would bolt out the front door. "She asked if she could join tonight."

"Of course," I said again, with a metric ton less enthusiasm. "Having dinner with my ambivalent husband's ex-girlfriend turned current business partner was exactly the kind of night I had planned. It only enhances the after-dinner drinks I'd planned with my isolationist brother and his reluctant finance bro turned Uber-driving-film-school boyfriend, a match made through the dating app that is my mother. No, Dev, all of this is completely normal."

Dev sighed. "Look, Charlie, she was talking about how many friends you already have here. How you're always doing something new. It was either say *Yes, sure, Elvis, take one night off working for the past year and join us*, or say something along the lines of *Actually, let me check first that my wife isn't going to* Mission: Impossible *her way into the walk-in freezer because she's high as a kite—*"

"That was *one time*," I hissed. "Every other night I'm home, with our kids, by myself, wondering where you are, why you're suddenly training for a marathon, where you go after work that you won't tell me about. Why you can't seem to be able to be around me anymore without a buffer of, like, ten thousand Norwegian mushrooms—or your emotional support best friend over there."

Dev's jaw clenched. "I'm not the one who practically itemized Elvis's bank account statements for Lacy. Do you really think you're in a position to talk, Charlie?"

His words hit me like a truck. He wasn't wrong. But neither was I. I punched back with the only thing I had left.

"You're right," I said. "I guess I'm just not as good at keeping secrets as you are."

Dev flinched, then let out a shaky exhale. His fingers gripped the countertop of the bar. His face returned to being unreadable, a closed door. Simon called us over, and Dev blinked, like he'd forgotten where we were for a second. Wherever he'd gone in his head, I wasn't with him. It seemed like I never was. Where did that leave us?

We sat down at the table, not making eye contact. I prayed Simon had already ordered wine.

When a young man dressed in black brought the bottle to the table, Presley almost jumped out of her seat. She put both palms on the table, as if to anchor herself in place. The waiter was in his twenties, skinny, with a shaved head and goatee, and Presley stared like he'd brought her a goldendoodle instead of a bottle of Malbec.

"Casper!" Presley said. "Look at you."

She put her hand on Dev's arm. I looked away and put my hands in my lap. Presley and Dev looked like proud parents. To my credit, I tried to copy their faces, because, if nothing else, I was genuinely happy that this man brought wine.

"This is what you were rushing to get to today, Casper?" Dev said, genuine surprise in his voice.

The young man smiled. He looked at the table and held up the wine. "You got me, Doc. What did you think it was?"

Presley beamed, almost forcefully. "Casper, you didn't say. This is really so great. Except, shit, do we have to leave a big tip now?"

Presley and Dev both laughed in a weird, relieved way. Simon looked at me with raised eyebrows. I shrugged.

"I'm usually at the bar, but I said I'd bring the wine over to you guys," Casper said. "The tips at the bar are decent, though, so no pressure."

He poured wine into each of our glasses. Presley watched him closely, and I noticed his hand shook a little as he poured. Perhaps the attention made him nervous? A line of sweat beaded his hairline.

Sometimes I still missed the straightforward physicality of tending bar—being on my feet for hours, hefting crates of wine and booze up and down the stairs. It could be a slog, but the mindless ease of tasks had often been reassuring, the value of the result direct and tangible. There were instructions for how to make a Manhattan, and if you messed up, you could simply toss it and start again. Less so for other things in life.

Dev hadn't taken his eyes off Casper. It seemed like he was about to say something more, but he looked around the table and suddenly remembered he was sitting with me, Simon and Victor, not just Presley. He cleared his throat, breaking some kind of spell.

"Casper, this is my wife, Charlie. I told you about her. We know Casper, Elvis and me, um, from work."

"Of course!" I said. It was a brilliant strategy, this one response. I should use it more often. "Nice to meet you, Casper."

Casper smiled at me and nodded. Holding the now-empty bottle, he looked over his shoulder, to the back of the restaurant. He seemed anxious, understandably, like he needed to get back to work.

"Enjoy the wine, folks," he said. "Good to see you, Doc. Docs." He smiled quickly and nodded at Dev and Presley. Then he walked back to the bar.

"I was worried, weren't you, Dev?" Presley said, swirling the wine in her glass, her eyes laser-focused. "Today, the way he popped in."

Dev nodded. "I know."

"I know it's been a good run, but, you know?"

"I know," Dev said again.

I didn't know. There was so much Dev and Presley knew that I never would. I reached for the bread.

"Did you see?" Presley's eyes were still on Casper, at the bar. He took a small towel and wiped down the counter.

Dev said softly, "Yeah, I did."

Now I felt like I was intruding on a private moment. Simon said something to Victor, and he smiled. I felt like a fifth wheel.

Watching Casper mix and pour a dry martini as a server came over to take our order, I wondered if he and I had more in common than most of the people I'd met in Rumford. Would he ever guess? Or would he take in my white jeans, my necklace with the pink tassel, my mailing address, and assume I'd never counted on tips to pay rent on a shitty apartment? How did Dev see me now?

Sitting next to Presley I suddenly just felt like a fraud. I'd always thought of Presley as the Southern belle who didn't know her way around a scholarship application. The woman had literally been a debutante. But while I replied to a group chat about the yacht bacch and color-coordinated bedazzled eye masks, Presley told Simon and Victor about how she played basketball with kids at the YMCA every Thursday. *Dev isn't the only one who doesn't recognize me*, I thought, my stomach souring on the wine.

"The clinic is part of Bradley," Presley was saying, waving around a breadstick. "And I want these families to trust me. I want the kids to know me, to come to the clinic for help when they need it, for themselves, for their parents. I know I don't look the part, but I'm not some shrinking violet. I'm fighting for this place. Plus, I played club basketball at Villanova." She cleared her throat. "I kick their little butts."

Victor laughed. "I played, too. We should organize a game tomorrow. Charlie, does that beach club place have a court?"

"What?" I looked up from a text about gemstones versus rhinestones. "No, um, we have bocce."

Presley waved her hand. "I'm sure y'all want to have your visit, anyway. I'll stick to playing with the kids; it's better for my ego."

"She makes it sound like she just volunteers," Dev said. I put my phone away.

"Elvis is a hustler," Dev continued. "Because of her, we have a network of detox centers, relationships with other outpatient clinics, shelters, social workers. She networks with everyone—*everyone*—on and off court."

There was such clear admiration in his voice. I felt a lurch inside my stomach and reached for my wineglass.

"Oh, it's not all that," Presley said. "But it'll pay off soon, I hope. If this grant comes through, we can hire on more people, maybe even think about expanding our services. Since Dev came on board, he's been reaching out to physicians who specialize in MAT—sorry, that's medically assisted treatment. It means we offer medical options for opiate addiction and support our patients in-house instead of giving them pamphlets and bus passes to other clinics and crossing our fingers they follow up."

She'd just dropped more info on what they were trying to do at the clinic than I'd gotten from Dev in weeks. Why on earth would he keep it from me? Did he think I couldn't handle it? *He just doesn't need me,* I thought. *He has her.*

"Sorry for the shop talk," she said, but she wasn't embarrassed; she was practically beaming. "It's what fourteen-hour days'll do to you."

"And I thought I worked long hours," Victor said. "Are you ever home? Is this your first dinner out in a year?"

"Maybe. It sure feels like it," Presley said. "I also moonlight at the ER a couple of times a month. They always need someone to pick up a night shift. And it's not like I have anyone waiting up for me, but honestly? I'm just *over* going into an exam room to get a tongue depressor and finding someone who's stopped breathing."

With that, Presley excused herself to go to the bathroom.

"That's fair," Simon mumbled.

"Damn," Victor echoed. They looked at each other somberly.

Dev looked down at his plate, like he wasn't sure how to take over from there.

"Dev, does that really happen?" I asked, slowly. I looked at him until he answered.

"Not all the time" was all he said. We were silent, then, as the server returned and delivered our meals.

I was about to ask if we should wait for Presley, when a door slammed. The sound of wood on tiled wall echoed across the restaurant. It sliced through the ambient murmur of other diners, the clinking of forks hitting porcelain. A handful of people dressed in black, servers and busboys, flanked the door of the men's room. They were shouting.

Was someone choking? Having a heart attack? Time felt like it slowed down, and I found it hard to lift my gaze from two drops of red wine on the white tablecloth. Then, the sound of a chair scraping wood, and Dev was inside the men's room, too. The other servers kept yelling. A woman said, "No, I don't know what happened. There's someone on the floor. I don't know."

I stood up, but I couldn't step forward. I gripped the edge of the table.

When the people crowded by the men's room stopped shouting and simply watched, when their hush was worse than their panic, I forced a deep breath into my lungs and moved toward the open door. I heard sirens. I nudged my way through. Our server leaned against the doorframe, the color drained from his face. I flattened myself against the wall inside the restroom. What I saw was Dev, straddling a pair of legs on the bathroom tiles. The stall doors obscured the top half of the man on the ground. He wore black pants. Black shoes. He'd either fallen that way or Dev had dragged him half out of the stall. Dev's shoulders moved up and down. Part of his shirt came untucked. He wasn't wearing a belt. Kate was always taking his belts. I didn't understand how both things could be true at once—our daughter and her pretend survival training, and this man, lying still on the bathroom floor.

Dev pumped his layered palms on the man's chest. My arms prickled with goose bumps. I moved along the wall until I could see over Dev's shoulders. The man's face looked gray. He was young. I realized, my insides turning to lead, it was Casper.

Something foamy and white dripped down his cheek and pooled on the floor. His head bumped up and down in rhythm with Dev's compressions. Someone had placed a bar towel under his head. Dev repeated, "One, two, three, four, five," eyes fixed on Casper as he tried to pump air into his lungs.

For a moment, I didn't hear anything but Dev. The servers around me moved their mouths. One was crying. But I only heard Dev. I focused on his hands moving up and down on Casper's chest. Casper's hands lay at his sides. His fingernails were blue.

"One, two, three, four, five."

Dev cursed. His shoulders moved up and down like waves. Then Presley was there, too. She kneeled beside him. Her face was inches from his.

"Dev." Presley was the one to say his name out loud.

"Over there." Dev nodded to the metal stall door. Under it, a syringe pointed to the wall.

Presley's face set, like she'd swallowed an expression. She had something in her hand. She peeled the back off a small plastic package. It looked like a long white bullet set into a tiny white table. Dev paused his chest compressions and Presley tilted Casper's head. She put the tube into his nostril. She pressed the plunger.

I wasn't sure if everyone was still yelling or if it was silent. I didn't know if I stood there for a minute or an hour. I was sure Casper was dead. I'd never seen a dead person before.

Then his chest heaved, a violent inhalation. He coughed. Dev rolled him to his side. Presley kept her hand on his shoulder. It was like he'd been drowning right there on the bathroom tiles. His lungs sucked and choked on air, set into motion by whatever Presley sprayed up his nose.

She saved him, I realized. She saved his life, like it was something she did every day.

"Where did you get Narcan?" Dev said, still breathing quickly. He sat back on his heels.

"I keep it in my purse."

Dev let out a small laugh of surprise, and relief, but it didn't come close to reaching his eyes. "Of course you do."

The volume around me slowly rose then. Two EMTs pushed past. They moved Casper onto a stretcher, put a plastic oxygen mask over his mouth. Presley went with them in the ambulance. The bathroom cleared out. I stood with my back pressed to the cold tiles, still in the periphery of where Casper had lain. I reached my hand forward, toward

Dev, who remained on the floor after everyone else left. He hadn't registered that I was there. My hand hovered in the air.

Dev used the toe of his shoe to pull the needle toward him. But instead of leaning down to pick up the syringe, his body moved swiftly forward. He thrust his open palm into the stall door, banging it, hard. I must have made a noise over the clang of metal. Dev turned.

"I didn't know you were there," he breathed, so quiet I hardly heard him.

He wiped a bead of sweat from the side of his face.

"So, this is what you and Presley seemed concerned about," I said.

"Yeah." I wondered if it was all he was going to say. But then, "He'd been clean for a few weeks."

"I'm sorry," I said. For what, exactly, I wasn't sure. I was sorry for a lot of things.

"We should go, Charlie," Dev said. He walked out of the bathroom.

Simon and Victor stood beside the table. I didn't realize I was shaking until Simon put an arm around me. He'd put the food in boxes and laid cash on the clean tablecloth. Dev waited, holding his car keys. Before we left, I stacked the bread plates. I put the silverware in a pile. Someone would still have to clear the table.

chapter 30

When we returned home from the restaurant, Dev was restless, adrenaline still winding its way through him. Simon and Victor followed him to the back patio for a beer, and I hovered in the doorway.

"Does that kind of thing happen often?" Simon asked softly as Dev paced. "An overdose. That you have to—I don't know what you'd call it . . ."

Dev shook his head. "No. But it happens when my patients leave." He sat down in a creaky Adirondack chair, tapping his leg. "There are bad batches, stuff people get from the street. There are pills mixed with fentanyl. Elvis sees it in the ER. I haven't . . . I hadn't done that in a while."

My nonmedical brain was stuck on how it wasn't at all like television. There was no practiced choreography of positions, or semblance of order. It was just a guy mixing drinks, it was nothing, then it was everything.

All night I struggled to sleep. Every time I closed my eyes, I saw Casper's legs on the floor, Dev above him, his shoulders moving up and down. I wondered, *Would Dev have told me about it if I hadn't been right there?* He'd be right that I couldn't handle it, not like Presley had, anyway—casually pulling an overdose-reversing agent from her handbag, then trading basketball stats with the EMT as they readied the ambulance. I wasn't sure when Dev finally came to bed, when he got up to go running, or if he'd slept at all in between. The next morning, he went to work like he hadn't spent the previous evening doing chest compressions on a young man who'd collapsed on the men's room floor.

Simon and Victor got up early, too, to drive back to Manhattan. Simon pulled me aside before he left, while Victor put their bags in the car.

"You going to be okay?" he asked. "I don't think *The Official Preppy Handbook* covers this stuff." He was smiling, but his eyes were full of concern.

"If I'm being honest? I don't know," I said. "But I'm glad you were here." I meant it. I thought giving Simon a front-row seat to the disconnect that was my world and Dev's would have simply compounded my feeling of being alone, but the opposite ended up being true.

Simon squeezed my arm. I promised we'd visit. He promised Kate she could lead a hike.

—∞—

It was STEAM day at the beach club—no matter that I felt like I'd already been run over by a steamroller. I'd signed the clipboard for Kate and Toby to participate weeks ago, and while the space between then and now felt like eons, she'd prepped all week. I couldn't tell her no. The bacch was all systems go as well, and I felt like I was straddling a crack in the ground. I wasn't sure which side to jump to—I could allow myself to get swallowed up by the yacht club and the weekend's inevitable (and seductively distracting) drama, or face head-on the reality of my rocky marriage and the uncertainty of what that meant. I knew which one I preferred. I also knew which one I had to choose.

At the club, I stared at Kate and Toby, at the healthy flush in their cheeks, until they noticed me and giggled. More than anything that morning, I wanted them to always, always be okay.

"Kate, you look very professional," I said.

"I changed my idea last minute, Mom," Kate said. She wore her khaki jumpsuit, pants tucked into hiking boots. "It's a surprise."

"I can't wait to see it," I said, trying to act like it was the only thing taking up an obscene amount of real estate in my mind.

Kate carried her lime-green poster board folded under her arm, with Toby in his bathing suit trailing behind her, a reluctant accessory to her master plan. Tables lined the concrete patio, and folded cards bearing children's names sat three feet apart. Kate used rocks to prop her poster to standing. In bold, black letters, the top read: How To Escape From A Sinking Ship.

I had never felt so seen.

Kate read the bullet points under the title of her project out loud: "Stay calm, think clearly, move fast." She pointed to a picture of a red life jacket as well as a circular flotation device. There was a whistle, a long-sleeve shirt, and a lifeboat. In the corner, Kate had pasted a magazine cutout photo of a woman doing yoga. She said it was for staying calm and taking deep breaths. I said it was the best project I'd ever seen.

Stay calm. Think clearly. Move fast.

Enough, I thought. *I need to stop rearranging lounge furniture and face the fact that our ship is sinking beyond my control.* I would go see Dev. I'd make him talk to me. I'd schedule a walk-in appointment with the receptionist if I had to. I'd go now, while the kids were engrossed in STEAM-day activities.

"And Mom, if the boat is *listing*—that means leaning over—you should go to the highest part of the deck. Toby! Where's your life jacket?" Kate posed with her hands on her hips, like a lifeguard on duty. "Take a picture and send it to Lilly and GE"

I did as I was told, though I knew Lilly wouldn't see the text until she retrieved their cell phones from the "mindfulness locker"— they'd followed their impromptu tour of downtown Manhattan with a silent retreat at Kripalu. I had to keep reminding myself they were unreachable.

Three tables to our left, Heidi leaned over a robot as it walked on legs made of spatulas. Ellery poked it with a toothpick. Heidi hissed,

"Ellery, Grandpa didn't make his intern work the weekend so you could break the robot before the judges even see it."

Now was my chance. Kate would be all set with her project for a few hours, and Toby had already abandoned his, choosing instead to play tag in the sand, corralled on either side by his favorite lifeguards, the ones who ran camp. If I was going, I needed to do it now.

"Charlie, can you give me a hand?" I jumped. I hadn't even seen Lacy striding over to us. She took my arm and led me to the cabanas, in the opposite direction of the club's exit. We passed the cabana where I had run into Oliver, then Lacy's, and we stopped outside of a tiny house on the far corner, next to the sand.

"You haven't even used it yet," Lacy said. "What's the point of winning?"

Lacy opened the door to the cabana that I'd "won" in the bonfire lottery. The truth was, it felt like more trouble to put something in it for only one week, to pretend to own something to which I really had no claim. Besides, I didn't actually have more than what was already in my bag. I didn't have kayaks or paddleboards or mini bars that were simply waiting to occupy beachfront property. If it didn't come with a crystal ball or a time machine waiting inside, it was of no use to me.

Lacy ushered me inside the empty cabana and let out a huff. She closed the door behind us. The enclosed space reminded me of being in the restaurant bathroom the night before. I wanted nothing to do with it. The kids would be okay for a few hours, but I had to get home, drive to Bradley, possibly wait my turn to get a moment alone with Dev . . . I didn't have time to waste with Lacy enclosed in a tiny cabana, breathing in her perfume. Had she always worn perfume at the beach? What other signs of obvious psychopathy had I overlooked?

Lacy stood with her arms crossed over her chest, a medium-size white tote at her feet.

"Your husband's place of employment is turning into a huge pain in my ass," she said. "I still can't get ahold of Teague at the goddamn rehab. Who do they think they are, Kripalu?"

I almost laughed as I imagined Teague in silent meditation next to Lilly and Edgar. I had ignored four of Lacy's calls the night before, after coming home. The first voice mail said she needed to see me. She hadn't left another after that; she just kept calling.

"You want to be in the know, Charlie? Well, here's the whole deal," Lacy said. "Heidi doesn't even know all of this. Teague was fully in charge of our investments. Warren's and mine. When his *habit* got the better of him, we didn't know it until it was too late. Warren and I lost a lot. I understand that it's a *disease* or whatever, but *we* didn't have insurance for Teague to go off the deep end. These condos have to go through. Do you understand what I'm saying? I'll do whatever it takes."

I sat down on the cabana's patio floor, next to the bag. I was suddenly so very tired. "Lacy, why are you telling me this? Can't we just go back to it being none of my business?" If not for Dev's "place of employment," Casper might have died on the bathroom floor.

Her face changed. Gone was any facade of a smile. "Why else are you here if not to make everything your business?" she said. "The investor will be at the bacch tonight. He's adamant about the deadline. He's going deep-sea fishing in the Keys, and he doesn't want to be bothered after the season ends here. Between you and me, he's kind of an asshole. But I can't do this without him. I have *obligations*."

"Like what?" I said, still on the floor, eyeing the closed door.

"Like I want to design those condos," Lacy said. "If I have to sit through another year of tennis club and technology board at the school, I'll lose my fucking mind. And if we lose the ski condo, I'll actually die."

"Do you really want to decimate the health care of an entire population to pay the mortgage on your ski chalet and assuage your identity crisis?" I said, trying to keep my voice level. "Lacy, you can't be serious."

"Charlie, we've been over this. The solution here can be good for us both." She stood facing me, then started rustling around in the tote bag.

"But your problem is not my problem," I said. "Not anymore. It never really was. And your 'solution' is delusional. I'm not going to sabotage my marriage—not to mention help take away necessary health care from *real people*—because your lifestyle suddenly feels unstable, for the first time in your life, and that's just not your vibe."

As I stood and reached for the cabana door, Lacy pulled her phone out of the bag. She stepped forward, blocking the door. I willed myself to not stumble backward, to not shrink in her shadow.

"Let me give you some motivation," she said. "I thought you might feel some allegiance to the clinic because of Dev. I get it. I do. We have to look out for our husbands. Without their jobs, their egos, what are they? God knows, Warren is a mess over this deal. But, speaking of ego, I'd hate for Dev to see something like this."

She gave me the phone, but I couldn't make sense of what was on the screen. It was a picture, but it couldn't be real. I was in a white dress, seated on the bar at the yacht club, and Oliver stood close, nearly between my knees. His hands were on the bar's countertop, on either side of my hips.

I dropped the phone like a hot potato. It clattered to the concrete floor, and Lacy dusted it off. She probably had extras in her boat closet. My hands shook, while Lacy looked like she was waiting in line at Nordstrom, like planting a ticking bomb in my marriage was nothing to her, a bump in her day she hadn't planned for. She handed the phone back to me. "You can scroll," she said.

There we were, facing each other at the bar. He was handing me a drink. There was Oliver with his hand on my leg, his fingers at the hem of my white dress. No. No no no. The last showed my hand on his chest, our heads bent toward each other. There was no way to know I was stopping it. What I'd intended didn't matter anymore.

I felt so small, like I lived in that tiny stupid house. I'd gotten so caught up in needing reassurance—that I was good enough, that I was wanted—I'd turned into someone who was neither.

"Are we clear?" Lacy said. "Because I'm on a deadline here."

I nodded.

"The kids are staying for camp, right? STEAM day and all that bullshit?"

I nodded again. It was all I could manage.

"So go to the clinic now," Lacy said, like she was doing me a favor. "See that Elvis person. Convince her to cave. Or get me some kind of financial records. I don't have time to play games. We still need Teague's approval, but I can't reach him. Warren is working on it, but I'm not relying on him. If I can show how the clinic is doomed anyway, our investor will go ahead with the deal. He'll agree to front his own capital and use his connections to push the deal forward if he knows we have an upper hand. You can have a future in this town, Charlie. You, Dev, the kids. But it's like I said, we have to be able to look out for one another. Don't let me down. Don't let the bacch be your final party."

Lacy stepped away from the cabana door. She opened it and stood there impatiently, like I was the one who'd been stalling. I blinked in the sudden sunlight. The water was calm and such a ridiculous shade of dark blue, I felt like it was mocking me. How was it possible that everything out there was the same as it had been when I'd entered the cabana?

Lacy sighed, taking in the same view. "We're just so lucky to live here."

chapter 31

From Rumford I turned the car onto the highway but instead of taking the exit for the clinic, I kept driving. I followed the highway until I reached a small town in southeastern Connecticut.

Stony Hills was glass and steel, like a snow globe nestled in the woods; I imagined it raining down quinoa instead of snow. Walking trails spread like spider legs from either side of the property. Inside there were no stacks of old magazines in the waiting room, no TV perpetually tuned to a cooking show. The decor made me feel cleaner, more fortified, just by walking in the door, like an architectural cleanse. Even the recirculated air felt nourishing.

Succulents in tiny white vases lined the front desk where I asked for Teague. The receptionist, in a deceptively bright and promising tone, told me no, it wasn't possible to see Teague Anderson under any circumstances. She said it like I had ordered the sea bass, and, so sorry, they'd eighty-sixed it an hour ago.

"You have to be family," she repeated.

"Please, could you tell me if he has, like, a scheduled break? Just thirty seconds?" I'd practiced my spiel in the car, but now I could hear the pleading in my voice. "I'm here for his wife. She's my friend. I really like her. I never thought I was good at, well, people. But I'm realizing how much she matters to me, and I'm here, and it sort of feels like a rom-com, like I drove all this way to make a grand gesture, even though it's Teague I need to see. But I do *not* want anything romantic with him.

What I mean is, I'm trying to do the right thing, not just the easy thing. And isn't that kind of . . . your thing here?"

The receptionist looked at me like she wasn't sure if she should actually respond.

"I want to help my friend," I said. "You have to let me help. It's the only thing I *can* do right now."

I realized it was true as I said it: both that Heidi was my friend, and that if I stalled this deal, she wouldn't remain beholden to a high-stakes business agreement to which she never agreed, one that would otherwise slip through the gates thanks to my low threshold for transgression and Lacy's low threshold for blackmail.

For all Lacy knew, I'd followed her orders and fled straight to Dev and Presley. While Lacy could still ruin my life in Rumford, she couldn't take everyone down with her. I was sure I could convince Teague to refuse to sign whatever Faustian papers Warren had when he heard what the trade-off would be. And it was the only move I felt I had left. Teague was the opposite of an outsider to Rumford; we weren't the same in any way. But he *was* on the outside now, literally. And he was my only hope.

He was at Stony Hills for a reason. Teague spoke the language of privilege and deals and wire transfers, but didn't he also know what it meant to let things go way too far over the line? To make decisions that needed mending? If I could get him on my side, on *Heidi's* side, he could create some kind of logjam, and the investor would walk. It would buy us some time, at least.

Fleeing to Presley like Lacy commanded wasn't going to change anything—I knew that much. Anyway, Presley was the last person on earth to whom I wanted to confess. In the end, I knew I couldn't control whether Lacy showed Dev the photos. It was all a game to her. But none of it felt like a game to me, not anymore. Part of me—down, down, deep down—almost wanted to admit to Dev how lonely I had been, how much I missed him, and just see where it left us. But being that honest scared me in equal measure.

And first, I had to lie to this receptionist.

"Does she know you're here?" the receptionist asked.

"Who?"

"Mr. Anderson's wife," the receptionist said. She tapped her pen on the glass countertop. I felt like Toby, caught trying to steal a snack from an upper kitchen cabinet.

"No. Not exactly."

Stalling for time to think and distracted by the tapping, I looked down at the receptionist's fingers. She wore a diamond engagement ring on her left hand.

"Wow, your ring," I said. "Congratulations!"

She admired it herself, and her face lit up. She met my eyes again, so I lowered my voice.

"The thing is, I'm here to surprise Heidi. It's her anniversary. And Teague is *here*. I mean, can you imagine? Not that this will happen to you, of course. Your marriage will be spectacular. Please, I promise, you won't even know I'm here."

The receptionist looked down at her ring again and sighed. "I'll check his schedule. I really shouldn't. But I did talk to Mrs. Anderson this morning, and she's so very generous."

I held my breath. The receptionist clicked a few keys. Her face scrunched in on itself.

"I'll be so quick," I promised again. I was so close! "Meep meep. Like the Road Runner."

But the receptionist just stared at the screen. "I'm sorry," she mumbled. "It won't be possible."

"But—"

"It's not possible at this time," she said again. She wouldn't meet my eyes now. She looked confused, but she wasn't budging. "I'm sorry."

I wanted to cry. I wanted to stomp my feet like a child.

"Please," I said again. "It's really important."

The receptionist said quietly, "I'm very sorry. I can't help you. If you don't leave, I'll need to call security."

I wanted to say, *Listen, I'm not the one doing the blackmail here*, but I didn't think appearing even more unbalanced would help my cause. Security was one way to avoid having to go to the bacch, but it would be a lot harder to explain to Dev.

"Charlie? What are you doing here?"

Presley stood at the sign-in desk. *Presley*, all six feet of her, was there in the lobby. So much for driving all the way to Connecticut to avoid running into her at the clinic. My shock at seeing her was exceeded only by my surprise at seeing whom she was with: Jeannine. I stared, waiting for my brain to move the pieces into a sensible order. Presley put her hand on Jeannine's back and guided her to a couch with a pile of paperwork. Was she moonlighting at the rehab, too? Presley looked like she hadn't slept since the restaurant resuscitation. She wore basketball shorts and a Bradley YMCA T-shirt. Her hair was in a messy bun, and round-framed glasses sat askew on her nose. I never knew she needed glasses. She motioned to the wall of windows.

"I keep basketball clothes in my car," Presley said after I asked my least pressing question. "We came straight from the hospital."

"We?" I looked back at Jeannine, hunched over the paperwork and filing through her wallet for ID and health insurance cards. Was she here about something for Teague? She moved slowly, like someone had siphoned off the energy that usually buzzed around her. "You and Jeannine?"

"And Casper." Presley looked out the window, so I did, too, as if I'd see Casper out there, leaning against a station wagon.

"Casper? Why? What about Teague?"

Presley blew air out of pursed lips, making loose strands of her hair lift and fall. "Of course, Casper. His mom and I spent the night in the hospital, calling inpatient rehabs. They had a sudden opening here, so we came straight over." She rubbed her forehead with her hands. "Charlie, who the heck is Teague? How do you know Jeannine?"

I felt like my brain was made of taffy, expanding and contracting. Casper's mother was Jeannine. Jeannine was Casper's mother. Casper was her son, the one who left town for a while, then returned. He was the patient Dev told me about, the one he worried about, the one who was going to meetings and got penicillin for his girlfriend's kid because he was in recovery and trying to live his life. The one whose chest Dev had compressed the night before. Jeannine was so happy when I saw her at book club, happy Casper was home. I thought her son had just been at college, maybe doing some traveling. I remembered Dev saying it all defied prediction, his patients, what they struggled with and how much.

"Is Dev with you?" Presley looked for him. "He could have called me."

"No," I said, shaking my head. "That's not why I'm here. Dev doesn't know I'm here."

Presley put her hands on her hips. "Charlie, I haven't slept in forty-eight hours, so you better just spell out what's going on."

I hesitated, but had to come to grips with reality: I wasn't making any headway on my own. I was up against a wall for the second time that day. So I explained what I could—how Teague was Heidi's husband, how Jeannine worked for Heidi, and Heidi was my friend, and how I desperately needed to speak to Teague about something. Something time sensitive. Something I couldn't tell Dev, not yet.

I'd spent so much time avoiding Presley. Years, really. Now, Presley was the only one who could help me. I put my hand on her arm. I didn't look away, even as I felt my eyes well up with tears of shame, hurt, and desperation.

"They won't let me see him," I said. "It's really important. Can you use your doctor membership card? Please, Presley, I only need five minutes. I've never asked you for anything."

And I've given you so much is what I wanted to say, but I didn't. I wasn't sure I believed it anymore, at least, not enough to use Dev as an excuse for my own poor behavior.

Presley slumped into the window. But then, like someone changed her batteries, she straightened up. It reminded me of that first time seeing Presley at the clinic, how it was like she zippered herself up before returning to work, growing two inches and setting her jaw, ready to vanquish whatever exhaustion or insecurity she felt on the inside.

"They're already doing me a favor, getting Casper in," Presley said. "But fine. Let me see what I can do."

Presley walked right through the double doors, not even glancing at the receptionist. I sat across from Jeannine on the slippery beige couch. I put a hand on the window, as if the cold glass could anchor me. "Jeannine, I didn't know," I said. "I'm sorry."

Without looking up from the forms, Jeannine said, "I heard you were there last night."

I nodded. I couldn't fathom what to say about it, what Jeannine could possibly want to hear. Jeannine set the papers on the table next to her. The circles under her eyes were dark, almost purple. "He's a good boy."

"I know."

I thought about Toby, how I spent so much time worrying about keeping him out of the road, away from the water. I stressed about screen time, avoided buying laundry detergent pods that looked like oversize Mike and Ike candies. What must Jeannine worry about, with an adult for whom she could no longer childproof the world? The scale was unimaginable.

"He had a scholarship to play baseball," Jeannine said. "But he tore his rotator cuff senior year. He lost his scholarship. He worked on his uncle's fishing boat to save for tuition. I couldn't cover all of it; I wish I could have. Then he worked construction. I didn't know he was still taking the pills." Jeannine took a shaky breath. "I didn't know he made the switch to needles."

Casper's body on the floor of the men's room flashed into my mind. His black shoes, black pants, laying still against the white tiles. I pictured his hands, fingers slightly curled. He was Jeannine's little boy. My eyes began to fill again. My body felt as cold as the window. I forced myself to breathe deeply. This wasn't my place to fall apart.

"Does Heidi know?" I asked. I wasn't sure I was capable of keeping one more secret.

Jeannine nodded. "How do you think we're here?" She chuckled, but it sounded like tin. "Heidi is covering Casper's stay," she said softly. "I promised to pay her back. She said she won't let me, but I'll try."

I moved to sit next to Jeannine and put my hand on her back.

"He'll be okay," I said, having no idea if it was true, but desperately wanting it to be. I didn't try to fill the silence after that. I sat with Jeannine until Presley banged through the double doors and gave me a hard look. It was enough to make me stand, like a child awaiting instruction. Presley softened to speak to Jeannine.

"We should go. I'm going to catch a ride back with Charlie. Jeannine, will you be okay driving home? You can take your time here. I asked the coordinator to come out and speak with you. They'll take good care of him, I promise. You can call me any time. You have my cell."

Jeannine thanked Presley, and she hugged us both. Then Presley took my arm, not lightly, and tugged me through the glass double doors into the parking lot.

"You drove, right?"

I pulled my arm away. "Sure, but what about Teague? What did you find out? Can I talk to him first?"

"It's not possible," Presley said, not slowing her stride.

"Wait, did you try? I know we're not best friends, but Presley, please. I really need this. Can you just get him to come out for a walk or something?"

"Look, Charlie, we can't do a walk and talk with him. I'm not fucking Aaron Sorkin. You have to trust me on this one. I'll explain in the car." Presley power walked to the Subaru. I followed her, out of options except to return to Rumford like I'd left it—empty-handed, but with an unexpected riding buddy in tow.

chapter 32

We were two hours from home. Two hours to figure out what to do once I returned, without any wrench from Teague to toss into the plan, apparently. As I waited for Presley to explain why we'd left without seeing him, she leaned her head against the passenger-side window and closed her eyes. I was so accustomed to her sunny disposition that the silence, and her obvious exhaustion, was jarring.

"Have you really not slept?" I asked, once we were on the highway.

"Sleep is overrated," Presley said, rubbing her eyes.

"Have you showered?"

Presley shifted to face me. "Do you care?"

"No. Yes," I said. "I mean, it's just—"

"What?"

"Nothing."

Presley raised her eyebrows. I fidgeted in the seat. I slapped the radio on to a pop station.

When I started softly singing along to Maroon 5, I thought, *Oh God, is this rock bottom?*

"What you did for Jeannine . . . and for Casper," I started to say. And then, strangely, got choked up. I wasn't the one who'd had to save him. I wasn't the one who had to get the call in the middle of the night. It just hit me, how heavy it all was. How much Presley, and Dev, must be carrying. "I'm glad you were there."

Presley's face softened. "Me too."

The high-pitched voice of Adam Levine filled the car. I turned the volume up to fill the silence between us that followed, but then Presley spoke over it. "And I'm glad you're here giving me a ride home, Charlie, even though I still don't fully understand why you came."

Join the club, I thought. There was still so much I didn't understand.

I raised my voice over the radio before I even could process what I was saying. I really hated this song. "Presley, why did you even ask Dev to come up here?"

"Why did I what?" She looked genuinely confused, and I remembered how little she'd slept.

"No night shifts," I said. "No being on call. You promised Dev it would be better up here. We were supposed to be okay here. That was the deal. Why did you convince him to come if it would still be billion-hour days to keep the place afloat?"

A long-haul truck passed on my side of the car, making me feel like I was driving in a tunnel. The car accelerated before I realized I was pressing my foot down. Trees blurred in the windows.

Presley threw her hands up. "Holy shit, Charlie. I didn't *promise* anything. I said we had an unexpected opening, and I needed to fill it. I thought Dev would recommend some hungry new grad. That was why I came back for graduation, to snag someone for the next year. Then Dev signed the contracts so fast, I don't even know if he read them. I didn't pressure him, Charlie. He *asked* if he could take the job. I assumed—"

"What," I snapped, only partially aware of the angry, confused tears now running down my cheeks. "What did you assume? That he wanted out? From me? From the life he didn't exactly plan, or wouldn't have chosen if he actually had the chance?"

"What? No! I *assumed* you told him to do it," Presley said, looking at me with genuine surprise.

"That's ridiculous!" I shouted. "We both know you're the one he listens to."

"Dev *asked* for the job, Charlie. He asked me. I'm sorry if you got the wrong impression, but that's between him and you. Y'all have a lot you need to talk about, yet you're out here trying to find Teague Anderson? What on earth does he have to do with anything you have going on? What could possibly be so urgent?" This time, Presley looked at me, her eyes sharp.

I opened my mouth, to say what, I had no idea, but Presley wasn't finished.

"And listen. Life isn't peaches for me either right now. I bust my butt for that clinic twenty-four seven. It's not like Dev and I are at happy hour. We're not 'hanging out.'" Presley shook her head. "I don't even have houseplants. No one is waiting up for me. I'm not breaking even in the personal life department either, in case you haven't noticed."

I gripped the steering wheel. Of course I hadn't noticed. I hadn't thought of anyone but myself. "Why was he so eager to drop everything then? Why was he so desperate to get away from *me* and join you?" I cringed at saying it out loud, but there was no holding back now.

Presley raised her hands in the air. "Charlie, don't be ridiculous. Dev has *never* chosen me over you. And if you didn't want to be here, why did you agree to the move? Why move here to start over if you're just going to be miserable all the time?"

"I'm not! I'm *happy!*" My breath came in waves. My hands felt sweaty on the wheel.

"Sure," Presley muttered. "Me too."

We looked at each other then, Presley in her glasses and tangled hair, me with my eyes wild and still wearing my beach club coverup. We burst out laughing. We laughed louder than the blaring radio, until we both had to wipe our eyes, until I was afraid I'd veer off the road if I didn't catch my breath. On the list of things I didn't want to explain to Dev—which was, to be fair, growing longer by the minute—going full *Thelma & Louise* with Presley "Elvis" Keen was up there.

I knew Presley wasn't really the one I was angry with or hurt by. She wasn't the one I wanted to scream at. And she wasn't the one from whom I needed reassurance, or at least an explanation.

Still, there was one thing I had to ask, and if the answer wasn't one I could deal with, I could still spare the time to ditch her at a Dunkin'.

"Presley, when you came over . . . the other night. At the cottage. When I was at book club. Was it just coffee?"

Presley looked at me like I was driving without hands. "What? Charlie, of course. I mean, we talked. You should ask Dev about it. You should talk to your husband—make him talk to you. But nothing *happened*, Charlie." Her eyes were softer now, behind the glasses.

I didn't know what I thought I should do anymore. I didn't know who I'd become since moving to Rumford, or maybe even who I'd been before. Maybe I didn't really know Dev either. If I did, I wouldn't be interrogating his best friend on I-95 instead of talking to him. But we hadn't really gotten to figure that stuff out—what we wanted, how to even talk about what we wanted—before life had swooped in with other plans, two of them, to be exact.

When Presley put her hand on my shoulder, I stiffened reflexively. I steeled myself for her voice to fill with pity, like caramel, trying to soften the blow of the dissolution of life as I knew it. For her to say *Sometimes things just don't work out the way we want, no matter how much we still, desperately, want them to.* Had I even made that clear to Dev? How much I wanted us to be okay?

But she used her no-bullshit voice instead. I was beginning to like that voice.

"Charlie, don't be stupid. Dev has always loved you. What he's going through, the way he's acting, it isn't *about* you. You're going to have to get over yourself, first of all. And you've got to say this stuff to him, not me. You need to use your words, girl. You both do."

Presley turned the radio off. We sat in silence for a few minutes. My back was wet with sweat. I fiddled with the air-conditioning vent, and cool air started to fill the car. I took a deep breath. "When the twins were babies, Dev and I tried to take them and James Dean for a hike. My friends were off becoming graduate students and artists and professionals, and I didn't recognize myself anymore. So Dev said we had to get outside and accomplish something, as a family. That's how he is, right? Got a problem? Don't overthink it. There's the parking lot, and there's the summit, and you just walk from point A to point B."

Presley smiled in recognition. She knew Dev like I did. It actually felt good to share that with someone.

"Anyway, we were halfway between the apartment and the trailhead when we realized neither of us had remembered to make sure James Dean had pooped before putting him in the car. We didn't realize he'd pooped *in* the car until there was traffic, and Dev braked suddenly on a descending road."

"Uh-oh." Presley brought her hand to her mouth.

"Dog poop *flew* from the hatchback into the center console air-conditioner vent."

"Charlie, no."

"Oh yes," I said. "I froze. I stared at it in horror. I started crying, because—gross—but also, it felt like an indictment. The twins were crying in their car seats, because they were always crying, and I remember *shouting*, 'How are we supposed to be parents? We can't even take a dachshund for a hike!' I was fully freaking out. But Dev, he reached for my hand. And you know what he said?"

Presley leaned back in her seat.

"He said, 'Shit happens, Charlie. We can still go hiking.' We were still in traffic, and there was dog shit in the AC vent, and there was nothing to do but keep driving."

"He's always so fucking calm, isn't he," Presley said.

"He's kind of an asshole that way, right?" I said, smiling now.

"You're right that Dev likes a good point A to point B," Presley said. "But I think that's why you've always been good for him. You're just the right amount of zigzag. I'm sorry he hasn't been honest with you, Charlie. And it's not my place, but I hope you do hold his feet to the fire sooner than later and get him to tell you what's really going on with him, because it sure as hell isn't an affair."

I let Presley's words hang in the air between us.

"This place, Rumford, I mean, I think it makes people lose touch with reality," I said. "It makes me feel like a character in a movie. I've let stuff happen here that feels like a fever dream, like it was happening to someone else. But it was me. The whole time, it was me."

I was so tired of something else having power over me: Lacy's secrets, Dev's secrets, the growing pile of my own. So I did it. I told Presley about Lacy's vendetta against the clinic, watched her eyes grow wide and angry. And then, the words wouldn't stop. Everything spilled out: Oliver and the photos, how I'd convinced myself of an affair between her and Dev at the same time I'd acted like my own actions had no consequences. I told her why I'd hightailed it to the rehab, what I'd hoped to get out of Teague. I told her about the book club, the pot gummies, how—high and hurting—I'd disclosed to Lacy that the clinic was hanging by a thread.

It felt terrible, but also really good, to finally put it all out in the open, outside of my own head, like a steaming pile of dog shit that at least, now that it was sitting there between us, I could actually begin to deal with.

"I'm sorry," I said. "I'm really sorry. I thought if I could convince Teague to stonewall the condo deal, I could buy more time, figure something out. I don't want to lose Heidi. I don't want to lose Dev." I felt my eyes well up again, and I swiped them angrily.

"Charlie, don't be so sure Dev is going to up and leave you. Are you going to tell him what happened with Oliver?" Presley's voice was gentle. I wasn't sure I deserved it.

"I have to, right? That's what adults do. I need to take responsibility. It felt good to feel wanted, and I think I'm allowed that. But it could have gone so wrong."

Presley sighed. "You need to grow up, yes, but you also need to accept the squiggly, awkward truth that being a grown-up means making choices, girl. And sometimes making mistakes. And taking responsibility for them, yes, but not just pawning them off on the person you hurt so they can feel shitty and punish you, like that solves the problem.

Shit happens, right? But shit gets put back together. So how are you going to clean it up, Charlie? How are you going to keep it going? You got me?"

If all that happened to put us in the car together that day wasn't surreal enough, I couldn't believe it was Presley "Elvis" Keen, of all people, giving me permission to not tell Dev about the night at the yacht club, but to carry it myself, and to figure out what I wanted, what it all meant, before I let it blow up our lives together.

"Okay, Coach," I said. "I hear you."

"And Charlie. Teague is not going to help you."

"What? Why? Did you talk to him?" God, had Presley been sitting on this info this whole ride?

"Not exactly."

Presley told me what she knew. I kept driving. When she was done, I turned the radio back on. I would drive straight to the yacht bacch. I could take care of everything there, one way or another, but I had to hurry.

chapter 33

Dev called when we were twenty miles from Rumford. I turned to Presley and pressed a finger to my lips, not knowing how exactly to explain our presence in the car together, blasting Journey on the classic rock station. I told him to meet us at the club, to bring my dress. Screw the mask. Kate could handle her and Toby's costumes. Dev could wear or not wear whatever he wanted.

"We don't have to stay long," I said. "There's just this one thing I have to do. Then you and I are going to talk. Really talk. Okay?"

I hung up before he could answer. Presley slapped her palm on the dashboard and sang along at the top of her lungs to Tom Petty.

It was tradition for the kids to have a costume party at the club before the end-of-season revelry of the yacht beach peaked. The kids' party would end at seven. I aimed to leave by 7:05. As I took the exit to Rumford, I meditated on two intentions: avoiding Lacy until I could talk to Heidi, and avoiding Oliver entirely.

When we arrived at the yacht club, I grabbed my dress, a slip of white overlaid with gold lace, from the back of Dev's car.

"Do you think the bar has coffee?" Presley yawned.

"How do you feel about mudslides?" I offered.

Presley was still wearing the workout clothes she'd thrown on at the hospital. Her hair spilled from the messy topknot she hadn't bothered to redo. She winked at me. "You got this, girl." Then she hitched up her basketball shorts and walked into the club like she'd been there a million times.

I dressed in the concrete changing room, the one from which I'd seen the group of boys emerge that first night. I remembered how they'd seemed like an entirely different species, a genetically engineered breed of teen, birthed in sepia tones. I peered in the mirror and tried to muster some swagger of my own.

I found Dev and the kids at the corner of the club. Dev gripped Toby's hand as Kate climbed the deck railing and jumped the few feet to the ground. She still wore her khaki jumpsuit and hiking boots. Toby was a crocodile, and the felt teeth of the costume's open mouth flapped over his face as he tugged on Dev's hand, desperate to be set free.

"She practiced saying 'Crikey!' all afternoon," Dev said as I gushed over their costumes. He wore the same gray pants and white button-up as the night of the gala.

"Still no belt," I said, hooking my thumb into one of the empty belt loops encircling his waist. It made Dev look up from straightening Toby's alligator head. *We could just leave now,* I thought. The four of us. I could avoid Lacy entirely. I could send Kate to pickpocket Lacy's phone at the beach club the next day, then drop it in the ocean. I had options. The noise of the party faded as Dev looked at me. He was the place I felt safe. I knew if I ran away from what I needed to do, I'd never find my way back there.

"Put your party face on, bitches! Dr. Dev, where is your party face?" Heidi rounded the corner of the deck with Poppy at her side, and I dropped my hand. Dev took a step back, clearing his throat.

"I think it's at the bar," he said.

"Where's Ellery?" Kate squealed. Heidi pointed around the side of the club, and Kate ran to find her friend. There was no escaping now.

"Stay with Toby!" I called. "There's someone watching them, right?"

Heidi waved her hand, like I was silly for asking, even though it didn't exactly answer my question.

"Elvis is at the bar, by the way," I told Dev. "She doesn't know anyone; you should go help her out. I'll meet you there." I waved my hand as if to shoo him away.

Dev gave me a confused look. "You just called her Elvis."

I grinned and said, "I know. Don't make it weird," as he walked around the side of the club.

Heidi's dress was a deep blue. Her mask was a peacock. Poppy's dress was solid black. It was the first time I'd seen her wear a dark color.

"Are you in mourning?" I said.

"It's the last party of the summer," Poppy said, like it explained everything. When I continued to stare, she explained, "Nothing counts tonight. It's like, existential. So I wear black."

"This is a new side of you," I said. "I think I like it."

Poppy sighed. "After this, we're stuck looking down the barrel of the next school year. Lacrosse practices, Russian math tutors, family dinners. Tonight has to last us until next summer. Go bold, then home."

"Well, you're not going straight home. Are you packed?" Heidi nudged Poppy.

Poppy giggled. In addition to her bold fashion choice, I didn't think I'd seen her this loose before. "I've been packed for a week."

"Where are you going?" I asked. "I meant to ask you this morning. Sorry, I was, um, distracted."

"LA," Poppy said. She broke into a smile. "I'm visiting an old friend."

Heidi snorted. Poppy slapped her on the arm, giggling again like a teenager.

"It's a special trip," Poppy said. "A special friend."

"Poppy gets an extended bacchanal," Heidi said. Then she walked up the deck stairs and into the club before I could talk to her. I wasn't ready to follow her and confront that particular bar location. I'd catch her on her way back outside, thanks very much.

"Poppy," I said. "How . . . ?" I wasn't sure what I was trying to ask.

"He only realized a few years ago," Poppy said. "Davis. It's what you're asking, right?"

I nodded. I did want to know: *How does she do it? How does he? How does it work?* Their marriage—any marriage, really.

"We were in a rut, so I asked him what was up. I don't let things go, Charlie, you know that. And he told me."

"And you're okay with it?"

Poppy shrugged, but she was smiling. She wasn't faking it. Her marriage wasn't a competition to her, I realized. It wasn't something to win. It was more than that. She put her hand on my arm as she spoke.

"The thing is, we love each other. We're a good team. We still have chemistry. And we have the boys. For now, it works. Who knows if we'll say the same thing next year. I just don't think we need to rush things, to play by anyone else's rules, you know? It's why I like you, Charlie. You do you." She gave my arm a squeeze.

I blinked. "That's what you think of me?"

"Of course!" Poppy raised her hand for a high five. "That first time I met you, at the coffee shop, I thought, here's someone who isn't trying so hard to come off as perfect."

"Poppy, I've tried exceptionally hard," I said. "I've just consistently failed."

Davis brought Poppy a glass of wine, and she kissed him on the cheek. I tried to keep my face neutral, like Poppy and Davis were packing for their college reunions, not to top off their sex banks before they returned to a marriage built in part around a trust fund and the shared cultivation of elite college athletes. And yet, I watched Poppy hold Davis's hand as she followed him into the tent. Meanwhile, Dev was, I assumed, at the bar with his ex-girlfriend turned best friend. And I was the one hell-bent on not running into the man I'd almost made out with. It was entirely feasible, all in, that Poppy and Davis had a better marriage than I did. They were honest, and they seemed attuned to each other's needs in a way Dev and I certainly hadn't been lately.

If I could just spot Heidi, I'd ask her to walk to the water, away from the crowd for a few minutes. That's all it would take. But Lacy broke into my line of vision instead.

"Charlie, I don't see your party face."

I wanted to tell Lacy where she could put her party face. But I moved the edges of my mouth into what I hoped passed as a smile instead, as I waited for Heidi to reemerge from the club.

"Ivy, go find your friends," Lacy said. Ivy puffed out her lip and huffed.

Before she ran off, I told Ivy she looked very chic. She wore a black sheath dress, pearls, and giant black sunglasses. Her hair was in a tight bun on top of her head, hugged by a tiny tiara. "I thought Holly Golightly was a superhero," Ivy said, hands on her hips.

"It's a costume you'll never regret being shown in your wedding slideshow," Lacy said. "Now get over there. The contest is about to begin."

Lacy was the last person I wanted to be alone with, but before I could slink away, she put her hand on my arm. "We need to talk."

"Sure, I just have to—" I pointed in the general direction of the harbor, anywhere that was away from her.

"Did you talk to Ringo?"

"Elvis?"

"Whatever."

"I did, actually," I said. "We had a good talk." It was true.

Lacy nodded once, assuming we'd talked about what she wanted, and she lifted her mask. Her smile seemed disconnected from the rest of her face. "That wasn't so hard, was it?"

Heidi reappeared with Poppy, hands full of mudslides. Crisis or no, I was not going to drink another mudslide. I used their return to excuse myself before Lacy could press me to go into details. I could find Heidi again—alone—after I checked in with Dev and Elvis.

I stared at the white tent covering the back lawn, sides draped to the grass. A red velvet rope led from the steps of the yacht club deck into the entrance.

"Abandon all hope, ye who enter here," I muttered.

"That's dark, Yellow Elephants."

I froze. I imagined running straight for the tent, leaving a body-shaped hole in the flap like the Kool-Aid Man. Oliver looked so good it made my eyeballs ache. He wore a white linen shirt that skimmed the waistline of his pants. He stood next to me with one hand in his pocket, half smile armed and ready as he brought a glass of something clear and fizzy to his lips. I flailed for something to say that could not possibly be construed as flirting.

"I ate too many pot gummies and got locked in the wine dungeon you built at Heidi's house."

Oliver choked on his drink. Mission accomplished.

"I'm glad you made it out." He coughed into his elbow. I hated him for being attractive even while aspirating a tequila soda. "This was supposed to be for you, by the way." He offered me the glass.

I knew, first of all, I should not take a drink from Oliver. I shouldn't care that he'd just sipped from it, and I certainly shouldn't kind of want to put my lips right where his had been. The allure of the bacch was strong, but it wasn't real. What happened there had real-life consequences, even if I wore a dinky gold mask, even if the reigning members of the Rumford social hierarchy put up an overpriced white tent with siding. A summer in Rumford was not a special vacay I could use to escape the less glamorous parts of my real life.

"Oliver, can I ask you something?"

He handed me the drink again, and I took it this time. "Anything."

"You and Heidi?"

He actually blushed, pink rising to his cheeks, but he didn't deny it.

"You know she's married, right? You know why her husband wasn't there?"

Oliver looked at me for a beat. "She seemed lonely," he said. "Like you."

He reached out, for my arm or for the drink, I wasn't sure. I shifted both away from him.

"Is this, like, a service you offer?"

Oliver put his hands in his pockets. I glanced behind him and saw Dev and Elvis talking at the bar. I needed to get over to them, but I needed his answer first.

"Not officially," he said. "It's just, I come here, and the women—some of them, anyway—seem like they're searching for something. Sometimes, they think that something is me. Who am I to get in the way of their journey?" His mouth lifted into a half smile, the one that, when we first met, made my knees feel drunk. I wanted to slap it off his mouth, leave it hanging crooked from one of the maple trees.

Oliver shrugged. "It's like they stay because they think Rumford is some kind of center of the universe. It's really not."

Now I kind of wanted to slap my own face, too. He might be a smug asshole, but he wasn't totally wrong. "You are different from most of the women here, Yellow Elephants," he said. "I'll give you that."

"I will take that as a compliment, but it needs to be the last one you give me," I said. A bell rang, and children in costumes started to gather near the flagpole. *Shit,* I thought, I still hadn't talked to Heidi.

"I have to go see a costume contest now," I told Oliver. "Do me a favor. Try not to talk to anyone with a slight British accent tonight—tall, dark hair, glasses, shoes."

Oliver flashed me a knowing grin as I stepped away. I looked for the kids, but all I could see were adults in glittering dresses, fitted blazers, and masks that made them look luxuriously demonic. From the bar, I spotted Dev with Elvis near the ledge separating the lawn from the harbor, that infinity pool of manicured grass. I headed over to join them, intending to usher the three of us to the flagpole for the costume contest where I expected to find Heidi.

"Charlie! Over here!" Lacy called from the opposite direction. I gave Dev and Presley the one-minute finger. I noticed that Dev had a bottled water, not a beer. Presley hit him on the arm and mouthed *Talk to her!* My heart and stomach felt like they'd flipped places.

Lacy, Heidi, and Poppy stood on the other side of the lawn, at the corner of the white tent. I felt like a snake trying to shed one layer and find another. There was who I'd been before, who I'd been this summer, and who I wanted to be. All these different versions of me, and none quite fit comfortably, not without effort. It was probably how Lacy felt about retail.

"Great timing, Charlie," Lacy said, as if she hadn't just sharply summoned me. "Our investor is due any moment. I'll introduce you. You really have been pivotal in the success of the development. It won't go unnoticed."

Lacy still thought I'd sealed the deal. And there was Dev, walking over. I didn't have any time. I pushed the words out. "Heidi, I have to talk to you. It's about Teague. Can we go someplace?"

Lacy threw me a reproachful look. She turned to Heidi. "It's nothing."

"Charlie?" Poppy asked evenly.

"It's not nothing," I said.

Lacy groaned impatiently. "It's just the condo development, Heidi. You know, the one Teague and Warren partnered on. Charlie helped with a small detail. That's all she's trying to tell you. Isn't that right, Charlie? Now Teague doesn't have to worry about it. And neither do you."

"That's not it," I said. "Heidi, I'd really rather talk to you alone."

Lacy looked at me like I should join the children's costume contest. "This part really isn't your business, is it?"

"Ugh, can we not talk business at the bacch?" Heidi said.

Poppy pumped her fist in the air. "Second!"

"I couldn't agree more," Lacy said. "Heidi, let me get you another mudslide."

"It's not business," I snapped. *Enough of this.* "He's gone. Teague is gone, Heidi."

Heidi dropped her drink into the grass. Her mouth went slack. She closed her eyes behind the peacock mask.

"They would have told me," Heidi said. "They can't not tell me if he's fucking dead."

I shook my head. "Oh God, no! Heidi, he's not dead! He's just . . . missing. He left rehab. He's AWOL. Warren paid them to wait twenty-four hours before contacting you. But I found out today."

"How did *you* find out?" Heidi said. "Charlie, what's going on?"

"I was there. I'll explain. I was trying to get you alone first, but . . . I'm so sorry, Heidi."

Heidi turned on Lacy before I could say more. "Is this true?"

"That's absurd," Lacy said. "I—Warren—would never."

"They wanted to finish this condo deal first." I talked as quickly as I could, looking only at Heidi. "Lacy wanted me to throw the clinic under the bus, prove that it's going under, so her investor would cover Teague's share and keep the deal moving forward. But I guess Teague's name is still on the project. And Heidi, if he's missing, or, um, compromised, you can argue he's not legally competent. It becomes your decision."

"What the fuck," Heidi muttered.

"Poppy, go get Heidi a drink," Lacy barked.

Heidi put her hand up. "Don't you dare."

That was when I noticed the shimmer behind Heidi. Ellery was dressed as a fairy, ephemeral with her icy-blonde hair and light-green tulle. I wasn't sure how much she heard, or understood, but she took Kate's hand and ran. Heidi watched them go but stood frozen.

"Heidi, I'm so sorry you had to find out this way," I said. "I went to Connecticut this morning, to convince him not to sign, to block the deal. I thought I could try to save . . . something."

Lacy turned on me. "Charlie, you went *there*? We had an agreement."

I threw up my hands. "Did you really think I was going to sell out a business that literally saves lives so you could get an interior designer discount at West Elm?"

"You were happy to sell out your marriage," Lacy hissed.

"What's that supposed to mean?" Dev said, from directly behind me.

I whirled. He held a water and a clear bubbly drink, still full. He was even wearing a mask, pushed up on his forehead. Presley must have found it for him, and he'd put the stupid thing on, for me. It had rhinestones around the eyes and was probably meant for a woman. And I knew, had known all along, that I still really loved him. It made everything else I knew I had to say feel a thousand times worse.

chapter 34

"It's nothing," I said to Dev. "What Lacy said is nothing. But Elvis *was* in Connecticut, and Teague *is* AWOL." I sounded like I was high again.

"I need to find Ellery," Heidi said. She looked back and forth along the lawn.

"Heidi, I thought the kids were all getting ready for the contest. I'm sorry." I spotted Toby by the flagpole. At least he was accounted for. Ivy sat on a low branch of one of the maple trees, legs crossed, a miniature Holly Golightly surveying the crowd from on high.

"I'll check inside," said Poppy. "You hang tight." She handed Heidi her mudslide, and Heidi threw it over her shoulder like it was a balled-up piece of paper, not a half-full cup of twenty-proof chocolate sludge.

Heidi stared at Lacy while Poppy sprinted away. "How could you."

"I didn't know for *sure* he was missing," said Lacy. "I'm not a monster."

"But you suspected?"

"Warren was there," Lacy said. "At the facility." She made air quotes with her long fingers for the word *facility*. "He tried to meet with Teague for three days, but Teague refused to talk to him. So, Warren offered to sweeten the deal."

A storm was gathering inside of Heidi; I could feel it. Her forehead remained placid, but her hands shook. Her mask looked menacing, like a peacock about to go off the rails.

"Sweeten the deal. You mean, like a Big Mac? A Snickers bar? Like a *treat*, Lacy?"

"Something like that."

"Let's be super clear. Warren brought my husband, who is in rehab, drugs."

It was the first time I'd seen Lacy look contrite.

"He didn't *bring* Warren drugs. Don't be ridiculous. He brokered an early release. A fast one. Whatever Teague is doing now is his decision. He's not a child, Heidi. You've known that for years."

Lacy tried to take Heidi's hand, but Heidi slapped it away. "His doctors just determined he wasn't ready. What do you *think* is happening now, Lacy?"

Lacy smoothed her dress self-consciously, but she didn't retreat. "It's a setback, absolutely. But I'm sure he'll turn up. He always does."

Heidi ripped off her peacock mask, and Lacy took a step back.

"You said yourself it was almost a relief when he was gone," Lacy said. "Like you could breathe again."

"That doesn't mean I wanted him to go missing!"

Lacy rolled her eyes. "I'm not a mind reader."

Heidi growled. "I wasn't happy. Most of the time, I forgot I had a choice in the matter. And we had the kids. But Jesus Christ, Lacy." I reached out and took Heidi's hand. She looked at me like she just remembered I was there, that there was still a party going on around us.

"Shit. Charlie, where *are* the kids?"

"Poppy will find them, don't worry," I said, squeezing her hand. "There she is."

Poppy glided across the lawn, but she only had Davis in tow. "I can't find them anywhere."

I looked at Dev, feeling wild panic in my chest. But Dev pointed calmly. Toby was still playing next to the flagpole, pretending to chomp the metal rod with his floppy alligator teeth.

"They took the boat," called a voice from above. It was Ivy Golightly, perched in the tree.

"Ivy, what are you talking about? And why are you up there? You'll tear your stockings," Lacy said.

Ivy rolled her eyes. She looked remarkably like—and also wholly unlike—her mother. "Ellery and Kate," she said. "They took one of the dinghies."

"What?" Heidi called. "Where? Did you see where they went?"

Ivy shrugged. "I saw them take it from the lawn. But I can't see the water from the tree. The stupid tent is in the way."

Kate was in a boat. On the water. With another child. Was she wearing a life jacket? It was Kate we were talking about, so yes, they would wear life jackets. But where on earth would they go? Were they just motoring around? Should I start swimming? I couldn't think. There were too many things that felt impossible, and yet were very much happening. I saw Heidi's mouth moving. I squinted, waiting for something to make sense.

"The island," Heidi repeated. "It's where Teague took Ellery to dig for clams, before he went away. It was their place."

I grabbed Dev's hand and pulled him to the dock while Presley promised to stay with Toby. The launch boat bobbed in the calm water, lines secured to metal cleats.

Poppy, forever my Rumford whisperer, grabbed the keys from a small metal box affixed to the dock.

"You can drive this thing, right?" I didn't wait for him to answer before starting to release the lines. Dev jumped onto the boat and held it to the dock so I could climb aboard.

"Get in," he said.

"I'm trying. It's these stupid heels."

Dev took me by the waist and hoisted me onto the launch boat. He pushed my hips onto the inlaid bench so I was sitting. Then he leaned down, took off my heels, and threw them overboard. I had to admit, it was hot—if under less-than-ideal circumstances.

—∞—

275

"I see it!" I pointed to the dinghy; it was tied to a tree close to the shore of the island. No one was on it. Dev slowed the launch boat. He killed the motor, grabbed a line, and jumped over the side into the murky calf-deep water, soaking his pant legs. I looked down at my gold lace dress and hugged my arms. The sky was turning pink, and the air was cool, especially away from the mainland. We had an hour to return to the club before it was too dark to see clearly.

"Are you coming?" Dev said from the shore of the small island.

I threw my legs over the side of the boat. I lowered myself into the water and sloshed toward him, the muck under my feet both sticky and slippery, as Dev secured the line to a small tree. The girls had tied the dinghy up, too. When we passed, I saw that Dev's and Kate's knots were identical.

The shoreline was dotted with smooth, round rocks, but the interior of the island was a mess of small trees, bushes, and beach grass. It wasn't big, but the brush was thick enough that we couldn't see much. My thoughts still swirling in every direction, I plunged into the beach grass swinging my arms like machetes and started calling Kate's name.

"Charlie, wait," Dev said. "Maybe we should split up."

I spun around and sputtered, "What? I told you, I can explain what Lacy said. Just, you have to hear me out."

Dev looked at me like I'd missed a step. "I meant here," he said calmly. "On the island. To find Kate."

I felt my feet sink two inches farther into the muck. A tiny crab scuttled past my big toe. I looked at the skyline again. The bright pink was growing deeper, darker. No, I decided, I wasn't letting Dev out of my sight. I wasn't going to let him walk away from me.

A flash of green caught my eye, brighter than the leaves or grass. Tied to a low branch of a tree, lilting in the breeze, was a piece of jewel-toned tulle.

"We don't have to search," I said. "Kate left breadcrumbs. This is from Ellery's dress."

I pulled up my feet, one at a time, and the muck made a sucking sound as I plodded toward the branch. Dev walked to the tree where the tulle shimmered. "There's a path behind it," he said.

Path was generous. More seagrass tickled my arms as I pushed it out of my way. I cursed as I stepped barefoot on a sharp rock. Would it have killed someone to leave a spare pair of Sperrys on the launch boat? Dev tried to hold branches out of my way, but as we kept pace, some still whipped back in my face, showering me with water and leaves.

We followed the trail of tulle, and dread settled around me, thick as the humid evening air. Had they gotten lost? Were they scared? Hungry? Kate was capable, but they were children. In the car, Presley had told me to grow up. She wasn't wrong. When was the last time I had really shown up for anyone? I stepped up onto a rock blocking the path, but my bare foot slipped down the side of it. Part of my right leg disappeared into a patch of mud, and my left knee buckled.

"Goddammit," I said, near tears. I slammed my palm onto the ground, splashing more mud onto my dress. My lower half, from the hem of my dress to my feet, looked like I'd been dipped in a chocolate fondue fountain.

Dev stopped walking and turned around. "You okay?" The way he stood there, like he wasn't sure if he should approach, like he wasn't sure if I wanted him to, made something in me come apart.

"I'm really not okay, Dev." My voice wavered.

"Hey, we're going to find them. You know Kate. She lives for this stuff. I'm sure they're fine. This is still Rumford, Charlie; it's not the Everglades."

I wiped at my eyes angrily, smearing mud on my face. I was out there to rescue Kate, not myself, and I felt my exasperation turn to something more heated.

"You can add traipsing through an island to the list of things I cannot get right about this place," I sputtered. "I'm so scared that I've already lost you, and now I've lost Kate on this stupid island, and I sure as hell lost myself somewhere in this gingham-filtered playground."

Dev looked like he was going to say something, but I couldn't stop myself. Whatever reserves I'd had for keeping things inside, I'd left them somewhere along the shore.

"Why didn't you tell me it was *you* who asked Presley for the job? Did you need to get away from me so badly? If I'm not enough for you, if it's not right, Dev, just tell me. I just need to know. We can find the girls and ride back in that boat, and it'll be super fucking awkward, but after all this, at least I'll know."

Dev took off his glasses, like he was about to wipe them on his shirt, then thought better of it and put them back on. He shook his head.

"It's not that," he said. "It's not any of that."

I looked at him. We needed to get the girls. We needed to get back to the club. But it felt like, for just a minute, there were things we could only say on this island, in this moment.

"I did ask to take the job," Dev said. "Something . . . happened at the hospital. Before we moved. Something I didn't tell you about. Then Elvis showed up, and I thought, I can just leave. Before we moved, I felt like I couldn't breathe, Charlie. I had a panic attack at work, in the break room. I was just working all the time. And then I screwed up. I thought it would be different here. Easier." Dev pushed his hair out of his eyes. "I thought I'd feel normal again. But it's not. I'm not. Obviously."

I motioned for him to keep moving. I shuffled beside him. The path was narrow, and I had to squeeze close. It wasn't the worst feeling, his arm warm against mine. I felt a wet drop on my forehead. I hoped it came from the tree overhead, and the sky wasn't opening up. Then I felt another.

"What happened at the hospital, before. Whatever it is, you could have told me," I said more gently this time. "Even here. I saw you with Casper. I know it's not all *Real Housewives of Rumford.*"

We passed another piece of green tulle. We had to be close. Rain pattered through the trees now and soaked my bare shoulders. I tried to walk faster without losing my balance and toppling over again. We both had so much we hadn't shared. I slid in the mud again, but this time I grabbed on to Dev's arm before I could fall. Water dripped from his hair, and curls were plastered to his head, framing his soaked glasses. I reached for his hand. It was warm against the cool rain still smacking the leaves above our heads.

Dev looked down, and instead of answering me, he stopped. "Charlie, you're bleeding."

chapter 35

My calf was smeared with blood. I sat down on a rock. "Is it gapey? Can you tell?"

Dev knelt and lifted my ankle to examine the cut. I couldn't look or I'd pass out, and he'd have to carry me to wrangle the girls, or simply leave me behind. "Just save yourself, and the girls. I'm sure I can forage a mudslide out here," I said, eyes closed.

"Don't be dramatic," Dev grumbled as he used his shirtsleeve to wipe my leg carefully, so as not to spread more mud. "Shame I didn't bring my cashmere scarf."

"Kate probably has a first aid kit," I said, wincing.

Dev held out his hand and pulled me back to standing. "It's a little gapey, sorry, but I think you'll live to see another party."

I groaned, but I held on to his hand. We trudged ahead. In the car on the way home from Connecticut, Presley had said Dev was burned out, like a fire that didn't have any more fuel. I knew the phrase, but Presley had emphasized that it was clinical, or could be, when it was more than a bad mood. Especially when it went on for months. Even as she'd recited a list of red flags—exhaustion, compassion fatigue, moodiness, poor coping—and even as I'd told her about the empties filling our recycling and how Dev had less patience with the kids and woke up already exhausted, I hadn't been 100 percent convinced his behavior didn't still go back to me.

"Dev, you can tell me what happened. It can't be that bad," I said, like nothing could be more obvious. "Failing is my job."

"What are you talking about? I fail at plenty of things, Charlie," Dev said, exhaustion fully apparent in his voice. "We moved here, I took this job so I wouldn't be so overworked and underslept and checked out that I'd nearly kill someone I was supposed to be helping."

My mouth dropped open. What was he saying? If this was true, how could he not tell me this whole time? My leg brushed against a tree limb and stung like hell, but I only gripped his hand harder as we passed another scrap of tulle.

Before I could press him for more, Dev smacked a tree branch and rainwater splattered onto my shoulders. Then he pointed to a clearing.

The shelter, a three-dimensional isosceles triangle of sticks and branches, leaves and beach grass, was the length of a golf cart, though half as tall. Through the brush piled on top, I could see one long stick propped onto two smaller sticks that were each tied together, secured with a leather belt on one side—Dev's belt! A collection of strings sinched the other, my shorts' drawstring likely among them. The sticks framing the front and back were joined in an upside-down V, the apex of which the longer stick rested upon. Smaller branches filled out the sides, leaves, moss, and beach grass unevenly covering the surface.

We ran, the mud squelching under our feet.

Kate sprang from the shelter, looking perfectly at home in her khaki jumpsuit and boots. "Hey, Mama! You found us." I felt immense relief jumbled with pride at seeing this independent, daring kid I'd somehow produced.

Ellery emerged next. Her eyes were puffy and red. Her dress was missing patches of tulle. Mud caked the Mary Janes on her feet. But otherwise, the girls seemed perfectly fine. They were calmly eating cookies, like the marshy island was a Girl Scout camp.

"Kate, did you make this?" I patted the shelter. It didn't budge.

"We both did," Kate said.

pink whales

"How? Tonight?" They couldn't have gathered all those sticks and leaves in the last hour. It was impossible, even for Kate.

"No, Mama, don't be silly," Kate said. "We've been working on it during beach club camp. When the lifeguards go in the cabanas."

Dev cursed, and the girls giggled. Poppy would tear those teenagers a new one when she heard this. "And the cookies?"

"Mama, why do you think my jumpsuit has pockets?" Kate said like it was the most obvious thing in the world.

"Are we in trouble?" Ellery asked.

I put my hand on her shoulder. "No, sweetie. You're not in trouble," I said. "We were worried."

"Do we have to leave now?" she asked.

Did we? Couldn't we all just crawl into the shelter? Tell stories and eat cookies and pretend nothing else mattered? *No,* I thought. *No more hiding.* The rain was letting up, but the sky was dark pink as the sun closed in on the horizon line of the bay. "The sun is almost down," I said. "It's time to go home."

chapter 36

Kate led the way out, holding Ellery's hand. Dev and I trailed behind.

"I had no idea," I whispered, once the girls were a few steps ahead of us. "About what happened. About you. I'm sorry."

"I'm sorry I didn't tell you," Dev whispered back. "And I'm sorry it ended up hurting you, too."

I ducked under a branch, and he moved another out of my way. I took a deep breath, and took his hand in my mud-covered one, even though this time I didn't feel in danger of slipping into anything. I held it tight as I kept talking.

"I know *I'm* not exactly the picture of balance here. I'm not trying to compete with your job," I said. "And I'm not going to compete with Elvis anymore either. I like her, it turns out. I guess I always thought, in the back of my mind, you should have been with her, that you would have ended up with her. But I got pregnant with Kate and Toby, and, well, that was that. Fortunately, I've been informed by Presley herself that I'm an idiot. But if *you* want it to be us, Dev, you can't use work or Elvis or whatever to avoid me when something's wrong."

I glanced up at the kids, who were walking ahead of us and busy whispering secrets of their own.

"Do you want to tell me what happened?"

I held my breath, then Dev spoke without looking at me, his voice low. "Back at the hospital, before we moved, there was a patient," he said, not meeting my eyes. "She had shortness of breath, and I blamed it on asthma. I wrote up the order, then I moved on. I was on three hours' sleep. I had so much work backed up, charts, a research grant, and so many other patients. I missed the note from the nurse about how she'd just come back from a trip overseas."

I waited a beat, then admitted, "I don't get it. What's so wrong about that?" Rain still fell around us, but I hardly noticed it anymore. It was beading off Dev's hair, soaking his glasses, but he didn't move to wipe them off.

"She had a blood clot," he explained. "It's the kind of thing you *should* think of after someone's been on a long plane ride. She went into respiratory distress, ended up in the ICU. She almost died, Charlie, because I was checked out on notes and paperwork, and I couldn't keep up, and I let myself make a mistake. This is the only job I've ever wanted to do. But what if . . . what if I actually kind of hate it? So much so that I almost cost someone their life instead of saving it? Where does that leave me? I didn't take the job here to get away from you. I did it to get away from myself."

Dev kept walking while I trudged carefully by his side, letting this new truth seep in. Kate and Ellery jumped over a puddle along the path, then I stepped right through it. "I had no idea you felt that way," I said quietly. "I wish you'd told me. Or that I'd just asked, instead of being afraid. But what about now? What about here?"

"Here? I'm treating a sixty-year-old woman who can barely afford her blood pressure medication. Meanwhile, her grandson is stealing her jewelry to buy pills. He's self-medicating for psych issues, ones the system isn't built to adequately treat or support. There are layers upon layers that I can't fix by just writing a script. Yet every day, I go in and do it all over again. Sometimes I feel like . . . you want a smiling doctor husband with charming anecdotes to bring to parties. I don't think I can be that person for you anymore."

"I don't want you to be," I said, then I caught myself. He wasn't wrong. Since we first met, I'd put Dev on a pedestal that was so high, there was no possible way I could join him on it. And as our lives got more complicated, I'd just left him up there. I'd grown so insecure about whether I was the kind of person I thought he was supposed to end up with that I hadn't seen him clearly at all.

"You're right. When we got together, I thought you were invincible, and I let you keep being that person for me, because I didn't know how to be honest, with you or with myself, about how lost I felt," I said, wiping mud from my forehead. "But I don't need that, or want it, not anymore. I'm sorry I made you feel that pressure in the first place, that you had to keep being this kind of invulnerable cardboard cutout of yourself." Thinking of the white party gala, I added, "I see, too, how just because you can walk through these spaces with more experience than me, there are no fairy tales."

The girls kept pace ahead of us, so I let myself keep going. Presley told me it was time to use my words, and I found they came more easily than expected, once I gave myself permission to let them out into the open.

"Listen, if there's one practical thing I've learned this summer, it's that people here walk around behaving as if the only kind of whale that matters is a little pink cartoon who winks at you instead of a huge gray sea beast that can crush you like it's nothing. But I don't think it's that simple either. For anyone."

Dev looked at me and nodded. When he spoke, his voice was rough. "You're right. It's not. I feel split in half all the time. It feels like, whatever I do at work, it's not enough to really help anyone. Then when I'm home, with you and the kids, I'm not enough there. I put Band-Aids on hemorrhages, and I have to tell myself it's good enough. Either I'm too numb at home or I feel too much at work. I fail at both."

I stepped on a log and felt it crunch under my foot. "Dev, do you want to quit?"

He smiled, and there was sadness in it, but I couldn't help thinking about how I'd always loved his smile. His, not anyone else's.

"Presley told me about how you're feeling. Some of it, anyway. If you're not okay . . . It's okay," I said softly. A few feet in front of us, the girls were crouched down, staring at a small flower in the mud. "I mean, it's okay with me."

All this time, I'd been chasing some version of myself that felt good enough for Dev. In my eyes, Dev had always been the one with confidence and direction. But I'd simply assigned him that role, as if only one of us could carry it. I didn't give myself the chance to ask what he wanted—what either of us wanted.

"I wonder if we both need to let ourselves grow up a little," I said. "When we got married, when it was like Kate and Toby just dropped from the sky, I think I stopped asking myself what I needed. It just morphed into what did everyone else need from me, and, bonus, I didn't have to figure it out for myself anymore. I've been thinking, though, maybe I want to get back into art. I mean, I do want that. I want something for myself. I was going to apply to grad school before I found out I was pregnant. I never even told you." I squeezed his hand. "You're allowed to want something different for yourself, too. You're allowed to ask yourself what that might be."

He looked at me, as if to gauge whether I was serious. "I don't know. Am I? I wanted to do this, to be a doctor, since my father died. I figured, if I didn't get to have him, I could be like him. I thought it would be what made him proud of me. And now, he can't even say it's okay to let him down, because he's not here."

I put my arm around him and squeezed. His shirt was soaked through. "That's an awful lot of pressure to put on someone who's not around to tell you how he really feels," I said. "Maybe you could start by asking the people who are in your life how they feel. Not about what you do, but just about you."

"You're telling me to use my words. Is that it?" Dev said, breaking into a tentative grin. "Is that what we're supposed to be doing here, the thing we tell the kids?"

I laughed. "I think so. I'll have to practice. Honestly, we should know by now to follow Kate's lead on most things."

I could see the water from the trail now. We were close to the boats. The girls were playing a guessing game. I marveled at how they could simply be in the moment, letting all that was behind and before them fall away. I wanted to remember how to do that, too.

Dev took a deep breath. "Charlie, I'm talking to this therapist—sorry, that's what the Wednesday meetings were for, by the way—about being burned out, from practicing medicine. But I think it's more than just that."

It was like a bungee cord releasing from my chest. My mouth hung open, and I smacked Dev on the shoulder. "You're doing therapy?"

Dev looked at me sheepishly. "It's the Wednesday secret meeting. I didn't want you to think the move here was a mistake. Like, we got here and, boom, there I was in therapy. Elvis pushed me into it. That's why she came over to the house that night, Charlie, to make sure I was going. I wanted to tell you, but . . ."

"I know, I know," I said, wincing. "We don't have to rehash my freezer reconnaissance mission."

He laughed, sounding relieved. "I didn't mean for it to come off as some secret thing, Presley coming over. I was kind of embarrassed. It was basically an intervention, an entirely unsexy, overcaffeinated assault on how I wasn't dealing with how hard our job is, wasn't being honest with you, was drinking too much, wasn't giving myself enough credit for the good things we both did get to accomplish each day, even amid all the shit we can't possibly control."

"Wow, I agree with all of those things," I said. "I guess I'm fully Team Elvis now, too."

"She said she'd fire me if I didn't start opening up, which, I don't know if she technically can do that, but she can be a little scary," Dev admitted.

I laughed, the simple relief of the truth flooding the parts of me that had been coiled with tension for weeks. It made me feel wobbly, but in a good way this time. "I can't disagree with you there either."

"Also, if I told you about what I was feeling here, I thought I'd have to tell you about everything."

"That's the idea!" I said. I leaned into his side.

"Okay then, I have one more thing to tell you," Dev said. I steeled myself. What else could there be?

"Charlie, I fucking hate running. The therapist told me to try it. And I think it really helps, and I'm trying to drink less, too, but I don't like it at all."

I wasn't even sure if it was funny this time, but I laughed, and Dev threw me a small smile. "Okay. Noted," I said. "And no judgment. I hate running, too. Maybe we can hate running together. My free month at the Garage is almost up, anyway."

We reached the shore, and Dev tied the dinghy to the launch boat. I waded out into the mucky shallows, and Dev carried each girl onto the boat. They sat side by side. Kate offered Ellery the last cookie from her pocket. Ellery broke it in half. I thought about how each of us had made real friends here, despite, well, everything. Wasn't that what made a place feel like home, more than anything that required a membership agreement?

It was a short ride across the harbor until I could see the dock at the club. We were close.

"I don't want to quit immediately," Dev said as we approached. "I don't want to leave Elvis high and dry. Or the people we're trying to help. I don't want the clinic to go under. But maybe I want to see what else is out there."

I breathed the salt air deep into my lungs. I pushed myself up from the bench, and holding on to the side of the boat with one hand, I stood next to Dev as he steered us toward the dock. "Do you want to run from *me*?"

Dev shook his head. He lowered his voice. "No. I don't want to run from you."

That was something. Maybe it was everything.

"Elvis interviewed another doc who can join us if we can find the money. If the grant comes through, we'll hire him, and I'll work less, for now. It won't be perfect, but it'll be better. And we can talk about it when it's not."

"With all that free time you can help me fix up the cottage," I offered.

"Yeah, or we can go sailing and get that guy who did Heidi's wine cellar to work on the cottage instead. What's his name?"

"Nope!" My voice was high and sharp.

"Jesus, okay, I'll do it myself," Dev mumbled. "What I mean is, I'll be there for you guys. I'm working on it."

"That's all I need," I said, and I meant it. I added, "Me too."

The wind blew Dev's shirt back against his chest as he stood at the center console. His legs were planted on either side of the wheel. He looked so solid. But I knew, now, he was a lot of other things, too.

Ellery leaned her head on Kate's shoulder, and I thought of Heidi. I realized I very much wanted to hear about Poppy's trip when she came back. I wanted to help Elvis fight to keep the clinic open. I wanted Casper to live his life and someday make an appointment for cholesterol meds or something equally boring. Without fully realizing it, I had made a life for us here. And it was time to make my life here, too, in a way that felt real. *Authentic,* as my mother would say. When Dev spoke again, I could hardly hear him over the sound of the boat's engine. "So what happens now, if I fuck up?"

I wrapped my arm around his waist and steadied myself next to him. Then I pulled him to me, and I kissed him, mud and salt spray and all.

"I guess we fuck up together. Then we figure it out."

—∿—

Heidi was waiting for us at the dock, standing in the rain. Elvis stood with her, each holding on to one of Toby's alligator paws. Ellery popped up out of her seat and waved. Heidi put her hand to her mouth when she saw us, then she waved back.

Climbing onto the dock, I felt like a swamp creature. But after Heidi checked every inch of Ellery, making sure the only thing she was missing was some tulle, she wrapped her arms around me, too, and squeezed. When she pulled away, we were both streaked with mud and tears.

"They were fine," I assured her. "Kate and Ellery built a shelter."

Heidi laughed and wiped at her face. "Of course they did." After Heidi gave Ellery another hug and told her they'd go home soon, Dev took the girls and Toby to get ice cream sandwiches. They passed Poppy as she ran to the dock, and Dev lifted his hand automatically for a high five. I wasn't sure if I'd ever loved him more.

"I knew you could do it, Charlie," Poppy said. "Davis is inside, too. He'll make sure no one disappears again." She cringed. "Oh God, sorry, Heidi. Did you find Teague?"

"He's at his family's country house in Connecticut," Heidi said. "Wasted, but accounted for."

"I'm sorry," I said.

"It happens," Presley said gently but with her signature no-drama assurance. "It doesn't mean it's forever. We can go there with you, if you want." She raised her eyebrows at me, to confirm, and I nodded.

Heidi waved her hand. "His parents are nearby, and they're adamant we all let him be for now. Anders Anderson does not want to make a fuss."

"He'll come around," I said.

"Maybe," replied Heidi. "But either way, I'm certain about two things. I want a divorce. And I'm matching the grant to fund the clinic."

Presley's mouth dropped open. It was the first time I had seen her at a loss for words.

"I can't change what's already happened with Teague," Heidi said. "But Jeannine said you fought hard to get Casper into rehab on short notice. He'll be lucky to have your support when he's back home. So should anyone who wants it. I've already spoken to my lawyer. It's taken care of."

"Oh, Heidi." Presley wrapped her arms around both of us. Poppy clapped her hands. "Anything you need, girl, I'm here for you. Just say the word."

Heidi wiped her eyes again, but she was smiling. "For now, will you go into the club and tell the kids I'll be right there? There's just one more thing I need to do."

Presley scanned the clusters of masked club members before walking away. "I just hope I don't run into that shoeless guy again. He hit on me something fierce, but I am *not* in the mood tonight."

Heidi laughed while tears ran down her cheeks. Before I could ask what she was waiting for, Lacy approached us with Al Westinghouse. His bow tie was red. It made him look like a wrinkled, pot-bellied vampire.

"Lacy, it's not happening," Heidi said. "I transferred the money to my lawyer. Teague isn't involved. The clinic is staying, for now at least."

"I didn't see you make a phone call," Lacy said. "I've been watching you all standing here. You're bluffing. She's bluffing," she told Al Westinghouse.

"I didn't need to call anyone," Heidi said. "I *am* my lawyer." Her peacock mask was pushed up onto her forehead, and she pulled it off. I whooped as Heidi tossed it onto the grass beside Lacy's feet.

Lacy turned to Al Westinghouse. "Dad, we can still make this work. Give me more time. I'll show you."

Al looked at her like she was a child, which, I realized, Lacy was to him. Her big-time investor, the one who was going to save Warren's postindustrial real estate empire, was Lacy's father. He was also the one who couldn't be bothered to help beyond that night.

"A deadline is a deadline, you know that," he said. "I didn't build a company with second chances. Tell Warren to go back to the drawing board. He'll get it one of these times. We'll see you for Thanksgiving." He spoke to her with the rapid clip of a business supervisor.

Lacy opened her mouth to respond, but Al turned and walked away.

I had to admit, I felt a pang of pity for Lacy, as much as I tried to swallow it like a sour blueberry. My own parents always had more faith in me than I felt I deserved. My mother thought I could land on the moon if I put my mind to it, and despite that, she never made me feel bad for tending bar instead, for making tiny paintings I refused to share with anyone. She trusted I'd get it right, or wrong—then she gave me space to do either. It was the kind of grace I was extending to Dev now, and also, finally, to myself.

The world is big, but if you define yourself by the story of a small town, that could be easy to forget. I knew this firsthand. If Lacy lost her power as queen of Rumford, even in the eyes of Al Westinghouse, who saw the world through the perspective of a pinhole of his own experience, what did she have left?

I thought about all I had—all I'd almost thrown away. I'd ignored what was right in front of me, not because it wasn't good enough, but because I thought I wasn't. I took Heidi by the hand, and we walked to get our children. I didn't care one bit whether it was the last time I set foot in the club. I had all I needed. And I wanted to go home.

epilogue

Kate was standing in the middle of the living room with a metal detector when I heard my mother announcing herself through the open window. "Helloooooo, and surprise!"

James Dean yipped as Lilly shuffled through the door, arms full of reusable grocery bags. She wore tie-dye overalls with a Kripalu tank top underneath. I'd say I was surprised to see Bessie taking up half of Cedar Street again, but after the past few days, not even my parents could shock me.

"Hi, Lilly!" Kate and Toby shouted in unison.

"Well, hello, you two!" Lilly said. "What's shaking?"

"I'm going to find an artifact. Maybe a dinosaur bone," Kate said. "Do you think there's one at the beach?"

"I think if there's a dinosaur bone anywhere in New England, *you'll* be the one to find it."

"I thought you had another day at the retreat," I said.

"I just couldn't take another day of *silence*, sugar. I am all for unplugging. But there are apps for that, and we have a business to run. We found our zen by day two—we really didn't need seven."

Lilly set the grocery bags on the floor, and James Dean sniffed around them. His fabric lobster collar, the one I bought our first week in Rumford, was looking worn. A lot had happened since I'd picked it out.

My father walked in, and I waited for him to say something as he stood and looked at me, a beatific smile on his face.

"Your father is determined to observe the week of silence to completion," Lilly explained. My father brought his palms together in front of his chest and nodded at me.

"Namaste, Dad," I said.

"We won't be in the way, of course," Lilly said. She winked at Edgar. "Kids, would you like to come with GP and me today? We have some work to do at the beach. You two can dig. The more hands the merrier."

Toby jumped up, and Kate looked at me with bright eyes. She waved the metal detector in the air for emphasis, and they were off.

When Lilly texted two hours later, I didn't see it. I'd pulled out my box full of canvases and paints, and I'd spread the sea glass Kate had collected—the entire jar of it—over the coffee table. I envisioned little creatures, made from sea glass and paint, on canvases the size of Post-it Notes.

I knew from *The Official Preppy Handbook* that rich people loved charmingly miniature animals—and would likely pay an arm and a leg for something Kate picked up from the town beach, with the right packaging. It felt like the start of something.

Lilly: Your father is waiting for the rocks to heat up, so I'm dropping off the kids but must rush back.

"What rocks?" I said out loud, to no one. "What heat?" I asked James Dean, as Kate and Toby burst into the cottage, cheeks flushed and feet sandy. Then the back door opened, and Dev ducked inside from the patio. The kids squealed as Dev hoisted them up, one on each hip.

"Daddy, we found soooo many rocks," Kate said. "But no fossils yet."

"I filled my bucket with seaweed over and over and over again." Toby giggled.

"And we dug a huge hole, Daddy."

296

"Sounds impressive," Dev said. He set them back onto the kitchen floor, sand still falling from their clothes. Presley pulled open the patio door next, holding a bottle of wine.

"Hey, y'all, this has been sitting in my car all day so I'm just going to help it get cold," she said, going straight to the freezer. She opened it, then leaped back. Next to a stack of frozen pizzas sat six lobsters, cold and still, blue rubber bands around their immobilized claws.

"You found our dinner guests," I said. "It's supposed to put them to sleep. Before we . . . you know." I gestured to the pot of boiling water on the stove.

"Boil them. We're going to boil them, Charlie," Dev said, hooking his arm around my waist and leaning down to bury his face in my neck. He whispered into my ear, "They can't hear you."

I dumped a palmful of salt into the water. "Well, it eases *my* psychic pain. We didn't all get off on dissecting a frog in seventh grade."

"Busted," Presley said, smiling. She winked at me, and I smiled back with genuine affection. I was liking that feeling so much better than insecure jealousy, and I was certain I'd feel that way even if she hadn't—while securing ice cream sandwiches for the kids after our island rescue—swiped Lacy's phone from her tote bag, asked Ivy for the passcode, then successfully deleted the photos of me in that very clubhouse from both the phone and the cloud.

Just as Dev reached into the freezer and placed the lobsters one by one into the pot of boiling water and I covered my ears, the door from the patio swung open once more.

Heidi put a bowl of salad down onto the counter and didn't miss a beat. "Charlie, it's the steam escaping from their shells; it isn't their goddamn souls. Have some prosecco."

I left Dev and Elvis to the lobsters and lit candles on the picnic table out back. Heidi had extra paper lanterns from book club, and we hung them between the maple tree and the roof.

"Have you talked to him?" I asked Heidi.

"The kids did, today," she said. "I'm not in a hurry. But I will. He's working again, from the Connecticut house. But whatever else he's doing there, it's not my responsibility."

I took Heidi's hand and squeezed it.

When Dev placed the steamed lobsters on the table, Kate, Toby, Hayes, and Ellery sat at one end, with Dev, Elvis, Heidi, and me at the other. Poppy was still in LA and texting regular updates with multiple high-five emojis. They each had become someone different to me than when we moved to Rumford two months before. I supposed I meant something different to myself as well.

As we dug in, the paper lanterns glowed over the table, making Dev's glasses shimmer. His hands were covered in lobster debris, so I pushed his hair out of his eyes, running my thumb along his forehead. I found myself wanting to find an excuse to touch him every few minutes, like we were new to each other. In a way, we were.

I'd signed the papers to be a member at the beach club—but just the beach club, for now—on the same day we extended our lease on the cottage. Bitsy van der Koff sponsored our family membership after Dev treated Bart for a broken collarbone—the result of a DIY ninja warrior course. I enrolled the kids in public school. I'd be there, too, as it turned out—they needed an art teacher. Dev would stay on at the clinic, but he was applying to grad schools for public health. The only other place we joined was the YMCA, so the kids could learn to play basketball with Presley.

As Presley told us about the new doctor she was hiring—it was Jake, with the abs, from basketball, he'd been an EMT in Bradley before med school, and he was single, not that she cared—Heidi pulled her phone from her bag, next to the table.

"There's some kind of situation at the beach club," she muttered.

Dev set down the lobster tail he was wrenching apart. "Is there always a situation?"

Heidi scrolled through the messages on her screen. "Something about a fire on the beach . . . probably teenagers."

"Um, are you on curfew patrol or something?" Presley said.

"It's a group text," Heidi said. "I'm on the board. If they're doing it close enough to the club to get noticed, it must be amateur hour."

"She means they must not be members," I loud whispered. Then I picked up my own phone and realized I had five missed calls from my mother.

"I'll be back in twenty minutes," I said, motioning for Heidi to come with me.

—⁓—

I smelled smoke and could make out my parents' dark silhouettes on the fine white sand beside the cabanas. "Charlie, there you are!" Lilly called. She held her hands in the air. "There she is, Ed. We'll get this all straightened out."

"What's going on?" I looked to my father. He mimed something. Digging? He pinched his fingers together. Digging for small coins? Buried treasure?

"He has another ten minutes of silence," Lilly explained. "We had this inspired idea, Charlie. Very on brand. Something real people can do."

"A bonfire?" I asked. Smoke escaped from the edges of a tarp. "Should you cover fire with a tarp?"

"An old-fashioned clambake, dear. Kate said you cook at this beach all the time," Lilly said, gesturing to the grills by the bar patio. "How are we supposed to know it's private? It's sand and water, for crying out loud."

Lacy's voice sliced through the night air. "Everyone knows it's private. It just *is*."

"Clearly not everyone," Lilly muttered. My father nodded in agreement.

I surveyed the scene, beyond my parents and the tarp. Seaweed, a handheld butane lighter, squares of cheesecloth, newspaper, and some kindling. A shovel stuck out of the sand next to a pile of what looked like burned firewood. Was there even a fire? I worked to put the disparate ingredients together, like paint by numbers, willing some picture of understanding to emerge.

"I still don't see what the big deal is. Do you, Ed?" Lilly said. "We should be setting up the spotlight by now to get the big reveal on film."

Lacy started indignantly jabbing her index finger in the air. "There are bylaws. They clearly state that this is private property. Even club members must get permission *in writing* to hold private parties. I put a copy in your practice cabana when I *thought* I'd be welcoming you into the club." She stomped into my lottery cabana.

"Kate helped us dig this hole to your father's exact specifications. Toby gathered all the seaweed to layer on top." Lilly gazed at the steaming mound like it was a third grandchild they'd conjured from fruits of the sea. "We'll remove the tarp and record the whole shebang. The best part is, our followers can do this themselves. It's not rocket science. The clams will be perfectly steamed, the potatoes fork tender. You'd know all of this, Charlie, if you ever checked our Instagram Stories."

Edgar raised a finger. "One minute to go," Lilly confirmed.

Lacy slammed the door of the cabana so hard it swung back open. She stomped her way back to the firepit, gripping a pile of papers. A ding sounded from my father's watch, and he pulled back the tarp. Steam climbed into the dark sky. Lobsters, packets of potatoes and clams, and ears of corn lay steaming underneath a layer of dark-brown seaweed.

"Ed, it's gorgeous. Well done." My mother took a step back and clapped her hands, delighted. "It's just a shame we don't have the reveal on tape to share." She sounded disappointed, but she reached for a pair of metal tongs and pinched a lobster, determined to make the best of it.

"I got it on video," Heidi said from behind me. Lacy stood gripping the papers, shadows under her eyes.

"I'll AirDrop it to you," Heidi said brightly.

"Aren't you sweet," Lilly said. "We brought a blanket. Should we dig in? You can join us," she said to Lacy. "Surely we can work this out. We won't leave a trace. You won't even know we were here. If we don't have community, dear, what do we have?"

I looked out at the water. *Leave no trace,* I thought. I'd been trying to do just that for so long. I'd been afraid to make a mark, to let roots take hold. If my mother had staged an after-hours clambake at the beach club when we first arrived in Rumford, and Lacy took me to task for it, I would have simply walked into the sea.

I heard the waves kissing the sand as tiny ripples moved in and then back out, incrementally smoothing the stones in their path. I gave Lilly's hand a quick squeeze, plopped down onto the blanket, and reached for a piece of corn.

"This is not how it works," Lacy said. She shook the stack of papers. "There are *rules*. You can't just come here and disrupt what was working perfectly fine. You can't change what's always been. You can't—"

Edgar's watch alarm sounded, and he finally spoke. "You might want to watch those papers, dear."

In Lacy's tirade, as she shook the stack of bylaws, a few stray sheets fluttered onto the pile of coals. I watched as a single piece of paper, carried by the wind, its corner glowing orange, flew into the open door of the lottery cabana.

If the tote bag inside hadn't contained Lacy's secret stash of sugar—candy, Oreos, an extralarge container of sugar substitute—and if the flaming piece of paper hadn't landed on top of a spilled pile of highly flammable, vanilla-flavored coffee creamer, it would have been fine.

Instead, orange flames consumed the cabana as they rose into the night sky. Heidi caught the whole thing on her phone.

Later that night, I squeezed next to Dev on the couch as Kate made us watch the uploaded segment for the millionth time. It was like the unexpected fire validated the months of her intense survival research. She'd insisted my father bring a fire extinguisher, and he'd dutifully put the fire out before it spread beyond the one cabana. Still, *Senior Moments'* viewership was soaring.

Kate hit play again as Toby fed James Dean a granola bar he found under the couch, and I pressed my cheek to the sharp curve of Dev's shoulder. When he lifted his arm, I leaned into him, letting the chaos of my little family fall over me like a weighted blanket. Of all the clubs, this was the only one I really needed.

acknowledgments

I wish I could throw a big, ridiculous party for everyone who had a hand in helping this book make its way into existence.

Laura Van der Veer and Amy Zhang are dream editors. Thank you for making this story and these characters come into greater focus with depth, clarity, heart, and, always, humor. Laura, thank you for your vision and confidence, in this book and in me. Thank you to Alexa Stark for welcoming me on board, and for your decisive insight and support.

I owe endless thanks to the team at Little A and Amazon Publishing, especially Patricia Callahan, Ashley Little, Tara Whitaker, Elizabeth J. Asborno, Nicole Burns-Ascue, and Georgina Kamsika, for reading and editing with such care and precision. Joanne O'Neill designed a cover that makes me smile (and laugh) with my whole heart every time I see it. Thank you to the fine folks at Heidi Pitlor Editorial, especially Nicole Lamy, for support in all the ways. And wild thanks to Katie Kurtzman for launching this baby into the world.

My year in GrubStreet's Novel Incubator opened up and changed my life. Michelle Hoover's insight and generosity make an absolute dream feel within reach for anyone lucky enough to be in her orbit. These pages would not exist, and I would be absolute dust, without Nicole Vecchiotti, Aube Rey Lescure, Kasey LeBlanc, John McClure, Juliet Faithful, Cameron Dryden, Michael Giddings, Joan Nichols, and Susan Larkin. The real dream come true is having you all in my life.

I'm so grateful to organizations like GrubStreet and LitArts RI for making space for and cultivating belief in writers at every stage of the game. On that note, a heartfelt thank-you to Annie Hartnett, Liv Stratman, Heidi Pitlor, Julia Claiborne Johnson, Byron Lane, Christine Simon, Shari Goldhagen, Rachel Barenbaum, Julie Carrick Dalton, and Jodie Noel Vinson for the ways you made me want to keep showing up, even if you didn't know it.

I'm lucky to spend my days with brilliant and thoughtful colleagues and friends like Cloe Axelson, Kate Neale Cooper, and Kathleen Burge. Thank you for helping me hold the both/and of life, and for making hard work so much fun.

Writing with three young kids is an odyssey, and I'd also like to dedicate this book to noise-canceling headphones and Gregory Alan Isakov. And to Connie Enos, Crisana Roussel-Heroux, Lisa Orfan, Lori Meyerson, and Kathy Kirshenbaum for being part of my village along the way.

Thank you to Curtis Sittenfeld and her seminal novel *Prep* for making me aware of the existence of *The Official Preppy Handbook*, a true gift, and to eBay for holding on to a copy I could afford. On a more serious note, I'm indebted to *Dopesick: Dealers, Doctors, and the Drug Company that Addicted America* by Beth Macy. And to all of the doctors I'm privileged to call friends who've shared stories with me over many, many years: this world is better (and darkly funnier, and less gapey) for having you all in it.

Danielle Zavada, Erin Rose, Erika Werner, and Abby Colombo, I would happily be trapped in a wine dungeon with you. To my other friends, a reminder that I made all of this up, so don't stop inviting me to your parties. And if you're having parties like the ones in this novel, please start inviting me to them.

To my parents, James and Lois Johnson, thank you for believing in me with such abandon. Thank you for making stories and a sense of humor part of what makes life worth living. Anita McGinty, and Ramesh and Joann Shukla, thank you for cheering me on.

Maya, Noah, and Leo, you are my favorite people in the whole world. Our friend Mel Brooks says, "If you can laugh, you can get by," and that's one thing we get right every single day. Anil, thank you for telling me I could do something like this when I insisted you were delusional. Thank you for laughing at my jokes, for making space for this dream in our lives, and for being a fan of my writing before we even met, which was a million years ago. I love you. I promise I'll learn how to sail this summer.

about the author

Photo © 2022 Melissa Sepulveda

Sara Shukla is an editor for WBUR's Cognoscenti. You can find her writing at WBUR as well as the *Los Angeles Review of Books*, *McSweeneys*, and elsewhere. An alum of GrubStreet's Novel Incubator and the University of Virginia, she lives in Rhode Island with her family.